LAST RITES

PERRY MICHAEL SMITH

Last rites

NEW YORK
CHARLES SCRIBNER'S SONS

Printed in the United States of America
Library of Congress Catalog Card Number 73-140774
SBN684–10554–3

For Lois, who made me do it for the first time

Liber scriptus proferetur,
In quo totum continetur,
Unde mundus judicetur.

Fiat justitia, et pereat mundus,

Let justice be done, though the world perish

—FERDINAND I
et al.

Part One

Deus ex

Thou art beautiful, O my love . . .

as terrible as an army with banners.

But our side uses guns.

MEMORANDUM TO: DANIEL TAMINO, DIRECTOR
FROM: ERLAND IVANSON
CONCERNING: RECENT OBSERVATIONS OF QUASAR BEHAVIOR, LACK OF COOPERATION FROM THE COMPUTER CENTER, AND SUNDRY OTHER MATTERS OF CONCERN TO DR. IVANSON.

My annoyance, you see, has reached a new peak. Never before, not at Upsala, not in Berlin, not at Jodrell Bank, not in Houston, have I been forced to put my complaints in writing. A word here, a word there, a gentle admonition; these have always proved sufficient in times past to remove annoyances, to still troubled waters, and to obtain the cooperation so necessary for the pursuit of my work. We all are agreed, I believe, as to the importance of my previous contributions to astronomy; we all recognize the significance of my discoveries, the perception and accuracy of my theories. Otherwise I would not have been solicited to join the Fellowship. All in all, I have found the time at the Center most agreeable. But, at this moment, standing on the verge of a breakthrough of *universal* significance, I have been totally frustrated. My constitution, as you well know, cannot endure frustrations. You promised me that my labors would be able to proceed unhindered by lack of funds or equipment, that I would receive both absolute cooperation and complete privacy from the other members of the Fellowship. I have received neither in the past days and I must register an emphatic complaint. Put bluntly, Mr. Tamino, either you restore order or I shall kill myself.

A bit of background to the present crisis:

As you know, I am an exponent of the "big bang" theory of the origin of the universe. That is, I support the thesis that the universe is merely the shrapnel thrown off by the explosion of Aristotelian ylem (consult your dictionary), ignited through the agency of some first cause at present unknown (my vestigial Lutheran conscience says *God*, my intellect says *who cares?*) since it resolves most of the problems of the receding galaxies, which are observable by virtue of the red shift in their visible spectra as the result of a Doppler effect in the trail of light waves left behind them as they approach the speed of light. I would cite sources for you, but suggest you do your own research if you have the inclination. You, I am sure, are aware of the work of Hubble and Humason at Mount Wilson, which correlated the red shift and the intergalactic distance scale to date the age of the universe, Baade's correction of their work, and my own small paper in which I fix the figure at twelve billion years, give or take two billion. I suggest you examine my old friend Arthur Eddington's *The Expanding*

Universe for a simple, elegantly phrased (if outdated) look at the entire problem.

Young Bob Dicke at Princeton, following my lead in the ylem hypothesis, more or less confirmed the big bang theory by suggesting that the universe's source might have been a primordial fireball which blew up. If so, surmised Bob, then some of the radiation from that fireball should be lingering around, waiting for somebody with good equipment to stumble across it. And that is precisely what was taking place while he was brushing the chalk dust off his coattails. Two lads at Bell Laboratories (Messrs. Penzias and Wilson, if memory serves) were testing the range of their radio telescope and found just what Bob said would be there. Naturally, I personally confirmed their discovery.

For the next few years we sat back and rested on our collective laurels. What a happy, neat picture of the universe: it began with a bang and would end with the assorted galactic flotsam shooting outward at the speed of light. Curtain. *Exeunt omnes.* Naturally, some of my colleagues found this conclusion less than pleasing and have propounded a number of clever alternatives. One group—my friends Gold, Bondi and, preeminently, Hoyle—declare that as the galaxies speed out of existence (from our point of view, at any rate), static hydrogen continues the process of creation, maintaining a balance of matter within the universe. The evidence to date, alas, does not support them. Another group predicts that while the universe will continue to expand, it will do so only to prescribed limits and then contract in on itself, finally coalescing back into a massive pocket of ylem and the whole process of explosion, expansion, and contraction will begin again. While this latter hypothesis has a rhythmic quality which could be particularly appealing to a certain monotonous turn of mind, I, until recently, had not given the matter much thought, my own predilections leading me to feel that repetition of this sort could indicate only a morbid lack of imagination on the part of any intelligent First Cause.

With Schmidt's and Oke's work on quasi-stellar bodies (quasars), our peaceful moratorium on confusion came to an end. These gentlemen analyzed and demonstrated beyond debate the presence of *starlike* bodies at the far reaches of known space, traveling at unheard-of speeds, producing, in some cases, radio waves that would require amounts of energy almost inconceivable when compared to our previous experience. Shortly after these discoveries, I began to despair of anyone making sense out of anything and, as an alternative to sleeping pills, accepted your invitation to come here and work things out at my leisure in return for operating the Fellowship observatory. At long last, I thought, I will have at my disposal the largest radio telescope in the world, with no committees to review my work and make me wait months or even years for a quick glimpse at the heavens. I was to be given access to computers with an almost infinite capacity for correlating data. I was promised no interference, I was encouraged to compress years of theorizing into days of action.

The discoveries over the past months have been astonishing. Permit me to bring a few of them to your attention once more because they have a direct bearing on our present difficulties.

At one time, it was believed that the quasi-stellar bodies could not be galaxies because of the noted fluctuations in visible brilliance and in their radio transmissions. This short-term periodicity seemed to support the point of view that they must be merely stars because of the enormity of a galaxy in size and the fact that no fluctuation could span the necessary galactic space in a few years, even at the speed of light. With techniques too recondite to mention here, I have succeeded in proving (to my satisfaction, which, I should think, says a great deal) that the quasars are indeed galaxies or, in some cases, parts of galactic systems. How then does it happen that they fluctuate in intensity? For the simple reason that they are, in a variety of timed cycles, alternately retreating from us and advancing toward us, or rather *were* since we are now receiving evidence of events that took place millennia before the existence of this solar system. More plainly, *they seem to be bouncing.* Short of the speed of light, these strange systems hit some kind of boundary, recoiled slightly, and then plunged back *as if stuck to flypaper and unable to escape.*

Three weeks ago, to my astonishment, I noticed that I had lost the signals from Quasar 9F 466. That fact alone is of momentous import. But, realize my shock when I discovered through a study of the monthly reports from Manchester to the Royal Society that 3C 273 also seems to have disappeared. Since these two bodies occupy locations in the heavens which permit their disparate observation only after the earth has made a turn of exactly 180 degrees, it is conceivable that they vanished into the outer reaches of the universe simultaneously. In other words, *they had reached the end of space and time together.* Naturally, I made no attempt to establish contact with my British colleagues (I have the heartiest respect and gratitude for our security procedures), but I put through a standard terminal call to the computer chamber, requesting an analysis of the probability of further quasar disappearances; if such was the case, I asked in addition for approximate times, locations, etc., if predictable. I then turned the radio telescope over to automatic guidance from the computer chamber and waited. Within a quarter of an hour after I had typed the request, the motors went on and the aerial started to lift from concealment. Suddenly, the power stopped and I realized that my receivers were no longer in operation. I called the computer chamber for an explanation and received neither answer nor acknowledgment.

No doubt you have been alerted to the fact that Miss Deckstewer has vanished and that the computers cannot be run without the guiding presence of a person at least equally competent. But, are you aware that because of Miss Deckstewer's defection a joint effort involving three of the Fellowship has been curtailed, an effort of such great significance that I have permitted the other two participants to meet with me *in my quarters* even though *one of them is Miss von Helsing?* Miss Feuer is sufficiently inoffensive scarcely to elicit notice, but I trust you realize how much significance I give this enterprise willingly to allow that other woman within ten feet of me.

Mr. Tamino, for some months I have been charting astonishingly regular transmissions from one of the radio source stars within our own galaxy (approximately eighteen light years distant). Upon Miss von Helsing's request, we have been debating the best course of action for laying out a program of response in the event that the future should prove these signals to be a consequence of a deliberate attempt to establish communication by extraterrestrial life forms. We had reached the point in our discussions of devising a universal symbology of numbers by which contact could be made and the priorities which should be placed upon any "conversations" that might occur. This, of course, is immensely speculative, but then isn't that the particular asset of the Fellowship, that all speculation is self-rewarding? Naturally, the computers would be necessary in our work, not only in helping us to code and decode initial exchanges but, in themselves, carrying on the steady and unceasing stream of such contacts as might be common in a mere thirty-six years. Here again, our work is at an absolute standstill. Without the computer, Miss Feuer cannot make the obligatory computations for anything so basic as the construction of an adequate transmitter with which to make our first response. Miss von Helsing for once has virtue on her side, although her motives in reaching to the stars to find what she calls a "nonhuman control group" for her ethnopsychological studies, I find somewhat distasteful.

Now, in quite another vein, I will draw your attention to one last bit of information and one ultimate outrage to my work. Since the computers are no longer operative, I have been searching out the major known quasars by manual operation to see if they are still out there. So far, alas, we have lost six, and because of our nonfunctioning computers, I have not audited a single disappearance. But, to the point, yesterday evening, as I leveled the telescope at the horizon in an effort to find 8C 22, an enormous spurt of static crashed through my earphones, deafening and, I must confess, terrifying me. After long years of experience, I at once recognized the emission as coming from the motor of a large vehicle passing directly in the line of the telescope's aim. From my wartime espionage training, I also

9

realized that the vehicle in question could only be a tank. Knowing your rule that armored vehicles would be deployed exclusively in time of attack on the Center, and fearing that the computer malfunction had caused a delay in the 1-A-Zed Alert, I immediately snatched the revolver from my desk and pressed it to my temple. Fortuitously, I had not removed my earphones and, before I had time to pull the trigger, I found, to my astonishment, that the tank (and there can be little doubt that it *was* a tank) was moving away from us, and that it seemed to be alone. Tense but curious, I listened and tracked it. As best I can judge, it moved approximately seven miles into the desert and stopped. It remained still, engines idling, for the better part of two hours, then returned. Despite the time lost for research, I could overlook this incident were I not under the strain of being unable to finish so much that currently presses on my mind. Further, at least two members of the Fellowship are passing, independently and apparently without the other's knowledge, petitions demanding Miss Deckstewer's immediate replacement. Since we are only a senior staff of five (excluding Miss Deckstewer and yourself), this means that I have been solicited twice for my signature in one twenty-four-hour period, wrecking my concentration, shattering my nerves, and throwing me into a personal despair such as I have not known for over a year.

Mr. Tamino, I can hold out for only a week, at most. You must get those computers running. You have my ultimatum.

ERLAND IVANSON, Ph.D., D.Sc., R.S.

Somewhere, outside and far away, the nuns were yelling their heads off. John assumed they were playing volleyball. He smoothed out the wrinkles on the front of his cassock, and extended a damp right hand to his guest.

"How nice, Father, how very nice to see you."

The ruddy young priest in the monsignor's rabat bypassed the handshake and gripped John's elbow instead. With his fingers sending a nervous tocatta into the bone, the monsignor steered John toward the couch and eased him onto it. He stepped back, hands on hips, and smiled. "And how nice to see you looking so well, I might add." As John watched from the couch, the other cleric walked across the room and stared out the grimy leaded-glass windows, one busy finger tugging and poking at his collar. "How I envy you these six months. The nuns took good care of you, I'll bet. Lots of good food? Card games on Sunday afternoons?

11

Ho ho. A real jolly time of it. And look, just look at that lovely view." John got a quick glimpse of the brown, autumnal Vermont hills before the curtains snapped shut. He didn't care; he had seen them before, every blessed inch on his grudging early morning strolls through the countryside. John squinted as the monsignor bumped about in the sudden gloom.

"Where the hell do they keep the lamps in this place?"

John reached across the arm of the couch, fumbled, and flicked a switch. "Better? It's only forty watts, but the Mother Superior is a skinflint."

"And doesn't give a damn who goes blind." The monsignor scraped a chair across the carpet and seated himself in front of John. "If it's all the same to you, I'm going to make sure this conversation is private." He turned his head and shouted. "Hand! Get in here."

Another priest, taller, looking more fit, backed through the door, darted to the window, and peeked through the curtains. He held a revolver. "Everything's clear," he said. "They're all on the other side of the hill trying to put out the fire in the guest house. I'll keep an eye open to see if any of them come back this way."

The priest in the chair settled back and smiled at John. "Looks like we're all right for now, at any rate. So. Time for introductions. My name's Tamino, Daniel Tamino. And I see you looking at my associate's gun. Forget it. Forget him. His name's Philip Hand and he's going to make sure we aren't interrupted. That's his job." He raised his eyebrows. "That clear everything up, Father?"

"Not quite." John studied the solid figure lounging in the chair across from him, wondering if he could trust anybody with cheeks so red, with eyebrows so heavy and

12

arched, with hair so black. Too much the face of a prosperous bartender, and John knew that they were never to be trusted. "Naturally, I'm pleased that you want to talk to me about a job. I want very much to get back to work. But the bishop's letter didn't get into any specifics."

"That's right." Monsignor Tamino's Adam's apple was having trouble clearing the edge of his collar; as a pudgy finger yanked the obstruction free, John noticed a raw abrasion running around the neck. Monsignor Tamino was doubtlessly more at home in a sport shirt. "Ouch. However, let's level on a couple of things, shall we? That letter was a bit of persiflage, I'm afraid. Isn't that a lovely word? *Persiflage.* It has a fine ring, I think. In any case, your bishop doesn't know about our visit. No one does"—he took the finger out of his collar and twirled it around his head—"except those of us in this room."

"Level ten," Father Hand said. John realized that the revolver barrel had wandered in his direction. He was halfway off the couch before he saw that Monsignor Tamino also had a revolver, which was pointing at him. John dropped back into his seat.

"I guess you're not from Notre Dame, then?"

"Hope really does spring eternal, doesn't it?" Monsignor Tamino chuckled. "Come on, Father Doffenbaron, think. You have a couple of little problems which would make most respectable places hesitate before they even gave you a broom and told you to sweep."

John did not need to be told of his problems. That little bell was clanging away at the back of his skull. Guns or no guns, John was leaving. "I don't want to talk with you any more. I may have problems, but I also have a certain expertise. I am aware of it; I have been told that I am

13

sinfully proud of it." The guns, unwavering in their aim, made it hard for John to think. The bell also tended to cloud his selection of adjectives and verbs, despite Dr. Klebo's sermons about fantasies, fixations, and delusions. People don't have bells in their heads, Dr. Klebo had said. Then why was this one ringing? Why were John's hands trembling? Slowly, ignoring the wobble in one knee, he got up. "I'm leaving. You can stop pointing your guns at me. Priests don't carry guns. Make him put that gun down. *Both of you put your guns down.*" A new horror occurred to him. "The nuns. They're tired of feeding me and have hired you to kill me! You don't have a job for me, you never had a job for me. Merciful God, help me." John's legs gave up the pretense of being in working order and collapsed beneath him.

Tamino poked his gun inside his pocket and tugged John back onto the couch. "Who said anything about killing you? I told you we were here to talk about a job. Let's talk."

John sat, mouth dry, bell banging in alarm. "The church will find me a job." He could barely whisper.

Tamino shook his head. "I wouldn't count on that if I were you. Face the facts. God knows, if anybody can be logical about this, it's you. The magnanimous church, the treasure house of eternal charity, has canned you and suspended you from your sacramental functions. Hell, the only reason you're not defrocked is because they've got too much of an investment in your education and treatment. Your professional society has acknowledged your abilities but blacklisted you from ever finding a decent position again. You're a prisoner in this convent because you can't be trusted out of it. We've done our homework on you, Father."

"I'm a drunk." John lowered his head and pressed his fists to his eyes. And he wanted a drink right this minute before the bell banged a hole through the back of his skull. He sniffled.

"Oh, no, you're not. And don't pull any crying jags on us because we don't have the time." Tamino snapped his fingers. "Hand, come over here and slap him around until he's ready to listen."

John blinked back his tears and recoiled from the figure advancing toward him. He showed his teeth in what he hoped was a grin. "Oh, I'm fine. Really, just fine."

Hand looked at Tamino, they nodded to each other, and Hand went back to the window.

Tamino stood up and considered John for a moment. "Just stay where you are, Father, and let me do the talking. Damn it, I can't stand this thing another minute." He yanked the collar off and turned into the shadows for a tussle with his throat. John thought of making a quick dash for the door, but remembered the gun by the window. He didn't need to look at it to know that it was pointed at him.

Tamino sat down again, his rabat replaced by a paisley ascot; a matching handkerchief bloomed in the breast pocket of his jacket. He no longer seemed quite so young. Nor, gun and all, quite so kind. "How do you people wear those things? Don't answer. That was rhetorical. Hand? Get behind the window and see what's up with the good sisters. I'll watch our friend here." His smile thinned. "See how I trust you, Father? Now, settle down."

John removed his fingernails from the sofa cushion and forced his spine back to meet the couch. An effort of the will was required to make his neck flex sufficiently to relax against the cushion.

"Stop gritting your teeth, Father, and listen to me while I tell you what I have to offer you. While I talk, think about what you're doing here, who put you here, why they'll never let you work again. And you want to work. We know that. It's the only thing you do want to do. All right, we're prepared to give you the chance to work with the greatest collection of hardware on the face of the earth. And it will be all yours. No administrators to scold you for using too much power, no snot-nosed graduate students lousing up your programs, no budgetary limitations, no interference." Tamino's smile had disappeared altogether and his eyes sparkled. "Do you like the sound of it so far?"

John chewed his lip, tasted blood, and stopped. The kinks were coming out of his muscles. "I'm an alcoholic, undependable."

Tamino's manner was two-dimensional, businesslike. John liked him better this way. "You're not an alcoholic. You're a spoiled brat. Ah, surprised that somebody has the goods on you? We raided your Dr. Klebo's files and looked you up. You're weird, all right, weird as they come. You've got a couple of quirks that make you unfit for normal society; I don't know how you survived in a convent. Somebody steps on one of your obsessions and you go on a toot, tear up a bar, break some heads, get yourself locked up. I don't know much about nuts, Father, but I've got an expert working for me who does, and she says . . . "

"Level six," shouted the draperies.

" . . . you're one in a million, one in a billion."

The bell stopped and John allowed himself a question. "And you deal in specialized personnel?"

"Right on the button, Father." Tamino left his chair and

16

paced off into the shadows until he was merely an especially mobile chunk of darkness moving hazily out of the range of the lamp. "And you're specialized. I know it, you know it."

John knew it, but he was tired of hearing about his obsessions. He had spent eighteen years leading semiannual guided tours for professional brain explorers anxious to map the backwater of his psyche, fascinated with the geography of his acknowledged genius, stymied by the impenetrable wastes of his so-called obsessions. He had heard the pat answers from a hundred different mouths. His first mistake (why did they blame *him?*) was being a coward at four, a crybaby at five, and a moral weakling at six. They sneered at him for using his prefabricated piety as the currency with which he purchased concealment behind an attendant nun's habit from menacing thirteen-year-olds on the parochial school playground. Recess, for John, had meant bullies and if a rattled bead, a sweetly piped Pater Noster assured him of a skirted fortress, then John rattled and piped. Regrettably, the nuns had not forgotten him when the dangers had passed on to chase girls and rob filling stations, but had dragged him, years later, into the custody of priests who had convinced him that his leaden adolescence could be transmuted into a golden vocation. The priesthood, or at least minor seminary, had sounded the promise of unparalleled peace with its enforced silences, its private cells, and its absence of pimpled enemies lurking in every alley on the way home from school. The decision to leave the world, which John still believed to be a precocious display of self-interest, had been unanimously condemned by the professional brain watchers as a failure to meet prepubescent responsibilities. But who wanted to be hit in the eye every afternoon? What was responsible about that?

Nonetheless, minor seminary had its disappointments. John's teachers were morons who substituted rote recitations for thought; his peers, sweet and gentle one and all, had paraffin for gray matter. Yet nobody clouted him so long as he said his prayers, made his confession, abstained from gossip, and passed his examinations. And that was a considerable improvement from John's point of view. So, in due course, John moved from minor seminary to major seminary or, rather, was moved with a kind of intestinal predeterminism against which resistance would have been impossible. Besides, John had allowed himself to fall in love. (Dr. Klebo said that the very phrase was obsessive. But wasn't Dr. Klebo himself insane? Wasn't he still wanted by the police?) Love, for John (and none of the doctors, except Klebo, believed that he had kept his cell door closed at night, ignored the scratchings, thumpings, and sighs which filled the dormitory darkness, really believed that a rectorial pat on the bottom was punishment) came as the *Summa Theologica*. Oh, John admitted to certain odd habits before he found it. His mind had shown tendencies to drift away on its own, uninterested in the unvarying beige of his intellectual surroundings. He actually had been frightened on occasion to find himself missing, his mind having evacuated lodgings which had become untenably barren. He had tried to fill the empty corners with the odds-and-ends clutter of a normative seminary curriculum, but his brain needed more inducement than that to stay at home. The *Summa* with its regular, regulated procession of questions and objections filled every niche of John's imagination.

Certainly, John's love was far from blind, but he permitted a certain astigmatism. If Aquinas ever seemed to be in error, John dismissed the evidence as insignificant, the result of inadequate data drawn from available given premises. The *Summa* was not only a love letter to John through the centuries; it was the clearest explication of God's relationship to man which man successfully had devised. John thrust himself into his passion and stayed there to the exclusion of all his other studies until the end of seminary. He never learned to preach. His liturgics were a blasphemy. Whatever rudimentary pastoral talents might have sprouted quickly atrophied and fell off without being noticed. John's love for St. Thomas was no ordinary love, he knew, it was a marriage, and he daily prayed to God to grant and sustain the life that John clearly had been created to live, a life spent caressing and stroking the hidden crevices, the deeper secret places of his love for the edification of the faithful and, if God would please cooperate, to acquire for John a penultimate place among the minor but uncontested contributors to the corpus of eternal truth. Love his Thomas as he did, John appreciated the *Summa* as a scuttled pirate's chest from which he could earn his way diving for tiny gems of scholarship; nor did he miss the fact that it was an extension of that unbreachable fortress in which he had hidden for most of his sentient life. John never had believed, as so many psychiatrists have charged in these later years, that he had schemed from the very first to use his love for his own psychotic ends. Rather, John felt that his compatibility with the *Summa* was proved by the happy consequences of the union: riches, fame, and privacy. As a result, he never doubted that, once the oil of ordination had dried on his hands, he would be shipped off to some graduate school or other and begin to live, after his fashion, happily ever after.

"To put this conversation in the proper perspective, let me confide, just between friends, that we need you as much as you need us." Tamino moved from the darkness and stood over the couch, breathing into John's face. "Our last expert has, well, retired, as it were."

"And who was that?" John had his pride. He couldn't replace just anybody.

Tamino hesitated, glanced at the draperies, pursed his lips, and finally pronounced the name very slowly. "Bonnie Deckstewer." He responded glumly to John's open-mouthed shock. "I take it you've heard of her."

John nodded. Miss Deckstewer had been one of the *best*, before John, before she had died in the plane crash. "But she's dead."

The corners of Tamino's mouth turned down. "We certainly hope so." Then, quickly, he presented John with a smile so patently forced as to be grotesque. "However, that's our problem. You've got your own troubles."

"He sure has." Hand moved into the lamplight. "You just leapfrogged into a level two."

Tamino waved his companion away and slid onto the sofa, his weight pulling the cushions down and making John catch himself to keep from tipping over. "We'll worry about that later. Get back to that window and watch out for nuns."

Hand slipped back behind the curtains.

"Now, Father"—Tamino slapped John's knee—"let's be frank with each other, shall we? I could offer you money but, after all, what's money when you've got what you really want, eh? I suppose there are other inducements appropriate to moments like this, but you're only interested in one thing, aren't you? You want to work, a chance to do what you can do."

John moved his knee from under Tamino's hand. "It would be a nice change." He had forgotten what it felt like to do what he wanted to do. Almost immediately after his ordination, the bishop had ordered John into his office and told him to stop his Thomistic studies. Hadn't anyone told John, His Excellency demanded, about the ancient compact drawn up by abbesses, mothers superior, and their hierophantic sympathizers? Didn't John realize that the study of Aquinas was a restricted province, maintained exclusively for the good sisters and any of their postulants who might be in need of a quick graduate degree? Poor John. Yes, for untold generations the *Summa* had been subdivided by paragraphs and these evenly apportioned among the major orders and convents. Hadn't anyone ever informed John that each nunnery applied to its mother house for an annual ration of Thomistic scraps and tatters to supply those sisters desperate for a thesis topic of sufficient tedium to anesthetize readers, orals committees, entire faculties, and boards of overseers into a numbed granting of the coveted degree? Dry those unmanly tears, the bishop had said, and think how wanton to have laid final claim to a single Thomistic semicolon lest some poor Cistercian or Sister of the Little Flower be denied her last and only chance at a doctorate and cause, God forbid, whatever good

21

Catholic academy, college, or prison which was stuck with her to lose its accreditation.

John's protests that he knew of, and had even read Thomistic studies written by men, were dismissed with a flash of the episcopal ring reaching for a cigar: if indeed any man had written on the angelic doctor's fine work, which the bishop himself recalled once having glanced over, then John might do well to investigate, for he would discover that within minutes after publication of the errant volume some sister was hammering out a refutation in partial fulfillment of her degree requirements; fourteen others were writing damning reviews for at least fifty-two scrupulously orthodox periodicals, and the Curia Romana had been presented with a petition, the ink still moist, requesting that this and any other work, previous or subsequent, by the same author be put on the Index; generally, the offending publishing house closed or burned down in a few months, depending on whether the Jesuits held any of the stock. Beating his superior's desk, John demanded to know what became of Protestants and Jews who did studies of Thomas. The bishop assured him that they were irrevocably condemned to exquisitely painful torments in hell, as John *surely* knew; then his excellency had mused as to what this poaching on sacred preserves would do to all the good nuns who would be driven to resort to studies of Abelard, or Augustine, or Scotus. So many, the bishop sighed, had started that way and nothing had been seen of them ever again except their abandoned wimples. He then offered John his blessing and the open door.

John had never done much drinking before, but he speedily demonstrated a natural facility. Many was the night, he was told (because he never remembered, mercifully), that he had polished off a good quart of gin and then tottered away to a tavern to settle his nerves and what was left of his stomach with a few beers. He recalled only too vividly the frequent mornings spent blinking at unsympathetic desk sergeants while some legate from the chancellery had sweet-talked him out of the tank.

The ecclesiastical authorities finally despaired of leaving John unguarded and had stored him in a monastery.

John climbed over the walls.

They locked him in convent attics.

John shinnied down rainspouts.

They sent him to Europe for a rest.

John was caught in Hyderabad.

He was sent to minister to lepers in Samoa.

John taught them how to ferment bananas.

John was counseled, psychoanalyzed, hypnotized, immunized, fed sugar, squirted full of insulin, dunked in hot water, immersed in ice cubes, bribed, tied up, scourged, tickled, tied down, brainwashed, recatechized, sent to A.A., thrown out of A.A.A., anointed, expunged and, at last, strapped into a strait jacket, locked in the rear of an armored car, and hauled to Dr. Klebo's clinic. In those few short weeks, Dr. Klebo solved the problem. Like a widower not quite through mourning his first wife but desperate for a little warmth on cold nights, John was willing to search for something to replace St. Thomas. Dr. Klebo arranged the meeting, supervised the courtship, and gave away the groom at the nuptials.

"You're a cybernetics genius," Tamino said. He clutched John's cassock and shook him. "Your career at M.I.T. was stupendous. Those months you spent at the Pentagon revolutionized war. Your work with I.B.M. and Rand is a legend, despite what the newspapers said. Your list of patents, your bibliography of articles, your singleminded dedication to those machines is a marvel in our times." Tamino released John, almost throwing him across the couch. "Yet you knew all the time that they never appreciated you, didn't you? How could they? How could any normal, functioning participant in this civilization of ours care about a man who loved computers when the civilization was worrying about smarty-pants ideas, big concepts, fancy issues! You talked transistors and they whined for peace; you miniaturized and they rioted for equal rights; you invented a universal cybernetic language and they worried about violence in the nursery; you polished your program techniques and they hollered for air they could breathe. Well, I ask you, what have they got for it?" Tamino jumped from the couch and raced across the room, waving his arms. "A great big nothing is what they've got!"

"I always sort of felt left out." John decided that he might learn to like Tamino if Tamino would keep his voice down.

Tamino was back on the couch, his right index finger menacing John's nose. "Of course you felt left out. You *were* left out. Somebody who wouldn't know how to shut off one of your machines shoots somebody else who wouldn't know how to turn one on and they closed your laboratory for a week. What else could you do with your time but go out and get drunk?"

"They weren't too upset about that. They thought I was reacting to the President's assassination."

"Ah, but they'd done it before and they did it again, leaving you alone, with nothing to do."

John nodded, wondering how Tamino knew so much about him. "Again and again," he agreed. "Christmas, Easter, sometimes for days at a time. It was awful. No one believed that I would get drunk because of Yom Kippur. Ultimately they distrusted me."

"So you beat up a policeman here and there, threatened a dean or two, blew out a whole state's power supply trying to run your computer with power rerouted over seventeen extension cords from a street light during a rainstorm." Tamino waved it all away. "Little things in themselves, but the humiliation of being driven to force must have been dreadful for you."

John tangled his fingers together, feeling tears sting his eyes and tumble down his cheeks. Everything Tamino said was true. All John had wanted to do was run his machines, day and night, and they wouldn't let him. "You certainly have a very clear picture of the problem. I think you understand."

Tamino pulled a handkerchief out of his breast pocket and dabbed gently at the moisture on John's cheeks and nose. "That's because I'm concerned about you and believe in you." He glanced at the handkerchief, then put it in John's breast pocket, patting it flat. "And I have lots of friends who will believe in you." Tamino sat back and folded his arms across his chest. "John, I'm going to make my pitch. How would you like to be able to work all the time, around the clock if you want to? I've told you that we have the best hardware in the world, and more of it than anyone else. It's yours." He cupped his hands and held them out; John looked to see what might be there besides air and skin. "How would you like to run programs like nobody has ever run before? How would you like to set up systems for people who won't even speak to you unless

25

they have to, who won't notice that you exist unless you stop working? Nice, isn't it? I like your smile, John. Your colleagues would be people responsible to no one, unconscious of anything around them except their work. None of my people will call you obsessed, John, because they're exactly like you, with an appealing individual variation here and there just to keep things interesting. Think, John, a little community without nuns to make you take walks and no place to walk to anyway. Nobody talks politics, or religion, or anything else nobody cares about unless they mean to do something about it or use it." Tamino lifted his head and stared off into the shadows, his eyes filled with a private vision. "This land that I'm talking about is unlike any other on the face of the earth. Where men and women do whatever it is they do best and they do it all the time because they're the best ones to do it. Yet what we do, John, could topple governments, move mountain ranges, turn this world upside down, all done by folks like you and me, bright people who want to be left alone to do our work because we know how important our work is."

"Is it Harvard?" John rubbed his hands on his thighs, trying to guess. "The State Department? The C.I.A.? Bell Telephone?"

Tamino chuckled. "You're not even close, John. We call ourselves the *Fellowship.*"

"Level one, and trouble coming up the driveway." Hand billowed from behind the curtains, beckoning Tamino with his gun.

Tamino yanked his own revolver out of his jacket and ran to the window. "Good God. The idiot must be doing a hundred."

John could hear a screaming engine whizzing toward the convent.

26

"What's that on the front of the bumper?" Tamino demanded. "It looks like some sort of electric grid."

"It's the wrought-iron gate we flew over this morning. Looks like he didn't stop to unlatch it."

Unsettled by the nonchalant manner in which guns were being waved in and out from behind the curtain, John crouched down into the sofa and closed his eyes. The car screeched to a halt and John heard a door slam.

"Shoot him," Tamino said.

"Argh!" John threw himself onto the floor and covered his head with his arms.

Glass broke, guns fired, Tamino shouted. John had never heard such loud noises in his life.

"Damn it, he's made it inside."

From the foyer below them a voice called, shrill and thin. "Sanctuary, good sisters! Sanctuary!"

"What in the hell . . . ?" Tamino came from behind the curtain and stepped over John on his way to the door.

"Father Doffenbaron," the voice called. Tamino stopped and glared down at John. "Help me. The nuns, bless them, are shooting at me. Tell them that I'm a friend, warm-hearted, generous to a fault. Jewish, but self-effacing. Father Doffenbaron, don't you know me any more?"

Tamino, no longer kind, no longer understanding, poked John with his toe, hissing between his white teeth. "Well? Do you know him?"

John gagged, then spoke far louder than he intended. "Dr. Klebo. He's the only Jew I know."

"I hear you, John." Dr. Klebo's footsteps, stumbling and running, pattered up the staircase outside the closed door. "Was that you shooting at me, John? Mustn't shoot your psychiatrist, John; you might need a friend someday. Think of all the good times, John, the hydrotherapy, the shock treatments, the phenobarbital. You just put the surrogate phallus down and welcome me, John. You'll feel better. I promise. Cross my heart." The footsteps stopped but the door didn't open. Tamino and Hand cocked their guns. "That was you shooting, wasn't it, John? Or was I right the first time? Sister? Who's in there with John?"

The door flew open and Dr. Klebo squinted into the dim room. His eyes bugged suddenly; he straightened and marched forward, a balding, round bundle of red fuzz and tweeds, every inch the Man of Action.

"What are you doing to my patient? John, what have they done to you?"

Before Tamino could react, Dr. Klebo had snatched his gun and thrown it behind the couch; he promptly kneeled beside John on the floor.

"No holes, at any rate. I don't think they shot you, John. You'll live, I'd almost stake my reputation on it." He glowered at Tamino. "The trouble with you laymen is that you can't tell a sick man when you see one. Look at you, persecuting him with guns. There ought to be a law." Dr. Klebo patted John's head. "What a brain in that skull; totally antisocial; but for me, a prize, a joy, speaking professionally of course." Dr. Klebo sniffed at Hand. "And you, a priest, still pointing that weapon." He grabbed at Hand's hand and missed. "Give me that! John, have a fit and show them how sick they're making you. John hears bells, you know. Still hearing bells, John? See him nod? Like a big drink to make the bell go away, John?"

Dr. Klebo lunged at Hand in earnest, tripped over John and slammed to the floor. Hand put his foot on the back of Dr. Klebo's neck and looked questioningly at Tamino.

"Not yet." Tamino glanced from Dr. Klebo to John.

"John and I have something to settle first." The lines and wrinkles on Tamino's face dissolved into a big smile. "All right, John. You've heard my offer. We need an answer. Do you join our enterprise or don't you?"

. John wanted to like Tamino, but the smile and Hand's gun didn't mix well for him. "How do I know that you're not lying to me?"

"Mr. Tamino doesn't lie," said Hand.

Hand's endorsement scarcely seemed without prejudice, but John had already decided that anything was better than being kept under lock and key in Vermont for the rest of his life. "All right. I'll give it a try. If everything is as nice as you say, then I'll take the job."

Placing a firm hand on each of John's biceps, Tamino helped him from the floor. "You've made a very wise decision, John. I think I can promise you, without the slightest reservation, that your troubles are henceforth over." Tamino moved his eyes and looked at Hand over John's shoulder. "That's that. Now shoot the other one."

John was aware of movement beneath him, but did not see how Dr. Klebo got to his feet, much less how he managed to knock Tamino down and position John between himself and Hand's gun. "Just one moment of your time, if I might," Dr. Klebo said. "Do I understand that you are offering my patient employment? *John!* How can you abandon me to be slaughtered and go off to a big successful job somewhere? You owe me too much, John."

"Klebo," Tamino said, "you're a phony."

"Ah" — Dr. Klebo waltzed John in a small arc as Hand maneuvered to get clear aim—"but recognized by the A.M.A."

Dr. Klebo and John fox-trotted across the room as Hand

darted back and forth trying to get Dr. Klebo in his sights. "My colleagues know perfectly well that I have never practiced medicine on anyone," Dr. Klebo declared. "My specialty is tests." The gun fired, Dr. Klebo did a tango dip, and twirled John away from the revolver. "Psychological tests. Didn't my tests make crazy John here a world expert? Huh? Didn't my tests expose a brain so crazed for regulation that an adding machine looks like Ezra Pound by comparison? Didn't my tests put this lunatic in M.I.T.?"

"Dr. Klebo," John complained, "I'm out of breath."

"You're out of condition, John. Have to give you a good look-over. Blood tests. Ah, there's a hobby for you. Hemanalysis." The gun discharged again, this time almost under John's ear. John tried to push Dr. Klebo away, only to have the doctor turn his resistance into a nimble cha-cha. "You can find the most astonishing things swimming around the bloodstream. I suppose you heard about my new clinic. John, I had one girl in there with more garbage in her blood than I could describe in a month."

"Is she the one they say you murdered?" Out of the corner of his eye, John could see Tamino crawling over the couch after his gun.

"Yellow journalism. Newspaper hysteria. Would I murder anyone, John? The poor girl simply ran out of blood before I ran out of tests. And the police. I refuse to describe what I have suffered at the hands of those Nazis. John, not more than half an hour ago, three police cars tried to run me off the road. And me, unarmed, except for a few hypodermic syringes in the glove compartment."

"Police cars?" A flash-card glimpse of Tamino pushing Hand's gun down whirled past John as Dr. Klebo spun him around the edge of the carpet. "Did that idiot say police cars?" Tamino shouted.

"That I did," Dr. Klebo panted. "No doubt they'll be along any minute, the fascists. That's why I dropped in on you, John. I thought my favorite patient might be able to offer me sanctuary for a few months until this foolishness blows over."

"That clinches it." Tamino and Hand jumped together and yanked Dr. Klebo off his feet. "We're getting out of here. Move, John."

Bundling Dr. Klebo between himself and Hand, Tamino shoved John ahead of him and out the door. They skipped down the stairs, Dr. Klebo's feet moving at their own irregular pace, missing one step, taking another twice. "I assure you, gentlemen, that while John might be of temporary value to your concern before his next break-down, someone with my experience in the dynamics of psychological testing could be a singular addition to your organization's long-term growth prospects. While no expert in the world of commerce, I have been left a few stocks and bonds here and there by grateful patients, and no one is more devoted to the concept of a prosperous America than I am."

They reached the door. Hand checked to make sure the way was clear, then dragged Klebo as Tamino shoved John out onto the convent grounds.

"That way." Hand pointed to a grove of trees beyond the barn. For the first time, John saw a pillar of smoke rising over the hill on the far side of the main building. They had been telling the truth about the guest house.

"Now, you might ask me what I would look for in the

31

potential young executive. Presuming, of course, that I had full charge of your personnel division."

"Shut up and run," Tamino said.

John listened. No, what he heard was not a nun screaming but a police siren, getting closer.

"After I had made sure that our candidate had not rented his clothes and his hair for the interview, I would put him through a stiff battery of tests, personally prepared by me," Dr. Klebo panted. He went gamely on. "Masculinity would be something I would hunt for in all the men, depending upon the nature of your business, of course . . . . A certain aggressiveness tempered by that kind of genial father-fixation which would keep our up-and-coming youngster from attempting to assassinate the chairman of the board or the president of the firm . . . . And which post, sir, do you occupy?"

"Run, damn you. Can't you hear those sirens?" Tamino grabbed Dr. Klebo away from Hand and dragged him forward.

"Of course I hear them. I've been hearing them at intervals for the past six weeks ever since that insipid woman had her daughter exhumed from my herb garden." Dr. Klebo scowled over his shoulder, stumbled, and was yanked back into balance by Tamino before he could hit the ground.

They skirted the pigpens and rounded the corner of the barn. Half concealed by the compost heap, a bright blue helicopter waited. Hand ran ahead, jumped behind the controls, and started the propeller into lazy motion.

With Hand pulling and Tamino and John pushing, Dr. Klebo was stuffed into the machine. Tamino lifted himself into the back by Dr. Klebo. John took the seat in front next to Hand.

"Where are the seat belts?" John asked.

"Oh, for God's sake. Get this thing off the ground."

Hand nodded, pushed something, pulled something else, and as John watched, the propeller began to beat the air with increasing fury. Hand gently maneuvered the stick in front of him and they lifted at a forty-five-degree angle and shot toward the treetops.

"I take it that I'm hired," Dr. Klebo said.

Tamino grunted. "You're lucky you're not dead. Phil, what security level did this character reach?"

The helicopter banked down into the valley and John could no longer see the convent; he realized that the convent could no longer see them, either.

"Well"—Hand pulled at his nose—"let's add it up. He knows that we were soliciting Father Doffenbaron. He knows that we were about to kill him. And, he knows my last name. That's about a level five, maybe four just to be on the safe side."

"That's enough justification to shoot anybody."

"I am four-square anti-union, procapital, and some of my best friends are landlords," Dr. Klebo squeaked.

"But we need another corpse like . . . " Tamino broke off and submerged into his own thoughts. When he surfaced, his voice was warm, affable. "All right, Doctor. I've always had a weakness for you men of science. As a matter of fact, I think I know a place where you can hide out and where I can keep an eye on you at the same time. Ever worked with old folks, Doctor?"

"Geratology has always been one of my first loves.

33

Given enough time and enough subjects, sir, I'll turn it into a money-making proposition." Dr. Klebo paused, then giggled to himself.

The laugh was so odd, John turned around to stare. Dr. Klebo rubbed his vest and grinned.

"Ah, John. The corporate mind is a wondrous thing. These moguls have more angles than a train wreck when it comes to seeing a man's true worth and dollar potential. Why spend your time reading forms full of demitruths, with forged letters of reference, if you are the sort of boss who can size up a deserving man down the barrel of a revolver?" Klebo sighed. "Sir, I commend you on the astuteness which has brought us together. I knew from the moment I saw you that we would have a great future doing whatever it is that you do."

"You flatter me, Doctor." Tamino smiled at a private joke of his own. "And yourself. The only reason you're here is because you would have been a spare body with a mystery involved. Bluntly, it was far simpler to walk you to the helicopter than to carry you here."

Dr. Klebo's grin faltered, then rallied. "As proof of my recently established but firmly entrenched loyalty to you, sir, permit me to point out that you could have blamed John."

Tamino shook his head. "No. Afraid not, Doctor. You see, John's dead. He died this morning. That right, Phil?"

John's hand stole to his throat.

"Yessir," Hand agreed. "Father Doffenbaron's charred remains will be found in the embers of the convent guest house. A terrible accident, the body unrecognizable except for dental work. Which, incidentally, is an exact duplication, filling by filling."

The helicopter lifted out of the valley and zoomed over the hills. John stared out the window, thoughts tumbling in his mind. Off in the distance, a silver sparkle against the gray pastureland caught his attention. As they hovered nearer, the outline of an airplane asserted itself through the bright reflections from its own surface. A man stood by one wing, waving up at them.

"Well," Tamino said, "here's where we change trains, friends."

The helicopter settled easily to earth. Tamino pushed John's shoulder, urging him out. John hopped to the ground and gave his shoulder to support Dr. Klebo's descent. "And *me*"—Dr. Klebo smacked his chest—"I suppose I'm dead, too?"

Tamino and Hand left the helicopter and walked to the airplane.

"What about me?" Klebo shouted. "When was I murdered?"

Hand exchanged whispers with the man who had been waiting for them, then crawled up into the plane.

"No, Doctor." Tamino smiled over his shoulder, clearly enjoying himself. "You're a little bit of luck we didn't expect. You're very much alive." He shrugged. "Wanted for two murders by now, I imagine, since you will no doubt be blamed for the fire at the convent."

Dr. Klebo scuffed his toe in the clotted pasture, making figure eights in the dust. "Well, I'm just not sure that I appreciate that. All things being equal, it seems to me that you and your friend here ought to get the credit for murdering John. You two must have murdered somebody to have a spare corpse handy to plant in burning buildings."

The stranger waved good-bye to Hand, accepted a pat on

the shoulder from Tamino, then climbed into the helicopter and accelerated the still spinning propeller. The machine lifted, its rear end tipped higher than the front, and wheeled south toward Massachusetts.

Tamino watched the helicopter disappear, shielding his eyes from the tin-bright glare of the sky. "All right. Let's go."

"Oh, no. Not one step." Body crouched, head thrust out, an indignant tortoise on the attack, Dr. Klebo lifted his fists and trembled. "Not until you give me a good reason why I should be the one who murders everybody and you two flap around, happy as jaybirds, with my favorite patient. It's an injustice."

Tamino sighed and reached for his gun. "I'm afraid that you are not going to find this a wholly satisfactory answer, Doctor, but you're going to have to make yourself happy with it. Mr. Hand and I can't murder anybody. We're in the same boat as John: poor forgotten dead men. Now, Doctor, please oblige me or I will entertain a motion for you to join the club. Get in the plane."

John slept until he felt the airplane begin its descent. He rubbed his eyes and glanced out the window. The earth beneath was a constant buckskin, speckled here and there with red hills which cast long, violet shadows. A picture postcard desert, but which one? Death Valley? Sahara? Gobi? Not that it should matter. John had awakened eager for his adventure, his hands tingling at the prospect of *work*. Stretching his arms and legs, he looked around for Dr. Klebo. Tamino was the only other occupant of the cabin and John presumed that the resourceful Mr. Hand was busy at the controls of the airplane. Straining against his seat belt, he leaned into the aisle. Ahead, just behind the cockpit, sticking out of the luggage compartment, a foot shod in a striped sock and unpolished cordovan bounced in time with the throb of the plane's engines. John did not remember what Dr. Klebo had been wearing on his feet, but striped socks and scuffed cordovans did not seem inconsistent with his general taste. He wondered if it might not be a good idea to see what else was in the luggage compartment —presumably the rest of Dr. Klebo—but was hesitant to leave his seat while the airplane was in motion. He was still weighing alternatives when Tamino spoke.

"Have a nice nap, John?"

"Very pleasant." He smiled across the aisle and stretched again. "The morning was more strenuous than I thought." The plane dipped abruptly and John clutched at the armrests. "I gather we've arrived."

"Well, almost. We have to . . . ah, look down there, John."

Throwing a wall of dust in its wake, a tan limousine played tag with the shadow of the airplane. As they banked to complete their landing, the car swerved on a course of interception. John braced himself and stared straight ahead as the ground rushed to meet them. They hit with a squeal of distressed rubber and the foot leaped up and down, one, two, three times.

"Everybody out." Tamino threw off his seat belt, jumped into the aisle, and ran to the front of the plane, neatly hopping over the foot on his way. Thumps sounded on the fuselage and the door of the plane swung open, washing Tamino in a glittering flood of sunshine and dust. "Hi there, Frank. Right on the dot."

"Yessir. Dr. Ivanson has been charting you since the Missouri Valley."

"Up and out, John. Lots for us to do today."

John started down the aisle. As he reached the luggage rack, he pulled aside the curtain and peered inside. Dr. Klebo, swathed in ropes, gagged, sitting on one foot, jabbing at John with the other one thrust into the aisle, rolled his eyes wildly and wagged his head. He did not seem grossly damaged, so John closed the curtain and followed Tamino to the door. "Are we leaving Dr. Klebo here?"

Tamino lifted his eyebrows. "Goodness, no." He called out the door. "Frank, we have some luggage up here. Could you help Phil load it into the car?"

"Yessir." A lean young man in a tightly fitting brown business suit bounded into the aircraft and followed Tamino's pointing finger to Dr. Klebo's visible foot. Tamino took John's arm and nudged him out of the airplane. A combined force of scorching heat and hard ground made John gasp and stumble. Tamino followed instantly, linked his arm through John's, and led him to the waiting car. "Sorry about your friend, John, but I think he'll be a more cooperative passenger if we leave him like that." Tamino stepped into the back seat, scooted across the upholstery, and nodded for John to follow him. "Ah, just a minute and we'll feel the air conditioning. That sun is a little much."

The interior of the car was dark and cool, with the tinted glass throwing a green, liquid mutation of the harsh desert light on their hands and faces. "To tell you the truth, John," Tamino said, "Dr. Klebo's conversation got on my nerves after a couple of hours. Besides, I didn't want him to disturb your rest—he was yelling quite a bit—so I tapped him and put him out of sight for a while. He'll be all right. The important thing is that we get you home as fresh as a daisy and raring to go." Tamino leaned around John and looked him directly in the eyes. "Want to catch a couple of winks while we ride? We've got time."

"No, thank you. I don't need much sleep, actually."

"Fine, fine." Tamino smiled and leaned back. "That's the kind of talk I like to hear."

A fat brown bundle rolled out the door of the plane and landed with a smack on the ground, throwing up a smokescreen of red silt. The bundle began to hump, inchworm fashion, away from the aircraft to shelter under one of the wings. Hand and the man in the brown suit jumped from the plane and snatched at the bundle, catching one of its feet. John recognized the foot.

Tamino laughed softly. "I'll bet you're going nuts wondering where we're taking you."

John looked away from the struggle under the airplane and stared at Tamino. "No, I wasn't."

"Hm, hm," Tamino nodded. "I admire your single-mindedness, John. We're going to get along."

The trunk lid opened and John could feel the jolt of a considerable weight dropping into the rear of the car. He turned around and watched a wrench rise and fall several times behind the raised trunk lid. The trunk was slammed shut and Hand and the thin man in brown shared a handkerchief to wipe the sweat from their faces. Then Hand walked around the car and crawled into the front seat. "Whew. Frank will take care of the plane," he said.

John and Tamino waved at Frank as the car jerked away and bounced across the desert. John stopped waving when the young man disappeared behind a rising cloud of dust.

As the ride wore on, and on, the monotony of the desert landscape would have been unbearable if John had not forced himself to concentrate on the glorious rekindling of his life that lay somewhere ahead of them. Still, the sand, the strangled clumps of anonymous foliage, the looming sandstone promontories viewed in haste through the green-tinted windows of the speeding automobile gave John the unpleasant feeling that he was trapped in the bottom of a mammoth aquarium. Tamino's eyes were closed and he hadn't spoken for over an hour, but John doubted that he slept. Occasionally, he noticed Hand studying him through the rear-view mirror, but he offered John no conversation. Now and then, as if to remind John that all was not yet well, the little bell began a far-off jingle. His hands incongruously clammy in the coolness of the car, John smothered the impatience which lodged, thirsty, in his throat with the willful assertion that inasmuch as he was on his way to work, he was as good as at work.

Despite himself, John wondered what *kind* of work. He prayed with all his heart and soul that he hadn't been bamboozled into another of those piecework jobs that the Pentagon used to hand out. Six months and then, pfft. How long, after all, should it have taken a competent systems analyst to discover the optimum site for a single rocket emplacement? Not that John ever quite understood what the generals had in mind when they told him to aim the rockets at New York, Boston, Washington, and Camp David, but that was their business. So, given alternative options, John's work led him to select a Kansas farm belonging to a pickle magnate. The magnate was flattered, the generals were delighted, and John was let go. John still felt hurt that, after all his work, they never got around to using those rockets, and wouldn't even let John include the work in his *vitae*.

Perhaps he would be expected to operate the same type of setup he'd had at I.B.M., training children in computer techniques. At least, he'd supposed they were children. They had certainly been eager to learn, darting out of that closed van which brought them to the plant every evening after sundown, chirping and chattering at each other in that perplexing private language of theirs. He had assumed they were orphans, probably foreign. He had never figured out why they were all bald.

For the last half hour or so the car had been aiming at a huge sandstone butte, a phenomenon of the desert which hulked solitary and abandoned by a former age when lost rivers and forgotten oceans had carved it out of a tropical forest. Perhaps that barren island of rock concealed another rendezvous where another Frank would relieve them of the automobile and provide them with still another means of transport. A steamship? A ballistic missile? A time machine? No, there was no confusion about their destination since what had been only a speck on the horizon now almost filled it, an immensity of crags, at least thirteen stories high, probably two or three miles long and half that wide. If they had been traveling on a road, if John had seen the scantest evidence of any sort of trail, he would have been sure that they would bypass the butte since no road or trail charted by rational men would start or end there. But Hand had not taken them near a road and John reasoned that where there were no roads there were no people. He glumly completed a syllogism: where there were no people there were no computers.

As they neared the sheer face of the cliff, Hand steadily aimed the car toward a rockslide that nestled several hundred feet high at the bottom of the precipice. John's eye was not satisfied with the picture. The pile of boulders was too uniform, almost spheroid in shape, and the rocks themselves were of a different composition from that of the butte against which they rested and from which, apparently, they had fallen. The cliff face was dull and pitted; the boulders glistened and shimmered in the sunlight. With a slap of recognition, John sat upright and leaned over the front seat, both elated and calmed. He was back in the realm of technological man. The boulders were fake, plastic, with visible seams.

Hand pressed a button on the dashboard and a section of the ersatz rockslide lifted out of their way. The car, barely decelerating, shot through the entrance. Craning his neck to see through the rear window, John watched the slab close behind them, fitting tightly into place. The rockslide had been nothing more than an enormous geodesic dome with its exterior camouflaged by translucent, acrylic boulders. Even through the bottle-green windows of the car, the light had a new character, a soft bourbon-and-water glow reminiscent of spring honey and perpetual sunset as it filtered down through the encircling globe which now surrounded them.

"You can stop anywhere, Phil." Awake and alert, Tamino threw a protective arm across John's chest as the car braked to a jolting halt. "Okay, fine. Take care of the car. John"—Tamino smacked John's thigh—"welcome to Beulahland. Come on, let's get cracking."

John stepped out of the car, grabbed a fender for support as he looked around, and froze. "What is this? Where am I?"

"Beulahland. Our charity. That old folks' home I promised Dr. Klebo."

On all sides, a mob of ancient Negro men and women in bandannas, gaily patched coveralls, sweeping skirts, bowed and, as best they could, curtsied as Tamino, waving to the right and left, slid from the car. Behind the crowd, like an especially well-constructed three-dimensional stage set, squatted a small village of unpainted shanties, fully equipped with boiling pots on grassless lawns, mournful hounds on broken porch steps and, covering everything, the geodesic rockslide.

John stared at the ring of withered black faces. Everyone grinned but displayed very few teeth. He pulled at Tamino's sleeve. "Are they real?"

"Sure they're real. Hi there, folks!"

A chorus of "Howdy's," "Hi y'all's," and "Yassuh's" answered. Two hats sailed into the air. Pulling John behind him, Tamino pushed his way through the crowd, shaking a hand, pinching a cheek, patting a topknot, until he and John reached the far edge of the dome. A steel door bisected itself and they walked through it into an elevator. Tamino jabbed a button on the panel and the compartment sank.

"Where on earth did you get those people?" John asked.

"Oh, here and there, Chicago, Detroit, Boston, Los Angeles, the big cities mostly. Poor, doddering things, trying to eke out their last years on public welfare dreaming about the good old days down South. Not that those days were ever much good, after all, but people have short memories and still watch old movies, John. Because of their general decrepitude, the turnover's pretty regular, but we keep looking. We only take the ones nobody will miss, the ones who've outlived their friends. We find them and bring them here, back to good old Dixie made all the better because the white boss is gone; in exchange, we let them cook for us and do light housekeeping and general maintenance. They're happy because nobody bosses them around and we see that they get good medical attention and a steady diet. We're happy because we need someone to look after us." Tamino smiled to himself. "What one of our boys, Professor Keruk—you'll meet him—calls a healthy ecological balance."

The elevator had picked up speed but John could not judge its rate of descent. No signal lights marred the surface of the cubicle; the control panel possessed only two buttons, and the increasing muzziness in John's stomach was not an accurate gauge. The ride was smooth, yet Tamino rocked back and forth, then side to side, as if he were adjusting himself to some private gravitational pull. Moving in and out of John's peripheral vision, Tamino's squat body described larger and larger arcs. John wondered if the elevator would stop before Tamino overbalanced and fell. Once, John almost reached out and snatched at him to save him from smashing his face against the door, but Tamino's internal gyroscope yanked him upright, only to hurl him into an even more precipitous swoop. The elevator slowed suddenly and the pressure on John's shoulders almost accordioned him onto the floor. Tamino swayed briefly, then stabilized as the doors slid open.

A sturdy, jut-jawed youth in a brown suit of the same tailoring as Frank's stood barring their passage.

"Good afternoon, Dean." Tamino led John out of the elevator. "I want you to meet Father Doffenbaron. John, this is Corporal Comstock."

"How do you do, Father." Corporal Comstock's eyes ran over John's face, then his torso, and then back for one last intense study of the face. Twisting his pale, pretty features into a quick, almost reluctant smile, he stepped out of their way.

John nodded at Corporal Comstock and caught up with

45

Tamino, who waited several yards away down a brightly lighted corridor.

"This way, John. Welcome to the Center."

John licked his lips. "Can I see the computer?"

Tamino stopped and laughed, clutching his stomach with one hand and patting John's back with the other. "Can you *see* the computer? Oh, my! John, my friend, we're going to put you to work." He pulled him along and hurried down the corridor. "Now, John, keep your eyes open. What do you see?"

John looked ahead, behind. "A hall with no doors."

"Very good, John. Now, what else do you see? Up there. No, John, *up* there."

"Television cameras. Little television cameras." John stopped to examine one more closely, but a push from Tamino kept him moving.

"Our guards use them to monitor the Center, John." Tamino shook his head and sucked his lower lip. "We're understaffed in our security division, I'm afraid. Not that we can't afford more guards; we can't find the kind of dedicated, relentless specialist who can do credit to the job."

"A specialist? At being a guard?"

Tamino gave John a shrewd, slit-eyed glance. "You're catching on fast, John. It's a big, wide, wonderful world we live in and everybody has his own little quirks. Some people run computers, some people guard them, and nothing on earth could make them trade jobs. John, I like a man to be serious about his profession."

John was puzzled. "I should think that doing nothing but guarding people would be boring. You must pay them a great deal."

"John, I don't pay them a cent. Like you, they're doing

their work for the love of it. And don't believe that it's boring work. Not around here."

As they walked, John's feet felt the stroll taking on the proportions of a hike. They moved from one corridor to another, they panted up ramps, they skipped down staircases, they made sharp turns, they eased around gentle curves. They pushed concealed buttons and where walls had been doors appeared, and vice versa. But all doors led to more hallways, never to a room with a computer in it.

A *beep* of doubt in John's brain had turned into a *blatt* of suspicion. "You never explained to me what you need a computer for?"

Tamino smiled. "For our work. For the Fellowship's work, that is."

"I've been wondering about that."

Tamino's arm reached out and pulled John to a stop. "John, I am constitutionally unable to lie to you. But the story is so long and so involved that you just wouldn't believe it. Besides, when we get you down to work, you won't have time to worry about history, ancient, modern, or future." Tamino prodded and they both moved. "Why worry if you don't have to, eh?" Tamino kept talking, although he paused now and then to gulp for breath. "We want you busy and happy, happy and busy. That's why we go to such pains to keep our people isolated from the hum and drum of that blathering frenzy those dingbats in the outside world call a social order. Now Hand is in charge of security. Any time you get worried about anything, you just call on Phil and he'll take care of it. Amazing man, Phil, just amazing the way he looks out for all this. I have absolute confidence in him, no matter what anyone says. One of the Fellowship is pretty cranky about what looks

47

like a security leak. But it's ridiculous. Nobody could borrow one of our tanks and go joy riding out in the desert without the guards getting wind of it." Tamino muttered something John did not catch. "Ridiculous," he added.

"You have tanks?"

Tamino opened his eyes wide. "Of course we have tanks. And cannons and rockets and heaven knows what else. John, we take our people very *seriously*, I hope you understand that. We don't want their work disturbed."

"Speaking for myself, I would find the sound of cannons highly disturbing."

Tamino cocked his head at John. "You wouldn't hear a thing. Not a single teensy pop." He waved at the ceiling. "We're under a mountain, John, buried like fossils under solid granite two thousand feet below sea level. Why, it would take an atomic bomb to crack even the plaster, if it could do that." They rounded another corner and walked down a long ramp.

John frowned.

"You don't look convinced, John. Something I said bother you?"

Gravely bothered, John hesitated, then spoke. "All things being equal, I can't understand why anybody would want to attack us. From what I gather so far, nobody can even find us."

Tamino lifted his eyebrows, nodding. "A point for the most part well taken. Yes, sir, you've got a good head on your shoulders, a fine analytic mind." They had reached a large steel door with a dial set in the center. Tamino spun the knob and ticked out the combination while unobtrusively blocking John's view with his shoulder. "Let me think about this for a minute. The whole world thinks we're dead, right? Oh, they do think that, John. We've worked very hard to make them think that so that our people could work in absolute privacy with no distractions whatever. We burned you up this morning. A couple of us, including Miss Deckstewer, died in plane crashes. Don't look like that, John, I don't mean for *real*. We've had a heart attack and a drowning, I think; anyway, you get the idea. And, as you say"—Tamino gave the knob one last twirl and the door swung silently and smoothly aside— "nobody even knows that this place exists." Tamino wagged his head for John to follow him. "I guess we don't have to worry about being attacked, after all. Good for you, John. You've cleared my mind."

They stood in a large square courtyard, at least eighty feet across, the skylight covered by blue glass masquerading as sky and almost succeeding in disguising the fluorescent tubes above it. Closed doors with brass plates set into them ringed the walls.

"Then what about the cannons and the tanks?"

Tamino put his hands into his pockets and smiled at John. "Guess we just won't ever have a chance to use them, that's all." He turned his head away, but John suspected that he continued to smile. "A shame, really. That sort of thing runs into money."

Tamino strolled across to one of the doors. He stopped and looked back at John. "Come on. This is what you've been waiting for. Don't shiver like that. Get yourself over here."

John swayed slightly and teetered toward Tamino. At this last moment, he was dulled by the conviction that all of it was a lie, that there was no computer, no tapes, no transistors. He would open that door and be back at the convent, where they hadn't even allowed him to keep an abacus.

"This is for you, John." John felt Tamino's hand bump his knuckles and he recoiled until he felt something cold being pressed into his tight fist. "Go on. Take it." John opened his hand and, his chin trembling, saw a key. "Now, my boy, use it."

Barely able to control the spasms running down his arm, John fitted the key into the lock. A hidden motor pulled the door open, dragging John, who would not relinquish his hold on the key.

The room was no larger than the average bedchamber, an effect immediately suggested by the della Robbia blue paint job and immediately belied by the wall of glass staring into darkness opposite the entrance and the two television cameras clinging to the corners of the ceiling. But John's eyes only skimmed these details; they fastened on a dream made real, which huddled in an enormous crescent in the middle of the room. He had once been asked by *Scientific American* to write an article describing what he envisioned as the ultimate computer, the machine he predicted would be perfected within the next hundred years. John had fantasized it, the magazine had printed it, and now somebody had built it. Words clogged in his throat and mouth. He could not move. "The technology . . . "

He felt Tamino's hand on his shoulder. "Our Miss Feuer. Your idea, of course." The hand patted John's back.

The crescent served as the desk console, just as John had known it would look, its surface arranged in seven tiers, the tiers cradling ranks of colored bars arranged lengthwise in steady gradations of the visible spectrum, like Technicolor piano keyboards with sharps and flats omitted. An outsize

I.B.M. Selectric typewriter with six extra rows of letters and symbols nestled in a well cut into the center of the crescent. To one side, other equipment that John did not recognize as part of his original plan clustered against the wall; teletypes, Xerox copiers, Datafax machines, all wired by a single thick umbilicus to the console. A black leather swivel chair sat in front of the typewriter, a tiny microphone on a supple arm reaching out from the back to a position from which it could catch and relay every word uttered by the chair's occupant. Six small green glass television screens, three to a side, covered the sharp points of the crescent. As John watched, numbers and words danced across these screens at a pace almost, but not quite, too fast to scan. "We're receiving data!" Summoning his courage, John took two steps forward. He still couldn't put out his hand for fear that his touch would dissolve the miracle.

He looked around the room, hunting. The machine commanded by this console would have to be monstrous, with a storage capacity of at least 10^{1500}. Unheard of; even with the best miniaturization techniques, the cabinetry would be as big as ten, maybe twenty Empire State Buildings. John turned to Tamino, stretching his hands out. "Where is it? The rest of the hardware, let me see it."

Tamino's face creased in taut sympathy and he guided John to the console. "Sit in the chair, John."

Careful not to touch the console itself, John eased himself down, ducking the microphone as it jabbed past his eye. Before him, through the glass wall, a soft light glowed, illuminating an endless corridor the size of a thousand hockey rinks placed end to end; ranked on each side, stretching to an invisible and unknowably remote vanishing

51

point, stood the twin rows of cabinetry, the open space between crisscrossed with a jungle of cables, wires, and circuits binding the two halves which faced each other off into infinity.

The typewriter sputtered and John jerked.

ARE YOU OF THE FELLOWSHIP?

The little aluminum ball threw itself across the surface of the paper.

IDENTIFY YOURSELF AT ONCE OR I SHALL FILL THIS ROOM WITH A CYANIDE DERIVATIVE GAS. IDENTIFY YOURSELF. MAMA.

Tamino reached past John and tapped his name out on the typewriter:

DAN TAMINO.

"Dear me," Tamino clucked. "More of that silly security business. Looks like we even have the machines in the habit."

John was less offended by the threat of being gassed than by the conclusion of the signal. *"Mama?"*

"Well, yes. Deckstewer christened it; MAMA for Maximal Amplified Mathematical Analyzer and it sort of stuck. Don't look at me like that, John. It was her computer, after all. And she had her own little peculiarities, just like everybody else."

John relaxed. These problems could be dealt with. "Miss Deckstewer's idiosyncrasies are tolerable in Miss Deckstewer; quantified, they merely take up space in the

52

memory banks. Not, I must admit"—he threw another disbelieving look at the line of cabinets—"that we don't seem to be well endowed." Biting his lip, John gently shifted the chair about to face the console. "What language do we use?"

"Eh?" Tamino raised an eyebrow. "Oh. English."

John let his fingers touch the keys of his typewriter but did not apply any pressure. "Basic? Fortran? Cobol? Argol? Synthic? Omniprog?" He tried to ignore the perspiration slipping over his eyelids. "It doesn't matter." He remembered. He had designed this computer, dreamed this computer. John reached to the third tier of keys and depressed a pale magenta bar, which promptly began to glow and pulse. The machine readied for a deletion command. John typed out the order:

SIGNATURE MAMA.

Almost before he could look up, a light flickered far down the gauntlet of cabinets and a tiny, distant spool whirled, made a reverse turn, and stopped. The magenta bar lifted into alignment with its companions and flickered off. John smiled, a release of the first true joy he had known for a long, long time. "That takes care of Miss Deckstewer's MAMA. Now, what else can I do?"

"John, you're all business." Tamino squatted beside John's chair and spoke in a low voice. "As a matter of fact, I would be extremely grateful if you would take care of one little piece of business that's been hanging fire for the past week or so. Apparently, the computer started to perform a job for our observatory and then stopped. You don't suppose you could get it back to work, do you?"

John rubbed his palms together. "Now, let's clear

something up before we go any further. The computer would not *stop* doing a job unless it had stopped altogether. My predecessor, Miss Deckstewer, might have stopped it, or perhaps the job was unperformable. However, we'll try."

"You're wonderful."

John surveyed the computer console and tapped the bridge of his nose. "Let's see. Be patient, Mr. Tamino. I'm going to have to get used to my equipment."

"Call me Dan."

Etched into the colored keys were tiny symbols, all of which John knew very well. He'd invented them. The trick lay in selecting the proper combinations—"chords" John had called them in his *Scientific American* piece—and the proper sequence. He struck three bars simultaneously and one by itself. Lights flashed in the far reaches of the corridor of cabinets. "Now, what I have done is call for the computer to retrieve its last instructions from the observatory and to disregard any subsequent cancellation order."

The typewriter chittered a note across the paper in the carriage.

CONFIRMED. LATER DATA NOW BEING PROCESSED.

John scowled. "Later data?"

"Oh, the computer is constantly on intake, John. We feed it every bit of information we can. Newspapers, periodicals, wire service reports, and so on. Frankly, I can't remember all the sources we draw on." Tamino used the arm of John's chair to pull himself to his feet. "Naturally, it absorbs everything that goes on here." He paused and considered John's upturned, slack-jawed face. "Why, John, I think I've frightened you."

No, not frightened. John was stunned. The amount of data which the computer absorbed over a twenty-four-hour period must be incalculable. John stared at the rows of lights darting back and forth across the twin rows of cabinets like jet-propelled fireflies. That was it! The computer had a built-in screening device, an almost incredibly sophisticated heuristic methodology which prevented it from considering irrelevant portions of its memory banks when given a problem. Through the window, the lights slowed down and resumed a random pattern of flickers.

TENTATIVE SOLUTION. CONSULTING HOUSTON I.B.M. 1975 FOR FURTHER DATA.

"Houston? The university?" Of course, now he understood how it worked. John's computer limited itself quantitatively by refusing to absorb information already programmed into existing hardware to which it was wired.

"Afraid not, John. The Space Center." Tamino had produced a nail-clipper and was giving himself a manicure.

"Do they allow that?"

Tamino grimaced and chewed on a hangnail before answering. "Well, John, they've never stopped us. As a matter of fact, I don't imagine that they know." He flicked a paring off his jacket. "Might be a wee bit of a problem for us if they did."

Clicks and whirrs from the typewriter drew John's attention away from Tamino.

SOLUTION PROBABILITIES HIGH. NOW ASSUMING CONTROL OF OBSERVATORY.

The four colored bars John had activated popped up and blinked out. Six more keys in the red end of the first tier depressed of their own accord and throbbed with light. John's face constricted with tears. He had never been so happy.

A disembodied voice bellowed over their heads. "Mr. Tamino. We seem, at long last, to be under way up here." John whirled and opened his mouth to speak, but a freshly trimmed finger over Tamino's lips silenced him. "If, as seems likely, we have someone working in the Computer Center, permit me to extend to him, or her, or them, my thanks, congratulations, and an invitation to join me in the observatory within the next fifteen minutes to enjoy the fruits of our mutual labors. If, on the other hand, the computers are at present operating without guidance, please be so advised and have the situation corrected at once. The radio telescope, at any rate, is in motion." The voice climbed an octave and spoke more rapidly. "Without any direction from *me*, Mr. Tamino." The voice shrieked. *"Do you hear me?"*

Tamino leaned over John, threw a switch on the microphone and shouted. "Loud and clear, Doctor. Glad to know everything's all right at your end. Our new man will be right up." He winked at John and flicked off the microphone.

"Thank God." Click.

Tamino walked across the chamber and shook his head at a grid in the ceiling. "We're going to have to tune those speakers down. They could scare a man out of a year's growth. I'll have it taken care of first thing tomorrow." Tamino moved to the door and waited. "Shall we go? A compliment from your colleague upstairs is a compliment indeed. And an invitation to the observatory, well"—he rolled his eyes—"you'd better hie yourself up there. If I know Ivanson, this will be your last chance to see what we've got going for us in the astronomy game."

John stroked the console, looking out through the window at the cables and cabinets. After so long a wait, he didn't want to leave, not even for a moment. "I'm so happy here." He tried to say "Dan" but couldn't get the name to fit on a tongue accustomed to calling superiors by official titles. "Do I have to go?"

Tamino folded his arms and leaned against the door-frame, an act of patience which translated to John as compassion. "Nope. But you've got to learn your way around, John. We won't stay long. We'll whiz you through the Center, let you take in our operation, meet your colleagues, and get you back here before you know you've been away." He measured John with a long look, then added, "Everything will still be here. It's all yours now, you know."

Despite himself, John could not restrain the tears which brimmed into his eyes, blinding him, then spilled over his cheeks onto his lap. He shook his head and waved away the blurred figure which moved toward him. "Don't. Please. I'm not sad. I'm happy." He warred with the muscles of his face, ordering them to smile while they insisted on crying. "I feel as if I'm alive for the very first time, ever."

"Attaboy, John. Maybe you are. Now, blow your nose. Oops, I already gave you my handkerchief. There. Blow."

John blew, twice, then stuffed the handkerchief into his breast pocket. "Thank you. I'm ready."

Tamino led him to the door. "You'll have to use your key, John." John pulled up his cassock skirts and retrieved it from his pocket, turned it in the lock, and dodged as the door pulled back to let them pass.

Tamino and John made a sharp left as they came out of the chamber and entered another elevator, this one moving so fast that John cried out as it shot up. Had they been descending at the rate at which they were rising, John would have feared for his life. His ears popped, his intestines fought rearrangement, and his pants threatened to fall off. The elevator came to an abrupt, no-nonsense stop and John continued to lift off the floor. He reeled, reached for a wall just as it slid away, and sprawled onto the pavement.

Tamino rushed to help, dusting John's knees, checking his hands for scrapes. "Gosh, John, I didn't think to warn you. Our astronomer likes his elevators fast. He doesn't mess around." Together, they got John off the floor, where he stood weaving, blinking, trying to coalesce Tamino and a ghostly twin into focus. "This way, John, right this way. We'll rush you through the observatory and get going. You didn't break anything, did you?"

John shook his head and let Tamino support his elbows as he stumbled down the length of a narrow hallway.

"You can't go all stiff like that, John." Tamino said. "Bend your knees, flex. This door here, John. I'll ring. Up, down, all around, like a boxer. I always do that in elevators. Even slow ones. Never hurts to be prepared."

John passed a hand across his face and nodded. "Yes, I saw you before. I wondered about it." He also wondered if Tamino knew the disconcerting effect he had on the other passengers.

A light on the doorframe ordered them to "Enter" and Tamino shoved John ahead as the door opened for them.

They stood in an enormous chamber filled with electronic equipment, dynamos, and girders stretching toward and through the ceiling; not since Baron Frankenstein's retirement from Hollywood had John seen such a room. Against one wall hung a large screen and on the screen John recognized the image of a parabolic antenna rising out of still another geodesic dome, this one on top of the butte.

"An astonishing mechanism, four times the size of the instrument at Jodrell Bank, a trifle over one thousand feet in diameter. I'm rather proud of it."

A frail, sandy-haired man in a white smock stained with grease moved from behind a nearby girder and approached them. "Pardon me for not greeting you more promptly, gentlemen, but I prefer to stay out of reach until I am reasonably certain of my callers' intentions." His eyelids, thicker than the skin on the rest of his face, movable calluses, dropped as he bowed to Tamino. "Mr. Tamino. And"—the eyelids flickered at John, then hung, almost too heavy to bear their own weight, at midpoint across his corneas—"the reverend gentleman is the font of today's singular boon, I gather?" He put his hands behind his back and gave John a slightly deeper, more profound bow than he had given Tamino. "I am Erland Ivanson."

A memory of a half-read notice in the *Times* rippled across John's mind. A sailboat accident in the Gulf of Mexico. John returned the bow. "I am familiar with your work, Dr. Ivanson. John Doffenbaron."

Dr. Ivanson half turned toward Tamino. "Is he now a permanent adjunct of our little family?"

"He burned to death this morning in a convent guest house."

"I see." Dr. Ivanson offered John a smile filled with

59

many things, none of them happy. "Let us devoutly hope that the nuns were well protected by fire insurance." He wheeled and shuffled away, talking over his shoulder as John and Tamino followed. "Am I right to assume that you are a Catholic priest?"

"Yes."

Dr. Ivanson stopped at a control board and examined an expanse of dials and gauges. John could not guess the function of the machine but he admired its complexity. "Well, then"—Dr. Ivanson pulled levers with both hands—"you no doubt have a vigorous curiosity about the nature of the heavens."

John wanted to go back to his computer, and Dr. Ivanson's manner, while much too urbane for the ghoul demanded by the setting, was scarcely an incentive to stay. "By your standards, Dr. Ivanson, I'm afraid not. I have certain fixed *beliefs* about the nature of Heaven but no particular interest in astronomy, save as a possible source of an occasionally challenging program for my computer."

Tamino winced. "Now, John, I'm sure that Dr. Ivanson didn't mean to . . . "

Ivanson silenced him with a slicing gesture. "No offense. On the contrary. Merely another case of intellectual stalemate." He considered John, eyelids sinking. "At least I have the assurance, Father Doffenbaron, that you won't be pottering around these premises asking impertinent questions like a female pseudoscientist of my acquaintance. We shall, if necessary, get along very well."

Unconvinced, John smiled and turned to Tamino. "Well, I'm certainly grateful to Dr. Ivanson for his time, but don't you think we'd better be going?"

Dr. Ivanson lifted a long, smudged hand. "I won't hear of it. An indulgence, Father, an indulgence of patience. I want you here to be a witness and, as fate would have it, a colleague, as we make history." The lifted hand swooped out and pointed at the screen. "That is my telescope being controlled by your computer. Today, for at least five more minutes, we are wedded." Without turning around, Dr. Ivanson felt along the panel until he found a switch; he threw it and the chamber boomed with static from a dozen loudspeakers, a mountain of cellophane being crushed by giants. John lowered his head and snapped his eyes shut. "Listen, Father, listen," Dr. Ivanson shouted, his voice high and reedy over the din. "Listen to the music of the spheres, radio transmissions from a billion galaxies pouring into my giant ear, guided by your giant brain."

John looked up and saw Dr. Ivanson clamp a pair of earphones on his head. "These are the exotic themes, a symphony of infinite variation, of mutually exclusive countermelodies." Dr. Ivanson laughed. "Strings, timpani, horns, a sound too full for our poor mortal minds to appreciate."

On the screen, the parabolic aerial moved more slowly, laboriously easing itself into position. The generalized static cleared away and, as they listened, a new sound echoed around them, a grinding, crunching noise: acorns squashing on sidewalks, corn submitting to a pestle, roaches mashing under a heel. Tape spools whirled into action as the sound swelled and then, with a last crescendo, became thinner and thinner. "Father," Ivanson said, a keening whine in his words, "do you know what you are hearing? That is your *tuba mirum*, the last trump, playing out its melancholy salute to the end of time. How many stars died to this music, I wonder? How many galaxies perished on that day a million eons ago when this solo began its journey through space to us?" The loudspeakers had gone silent, the tape spools had stopped spinning. Dr. Ivanson shuddered and braced himself against his control board. "I have heard a part of our universe disappear. Where? Why?" He glanced back and forth at John and Tamino, then allowed his eyes to be swallowed by their lids. "I see that you are impatient to go. Very well. The concert is over and I have a great deal of work to do." Without another word, Dr. Ivanson rewound the tapes and started them over, playing back the grating noises the aerial had just plucked out of space. Needlessly, John thought, he and Tamino tiptoed away under the thunder of the loudspeakers, crept down the hallway and into the elevator.

The plummet back to the courtyard was everything John had anticipated, and worse, his buoyant stomach rebelling at Tamino's bobbing and swaying. Gulping and nauseated, John lurched from the elevator as soon as the doors opened and leaned against the entrance to the computer chamber, pressing his cheek against the cool steel.

"Let's have the key, John, and get you back to work."

John belched and gagged.

"John, you're *sick*." Tamino cursed aloud. "And no wonder, after what I've put you through today. I'm an ass. I haven't even fed you. Come on, let's get you to bed."

A wave of cotton rolled through John's midsection. "No bed, no food," he gurgled. "Work."

"Here we go." Tamino almost shoved him over. John resisted.

Firmly, and not particularly gently, Tamino pushed John along the wall to another steel door. While Tamino fumbled with locks and knobs, John slid to the floor like a wounded bat, trying to force the memories of Tamino's ritual elevator dance out of his mind. Grunting, Tamino yanked John to his feet and dragged him through the door. John shut his eyes as he felt his toes dragging across carpeting, felt his knees hit a springy firmness. "A nap for you, buddy boy," Tamino said.

John was already toppling onto the bed before he opened his eyes. A pink quilted coverlet rushed to meet him and kissed his face. Silk. He cuddled into it. It cuddled around him. He felt better.

"You have to throw up?" Tamino moved beside the bed and flicked on a lamp somewhere. John lifted his eyelids and peeked through them.

"No, thank you. I'll be all right. Just a minute."

Tamino's ample rear momentarily filled his field of vision and then passed on out of sight.

"You'll find a button over here by the door, John. I'm pushing it. It'll bring your housekeeper and she'll tend to you. Her name is, uh, it's on the card here, Junta, Mamie Junta. Call her Mamie. She'll expect it."

John heard the door click shut. He waited, counted to ten, then pushed himself up on one elbow and looked around. Tamino had gone. His stomach, with occasional lapses, was settling, but he felt weak. He carefully pulled himself to a sitting position on the edge of the bed and explored the room with his eyes. Pink wallpaper, pink shag rugs, stuffed Steiff animals (three bears and a tiger), a copy of Krafft-Ebing on the bedside table, frills and pussy-cat bows on the lampshades, two television cameras, and a duplicate of the crescent console in the computer chamber. Numbers and words hopped and skipped across the surfaces of the little green television screens; queasy again, John turned away, belching. Not yet. He flopped backward, feeling the bedclothes embrace him, satisfied that the console was so close at hand, satisfied that he was near it. He conjured up happy pictures of programs, Omniprog equations, cabinetry, wires, and slid toward sleep.

"Well, now, what do we have here?"

Had John dozed? He couldn't tell. But he had no doubts about the shape that ballooned at the end of the bed, black arms on hips, white eyes twinkling in a chocolate moon. "Mamie," he said.

"You guessed it, honey." She swaggered across the room, her stride more of a thrust from the pelvis than a conventional lift of the knees. John guessed her to be no more than five feet tall but at least half that wide. Mamie's skirts sputtered over the carpet, a feather duster in her hand, which passed over the furniture like a magic wand, touching but not lingering.

"You the new one?"

"I've replaced Miss Deckstewer."

Mamie had her head in a closet. "My, my. They ain't even got that girl's clothes out yet." A blizzard of vinyl, taffeta, nylon, and wool sailed over her shoulder, piling up in the center of the room. John's stomach twinged but surrendered as he contemplated Miss Deckstewer's wardrobe. Bonnie had always been big on flesh tones.

Mamie swayed across the room to a credenza. Delicate spiderwebs of lace whizzed past John. "She was a sweet little thing," Mamie said, "but scrawny. Couldn't get that girl to eat nothin'." She pulled out a drawer and held it upside down over the pile of clothing. Pennies and a lipstick case joined the collection. Drawer hanging from one hand, the other arm cocked over a lard shelf in the general area where most women had waists, Mamie assayed John. "You won't be needin' any of this stuff, will you, honey?"

John shook his head.

"Well, I'll just take it off your hands, then." Bonnie's wardrobe, surrounded by a brown blur, tangled and folded into a bundle.

"Take those, too." John pointed at the stuffed animals and the book.

Mamie pondered the offer. "Can't think what I'd do with those, honey." She gathered up the bears, the tiger, and the Krafft-Ebing and shoved them through a panel in the wall. "This here's the incinerator. Anything you don't want and I can't use goes in here." A sense of wonder filled John, a conviction that he had touched the pulse of things totally unrelated to the basics of what he believed to be the full life. "What are you going to do with Miss Deckstewer's clothes?"

"Hee hee hee!" Mamie rocked and heaved with laughter. No doubt about it; John listened twice to make sure: she *did* go "Hee hee hee."

"Can't say that I have any notion. Hee hee. Habits is hard to break, that's all."

Mamie hoisted the bundle onto her shoulder and packed it toward the door. She opened it, took one step and stopped, the knapsack sliding over her buttocks and landing, plump, on the floor.

"Just one moment, Mamie." A slenderized Valkyrie wearing curls and suit of the same shade of taupe stalked across the threshold and dropped a briefcase on the carpet. "Have you taken care of everything here?" She looked at

John as if she suspected him of molesting children. "Did she unpack your things? Did she arrange a meal schedule? Did she ask you whether you liked this room?"

Mamie humped backward until she bounced against the computer terminal and stopped.

"I didn't bring anything with me," John said. "Nothing to unpack. I have an upset stomach, so I haven't thought about eating."

"Mm. Do you like the room? The decoration?" The woman fingered the pink bedcover. "I can't imagine this being to your taste. Do you have any color preferences?"

John thought, feeling rushed, harried. "Black, I suppose. Gray? White?"

An acid glint skimmed across the tall woman's eyes and she aimed a scarlet fingernail at Mamie, who cringed. "All right, Mamie. Get us a tailor from your place. He's to bring fabric samples." She squinted at John's cassock. "Wool, I think. Dacron. All black. And a painter; tell him we want a flat off-white for walls, ceiling, and a deep gray on the woodwork. And you might bring Father some light broth, tea, and toast. Oh, find that Sarah woman and tell her to put my dinner in the warmer and wait for me. I may be here for an hour or so and I want to discuss a few things with her." Her eyes spilled accusation on the bundle of clothes and then on John. "Did you tell her she could have those things?"

"She's perfectly welcome to anything that Miss Deckstewer left."

Pathetic longing vibrated between Mamie and her bundle.

"Very well. Take it and get on your way. And don't pout."

Mamie snatched up her spoils and limped out the door.

" ' . . . the rage of the vulture, the love of the turtle, now melt into sorrow, now madden to crime.' " The woman retrieved her briefcase and put it on the credenza, flipping the locks and removing a bundle of wires. "Lord Byron was right and you were wise to agree with him. She would have taken those things, sooner or later." She laid the wires aside and turned to John. When she had first come in, he had thought the smoke-colored hair to be an affectation, but he realized that the woman was old, extremely old, her handsome face cross-hatched with thousands of tiny valleys under a paste of make-up. John had been deceived by her erect posture, the light voice, the elegant body and legs. "I met Dan Tamino a few minutes ago and he said that you weren't feeling well, so I dropped by to give you some tests." She fondled the wires. "I have the basic reports on you which were compiled before you came but they aren't much help, I'm afraid."

"Oh, well, I appreciate your concern, but I don't think you have to bother. I just got a little queasy from all the excitement and the elevator ride from the observatory finished the job." John stood up and smiled. "I'm much better already. I'll be fine by tomorrow, Doctor."

Only at this moment did John realize how tall the old woman was. She had him by a good five or six inches. Her eyes darkened and thinned under lowering brows. "The crisis is over? Too bad." She tossed the wires back into her briefcase and clamped the lid shut. "I'm not a doctor, by the way, in any sense of that word. I have been doing some stress studies for my work and your little discomfiture might have been helpful." She snapped the briefcase off the credenza and marched to the door. "If you have any free time tomorrow, we might run you up and down that elevator and try again."

"I don't think I want to go back to the observatory." John tried to smile, but he didn't appreciate the humor in making him sick again.

"No, of course not," she said flatly. She opened the door and Mamie, who had apparently been poised outside, crept across the room carrying a covered tray. "That's the point. Dr. Ivanson and I are the only people who seem not to be disturbed by the elevator. He had it speeded up to insure his privacy; I have found it most useful in inducing temporary disorientation in my research subjects. Right, Mamie?" She lifted her briefcase, as if in salute, and left.

Mamie pulled a table out of the wall and spread it with steaming dishes and cups. "That Miss von Helsing," she mumbled, a solemn pause between each word, "that gal some kind of witch for sure."

John's fingers and fists whipped back and forth across the console, striking chords, typing out instructions, reorganizing the programs Mamie had brought in with his coffee and eggs, stuffing the computer with problem upon problem, ducking as Mamie tried to fork half a slice of bacon into his mouth. "I'll eat later." How long would he be awed by this equipment? He had set up at least seventy programs since he had pulled himself, gummy-tongued and blinking, from under the quilts and staggered across the bedroom to the terminal.

"You gotta eat your breakfast, honey. You didn't have next to nothin' last night." Mamie poked at the corner of his mouth with a triangle of toast. John nibbled and chewed. Mamie pushed a cup of coffee under his nose and he lapped at it.

"More sugar," he said and Mamie padded away. John

was not particularly surprised that the computer could handle seventy different programs simultaneously, but he was fascinated by the manner in which it did so. Most computers could do no more than say "Yes" or "No," but this one appeared to have some kind of "Maybe" regulator which allowed it to offer probable solutions to problems for which it had insufficient data.

"Your teeth gonna rot." Mamie blotted out one side of the room as she returned with the coffee and tipped the cup into his mouth. Much of the material he had been dealing with had already been set up into Basic, but he had retranscribed the whole lot into Omniprog since that seemed to be the language which the computer used with the greatest facility. Now John quantified a bundle of random facts which the computer filed and related with data already held in storage.

SEISMOGRAPH READING +9 AT 500 HOURS N. HEMISPHERE 53.75 LAT 6 LONG W. GREENWICH. CORRELATE WITH ANALOGOUS INFO REC 24 HOURS PREV AND SUBSQNT.

John typed the order and considered it. He had just instructed the machine to compare any sizable earthquake reports in the last twenty-four hours to one that occurred at 5:00 a.m. (this morning?) as well as any that might happen during the next twenty-four hours. He had presumed a delay restraint which would keep a goodly portion of the computer on a stand-by basis for the next day. He checked the order to make sure he had read it correctly, saw that he had, and added another line:

NOTIF. FEUER. EMERG.

70

He frowned A lot of people must take this machine for granted; they were using it as a communications center to keep themselves informed of current events.

"Honey, you don't have no shoes on." Mamie crawled across the floor toward his feet. "You're gonna catch your death." She struggled with the laces. "You could use you a bath, honey," Mamie said.

"Later."

Mamie pulled herself upright. "Before you go to bed tonight? Promise?"

How would the computer know about any earthquakes unless John gave it the information? His eyes caught sight of the chorus line of hieroglyphs entrechating across the television screens.

"I'll strip you nekkid and put you in the tub myself if you don't promise."

Data were being received which bypassed John, but he didn't know from where or how much. In other words, he had to assume that the computer had sufficient data to work out a problem, or had access to other information and had been preprogrammed to know where to search for it.

"All right, honey, you asked for it."

Shirt buttons popped and John moved his arms so that the sleeves could be pulled off. That, of course, was a Deckstewer trademark: how often had John argued with her during those steamy seminars at M.I.T. about the wisdom of using as much hardware to program a computer to hunt for data to solve a problem as to store the data in the first place. John had always agreed that Bonnie's approach would simplify the programmer's job, but he had objected on the grounds that he knew of no computer large

71

enough to give over that much of itself for search purposes and still function adequately.

"Lift your feet. I'm taking those shoes right back off."

John wiggled his toes in the cool air. The demands on the machine, the cross-referencing devices involved, the communications network required were inconceivable. Well, one way for him to find out what was confronting him was to ask. He struck two chords, one on the top tier, another on the far right of the fifth tier. The alphabet ball in the typewriter jumped up and down, then darted across the face of the paper roll.

DATA AVAILABLE FROM THE FOLLOWING SOURCES: SAN FRANCISCO EARTHQUAKE CENTER, YOKOHAMA SEISMOGRAPH, BRISBANE METEOROLOGICAL INSTITUTE, CAPETOWN UNIVERSITY SEISMOGRAPH, NAVAL OBSERVATORY, RAND CORPORATION 575 . . . .

John tapped a cancellation order and the typewriter switched off. Mamie made him stand up and walk. All very well and good that information was available from Yokohama, but how did the computer get it? And how was it quantified, made intelligible to the computer? Was the machinery somehow attached to a seismograph in Japan?

"You sure could use yourself some exercise. You getting yourself a regular little pot."

Naturally, communication between two computers was not only a possibility but a commonplace. Outside of some delicate diplomatic negotiations with the telephone company, no great technical problems were involved *there*. But had Bonnie preadjusted the hardware to scan, correlate, and assimilate sensor readings from other machines? Theoretically, John saw no great difficulties. Although he was a bit

72

vague on the mechanics of seismograph operation, he suspected that whatever it did could be reduced to electric impulses instead of carbon jiggles on a scroll.

"You're a real man, ain't no doubt about it. If ol' Mamie was a few years younger we'd both of us be gettin' a scrubbin'. Just lift up that leg, honey. Mmmmmm mmm. Look at that."

John was excited. Not that seismograph readings were all that great an academic curiosity, but if the computers were programmed to absorb them, then what else might they be prepared to assimilate? His own work with radar installations and cybernetic interpretation had been one of the first breakthroughs, after all. The Joint Chiefs of Staff had sent him a very nice letter. Oh, my!

"Do that feel good, honey?"

So much to do, to find out. John would run inventories. He would check out wiring. He would find plans. He would see Tamino. Nothing so wonderful had ever happened to him. He couldn't stand it.

"Whoops!"

Joy, his heart and soul bubbled over with joy.

"Bet you never had you a bath like that before. You just lie back and soak, honey, and Mamie'll lather you up and shave off them whiskers."

John would have to restrain himself. As large as the system might be, after all, it wouldn't have any emergent properties. That is, the computer was, could be, only the sum of its parts and no more. On the other hand, John really had no idea what that sum might be, was not sure that if he did know he would be any better prepared to predict the computer's capabilities. He needed some kind of topological approach, where he could isolate bits and pieces, separate the variables, and draw intelligent conclusions about what his equipment would do.

"This here's cologne, honey. Gonna make you the sweetest smelling thing from here to Memphis."

Sure, he could talk all he wanted about "the sum of the parts," but even if he spent a year creeping around inside the cabinets, charting the circuitry, counting the transistors, he still wouldn't know how far the computer would or could reach to establish contact with another part and, God help him, John hadn't the slightest notion what that part might be.

"All right, honey. Into your drawers. Now you gotta brush your teeth yourself. Ol' Mamie's done more than her share already."

An astringent thrill ran through him. Who could predict what channel capacities the computer might possess? Only the computer, and even if John asked, all he'd get as an answer would be a number, nothing related to specific programming needs. Certainly, it would be only reasonable to assume that whatever were the areas of principal concern to Tamino's Fellowship would be primary in the computer's memory banks as well. But what, actually, comprised the computer's environment? This morning John had run seventy or so programs, four involving the theory of games, seventeen analyzing the placement of NH_3 in hydrocarbon molecules, countless statistical surveys concerned with everything from the group behavior of senescent Zulus to paranoia among Jewish refugees, five separate metal stress analyses, and so on, not to mention the data on earthquakes.

"Honey, you're gonna have to pick up your feet if you're planning to wear pants under that black dress of yours."

Did the computer interview Zulus? Did it persecute Jews? Did it run a chemistry lab? A blacksmith's shop?

"Shoes. We got to get them shoes back on. You gotta help ol' Mamie."

Nonsense. But perhaps they made contact with computers containing data provided by people who did interview Zulus, who did persecute Jews. No, John rejected that as insufficient explanation. The computer would need access to more information than that stored by the totality of the world's cybernetic hardware at any given moment. How could they guarantee that computer X would be working on problem Y when they needed the data?

"Ah, John, good to see you up and at 'em." Tamino stood in the doorway squeezing in his stomach as Mamie hobbled past. "You look a little flushed, John. Don't you feel better?"

"Oh, yes, fine. I've been working."

Tamino strolled to the console and dragged a finger across the stack of program requests. "So I see. And the boys in the guardroom tell me that Mamie is looking out for you all right."

John glanced self-consciously at the television cameras tacked to the ceiling. "Oh, yes. I had breakfast promptly at six." The tray was gone; he presumed that he had eaten.

AWAITING CONFIRMATION FROM BRISBANE AND SYDNEY.

"John, you seem distracted." Tamino leaned over the top of the console, resting his chin between open palms. "Something bothering you? Be honest, buddy. Tell me."

John waved his hand at the terminal. "It's this, all of it, all that hardware buried under the desert. I don't know what it does. I used to think I knew how a computer

75

worked, but I can't figure out how this one gets and processes its data. I come up with theories, but the theories are crazy. They presuppose too much."

Tamino slapped a hand down on the console. "John, you stop worrying this minute, do you hear me? Just be glad that the computer does what you want it to. What more can you want?"

John slumped in his chair. "I don't understand."

Tamino made a face, then walked around the console and put a hand on his shoulder. "John, let me be your Dutch uncle for a minute. Don't get mad, just hear me out."

John stared at the little television screens. One was gyrating with wavy lines, another was flashing unpunctuated words in Cyrillic, another was cataloging mandible norms for a tribe of vegetarian Eskimos, and two others seemed to be computing the Dow Jones average. "Where is it getting all that data? *Why* is it getting all that data?"

"John!" Tamino pulled him around in his chair so he could not see the terminal. "You're not here to think, John. You're here to work. Now, I didn't want to tell you this because you're a sensitive guy and I understand, but you might as well hear it from a friend as from anyone else. The month before she disappeared—yes, John, *disappeared*—Bonnie Deckstewer went running around the Center grabbing people and asking them the very same question. 'MAMA's at it again,' she'd say. Things like, 'MAMA's just got hold of the first draft of the President's State of the Union Address,' and then she'd get mad when we asked her if it was any good. 'Where did MAMA get it?' Bonnie would say. 'This is for the State of the Union *next year!'* We tried to calm her down, told her that somebody was playing a practical joke, but old Bonnie didn't believe us. Not that anybody would do such a thing in malice, John, but some people have odd ideas about what's funny.

"Now Bonnie knew as well as the rest of us that when we put the computer together, we wired it into all sorts of things, microwave relays, telephone wires, party lines, taps on other computers, God knows what all. Anything with a wire, we're plugged into it. Bonnie should have known that, with time, the machine would pick up little tricks that none of us had counted on. Who knows, John, maybe a computer in Washington *does* write the President's State of the Union Address a year in advance and they rearrange the country to fit the speech; maybe our computer caught 'em at it, but that didn't satisfy Bonnie. She started to worry because she couldn't figure out *how* it was happening. John, that girl went to pieces." Tamino paused and closed his eyes, overwhelmed by a memory so vivid and so awful that it had to be savored. "She wandered around, this bug-eyed look on her face, gibbering about how she was going to find out if it took the rest of her life. Then one day, poof! No Bonnie. John"—Tamino searched John's eyes—"we don't want that to happen to you."

"What happened to *her?*"

Tamino thrust his hands in his pockets and slouched across the carpet, then back. "Nobody knows. She'd locked herself in the computer chamber, so we know she didn't come out. We had to use a blowtorch on the door and when we got inside, she was gone. We searched this place high and low, even sent a scouting party into the desert. Not even one gnawed bone that looked fresh enough to be Bonnie."

John rubbed his hand over the console, careful not to depress any bars. "I'll try to take my mind off it, but it's hard."

Tamino punched John's shoulder, so quickly that John was unable to dodge, and took the full force of the blow. "That's my John talking. Don't be inquisitive about things. Just appreciate your blessings. Look at it this way. If you found out how the computer did the things it does, you might be tempted to make a little change here, a little change there, and you'd ruin it. Changes are always destructive, John. Besides, half the fun would be gone, wouldn't it, if you really knew how it worked?"

"No," John said.

Tamino put his thumb in his mouth and bit it. "Hmm. All right, John. Look at it this way. Tell yourself, for the sake of argument, that your computer has at its disposal the accumulated knowledge and wisdom of the world—and, for all you know, it does—and that, in fact, the rest of the world exists solely for the purpose of providing your computer with data so that you can run programs. How's that so far?"

John twisted his hands in his lap. "Go on."

"I knew this would get to you." Tamino coughed into his fist. "All right. All over the face of the globe, little yellow people, little brown people, little red people, little white people are living out their daily lives thinking that they mean something, that all those passions and lusts, all those laughs and tears, all have some special significance in the scheme of things. But we know better. All they are, John, is a couple of hundred billion mobile sensor units attached to your computer. Every time one of them comes up with a new idea, or a new poem, or a new tumor, it

78

belongs to you, John. The idea gets reduced to seventeen hundred electrical impulses on a magnetic tape moving fourteen inches per second, the poem gets cross-referenced by title and author, and the tumor is a medical statistic."

"This is very helpful."

Tamino wiped beads of sweat off his upper lip. "Don't stop me now. I'm just getting warmed up. Okay, you've got all these little sensors running around and some of them own machines, or they think they own them, and these machines do jobs. Give me some machines that do jobs."

"Seismographs."

"Good one. So, some of them own seismographs, and they spend night and day watching for the seismograph to show something more cataclysmic happening to the earth's crust than traffic on the L.A. freeway." Tamino crouched, acting out the role of a mad scientist watching his seismograph. "Then, one day, eureka! A tremor some-place!" Tamino jumped up and down, waved his arms, loosened his tie, dropped to his knees and threw kisses to an imaginary audience. "The event of this character's life. But you, John, you knew about it all along. You get reports from thousands of seismographs, all of them better than this old fart's, because your computer finds out as soon as something of interest happens any place." Tamino scrambled to his feet, his smile shrewd and conspiratorial. "Which makes us wonder, doesn't it? Where do things really happen, John? In somebody's laboratory out in the sticks or down here, when your computer tells you they happen?" He extended a hand, fingers spread, toward John. "I think that's what it all means. All the world's just part of your computer and when you're seated in that chair, you're at the heart of the universe."

John's eyes lingered on Tamino, waiting for more. Tamino was right. Questions about *why* a thing happened were foolish when so much *is* was involved. His heart raced and his hands rubbed the sides of the terminal, leaving sticky tracks. "I'm a very lucky man," he said, a clot of emotion cracking his voice.

"John, don't cry on me again." Tamino wiped his face and threw droplets across the room. "We've got a big day ahead of us." He winked. "Come on. I've got a surprise for you."

Tamino pulled John from his chair and urged him to the door, one arm around his shoulders, the other gesturing expansively as they made their way from John's bedroom, around the ninety-degree turn, and ("Use your key, John") into the computer chamber. Tamino talked about his plans for welcoming John to the Fellowship: sherry parties, fireworks displays, a festival of the arts in Beulahland, "but none of them seemed quite right." John ducked the microphone, and sat down, scarcely listening.

ARE YOU OF THE FELLOWSHIP? the computer inquired.

John put the console on "hold" and the typewriter stopped short, buzzing and fidgeting in frustration.

He set up the "eradication" order, then typed

BONNIE DECKSTEWER, PLUS CYANIDE GAS, PLUS SALUTATORY INTERROGATION.

"Then I decided, John, that for a person of your turn of mind the best way to welcome you was to give you a full demonstration of our little operation in action."

The typewriter snapped back into action.

REPLACE DECKSTEWER.

Holding his breath, John made the necessary adjustments on the console and typed

JOHN DOFFENBARON.

"So." Tamino seemed to be getting further away. John didn't look up. "If you'll excuse me for a second, I'll see if the others are ready and we can get things in motion. Just keep your feet on the ground, John." He laughed as if he had said something very funny and the door shut.

Through the window, lights blinked and flickered along the computer cabinets, sparks in the Spanish moss of looping cables and interconnecting wires.

The typewriter ball trembled and jerked like an overactive fat boy limbering up for hopscotch, then tumbled across the carriage.

DATA FOLLOW. CONFIRM OR CORRECT.

The ball slapped back against the lefthand margin, then blurred around toward the right.

JOHN VIDO DOFFENBARON: BORN NOVEMBER 1, 1925, PURBLEIN, PA.
SECONDARY EDUCATION:
    ST. METHODIUS PAROCH. SCHL.
    ST. MARY OF THE SEA SEMINARY
COLLEGE: ST. MARY OF THE SEA SEMINARY: REC. A.B., S.T.M.

ORDAINED R.C. PRIEST MAY 1, 1951
GRADUATE DEGREE: M.I.T., PH.D., 1956
EMPLOYMENT:
  M.I.T.: 1956-7
  I.B.M.: 1957-9 (RAND CORP PURCHASED CONTRACT)
  U.S. DEPT OF DEFENSE: JULY-DECEMBER 1959
  BARNARD-COLUMBIA: 1960
  TULANE: 1960-2
  UNIVERSITY OF KANSAS: 1962-3
  OWOSSO COLLEGE: SEPT. 12- DEC. 24, 1963
UNEMPLOYED: 1963-8
  ACCTNG DEPT. WIEBOLDT DEPT. STORES: 1968-9

John couldn't look at the rest. Instead, he decided to watch the lights on the computer cabinets run up and down from infinity. At once, he had the curious impression that the corridor was sinking away from him. Reassuring himself that vertigo was not, could not be the keystone for any system of Christian values, he slowly stood up and walked to the window. A mechanical wheeze from overhead drew his attention. No, the corridor was not sinking. The floor of the computer chamber was lifting through a new hole where the ceiling had been and taking John with it. He wheeled and saw the floor lift past the top of the doorframe. He had no exit.

Conserving every ounce of potential energy, John steadied himself and went back to his chair, taking his seat with such caution that he scarcely felt his buttocks touch the leather. He reasoned with himself that no one who had taken such pains to bring him to this place would place him in any harm. With a determination, a courage he scarcely believed to be coming from the overdrawn account of manly reactions buried within him, he looked up to see where he was going. The floor of the room ascended into a four-sided glass box, a tray on which John and his equipment sat like condiments, lifted by a subterranean hydraulic arm. One glass wall was an extension of the window which looked out on the computer cabinetry, now at least thirty feet below him, the other three stared down on an oval amphitheater. Against the far wall of the amphitheater and at least fifteen feet below John's glass cage sat five small, two-tiered versions of his computer console. He did not notice the people who sat behind them looking up at him, but scanned the room. Directly across from him, behind and above the computer terminals, Tamino perched in an open bandbox, his feet crossed on an old-fashioned desk that squatted like a decorator's lapse in the swirls of plastic, Martian-modern functionalism which filled the amphitheater. Everything but the desk was adrip and asparkle with glowing fiberoptic strands which threw shadowless pastel light from unsettling angles.

"Surprise, John." Tamino lifted his feet from the desk and waved to him across the intervening space. His voice rattled from loudspeakers hidden in the new ceiling. They were, if anything, louder than the ones on the courtyard level. "Welcome to our Game Room."

Not quite frightened but, then, not quite comfortable either, John produced a weak smile and waved back. Nobody on the floor of the amphitheater waved at him. Instead, they seemed to be doing their best to ignore him. Perhaps they merely studied the blank surfaces of the screens opposite each small console.

"John, I decided we'd break you in the hard way." Tamino's amplified voice was more jovial and fun-loving than ever. "We're going to have a run-through of what it is we do here, John, the greatest enterprise of the Fellowship and that special work which sets us apart from the rest of the world."

John recognized only two of the people sitting at the small terminals on the amphitheater floor—Dr. Ivanson and Miss von Helsing. Ivanson busied himself scrawling notes on large sheets of yellow paper which he alternately banished to a plexiglass folder then retrieved for amendment. Miss von Helsing, sheathed in a tangerine dress which flattered her figure but warred with her hair, stared off into space, lighting a fresh cigarette from the embers of the last.

"Make no mistake, John," Tamino reverberated, an emotional or electronic hemidemisemiquaver distorting his shouts, "you are integral to our work, perhaps crucial, as this exercise today will prove. And what better way could we welcome you than by giving you an opportunity to have the kind of fun we all like the most: *work!*"

The other three people in the amphitheater struck John as an odd lot, to say the least. Although he attempted to give his full attention to Mr. Tamino, John glanced back at the trio of strangers, unable to discover what might have won them their place in this company. The Negro without a shirt couldn't be much more than twenty; the dark-skinned man next to him, an Oriental of some sort, slept fitfully; and the fat woman played with her fingers and talked to herself.

"Gathered together in the common endeavor, we have the finest minds on this little old earth of ours giving their all for the cause of total scholarship."

The Negro jumped from his console and ran across the amphitheater, long legs scissoring in striped, bell-bottomed trousers which closed four inches under his navel. He vanished from John's view for a few seconds, then returned dragging a tall white man in a brown suit. The Negro was talking so enthusiastically that he appeared to be doing a dance, his heavy chest weaving back and forth toward his companion whom he had clutched around the waist with one arm, the other arm carving flamboyant arabesques out of the air. After a brief struggle, the Negro allowed himself to be forced back down behind his console, while the other man, whom John now recognized as the guard he had met in the corridor the day before, stood aloof but smiling off to one side, just out of reach.

"Independent and unfettered by the tribulations of a confused world, we pursue *wisdom*. Pooling the vast resources of highly trained minds, impelled by the love of truth, we view the activities of lesser men for what they are." Tamino moved around his wooden desk and stood at the edge of the bandbox, striking a series of theatrical poses as he spoke, moving so rapidly into one that he scarcely had time to rearrange his muscles from the last. Nobody but John seemed to be watching him, much less listening to him. "Detached, Olympian, we abandon the relative for the absolute, we confront the infinite turmoil of the human condition, not out of fear, not out of concern, not out of need, but as a stimulus for those cerebral exercises which provide life with its only justification."

Miss von Helsing yawned and stubbed out her cigarette.

"In this room, at regular intervals during the week, we come together from our separate spheres of activity to join in the total Fellowship and play our games. John, ladies and gentlemen, when we play, the earth shakes." Tamino's fist smashed onto the desk top. The Oriental jumped upright and the fat woman squirmed and studied her watch.

Tamino returned to his seat behind the desk. "Enough

of that. Now for introductions. You've met Dr. Ivanson and Alicia and know what great folks they are. And they already think the world of you, too."

Dr. Ivanson wadded a sheet of yellow paper and Miss von Helsing lighted another cigarette. Neither of them looked up at John.

Tamino peered over the edge of the bandbox. "First, let me see, we have Leo Membozig, our tactics man." The Negro waved a languid, naked arm, never taking his eyes off the guard. "Leo's a born military genius. Our gain, West Point's loss, eh, Leo?" Membozig pulled a face and dangled a hand backward over his shoulder. "Now then, over there on the end, we have Jane Feuer." The stout woman stood up and narrowed her eyes to squint at John from under an awning of black hair. Her face, the color and texture of tapioca pudding, jutted from a body which seemed not so much badly cared for as totally forgotten. Edges and lumps of underclothing peeked shyly from unexpected fissures in her dress. "Jane, Miss Feuer, is the Fellowship's double threat. Earth sciences *and* mechanical engineering." Miss Feuer plopped down in her seat, a rosy blush creeping up one side of her face. "And, finally, between Jane and Leo, we have Professor Senid Keruk, late of New Delhi, now our biophysicist." Keruk smiled at John; an array of teeth the precise hue of his sallow skin dominated his features briefly, then vanished behind slit lips. He was not unhandsome, but ever so slightly desiccated, as if at some point in his career he had been left too long on a drying rack.

"Well, that about covers the waterfront. Professor Keruk, I guess you're the ringmaster for the day's exercises. It's all yours."

Keruk stood and lifted one finger toward heaven. "One point, if it is not out of place." He salaamed toward John. "Might we inquire whether our distinguished newcomer, whose presence brings us all so much joy, has perhaps a question, a desire for clarification?"

"Thank you. As a matter . . . "

"Oh, Christ!" Miss von Helsing buried her face in her hands, the cigarette between her fingers singeing a stray curl.

"Speak into your microphone, John." Tamino strained over the top of his desk, cupping his ears. "We aren't getting you out here."

"Thank you," John repeated, yanking the microphone around. "Nobody has told me what I'm supposed to do."

"Good for you, John. Better now than later." Tamino folded his hands on his stomach and leaned back in his chair. "Your job is to incorporate data from or to provide information for the five participants in the game, if you follow me. Each of them will use their own terminals to give the computer specific directions; you make sure that the computer handles the *entire* problem from second to second as they each feed in their respective portions of the program, make their plays. Got it?"

"I think so." John looked down at the five faces beneath him. Only Professor Keruk looked back. "In other words, the computer must correlate its individual output to Mr. Membozig, for example, on the basis of the total input of the group."

"John you're a genius. Anything else?"

John stared across at Tamino's bare desk. "What do you do?"

"I watch." A memory of that voice using that same tone from behind a gun barrel jammed into John's memory. "I like games. All right, Professor, take it away."

Professor Keruk consulted a stack of index cards. "Today we shall play the Food Game. Our premises are these: a blight has wiped out the entire winter wheat crop in the states of Kansas, Iowa, Nebraska, and the summer crops of North and South Dakota, Minnesota, and Illinois. A foot-and-mouth epidemic has stricken the beef cattle herds of Argentina, Australia, and Chile, and Soviet trawlers have poisoned Japanese shrimp fishing waters." He concealed a brown smile behind a brown hand and continued. "The computer has been preprogrammed with this information."

John automatically jerked around and looked at the console. He caught sight of the conclusion of his *curriculum vitae* jutting from the typewriter and tore it out.

SUSPENDED FROM SACRAMENTAL FUNCTIONS 1970.
RETIRED TO OUR LADY OF VICTORY CONVENT, FLETT, VERMONT.
AUTOPSY REPORT STILL PENDING.
CORONER'S REPORT STILL PENDING.
CONFIRM OR CORRECT.

John confirmed. Why was he worried about the computer? If Professor Keruk said that the hardware had been preprogrammed, John had learned enough in one morning to believe him. He tore the sheet of paper in his hands to bits, an exorcism of the past. He wheeled around and looked down at his future.

"Such events," Professor Keruk explained, "are possible from time to time, either through coincidental mishap or carefully planned exploitation of circumstance."

Membozig whispered to the guard and giggled.

Professor Keruk scowled at Membozig, then shuffled his index cards. "Now, from these premises we are to play a game with the following results: to arrive at a date when such disasters might be most happily implemented to occasion these events: the death of the Emperor of Japan, the conquest of Kashmir by the People's Republic of China, and the dissolution of the government of France."

"Man, why you so up tight about wheat blight?" Membozig snickered at the guard, who looked away and pored his concentration on his shoes.

Keruk swelled to full height and thrust his chin in the air. John guessed him to be a little under five feet two or three. "My own work with mycorrhizal mutations makes this game of special fascination for me. We have often played your games, Leo, pushing the pretty soldier boys in and out of cannon range. Kill, kill, kill. Now today we shall play wheat blight and we shall be interested."

"I shan't be interested"—Dr. Ivanson gathered up his papers and walked away from his terminal—"because I shan't be here. Anything you desire in the way of solar phenomena or meteorological projections can be gotten from the computer quite well without my presence. Good day, one and all." He left.

"All right, friends." Tamino's feet were back up on the desk. "The fun's over. Let's play."

Keruk jumped into his chair and hammered at the typewriter on his terminal. Miss von Helsing closed her eyes, a punctuation mark in her reveries, then dropped the cigarette onto the floor and stabbed it to death with a spike heel as her hands caressed the console keyboard. Membozig slumped in his chair and peered straight ahead through his fingers at the collection of screens opposite the line of computer terminals. John saw Miss Feuer make a tentative jab at her typewriter, when he heard a clatter from the main console. He turned his chair around and watched figures flash at varying speeds across the television tubes on both sides of him. The problem was simple, actually. He would simply act as a control to make sure that all the incoming data were correlated in the same bank and that any subsequent information drawn from other sources would be held in availability for the duration of the game. Pulling five knobs at the top of the console, he ordered the computer to open sufficient space to receive and process all input immediately; then he depressed, in sequence, five chords, clearing channels for whatever stored resources the Fellowship might need as reference. Working quickly, he also corrected errors transmitted from the five typewriters in the amphitheater.

POPULATION PROGRESSIONS BY COUNTRY FROM PRESENT TO YEAR A.D. 2100.

TACTICAL ARMORED STRENGTH: KASHMIR. AVAILABLE INFO RE. TREATIES SURROUNDING NATIONS AND WESTERN BLOC POWERS.

John watched the last order meander across the screen, then looked over his shoulder. He was right, Membozig was typing, but with only one hand. The other hand stole through the air, poised above the guard's thigh.

COMPUTE PROBABILITIES SPREAD OF WHEAT BLIGHT IN-FECTION THROUGH WIND CURRENTS, TRANSPORT, ANI-MAL CARRIERS, ETC.

Back and forth across John's typewriter carriage, the details of an international cataclysm spilled out in the path of the rolling typeface as the participants in the Food Game fed variables into the computer and the computer reduced the combined variables to high probabilities. Disguised as numbers, armies swept back and forth across mountain ranges hidden within the bowels of the hardware, the geometric progression of human life and death buckled and warped into a new dimension as equations were shifted and constants altered. Underfed nations starved and died in the twinkle of an electric charge because an imaginary cow had been exposed to a shower of imaginary virus, because imaginary wheat had fallen victim to an imaginary fungus. Japan honored treaty agreements to a besieged Kashmir and sent food which they could not spare precisely at the moment the Russians wiped out their fishing grounds. French concordats with Communist China prevented their assisting the Japanese, American grain prices soared; six Asian powers consequently enjoyed famine, and joined in the attack on Kashmir in exchange for rations of Chinese rice. Tumbling South American economies bred revolutions, perfunctory but paralyzing to the degree that unsteady governments in the Southern Hemisphere offered no aid to the starving nations of the East. All very interesting, but John preferred checkers.

The juggernaut of disasters regathered steam and churned across the face of an imaginary globe. Japanese students rioted in Paris, supported by Rightists, and the government fell in three days. The Emperor of Japan, who had been symbolically fasting as evidence of his anguish over the misery of his people, had a gall bladder attack and

91

died of complications during surgery. A combined Chinese, Laotian, Pakistani, Thai task force occupied Srinagar and the game was over.

"Stop," Keruk cried. "Give us the optimal date for the primary events, for initiating the wheat blight . . . "

"Baby, that cat's got wheat blight on his balls." Membozig leered in all directions.

Keruk trembled, then forced himself to address his microphone, holding onto the stalk as if he were throttling a chicken in ritual sacrifice. Miss von Helsing watched him and made notes. " . . . and the probable time lapse for the actualization of the objectives to this point."

John nodded, realized that his nod had not translated itself to Keruk through the glass wall and across fifty feet of amphitheater, and said, "All right." He opened the appropriate channels and typed the order. Microseconds elapsed before the typewriter replied.

OPTIMAL DATE FOR INITIATION OF GAME PREMISES: MARCH 3-10, 1981.
TIME LAPSE FOR ACHIEVEMENT OF GAME OBJECTIVES: 5 MONTHS, 2 WEEKS, 4 DAYS.

A collective groan echoed through John's loudspeakers. Miss von Helsing hurled an unlighted cigarette to the floor, Miss Feuer pursed her lips and pouted, and Membozig laughed. Professor Keruk slumped into his chair and rubbed his eyes deep into their sockets.

Apparently rapt in sour contemplation of his desk top, Tamino didn't look up. "That's too bad, Professor," he said. "I hate to see so many people disappointed."

"1981?" Miss von Helsing incinerated another cigarette

and spat an artillery shell of smoke across the top of her console. "1981? Senid, that was the most abominably premised game I can recall since I've been here. You know that the variables, certainly the ethnopsychological variables at any rate, won't hold that long?"

"There are things which we cannot predict." Keruk studied his lap, miserable and suddenly shrunken. He reminded John more and more of a piece of dried fruit.

"In 1981?" Miss von Helsing sucked tobacco fumes over her upper lip into her nostrils. "I doubt," she said, each word arriving wrapped in smoke, "that you'll live that long."

A melody whispered in the background through John's loudspeakers, as if he were picking up interference from a radio station.

If yuh love me, baby, if I'm all yuh got,
Then yuh better take me, take me while I'm hot.
If yuh leave me coolin', guess I'll haveta learn yuh;
'Cause when I gets cold, that's when I will burn yuh.

No interference came through his speakers. John could see Membozig, leaning back away from his microphone, crooning to an anguished Corporal Comstock.

Prim, offended, Keruk retaliated. "My health is most excellent, Alicia. I am sorry if this game is untestable and therefore uninteresting to you. I had little time with which to prepare the premises." He flared his tiny nostrils; John couldn't tell if Professor Keruk were acting fierce or if he'd inhaled a fly. "I might point out that my variables are not so inconstant and would hold quite serviceably until a possible test in 1981. Perhaps our problem is less with my

93

game than with your science, so-called, which would seem to be so sadly deficient in predictability over a long period."

"That isn't very professional of you, Senid." Miss Feuer's complexion had paled from ash to ivory. "That is not the way we talk to our colleagues."

The computer typewriter drew John's attention from the argument and the singing. Membozig had a nice voice.

BRISBANE SEISMOGRAPH REPORTS CONFIRMED BY SYDNEY.

"Don't let him worry you, Jane." Miss von Helsing showed long, straight teeth. "One of these days Senid is going to run out of new wheat blights to play with and he'll probably just go crawl in the corner and die." The possibility seemed to cheer Miss von Helsing immeasurably. "It's not uncommon for lower-caste Indians when the monotony of their lives catches up with them, you know. I'll drop my files off at your room tonight, Senid, if you're curious."

Professor Keruk formed a tent with his fingertips and peered inside. "Please do not trouble yourself. I have no doubt of the authority of your observations, coming as they do from one who has lived so very, very long."

+9 READING AT 500 HOURS S. HEMISPHERE 53.75 LAT 173.9 LONG E. GREENWICH

"Oh, goodness. First Dublin and now"—Miss Feuer squeezed her eyes shut and counted her fingers—"*Christ Church, New Zealand.*" She contemplated the screen in front of her console and chewed her knuckles. "How dreadful!"

Professor Keruk turned away from Miss von Helsing's inevitable riposte which at that moment was taking on shape in a swelling stormcloud of smoke and smiled at Miss Feuer. "Some mishap? A misfortune that distresses you? You have relatives in those cities?"

Miss Feuer had not removed her eyes from the screen. "Don't be ridiculous." She blinked a rapid semaphore as if she were trying to censor her vision. "I've never heard of anything like this before. *That's* dreadful." Pointing at her screen, she looked up at John. "Maybe you had this left over from the game?"

"No," he said. "Isn't this the data you requested?"

"Oh, agony," Miss Feuer said, pounding a pudgy hand on her temple.

Burn and burn and burn, till Ah've got my heart's desire;
Make muh Baby turn till yuh lights your daddy's fire.

"Oh, why don't you be quiet or get out of here. I'm trying to think things." Miss Feuer's head tipped sideways under the assault from her fist.

"Suits me, baby." Membozig twisted out of his chair and snagged Corporal Comstock with both hands as he pranced toward the door.

"Fill me in, Jane. I can't see your screen from here." Tamino lounged across his desk and rested one hand on the back of the other.

Miss Feuer sniffed. "This morning I learned that a severe earthquake had taken place near Dublin, totally demolishing the city and dropping Bray and a couple of other towns into the Irish Sea. So naturally, I requested the computer to be on alert for reports of any sympathetic tremors since, after all, everyone knows that Dublin isn't in an earthquake belt." Her face gleamed with a film of sweat. "Oh, mercy. Just now, I discover that, simultaneously with the Dublin earthquake, another earthquake of the same intensity occurred off the New Zealand coast." Miss Feuer clapped both hands on top of her console and shook violently. "That's almost exactly on the other side of the planet. It can't happen like that. That's not the way earthquakes happen."

"Perhaps all is not so serious as it seems," Keruk soothed. "Perhaps we have merely an amusing and stimulating coincidence."

"*Two earthquakes at exactly the same time, exactly opposite each other, of exactly the same intensity are not a coincidence.*" Miss Feuer erupted from the chair and hugged herself. Her eyes flitted back and forth from the screen to Professor Keruk. "See? See it? You have no right to say things like that. Earthquakes aren't even your field of competence."

Miss von Helsing slid from behind her terminal, bringing her briefcase with her. As she eased across the floor, she pulled long cords from apertures in the side of the case and held them tightly in her right hand.

"I meant no offense," Keruk began, but Miss Feuer would not hear him.

"All my life I have had people tell me that things didn't really happen when they did. Well, you foolish, nasty little man, this time I *know* it's happened and you are wrong."

Miss von Helsing crept up behind Miss Feuer and gently attached the cords with pink adhesive to various parts of her body: one over each ear, others on the upper forearms, another inside the front of her dress.

96

"Do you realize what this could mean?" Miss Feuer yelped. The wires slid in and out of the briefcase, adjusting themselves to Miss Feuer's movements. Ducking occasionally to avoid the sweep of a hammy arm, Miss von Helsing tiptoed to the nearest console and typed an order.

TRANSCRIBE ENCEPHALOGRAM, CARDIOGRAM, ETC. READINGS NOW BEING TRANSMITTED PLUS CORRELATE READINGS WITH ACCUM DATA RE CAUCASIAN FEMALE TYPE 43B FOR REF VON HELSING.

John watched the order appear on a television screen at the corner of the console. Three bars, two blue, one green, one on the second tier dropped and glowed. The words on the screen vanished and wavy lines replaced them.

"I guess that just about finishes us up here, John." Tamino sounded weary or bored or both. "I'll send you home." Gently, the floor of the chamber started to sink back toward the courtyard.

"A fault that ran through the earth from Ireland to New Zealand could mean that the planet is *about to split in half.*" Miss Feuer's voice cracked and John turned from the computer and watched her clutch her throat.

"Jane, dear," Miss von Helsing purred into Miss Feuer's ear, "you know damned well there isn't any geological fault like that."

Crimson blotches popped into relief on Miss Feuer's cheeks and legs. "I know it. Yes, there is, too. There can't be. There must be. *If there isn't any fault then it couldn't have happened.*" Miss Feuer stiffened, held her breath, and turned blue. John glanced at the television screen and observed that one of the wavy lines was now perfectly horizontal, not a bump in it.

Miss von Helsing opened her briefcase and twiddled with

knobs on a gray box nestled inside. Then she pulled a small camera from her pocket and, moving from one side of Miss Feuer to the other, snapped pictures.

"Now, darling." Miss von Helsing paused to change film. "What do you mean it couldn't have happened? You just told us it *did* happen."

Miss Feuer swayed and steadied herself against Professor Keruk's terminal. "I have the qualifications to handle this assignment, you know. My qualifications are among the best in the country." Moisture traced a smutty path down the side of her neck. "In the world."

"Don't move, Jane. The light's dim." Miss von Helsing clicked away, now from down on her knees, now from up on a chair.

Miss Feuer said nothing that John could hear, but as the chamber sank below the amphitheater floor level, he could see her lips working. He checked the console to be sure that the computer was still receiving data from Miss von Helsing's briefcase.

"Of course we get no results. We cannot run probabilities for something that has only a single precedent."

Miss Feuer looked from the computer console to John
and then back to the computer console. She had not
changed her dress since her collapse the previous week at
the game, not even dusted it, and it was as stiff and
wrinkled as crumpled parchment. Her agitation had swollen
into fat and the seams of her clothing were even more
tormented than before. "But Dr. Ivanson said that he
knows how to find out which quasar is going to blow up
next by asking the computer. Why can't I find out where
we're going to have more earthquakes?" Her eyes blinked
constantly, the left one a little faster than the right.

John sighed and pushed his swivel chair around in a
circle. "Because more than one quasar has disappeared, not
blown up, by the way, and the computer was able to

project a hypothetical pattern which, as it turned out, was successful. The probabilities of an event occurring are based on the frequency with which an event occurs." A run spontaneously appeared in Miss Feuer's stocking and ambled from her knee to her ankle. "You have given me *one case* of simultaneous earthquakes taking place at diametrically opposed points on the globe. The best we can do is speculate about the chances of its happening again, or if it ever happened before; we might even run a projection based on analagous geological phenomena, if such exist, but I cannot program the computer to do a job that is mathematically impossible."

"You're not very sympathetic," Miss Feuer said.

John let out a long breath he had been harboring ever since Miss Feuer came in. "I do not understand what I am supposed to be sympathetic *about*. We have insufficient data. Period. The end. I cannot comprehend this in terms of an emotional crisis."

"Now you're being hateful." Miss Feuer snatched her notes off the console and marched toward the door. "Can't all of you realize that this is the most important thing that's ever happened to me and I can't decide what it is and none of you cares?"

"None of which?"

"All of you. The Fellowship." Miss Feuer stamped her foot and the ravaged stocking collapsed around the top of her shoe. "You have absolutely no professional pride in my work. This place wouldn't be any better than those universities and those think tanks if it wasn't for the equipment and the time I have to carry on my research." She flipped her bangs up with the corner of a manila folder. "I would like some acknowledgment of what it is I'm doing."

John smiled for Miss Feuer. "I'm sure you are very good at earth sciences. And mechanical engineering."

Mamie slouched through the chamber door. She looked tired. "I gotta message for you, honey."

"Just a moment, Mamie." John looked at Miss Feuer. "Go on."

Miss Feuer pursed her lips. "Can't she deliver her message in front of me, or do you already belong to one of those cliques?" She shook her head before John could answer. "No, don't try. A person's accomplishments are just totally ignored around here, that's all. Do I get invited to Alicia's parties? No. Do I get invited to the special meetings? No. Why is it, do you suppose?" Miss Feuer gave John an emphatic nod, as if she'd just made her point.

"I didn't know Miss von Helsing gave parties."

"Secret parties." Miss Feuer laughed. "But she lets me find out." She sneered at John. "As if you didn't know. I'll bet you go all the time, to all of them."

John fought down a groan. "This is unfair. All of us are too busy to go to parties."

Miss Feuer let her head tip back as far as the rolls of fat on her neck would allow and roared, a hilarious bray that snapped off at the end like a sob. "Oh, mercy, that's what they all say, all right." She turned to Mamie. "I could be lots of fun at parties." Her voice softened and climbed three octaves. "I dance."

"Look, Miss Feuer, I am sure that nobody is giving any parties and if somebody has told you so they misled you. Who told you about any parties?"

Miss Feuer smiled, one corner of her mouth turning up at a time. She tapped her forehead mysteriously. "Oh, I hear," she chuckled.

John looked longingly at his computer. "All right. If it

will settle your mind, Mamie will give me the message right now, in front of you. Mamie?"

Mamie shook her head and shot a quick sidelong glance at Miss Feuer. "I forgot."

"Ha!" Miss Feuer said. "She's in on it, too." She glowered at Mamie, top to bottom, from bandanna to blue sneakers.

"Mamie! Out with it. What is the message?"

Mamie swallowed a mouthful of air and clenched her fists at her sides. "Miss von Helsing want you to come by her place about six." She paused, then blurted, "For dinner."

"Ha!" Miss Feuer yelled. "Ha! *Ha!*" She turned and staggered for the door and then whirled and glared back into the room, eyes fixed on an invisible point two inches in front of her nose. "I think you could run those probabilities if you wanted to. I think you like Dr. Ivanson more than you like me. I think that's all there is to it." She waved her folder at John. "Well, you just don't know what you're missing." Then she burst into tears and fled.

John closed his eyes.

"I didn't finish the message," Mamie said.

John kept his eyes shut. "Finish," he said.

"I ain't feeling too good and I'm gonna take off early. That's why you gotta have dinner with Miss von Helsing. Miss von Helsing said she had somethin' to talk with you about anyhow."

Reluctantly, but with a sense of inevitability, John looked up and studied Mamie as she rested her buttocks against the console. How long, O Lord, how long? "A party?"

"Miss von Helsing don't give no parties." Mamie slumped

and coughed into her hand, exposing a flesh-tone bandage, the wrong flesh tone, on the inside of her elbow. "Nobody else gives no parties either, far as I know."

"Thank you, Mamie," John said. "Tell Miss von Helsing that I will be there at six. Now," he tried to sound gentle but could feel the words coming out wrong, "why don't you go home and rest?"

"Nobody care about anybody," Mamie mumbled her way to the door. "You works your heart out for folks and a lot they cares if you fall over dead, just so you gets the job done."

"Mamie," John said, "stop it."

"I'm going." Mamie went, stumbling, or pretending to, as she left the chamber.

John hopped from his chair and closed the door after her, turning the key in the lock and pocketing it. He paced back and forth across the chamber, looking through the glass at the glittering cabinetry, shoving his hands under his armpits, taking them out. He did not want to keep the door closed all the time because people respected his privacy a shade too scrupulously; but when he left it open, Miss Feuer bounded in with new figures more incomplete than the last, then greeted every failure with a brief volley of accusations followed by an explosion of the tear ducts. John liked to have people visit him because they brought him new programs, or asked questions that provided an opportunity for him to show off his equipment. If the door was closed, Mamie would let him go without lunch and he would lose more weight. Already, his new cassock hung limp on him, flapping and billowing when he moved. He was working hard. Mamie should save him a sandwich.

But, even with all the work he had to do, John found

himself with spare time, odd minutes and leftover half hours between breakfast and bed which brought him close to frustration. With frustration came a quiet warning jingle off in the far distance of his awareness. Right now, he felt himself pacing faster and faster, his laps around the little room taking less and less time, while he waited for the computer to finish calculating zymogen variations for Professor Keruk. When those came through, he would have another too-short flurry of activity, calling down to the labs, relaying the results, receiving (maybe) new instructions, more work. His fingers itched, tingling for a new program.

John paused by a collection of copying machinery, teletypes, and microwave facsimile equipment. He shuddered. The computer was too efficient, that was his whole problem. Half the work a programmer could be doing was done automatically. Right this minute, the computer was setting itself up to receive and transcribe a copy of some article or book which was being transmitted on the National Interlibrary Microwave hookup. John could see the practicality of automatically acquiring data which might not have been quantified previously and stored in their own computer's memory banks, but he was displeased that all of it was done without his so much as throwing a switch. He had spent too many hours this last week in frenzied lassitude while the computer sent directives out across the continent, asking for information from compliant librarians on whatever topic might be missing from its own resources. John had visions of withered old ladies clambering up and down rickety ladders to find forgotten articles in bankrupted professional journals, plunging them into their Datafax copiers and nervously supervising as page after page was translated into electrons and spewed through the atmosphere to his omnivorous computer. He felt left out, bypassed while the computer carried on a life of its own with mildew-colored old maids whose sanity could be measured in Dewey decimals.

Worse, he had endured the cruelest of slights, setting up a program, glumly conscious that the computer was giving just as much of its attention to a new book, an old thesis, a misprinted monograph lately retrieved from the stacks by arthritic spinsters of assorted sexes and pumped by radio and magnetic tape into its excited innards. Tamino's suggestion that all outside sources were merely part of the computer's sensor system was not helpful; John saw these librarians differently, as a kind of round-robin harem, incessantly bent on distracting his computer from its true, primary, and ultimate object of attention: John. He stared at the Datafax, at the bland cipher of a mash note which ticked out of the copier in oh-so-innocent machine-readable type as it was absorbed simultaneously in hot, private electrical thrusts by the computer itself.

Yet, how could he blame the computer for deserting him when he had nothing to offer it, not even another of Miss Feuer's garbled excursions into mathematical fantasy. Neglected, the computer sought a little diversion, something on the side. John beat his arms against his ribs and cursed as he watched the Datafax cuckold him.

Requesting specific material from Widener Library, Cambridge, Mass. HA 1636.

Those numbers, those inexplicable numbers. John

groaned when he thought what the computer would do with those numbers, all without one bit of help from him.

Go ahead Pius X Library. Widener standing by.

John couldn't take his eyes off the monitor. Why did he torture himself like this?

Sister P. Vandercock of our graduate school needs for her thesis all materials—John felt the blood vessels in his chest constrict into a wriggling mass—*with reference to St. Thomas Aquinas' discussion of the conscience, with particular concern for his handling of the concept of synderesis (or synteresis).*
Stand by, Widener said.

Ghosts, phantoms, ghouls had attacked John; forgotten demons had assaulted him through his own computer. *St. Thomas.* He had forgotten this pain, this loss.

We are transmitting the thesis of Sister Hilda Cretark, submitted in March 1962, in partial fulfillment of requirements for her...

John backed away, flayed by nostalgia and bitterness. Idle, ignored by his computer, he did not think that he could bear being reminded of those wretched women and their suzerain possession of his first love. This place had promised peace, but he found quarrels; this place had promised work, but he found idleness; this place had promised thrills, but he found heartache.

He leaned his head against the glass wall and watched a workman far, far down the corridor of cabinetry darting back and forth among the cables. All that computer, more than anyone had ever believed possible, and the only thing that filled John was the growing conviction that he had been cheated. When was *he* going to get a break for a change? When would *he* have his turn? When would *he* get what he wanted?

He wanted St. Thomas back. He wanted his computer to pay attention to him and ignore those librarians and nuns. He wanted to be busy, to be happy. He wanted a drink.

The workman vanished in the distance. John stared down the awesome line of cabinets, more and more miserable as he thought of the potential within the computer. He thought of the *Summa*, forever gone, surrendered to hollow-cheeked women in starched veils and hair shirts. He thought of himself.

John, the computer, and the *Summa*—all rolled into one big thought.

John laughed; then he laughed and rubbed his hands together. Then he laughed, rubbed his hands together, and ran to his chair, pressing a button on the console as he sat down.

"Mr. Tamino, this is John Doffenbaron. I have a question."

"Sounds more like you heard a joke," Tamino's voice roared overhead. "I've never heard you laugh before, John. You *are* laughing, aren't you?"

John snorted and tried to bring himself back under control. Everything was much too wonderful. An epiphany. A miracle. "Yes, I was laughing. I want to find out if it is possible for me to order some additional materials."

"What sort of materials? Don't tell me the computer isn't big enough?"

"No." Plenty big enough. John bumped into the

107

microphone, stifling another joyous seizure. "Just some books."

"Can't you tap the Interlibrary setup down there?" Tamino did not sound too eager to help.

"I'm afraid that I need too many; it would tie up the equipment for too long." And might arouse suspicions.

"Hm. All right, John. What do you need?"

Gloria tibi! "I need the *Summa Theologica*, Vatican edition. And a few other things, but I'll give you a list."

Tamino did not answer for several seconds. When he finally spoke, his voice was heavy and suspicious. "Might I ask why?"

"Ah." Neurons scrambled in John's brain, searching. "Well. Now." *He had it.* "An idea of yours, really. You mentioned something about a computer writing the State of the Union Address, as a possibility. I've been thinking about testing our hardware's potential in handling abstractions, semantics, things like that. I thought I'd do my experiments in an area I knew a little bit about, mainly because I want to avoid upsetting anyone by ruining one of their programs, which I could do if I used material unfamiliar to me."

"For God's sake don't do that. Don't upset a *soul*. I've had Jane Feuer in here half the afternoon raving about some masquerade ball you and Alicia are giving and I can't take much more. Damn it, John, you and Alicia should consult with me before you start planning things which could upset morale around here. Besides, I don't see why you can't invite Jane. She claims that she does a mean frug and it might be fun for her to get her mind off those damned earthquakes."

"Do I get the books?"

"I suppose so. When do you want them? We can get somebody to fly them in tomorrow if you're in a rush."

Giddy lights danced before John's eyes. "Tomorrow will be fine."

"What about the party?"

John laughed. "We aren't having it. I'm going to be too busy."

"Good enough. I'll tell Jane it's canceled."

John flicked off his microphone and spun his chair around like a top. He was a man twice blessed. The plan was so absurdly simple, so patently obvious that a divine touch was indisputable. He would quantify the *Summa*, and then program the computer to respond to any Interlibrary call for information about St. Thomas with no less than 200,000 words of exhaustive explication on the specified topic. The computer would feed its handiwork back into the Datafax and he would have those nuns out of the universities and back to their convents within the year.

John would need the standard references, of course, for footnotes and that look of scholarly authenticity. He could scarcely contain himself. He would give the computer a style of its own, so niggling, so nitpicking, so overwhelmingly, unbelievably, absolutely *nunnish* that not one speck of remote degree-earning possibility would be left in anything from the verb tenses to the punctuation.

His bishop's injunction against John's continuing to work with the *Summa* rumbled into his memory. Not that it mattered, of course. And it didn't because, John assured himself, in this case the inhibition clearly could not apply. The computer would be working with Thomas, John was merely doing the job the church had prepared him to do: cybernetics.

John saw no reason why his conscience could not remain at rest.

"My, don't we look happy with ourselves." Miss von Helsing stepped back and gestured for John to come into her room. "You certainly are a picture of twinkling good cheer this evening."

"Thank you. I've had a splendid day." John stepped past his hostess and across the threshold. He had heard it said someplace that people filled their dwellings with extensions of their souls. In this case he hoped that it was not true. He barely had space to move after the door closed behind him. Miss von Helsing's suite (he realized she had two rooms) was crammed from floor to ceiling with furniture and pictures, no two woods, fabrics, periods, styles complementing each other. Plush leather couches squatted behind fragile glass lampstands, needlework cushions cowered under the assault of Jackson Pollock prints, baroque madonnas contemplated Zulu phallic totems, lace antimacassars perched atop water-filled plastic chairs. Only three notes of consistency were struck: dozens of photographs in tiny silver frames, all chronicling Miss von Helsing's disintegration through the decades; counter after counter in the far room crowded with a variegated collection of clinical steel boxes, each festooned with cords and sparkling with dials and buttons; and one wall covered with axes, tomahawks, and hatchets, all in their own plush-lined cases, every case labeled with a polished brass plate.

"Sarah left dinner in the warmer." Miss von Helsing wound a course through the obstructions and introduced John to a butterfly chair made of leather and decorated in a random pattern with curious designs showing hearts transfixed with arrows, florid but clumsy calligraphy, and naked women. "Make yourself at home and I'll get us a drink."

"Just juice for me, if you have it," John said.

"I have it," she said, and swept into the back room. Her gown, he noticed, was iridescent and successfully clashed with everything it touched. While Miss von Helsing tinkled glasses, John got up from the chair and examined the brass plate on one of the ax cases. *"Für die schönste ELEKTRA aller Zeits. Werner Rode. München Staatsoper. 14 Februar, 1935."* He looked at another *"For Darling Alicia. This Agamemnon never had it so good so often before. Your Nikolai."* The legend under the tomahawk was in pictographs and John went on. The case holding a heavily rusted woodsman's ax had no brass plate but a small tag hung by a string from the handle. *Exhibit A*, it read.

"All I have is pineapple. Will that do?"

Miss von Helsing deposited a silver tray on the inlay tortoise-shell top of a nearby table and poured John a drink from a large tumbler.

"Very nicely, thank you."

John returned to his chair and Miss von Helsing located herself and her shimmering silk on a teak faldstool. She sipped at length, considering John over the rim of her glass. "I can't get over that big fat smile of yours. I didn't think you'd be able to take it here."

How could a voice so beautifully modulated, with phrasing so perfectly enunciated, manage never to sound pleasant? "I have had difficult moments, of course, but things are working out quite nicely."

"I'm delighted to hear it." She sipped. "Naturally."

John already knew that he wasn't going to be able to eat his dinner. Miss von Helsing wanted to spar and John wasn't

111

very good at that. He would remember another engagement, get a headache, have work to do, need a breath of air, anything, but he would finish this glass of juice and leave. "You sound disappointed."

Miss von Helsing lifted her chin and smoothed the cords in her throat. "Not at all. Just surprised. You looked like such a delicate little thing the first time I saw you, all green and burpy from the nasty elevator ride, that I couldn't imagine you being much different under more stable conditions." She smiled and refilled her glass from a pewter beaker. "Clearly I was in error."

John tasted his drink. "You are the first person I have met here, besides Mr. Tamino, who has confessed that error might be possible."

"Really?" She rearranged her dress so that one spectacular knee popped briefly in and out of sight. "I'm flattered, I think. I have no idea what you feel about Dan but I assume you like him."

"Oh, yes." How odd that she would assume that because he liked Mr. Tamino he would like her. "But I don't understand him."

"Oh?"

"I don't understand what it is that he does besides recruit people like us." He hesitated, fearful that she would interpret his confusion as prying. "Not that it matters. He has been very helpful to me."

"Don't underestimate Dan, Father." Before John could stop her, Miss von Helsing had replenished his half-empty glass. "He's topnotch, just as much of an expert in his way as you are in yours or I am in mine. He's an administrator. A very good one. The best, probably. I can tell you one thing, I've been around." She smiled, as if remembering where. "And I can't remember anybody better than Dan."

A new question occurred to him. "Does he own the Center?"

Miss von Helsing laughed, a tidal wave from her glass slopping unnoticed onto the Navaho blanket which served as a carpet. "I wouldn't have the foggiest, if you must know, but I doubt it. He runs the Center and that keeps him busy enough. We've only spoken about it once." She contorted her face and squared her shoulders, a fresh arch in her eyebrows, a suggestion of stockiness in her frame already a successful transvestite impersonation of Mr. Tamino. " 'Alicia, baby, let me give you my philosophy of life. This is the age of the administrator, Alicia. We're the new priesthood, if you follow me, trained not to own things but to *administer* them, ordained not to govern but to *plan*, elevated not to rule but to *organize*.' " She relaxed and preened under John's applause. "Thank you. I'm rusty."

"You're very good." So long as John could keep her sights leveled on someone else, he didn't mind Miss von Helsing's company. "But if he doesn't own the Center, who does?"

Miss von Helsing pulled down the corners of her mouth. "Who knows? All I can tell you is that when I came here, let's see, about six years ago, everything was already ticking away like a bomb. No, I take that back. Membozig and Ivanson hadn't come yet. We got Ivanson in three years ago. Leo showed up last year." She licked the moisture off her upper lip and lifted one eyebrow. "All right. Ask me."

"What?"

"The next question. You'll ask sooner or later. Ask now."

John stared into his pineapple juice. "I can't think what it is that you want me to ask."

"Oh, my dear Father. How well you do fit in here." She rocked back, lifting her crossed ankles off the floor as she ran her laughter up and down the chromatic scale. "Just pleased as punch that you have a little corner of the universe where you can ply your trade with no interference. Never wondering where the money comes from, never worrying about the fact that nobody else in the world seems to know where we are, never worrying about how all this came to be in the first place." Miss von Helsing smiled at him, her smile curiously benign in the hard, lacquered face, the smile of the Mother of God under the cracking varnish of an unrestored icon. "Don't look so peevish. I'm not teasing you. I'm just fitting you into place, at last." Her eyes sparkled as she took a quick gulp of her drink. "No, Father, the question you should ask is, 'How does the Fellowship exist?' "

"As you say, the thought has never occurred to me."

"Well, it has now because I've planted it there between your little pink ears."

John put his glass down and covered it with his hand before Miss von Helsing could refill it. "Perhaps you shouldn't tell me."

She moved his hand and poured more juice. "Why not? God knows, I don't know that much myself, but you're welcome to it."

John ignored his glass and frowned. "I gather that whether I want to hear or not, you're going to tell me."

"Take it like a little soldier. And if you've got any cute ideas about sneaking out of here before I'm through with you, forget it. Drink up and make merry." She crossed her

114

legs and grinned. "My door locks from the inside and I've hidden the key. Of course, you could always overpower me and hunt for it."

John glanced around the room. He could spend days digging through this museum and never find anything so small as a key.

"Now, the way I've figured this out"—Miss von Helsing leaned sideways and draped an arm over the side of the stool, eyes half closed, a dowager empress waiting for her late afternoon fix—"the initial funds were raised through a confusion of jurisdictional rights in a number of government agencies. All had budget lines to cover the expenses of some piddling research grants for predicting things which seemed at the time to be of use to the country. The country I'm speaking of, by the way, is the United States, just in case you were wondering, which I doubt. Anyway, through a fluke, they managed to get all the money into the hands of one simple-minded assistant professor who, suddenly rich beyond his wildest dreams, ran off with it. Next, we go through a hazy period in which people get shot, kidnapped, robbed, the works, until the money, which has increased by the way, pops up as part of a court dispute between the government and this professor's heirs, of which, in his travels, he had begotten many. Further, to add to the general melee, the court bailiff somehow got his hands on the assets and grabbed the first plane to Brazil. Apparently, and the facts are none too clear, after landing and converting his currency, he was eaten by cannibals someplace in the Amazon valley. The savages kept the money, which they used as a poultice on sores. Now, the dollar, especially if it happens to be a municipal bond, is one of the germiest things around, and the tribe was, in

115

short order, wiped out. A wise missionary, discovering their bodies, realized that all this currency he found lying around the abandoned huts of his late parishioners was clearly a long-overdue gift from God, so he renounced the ministry and came home to make a killing in the stock market. Unfortunately for him, he couldn't keep his mouth shut about Providence's special benefits to those who bide their time, and he was promptly robbed and shoved off the New Orleans docks by a retired high school principal from Decatur, Miss Lena Fangell, who, being a woman of principle, I suppose, decided to use the money for its original purpose, research. She's the gal who got Jane Feuer to build the first computer, since she felt that no research was as worthwhile in this life as figuring out a system to beat the roulette wheels in Vegas. Which explains why we're out in the middle of a desert."

"It doesn't explain why she hired Miss Feuer."

Miss von Helsing finished her drink and poured herself another. "Been having a time with our Jane? Well, old Lena didn't exactly hire her, as a matter of fact. She borrowed her from a California asylum where she'd been committed as a result of some pretty unpleasant delusions she'd been acting out in the billiard room of the La Jolla Y.M.C.A. And, I gather, Lena just never got around to returning her. But, to get back to the story, somewhere along the line I get the impression that this Lena Fangell was just a front for a *very big operation*, if you follow me, because after she'd cleaned up on the wheels, Dan pops up out of nowhere to be her business manager. Now, did she hire him? Was he assigned by the home office? Did he blackmail his way in on the action? Your guess is as good as mine, because he doesn't say and I don't ask. Good old Dan. Well, after Lena drops off the edge of the butte one night (close your mouth, Father), Dan takes over. Here's the riddle. Dan apparently sat around here for years, all by himself, putting out food and water for Jane, who spent all her time tinkering with the computer and blasting more holes in the granite. Odd, isn't it? Well, I think it's pretty damned peculiar myself. So, at any rate, Jane got herself this article out of *Scientific American* . . . "

"I wrote it."

"Great. To continue, she found this article, uh, your article, and built herself the damnedest computer anybody'd ever seen. Of course, neither Jane nor Dan knew how to run it, so they sneaked out and found that strange little Deckstewer woman—God, what a zombie; did you ever see her clothes?—and dragged her back. Then, Dan and Jane went sneaking around all over the country stringing cables, wiring the computer into anything that looked like it might be useful, working like madmen for over a year."

John grimaced. "Two people couldn't possibly have made all our extramural contacts in a *hundred* years. With Miss Feuer assisting, I'd give them something under a millennium to get a good start."

"Well, maybe they got a little outside help from somebody or other. I told you that this outfit looks like a front for a very big operation. More juice? Sure you will. Frankly, Father, I think Dan got hooked on the basic research idea. A man likes to make a mark on his times, even if it's only a deep scratch and not a mortal wound, and the times cried out for research. So, he went into the market for geniuses."

John shook his head. "You still haven't answered your own question. How does the Fellowship survive?"

117

"No, I haven't. I can't say I know for sure, but I believe that Dan just lets his little collection of eggheads run wild, knowing that every now and then they'll come up with something sellable."

"To whom?"

Miss von Helsing winked. "Get smart, Father. Think about our games. Don't you suppose, using that abortion of Senid's as an example, that *somebody* might be interested in finding out how they could wipe out the French government, murder the Emperor of Japan, or unite all Asia behind the Chinese Reds? Sure they would, and I bet they'd be willing to pay a pretty price for it, too, up to and including their souls."

John struggled out of the butterfly chair and stood up. "What you're saying is treason!"

Miss von Helsing pointed John back into his chair. "Stop playing Betsy Ross. For us, it's just a game; we're scholars. For you, it's data; you're a computer analyst. For Dan, it's business; he's an administrator. Who gives a damn what anybody else thinks? You want a place to work, don't you? All right, so you have to make a little sacrifice here and there."

"A world war seems to be an exaggerated kind of sacrifice."

"Shit. They're going to have their war anyway. We can set it up so everybody wins; that's the fun of the game. Last month we had Kashmir invading China, and winning, for God's sake. About a year ago we eradicated Israel, just for laughs. What difference does it make to us? We'll still be doing our work the same as ever when the rest of the world is sucking marrow out of mouse bones and calling it a feast.

Speaking of which, if I don't have some dinner I'm going to fall on my face." She stood, unsteadily, then waved for John to follow her into the back room.

She piled a stack of metal boxes out of the way and brought two foil-covered trays from a wall oven. "Pull up a stool and dig in."

John scarcely tasted his food. He wished Miss von Helsing had kept the origins of the Fellowship to herself. Not that he was terribly distressed by anything she had said; John, as a priest, knew all there was to know about moral ambiguity. But, the great detail of her narrative contributed to a kind of mental clutter which he abhorred. He determined that he would put his mind to erasing from his memory everything she had said. He would be ill-advised to think about possible consequences of the games while programming them, wondering who would be bidding on what, whether this result or that result would bring more money. That kind of thinking was a distraction, and with the project he had laid out for himself, he did not have the time for distractions.

Nonetheless, he had to admit that it had been a good evening. He had watched Miss von Helsing tipple and he had never once been tempted to join her. He had kept his temper. And, best of all, he had not been frightened when she told him that she had locked him in. Clearly, he was riding the crest of a wave of happiness which had picked him up earlier that day. Nor did he have any doubts that it would continue.

Miss von Helsing put down her fork and slid off her stool. "Now. That's better." She pulled one of the steel cubes toward her and flicked a switch, humming to herself.

119

The box buzzed loudly, then quieted to a steady sizzle. "All right, Father. Time to get to work. Would you go over and sit in that chair?"

The chair was square, with a high, stiff back, straps on the arms, legs bolted to the floor and a heavy cable connected to a switch box on the wall. John had seen many just like it in the movies. "No," he said.

A faint hint of color spread through Miss von Helsing's make up, then dissipated. "Listen, you. You're not the only person here with work to do. I have my job and I need subjects. I can't go prowling around the countryside hunting for them, either, so I use my colleagues. We're all in research; we should cooperate."

John considered the chair; he contemplated the possible function of the steel cap attached to the back by a pliable armature. "What exactly is your research?"

"You're stalling, Father. I'm an ethnopsychologist and you know it."

"Never heard of it." So he was stalling. A little stall never hurt anybody. John could think of worse alternatives.

Miss von Helsing expelled a stream of breath in a teakettle hiss. "I'm not going to argue with you. I'll wait here all night if I have to and you know it. My field requires that I take individuals, observe them under a variety of environmental conditions, and make projections of behavioral patterns for the groups of which they are representative."

"Why do I have to sit in that chair for you to observe me?"

Miss von Helsing tapped her foot. "Because I need as complete an initial examination as I can get to classify you for type and group. You probably represent several subclassifications, most people do, and I need to know them all so that I can analyze your behavior in different situations." She raked a fingernail down her cheek and caught it with her teeth. "If we don't do this now, we'll have to do it later."

John tangled his feet in the legs of the stool. "I don't believe you. I've never heard of ethnopsychology. You made it up. Why don't you get my psychiatric records? They're complete."

Miss von Helsing's face stiffened and she glared at him. "What difference does it make whether I invented ethnopsychology? None, none at all. Because it works, and that, Father, is the only test of a true science, whether it works. And whether you can make people believe that it works. And I am not interested in your psychiatric records. My approach is entirely different from that shamanism, or didn't you listen to me? I take the individual and record his specific patterns for insights into the general behavior of the part of the population he represents; a psychiatrist would attempt to create a general princple and then try to cram an individual inside it." If Miss von Helsing had been the meagerest bit tipsy, she was sober now, her cheekbones standing in high relief through a taut checkerboard of skin. "Are we going to argue all night? My procedures are normally painless, Father, but they don't have to be."

"I *thought* so." John leaned away from her.

"I don't want to hurt you."

"I don't believe you."

Miss von Helsing flipped on a tape recorder and edged the microphone across the counter toward John. "Why?"

"That chair."

Miss von Helsing smirked. She crept closer to John,

insinuated a hand under his shirt cuff and clutched his wrist. His pulse was doing ragtime. "The chair is harmless. Merely a convenience and a souvenir, of sorts, which I remodeled for my own purposes. Do you often think that people are going to kill you?"

"Not for the past week. Not until this evening."

"Would you believe the chair is harmless if I sat in it first?"

"No."

"Would you get in the chair if I told you that I would shoot you if you didn't?" Miss von Helsing had lifted one of John's eyelids and was closing in on the pupil with her nose.

"Yes."

Miss von Helsing smiled. "I am going to shoot you if you do not get into that chair."

John got into the chair. Miss von Helsing strapped him into place, then pulled long wires from the metal boxes on the counter and attached them to contact points on the straps.

"Tell me about yourself, Father."

"I am very tired and I think I should go back to my room and get in bed."

"Not that sort of thing. Tell me about your life. Are you an only child?" Miss von Helsing typed somewhere behind John, probably at her computer terminal.

"I think so."

"That's certainly evasive, isn't it?" Another strap snaked around John's throat and held him fast. The steel cap lowered onto his head, chilling his bald spot. "What do you mean by that?"

"I left home at twelve. My parents could have had more

children, I suppose. I've never been much of a correspondent."

"Tell me about your parents." Miss von Helsing's hand threw the lever on the switch box. All the steel boxes on the counter lighted up and sang out in a chorus of beeps, hums, trills, clicks, buzzes, and crackles.

"I don't remember them."

Miss von Helsing walked down the counter, each box receiving a short benediction as she surveyed dials, readjusted knobs, and checked readings. "That figures. Do you remember anything about your family? About your childhood?"

"Bullies used to chase me until I went to minor seminary. Nothing much important after that, I guess."

Miss von Helsing turned to look at John, her face pensive and obscure. Chuckling to herself, she swayed past the chair and threw the lever on the switch box, then released John's straps.

He leaped away from her and ran to the other room.

Miss von Helsing passed him and pulled open the door. She needed no key. "Go on and get your sleep." Her expression was quizzical, displeased. "You probably need it. The little boy has had a very busy day."

Lights flickered in sequence down the corridor as the computer responded to John's query. He settled back into his chair and watched the typewriter putter out its reply.

WE ARE LEFT TO DRAW OUR CONCLUSIONS FROM ST. THOMAS' COMMENTARY ON THE SENTENCES, TO WIT:

LOVE PERTAINS TO APPETITE: NOW APPETITE IS A PASSIVE POWER.... BUT THAT WHICH IS PASSIVE IS PERFECTED WHEN IT IS INFORMED BY THE CORRESPONDING ACTIVE FORM: AND IN THIS DOES ITS MOVEMENT TERMINATE AND REST.... WHEN THE AFFECTIVE POWER OR THE APPETITE (AFFECTUS VEL APPETITUS) IS WHOLLY PENETRATED BY THE FORM OF THE GOOD WHICH IS ITS OBJECT, IT TAKES PLEASURE IN IT AND ADHERES TO IT AS IF FIXED IN IT; THEN IS IT SAID TO LOVE ITS OBJECT. THUS LOVE IS NOTHING BUT A CERTAIN TRANSFORMATION OF THE AFFECTIVE POWER INTO THE LOVED OBJECT. AND BE-CAUSE EVERYTHING WHICH BECOMES THE FORM OF A BEING, BECOMES ONE WITH THIS BEING; THE LOVER, BY

LOVE, IS ONE WITH THE BELOVED WHICH BECAME ITS
FORM; THAT IS WHY THE PHILOSOPHER SAYS THAT A
FRIEND IS ANOTHER SELF; AND THE FIRST TO THE
CORINTHIANS: "HE WHO IS JOINED TO THE LORD IS ONE
SPIRIT WITH HIM." NOW ALL BEING ACTS ACCORDING TO
THE EXIGENCY OF ITS FORM, WHICH IS A PRINCIPLE OF
ACTION AND A RULE FOR OPERATION. BUT THE LOVED
GOOD IS THE END, AND THE END IS A PRINCIPLE IN THE
FIELD OF ACTION, JUST AS FIRST PRINCIPLES ARE IN
KNOWLEDGE.... THE LOVER, WHOSE AFFECTIVE POTENCY
IS INFORMED BY THE GOOD HAVING THE VALUE OF AN
END, IF NOT ALWAYS OF AN ULTIMATE END, IS INCLINED
BY LOVE TO ACT ACCORDING TO THE EXIGENCY OF THE
BELOVED; AND THIS OPERATION IS EMINENTLY DELIGHT-
FUL TO THE LOVER, FOR IT SUITS ITS FORM.... BECAUSE
THE LOVER HAS ASSUMED THE BELOVED AS IF HE WERE
ANOTHER SELF, HE MUST PUT ON THE PERSON OF THE
BELOVED IN ALL THAT CONCERNS THE LATTER.... FOR
IN SAYING THAT LOVE IS A UNIFYING COMPACTING
POWER, HE EXPRESSES THE VERY UNION OF LOVER AND
BELOVED WHICH IS EFFECTED BY THE TRANSFORMATION
OF THE AFFECTIVE POWER OF THE LOVER INTO THE
BELOVED.

John ripped out the sheet and bounced up and down,
the springs screaming their protest. Nothing could be
better, although the libraries might object to receiving
copies typed solely in capitals. John could instruct the
computer in the intricacies of upper and lower case, but
why go to the bother? How like a nun to have locked her
shift key and typed four or five hundred pages without
looking up from her notes. John had other, more serious
problems to solve. The computer resisted translating Latin
into idiomatic English, preferring to leave words in their
original order. He had been forced to use the Interlibrary
Microwave to acquire some articles on semantics which he
was now transcribing into Omniprog for the computer's

reference. Maybe, for the time being, most of the quotations could be left in the original Vulgate, implying that the anonymous source of the manuscript hadn't bothered to find out what the original text really said. Or, long Latin passages could be interpreted as a specialized symptom of a general disease, intellectual snobbery. John didn't know. These things would have to work themselves out as time went on.

"Hi there, baby. Like some company?"

The voice was Mamie's but Mamie's voice buried in a bullfrog. Membozig sauntered into the chamber looking as if he had just fled an exploding paint factory, wrapped from neck to midsection in a phosphorescent blue-and-green turtleneck sweater with no sleeves; below that he was minimally covered by a diaper of red and orange cotton. A monstrous elastic lump presided under the diaper, metamorphosing with every step. He flashed an unlikely display of white teeth and spun a full three-hundred-sixty degrees. "Like my skins? Those cats over at Beulahland know how to take care of their own."

John had a choice. He opted for the obvious question rather than the obvious comment. "Aren't you cold?"

"Cold? This child cold? Baby, I'm always *hot!*" Membozig snapped out the last word with such eager ferocity that John jerked backward, one hand half lifted in defense of parts unspecified. "Oh, man. Looks like I just scared the reverend. Well, you just calm yourself down, little man. You ain't my type, by no stretch of the imagination. Now, if we could turn out the lights and I didn't have to look at you . . . " He exposed more teeth and undulated his eyebrows.

John turned his chair back to the console, shaking his

head. The stereotyped seduction and rejection had become a ritual in his relationship with Membozig. He gathered that much the same thing was endured by Tamino, Keruk, Hand, and even Ivanson; not that John would consider promiscuity, even *pro forma* promiscuity, endurable, but Membozig was. John appreciated his energy and the transparency of his programs; Membozig never argued about quantification techniques, he never expected more of the computer than John told him the computer would do, and when John told him to go away, he went away. Membozig's virtues were few and far between, but those he possessed were cardinal.

"Leo, do you have something for me or are you here to waste time?"

Membozig plopped down in a yoga squat on the floor. "I'm here to waste time, man. And I also want you to gimme those figures you were running on casualty potentials of first- and second-born sons of Anglo-Saxon urban families with incomes in excess of twelve thou a year."

John smiled. "I don't call that a waste of time." He produced an envelope from under the console. "Here you are. As I told you, I had to run the program twice since you wanted data on two separate groups. First and *second* born."

Membozig rocked from one buttock to the other and examined the contents of the envelope. "Naw, this don't help much. I must've done something wrong."

John retrieved the figures. The mistake could have been his own, not that he considered *that* very likely. "Let me see, Leo. What else do you need?"

Membozig beamed up at him. "Well, all that shows is how many are gonna be lost for combat. I want to know how." He counted off on his fingers. "How many by exhaustion, how many by losing their marbles, how many because they got scared and ran, how many by doing somethin' dumb, how many by getting their balls shot off, how many by getting killed dead, how many because they died at home first, how many because they got sick and couldn't get to the war, how many because they shot off their big toe so they wouldn't have to fight, how many because they got lost on the way to the battle"—he ran out of fingers and switched to bare toes—"how many by being shot dead by their buddies, how many by failure to obey orders and gettin' shot by their officers, how many . . . "

John lifted a hand and stopped him. "That was your fault, Leo." Leo smiled at him, clearly grateful that John was about to solve the problem. "You should have told me that when you brought the program in for processing. Naturally, I gave you *total* figures. We'll have to go into the basic data. I'll see what I can do for you." John tapped out the order on the typewriter and depressed a chord on the console. "A few minutes, Leo. Nothing too difficult, really."

"How'd you like a big slick kiss?"

John flinched.

"I'll save it and give it to somebody else I got in mind." Membozig reached under the diaper and scratched his bottom. "All right if I just wait for the results?"

John nodded. He didn't want to work on his project with Membozig around, not that Leo would know what he was doing, but the man was sufficiently unpredictable that he might say or do something which could cause John to make a mistake. These programs were going to be absolutely without error.

Membozig played with his toes, then looked up at John. "Tell me something, man. You ever been in love?"

"Yes." Could John ever forget that day when he had found the *Summa?* Would he cut from his heart those first weeks of discovery, the hopes for consummation?

"Did it ever make you sad?"

The bishop's office, the tears, the binges. "Oh, yes indeed."

"But it worked out all right, didn't it?"

John thought of the decision he had made last week, he thought of the computer and what it was doing at that very moment. "Better than I had ever hoped."

Membozig tucked his bare knees under his chin and hugged them. "That's what I like to hear." He grinned shyly at John. "Can I tell you something?"

"If you want to."

"I'm in love."

John was not surprised. He was not unaware of the ways of the world; he had heard confessions and dispensed absolutions from Pittsburgh to Borneo and back. "With Corporal Comstock?"

Membozig wrinkled up his face and tee-heed. "Yeah. Man, ain't he somethin' else?"

Vague phrases and disemboweled paragraphs floated through John's mind, adumbrations from his long-ago, half-started, never-completed readings in pastoral counseling. *Be responsive but not too* . . . Not too what? *Remember that the counselor's task is not to judge but to make himself ready for* . . . Ready for which? He considered how he could be responsive and not judgmental. "Well, I can't say that I really know Corporal Comstock. We have met at various times in the courtyard, in the corridors once, and so

129

on." John thought for a moment. "What do you think of him?"

"I wanna stick my tongue out and lick him like a lollipop, baby. I wanna peel that big, pink man nekkid as a wienie and wipe myself all over with him." Membozig stuck his legs out straight in front of himself. A whining teen-age girl had taken possession of his vocal cords. "I wanna be his *friend.*"

Establish early rapport, but maintain . . . something. "Why do you say that?"

" 'Cause that's what I want." Membozig hopped up on his knees and put a long black hand by the side of his mouth, ready to share secrets. "You know what I did? I got Tamino to fire that big mammy they had lookin' after my place. I told him, I said, 'Tamino, it ain't right for a nigger to clean up after another nigger. I want somethin' fittin' my station.' So Tamino, he says, 'Well, who's gonna look out for you?' And you know what I told him?" Membozig quivered with pleasure.

The counselor himself must be cooperative . . .

"That you wanted Corporal Comstock." John had the distinct feeling that he was bungling a job at which the computer would be a master.

"Yeah, and I got him!" Membozig threw his arms out wide and tipped over onto his back, kicking his feet in the air.

"Does this make you happy?" How did John start asking these questions? How did he *stop* asking these questions?

"Yes and no, man." Membozig stared at the loudspeaker grids in the ceiling. "He has to come in every morning and get me out of the sack. I pretend to be asleep, see, and then I grab him when he gets close. But he's big, man, he fights

130

me off. Then at night, when he's turning down the covers, I jump on his back and try to get into his pants. He don't hurt me or nothin', but he don't put up with it long. All I wanna do is suck him off."

"This pleases you?" John's mind reeled.

Membozig gawked at him. "That's the dumbest question you asked me yet. *Yeah,* it pleases me, and one of these days he's gonna give up and let me do it, too. Then, when I get him all hot and ready, that's the time when I'll ease myself around real slow, pull it out, and slip it in between his pretty little lips. Boy, that child's mouth ain't never been so full as I'm gonna fill it." Membozig pressed his thighs tightly together. "Mmmm mmm, will we have us a time."

John had run out of nostrums from his reading. One of Dr. Klebo's favorite interrogations bridged the gap. "Do you realize that this is a fantasy?"

"Of course I do. What else I got, baby?" Membozig sat upright, his bristles bristling. "You know how long I been here? One long year, that's twelve months. You know how long I been living a bad scene? All my black-ass life, and that's forever."

John saw the beginning of an autobiographical flood. Perhaps a word of encouragement would stem it. "But you've obviously been well educated."

"Who say that?" Membozig trembled and clenched his fists. "I was just a little kid, see, when, on accounta my brains, they say they gonna give me some advantages, give me a big head start on all them other darkies so's I won't end up livin' off somebody else's taxes. They got this thing called a SEEK program at this piss-poor little college where all the Polacks and Wops go. They put me in special classes,

131

see, just the same as if I was in Alabama, where I can get 'individual attention.' Oh, those were great courses and I sure could've made me a place in the world with what I learned there. Lemme see, first we had Afro music. Then, Afro history. And, oh, boy, Afro politics. And you know who taught 'en? Some fat-belly nigger who never even been to Africa much less to college. But he tell that college president he teach courses or he burn down that school, Wops, Polacks and everything. Now, baby, that's somethin' I *did* learn and when I learned it, I stopped wasting my time in classes." He sneered. "I just sat in my room, playin' some cards and, lo and behold, what should I turn out to be but some sort of bridge shark. Hah! I cleaned up off them Wops, did I ever."

John forced a tight smile. "You could have made a career of that, couldn't you? Gambling's better than killing."

Membozig spat on the floor. "Didn't life teach you that one thing lead to another? Well, it sure do. First thing I know, I'm skedaddled outta that college and run outta town because I soaked some Mafia type's kid for his tuition *and* his room and board. So, I go and start hangin' around with some cats who put me onto a little action in Los Angeles, where I meet some Panthers. I like the outfit, so I stays. Pretty soon, right up through the ranks, just like I learned to play bridge. Nex' thing I know, I'm bein' carted around the country as some sort of consultant. I don't mind. I'm getting fed regular and lotsa those ofay college-boy liberals just do anything for their black buddies, so's I'm gettin' laid regular, too." He shook his head. "But nothin' work out for po' little Leo.

"Lessee, they'd burned Detroit, Shreveport, and Newark, so we decided to try somethin' big: Chicago. Well, we wouldn't have had no trouble if they hadn't given me a bunch of hopheads to work with. The guy I gave orders to, he was so high most of the time, he forgot the orders. Anyway, one night the cops start machine-gunning their way through one door and nobody's there to stop 'em. Me, I hop out a back window and start runnin'. I'd barely got down the alley when who should I bounce off of but Tamino. With bullets buzzin' around my ears, that man talk a very convincing argument."

"And you came here and lived happily ever after." John started to turn away but Membozig wouldn't let him.

"At first. Everythin' was just *graaahnd*." Leo fluttered his eyelashes. "Oh, I was Mr. Prince Charming around here then, everybody's little black pal, *the* big expert. But I was just a baby. I'm only twenty-two years old now, Goddammit. I grow up and nobody likes me so much any more. I get me some muscles and some balls and nobody wants to spend any time with me. They tell me, 'Leo, you just do your job like you useta when you was a good little boy.'" The pink underside of his lower lip pushed out. "Can I help it if I know how to fight wars? You gimme a war, big war, little war, no difference, I'll tell you how to win it, fast or bloody, any way you want it fought." Leo's mouth twisted into a sinister circumflex. "You just tell me what men I got and what ammunition I got to give 'em and, man, I'll take over. It's a gift, like paintin' pictures."

His head dropped and the sickly girl's voice returned. "But that don't make me no friends, does it?"

"Why don't you leave?" John regretted allowing Membozig to wait for the program. John had work of his own to do.

"Nobody leaves here, man. Besides, when I figured out

133

what this place was really all about, I knew that I had to stay, no matter what." A mad glimmer wavered behind Membozig's obsidian eyes. "They tell you yet what we're doin' here?"

Not a twitch from the computer. "Miss von Helsing told me last night."

Membozig sneered. "You think they tell her the truth? She's nuts. Listen, baby, I got my troubles but every nigger's got troubles. I also got me a high-powered conscience."

"I believe you."

"You better believe me, man. Listen, when I found out that we were part of a strategic foothold for the Afro-Asian bloc nations, I knew that nothin' nor nobody was gonna budge me outta here, no matter what."

"What?"

Membozig made a savage face. "Didn't they tell you, preacher? Didn't you get the story from old Alicia?" He pushed himself back onto his knees, his hands doubled into fists resting knuckles down on the floor. "I bet she didn't tell you that your computer is nothin' more than a Chinese plant sitting here to guide rockets from the mainland over the Pacific to zap New York and all the big cities. Huh?"

John didn't want to hear this. He wanted the computer to finish Membozig's program so that he could get back to his own work. "No, she didn't tell me." Perhaps it was a conspiracy, a prank to confuse him. If so, he didn't appreciate it.

"Did they tell you about the cat who built this place? Did they tell you about General *Lee Flan Lang?*" Membozig uttered the name as if it were a privilege accorded only to the elect. "Did they tell you how he died bringin' this computer over wire by wire, wearing himself down to a bloody nubbin for the good of peace-lovin' peoples all over the world? Did they tell you about the sacrifices made by the proletariat masses of Asia and Africa to build this Center so that the capitalistic imperialist swine wouldn't get them first?" Membozig was sweating. "Did they tell you about all the *native American Chinese* who gave up their time off from a thousand little laundries to dig this place out of the mountain? No, man, they didn't tell you." Membozig paused and flared his nostrils. "But they told Leo."

Voices? Spies? Chinese laundrymen? "Who told you?"

"Back in Detroit, they told me. All the big daddies in SNCC and CORE and ESCRU and CUT and WHACK. They said there was gonna be a place like this someday." Membozig's mouth spread into a cave of jelly and he screamed. *"There just had to be!"*

John edged his chair closer to the console. "All right. You found it, you think. But who told you that business about the Chinese general dying and all the rest?"

"Oh, man, are you ever out of it!" Membozig had himself back under control. "Don't worry, baby, when it's all over I'll see that you're looked out for."

Despite himself, John grew uneasy. "Who told you about the Chinese general?"

Membozig chuckled sadly. "I asked that wild collection of tubes you run, baby."

"The computer?" John didn't believe it. He whirled in his chair and poised at the typewriter. "Give me that name again. Spell it."

Membozig spelled and John typed. The response from the computer was immediate.

LEE FLAN LANG
BORN HANTAN, HOPEI PROVINCE, OCTOBER 12, 1902
EDUCATED DARTMOUTH, WEST POINT, U.S.A.
JOINED COMMUNIST PARTY 1935 (?)
PARTICIPATED IN LONG MARCH
DIED OF HARDSHIPS INCURRED ON BEHALF OF WORLD
PEACE WHILE CONSTRUCTING THIS CYBERNETIC DEVICE
AND ERECTING AFFILIATED RADIO TELESCOPE. BELIEVED
TO HAVE LOST CONSCIOUSNESS AND FALLEN FROM
BUTTE. DATE UNKNOWN. LT. COL. NO MI TA OF THE ARMY
OF THE PEOPLE'S REPUBLIC OF CHINA ASSIGNED TO
COMPLETE THE ENTERPRISE. LONG LIVE THE THOUGHT
OF CHAIRMAN MAO.

"No Mi Ta. Ta Mi No. Get it?" Membozig stood looking
over John's shoulder.

"No Mi Ta! That's nothing but word games."

"That's life, baby. This one, anyway." Membozig
snorted. "And it's the only one we got, ain't it?"

Before John could think of anything to say, and he
desperately wanted to say something, another voice interrupted. "There you are, Leo. Good afternoon, Father. Leo,
I want to talk with you."

"Why, it's Super Fuzz. How do, Mr. Hand."

Hand lounged against the doorframe, arms folded across
his chest, frowning.

"Mr. Hand, could I speak to you?" John pointed at the
typewriter. "It's quite urgent."

"Just a moment, Father." Hand straightened and walked
slowly toward Membozig. "All right, Leo. We've got you.
Why'd you take the tank out?"

Membozig wrinkled his forehead and looked at John.
"Take what tank out? Who said I could drive a tank?"

Hand's face was set, his eyes narrowed. "If anybody can,
it's you. Don't horse around. Dr. Ivanson heard the tank

136

going out last night about eleven and you're the only person not accounted for. Why did you do it?"

"I didn't do it!" The moppet inside Membozig was back in control. "And I am so accounted for, man. Ask Comstock. He was making me hot chocolate at ten-thirty and saw me go to bed just as quick as I finished it. You ask him."

"We did." Hand sighed. "He said he didn't see you after seven."

All expression left Membozig's face and his jaw dropped. "He told you that?"

"He told us that, Leo."

"Mr. Hand, please." John ripped the sheet out of the typewriter and waved it at Hand. "This is *very* urgent."

"So is this, Father. Wait a moment, please." Hand put his hand on Leo's shoulder. "Look, Leo. We've worked very hard building up our security around here. Nobody knows we're here, nobody ever will unless one of us makes a slip. Driving a tank around the desert is a *real* slip, a bad one."

"Yeah, I see that." Membozig's complexion had diluted to a thin mocha. "I see that."

The computer typewriter slashed into action, recounting the untimely removal from battle of the prototypical sons of the urban middle-class white man.

Hand would not let up. "How in the hell could we explain a tank? How could anybody explain a tank, since, obviously, we're not going to go blushing into some sheriff's office and say, 'Sorry, sir, that we didn't let you know about our tanks. And we're also most repentant that we didn't mention that we're holed up out in your desert pretending to be part of the landscape.' Somebody might send tanks after *us*."

137

"I see that," Leo repeated, looking as if he saw nothing at all except some private tragedy unraveling itself on an interior stage.

"I don't want to sound like Mr. Tamino, Leo, but do you know how important our work really is?"

Leo returned to the surface of his skin for an instant, a tremor of awareness moving across his face, then fading gently away. "Yeah."

"All right, Leo." Hand stepped back from Membozig, as if snapping a bond that had tied them together. "Go on about your business. But this cannot happen again. Understand?"

"Please, Mr. Hand." John took advantage of the silence and stood up. Membozig continued to stare at the place where Hand had been. "Could I show you something that I think is extremely important?"

The console typewriter clicked off and the silence, as jarring as a scream, reminded John that Membozig's program had come through. He gathered up the results and passed them to Leo. "Take these with you as you go."

Membozig looked at the papers, looked at John, looked at the papers passing into his hand, looked at the papers in his hand, nodded, and shambled out.

"All right, Father, what's the problem?"

John could not decide whether Hand's manner was the result of an inept attempt to be affable or a deliberate display of patronization. The thumb in the belt, the posture so casual as to suggest a past as a fashion model or a future as a hunchback, the lopsided smile born either of shyness or contempt; these did not add up in John's mind to a convincing image of the ever-alert security officer. And since Hand did not equal the role in which John expected

138

him to perform, he abandoned the equation as insoluble.

He offered Hand the dossier on Lee Flan Lang. "Leo has been telling me a rather upsetting story about the origins and purposes of the Fellowship. I am disturbed that nobody bothered to tell me that I was going to be involved in the invasion of my own country before I came here. That is neither here nor there, of course; what's done is done. I am here, doing a job; I want it made perfectly clear, however, that while I am happy in my work and have no intention of leaving the Center, I do wish to be promised one of two things."

Hand glanced at the sheet of paper, then passed it back to John. "What?"

"Either I be told, once and for all, the absolute truth. Or that I be told nothing."

"I don't follow."

"The function of the Center is irrelevant to me. All I want to do is my job and to keep busy. If you tell me the truth, then I won't be bothered by the private mythologies of the other members of the Fellowship. If I know nothing, am told nothing, then I won't find my equilibrium being threatened by the latest piece of exegesis making the rounds."

"You've changed." Hand considered John, top to toe, and nodded. "Quite a difference from the little man we lifted out of that convent. All your nerve ends retracted, self-confident, a bit on the frisky side, no more hysterics. I bet I could pull my gun out now and—no?" Hand laughed. "Still, quite an improvement as improvements go. We've done you quite a bit of good, haven't we?"

John was not going to be detoured. "I want the truth. Or a promise that I will be shielded from speculation."

139

Hand's hand crept toward the inside of his jacket. "Then I guess you *do* want me to shoot you. You want to be dead."

John did not like this joke and he liked Hand's teasing manner even less. "My understanding, Mr. Hand, is that we are all already dead. A promise."

"Touché." Hand looked intently from one corner of John's face to the other, as if hunting for something that had caught his attention but disappeared before he could identify it. "I can't promise that you won't hear speculation but I can promise that you won't hear any from me. As for the truth, I have to take Pilate's way out."

"That is not satisfactory." John held out the sheet which Hand had given back to him. "All right, I'll ask specific questions. What about this business? Was there a Chinese general? Is this place going to be used to track down and direct missiles from China against American cities?"

Hand scratched his nose. "Would it matter to you?"

"I told you. I have my own work to do. But I have asked a question. I would appreciate the truth."

Hand appeared to wilt a trifle. "And I gave you my answer to that. All I can say to you is to suggest that you remember one thing, which you should know only too well, when someone uses data from the computer memory banks to validate their stories about the Center. The computer must be given data before it can give any back. Also, no matter whose story may or may not be true, keep in mind that the only person here before the computer was Dan Tamino."

"What about Miss Feuer? Miss von Helsing told me . . . "

Hand shrugged and made an idiot putty face out of his angular features. "As I say, it depends on the story you

140

heard last." He laughed, but not very heartily. "Maybe you ought to dream up a yarn of your own and scare hell out of Alicia with it. Then again, maybe you better not."

"Ah, how fortunate for us. Mr. Hand, whom I have sought for so long today."

Professor Keruk darted across the room, suggested a salaam in John's direction, then addressed himself to Hand. "I have run the tests which you requested on the scrapings from the interior of the turret of tank three. I have my analysis." He offered a brown smile to the room at large as he rummaged through his pockets. "Aha. Here." A packet of pink cards riffled through his fingers. "You see. The stains were as follows: human semen, saliva, perspiration, and feces, with a slight trace of human vaginal discharge." He flipped a card over and inspected it. "The hormones are perfectly evident." Two more cards snapped out of the deck. "Also pubic hair, blond, but from two people. Semen and vaginal fluids were most evident on these hairs." The cards fanned out for a final inspection. "The feces, I may note, was scarcely worth mentioning, but you requested the fullest possible report." Professor Keruk tapped the edges of the file cards together into a neat pile and presented them to Hand. "I do hope that my information will be sufficient to draw satisfactory conclusions."

Hand scratched an itch behind his left ear with the corner of the cards. "Why in the devil would anyone take a tank to go make love? Don't we have enough beds?"

Keruk clapped a hand to his heart and opened his eyes wide. "Sexual intercourse. Of course. A shrewd deduction, might I say. You are most clever, Mr. Hand."

Hand paced back and forth across the chamber. "I don't get it."

Keruk did not notice that Hand had long since stopped

listening to him. "The ways of men are strange indeed, are they not, Mr. Hand? 'Lord, what fools these mortals be!' " He turned and poised on tiptoe, tossing John a self-satisfied grin. "You are surprised, Father, that I am well read in the Christian scriptures?"

Hand stopped pacing and stared crossly at the computer console. "That's not scripture. That's Shakespeare." His eyes lifted toward John. "Excuse me, Father, but I'm going to have to look into a couple of things. Can I have a rain check on our conversation?"

"Naturally." John had no idea what more could be achieved by the kind of aimless chitchat he'd just had with Mr. Hand, but he saw no point in being abrupt. "Any time."

"Thanks." Hand waved and disappeared across the threshold. Professor Keruk flapped a tiny hand after him.

"Mr. Hand is such a busy person, do you not think? Or perhaps you do not choose to gossip?"

"No busier than the rest of us, I'm sure," John said. "Can I do anything for you, Professor?"

"Oh, yes." The brown smile never wavered but the eyes had shrunk to oily puddles. "For I am busy also, very busy. Only this morning, long before you were up if I am not mistaken, I audited some computer readings from Rumania which were most helpful to me."

"Rumania? The computer is wired into Rumania?"

Professor Keruk clasped his hands, knuckles up, a leper at prayer. "These are technical matters quite beyond my competence, and we would have to consult with Miss Feuer, but I do not believe that *wired* is the proper terminology. I do not understand it." A modest hand disentangled itself and fell to Keruk's side. "I merely accept it, you see."

John nodded. He could not go on allowing himself to be surprised. He would have to learn to accept.

"From these readings I have learned of a most—how do the young say it?—*sensational* new breakthrough in my field which has been done by my old teacher from Cambridge, I suspect, Dr. Nicholas Veltri, since the data bear those signal characteristics of his so clever and original work." Professor Keruk paused, out of breath. "Naturally, I am not jealous, only proud that after his abduction from an airliner ten years ago, and he is no longer young, he is still producing." He leaned over and breathed an herb garden into John's face. "You understand, please, that I shall improve on these discoveries."

John exhaled and moved away. "Of course."

"Yes."

"I gather you want the computer for your 'improvements'?"

"Yes, most certainly." Professor Keruk groped into his breast pocket and dragged out a scroll of paper. "Let me tell you our situation, to date. From the findings this morning, I believe that Dr. Veltri has succeeded in doing many astounding and delightful things with the *lymphogranuloma venereum* virus. A most distasteful affliction in itself, but"—Professor Keruk hid his smile behind quivering fingertips—"infinitely more ghastly since clever Veltri has done his work. You as a Westerner with your inscrutably inverted sense of humor will appreciate more than I the nuances of this advance. I, as an Indian, have known disease and death from a purely"—he tipped his head back, trying to roll a lost word into reach—"a purely *pragmatic* viewpoint." Professor Keruk's brows assumed a solemn trident of creases above the bridge of his nose and the mud-colored teeth disappeared. "We have too many

143

people in India, you know." The frown disappeared and Professor Keruk's face resumed the Dionysian leer which served as his passport through the blockade of Occidental social conventions. "But, you can be jolly and frivolous about such things which your culture does not actually depend upon for survival and which serve merely as inconveniences and temporary misfortunes. Do not be afraid to show your smiles as I speak."

"I, frankly . . . "

"No, no. Please. I have been long enough in the West to understand and to communicate. I shall laugh with you. Ho. Ho." He said each "Ho" as a distinct word. "Enough of such pleasantries for I realize that our work brings us sufficiently close that we are already better than friends: we are *colleagues*. If my reading of the data is correct—and I may, perhaps, require a further consultation with you on these matters—the genius Veltri has managed to mutate a hardy virus which survives in a variety of environmental conditions and is resistant to the known antibiotics. However, the symptoms will amuse you the most, I think. Rather than suffer the limitation of inducing severe ulceration solely in the genital-anal region after an incubation period of some many days, the improved virus is much swifter and far more generalized in its effects. Permit me, please, to give a graphic example by telling a make-believe story about a *lymphogranuloma Veltri* sufferer whom we shall call 'John.' "

John found it difficult to swallow.

"Our John is exposed to the virus in the late afternoon during teatime. By nightfall, as he slips into bed, he may discover a perplexing rash on his eyelids, ear lobes, and testicles. Ho. Ho. In the morning, when he is shaving, John

144

will discover that the rash has spread down the center of his back, over the entire groin, across his face and into his nostrils. This rash will burn John profoundly. His eyelids, ear lobes, and testicles will be showing small, yellow epigenous pustules with red centers. Ho. Ho. Ho. Please, feel free to laugh. I will pause and wait. John will not work this day because, I neglected to mention, he has a fever of 105 degrees Fahrenheit. By noon, a fissure will make its astonishing appearance down the center of John's back, exposing the muscle radiating from the lumbar region. John will be noticing a tingling sensation in his extremities, but this will soon pass and John will feel *nothing* in his extremities. He will not mind this inconvenience because he will be deeply concerned that he may soon lose his vision—which, of course, he will, but ignore this fact for now since it takes us ahead of our story—due to the large, violet boils growing on his eyeballs. Hee. You have magnificent restraint. Please, be gay. His joints are now frozen, I must add, and breathing is rapid and uncomfortable.

"In the event that John has not perished already from a cardiac arrest, he will begin to evacuate a constant flow of yellow gleet through anus, penis, ears, nostrils, tear ducts, mouth, and pores. The great likelihood is that John will go mad and kill himself, but perhaps not. Who can predict such things? His tongue has swollen to five times its normal size and protrudes several inches before his mouth. Now, surely, you must find this a droll picture. Ha. Ha. John's hair has fallen out and his skin is the texture of plaster of Paris in those places, that is, where skin remains. His spinal column is now visible to the naked eye. All this within twenty-four hours."

"Horrible." John's larynx scarcely functioned. He had to repeat himself. "Horrible."

"Yes, but you have not laughed a single time. I fear that I am not a good comedian. However, the signal of the end of the cycle comes with the advent of blindness. The optic nerves, you see, have dissolved. All is now over."

The tension left John's muscles and he sank back into the chair. "He's dead."

"Oh, no. That is the Veltri signature in virus mutations. They are very unstable and tend to disappear most speedily. John will never walk, see, feel, talk, hear, or, probably, think again, but if other factors have not intervened during the crisis, he will most certainly live. With proper medical attention, no doubt for many full years."

Miss Feuer peeked in the door, then plunged away as she caught sight of Professor Keruk. John couldn't take much more. "Please, Professor. I have a great deal to do. Could you get exactly to the point of what it is you want me to program for you?"

Keruk offered John the paper scroll, his smile a tidal basin of accommodation. "But, yes, of course. Merely inspect my directions. Since it is almost impossible for me to acquire samples of Dr. Veltri's work from Rumania, I shall be forced to duplicate it here. Much hard experimentation can be eliminated if you will run parallels on filterable virus mutation patterns for the *lymphogranuloma venereum* type. You will provide for me the map to a gold mine."

John took the scroll and nodded as he saw the amount of programmed data already presupposed. "You've done this sort of thing before, I see."

"Many, many times." Keruk's eyes dissolved under a wistful veil of moisture. "Miss Deckstewer spent two whole days of her last week with us running programs on a particularly useful little bacillus that does most alarming, but for you amusing, things to the human placenta." He sucked in his cheeks. "As a gesture I named it after her." He looked slyly at John. "Perhaps our virus may have a special name someday, too."

John's association with the virus had been of sufficient intensity already. However, before he could speak, Keruk had backed the three paces out of the chamber.

John studied the program in his hand, correcting the order and shortening and clarifying procedure. Reduced to numbers, the virus achieved a new dimension and a higher being. John's revulsion vanished as he apprised himself of this fact. In a few moments, this harbinger of spinal fissures and swollen tongues would be transcribed into Omniprog, assuming a stature no less than, but no greater than, Membozig's Anglo-Saxon warriors or Miss Feuer's earthquakes. In a few moments more, the Omniprog would be transmigrated into electrons, shooting through channels of transistors, registering on sensitized tapes, throwing switches; at that instant in space and time, its identity would be indistinguishable from a *quaestio* out of the *Summa*, a vanishing quasar, any of the other thousands, millions of bits of data absorbed by the computer during its existence. John felt himself on the verge of an insight but, push as he might, he could not force his imagination to take the last step. Somehow, the fact that the final reduction of human perception to the lowest common denominator of physical being resulted in the absolute oblivion of identity should mean *something*. But John did not know what.

He remembered what he had been doing before Membozig initiated the train of visitors, and his mind darkened with grievances against those who had robbed him of so much time. He hastily began to depress bars on the console, barely noticing if the pressure of his fingers had been strong enough to establish contact and start the pulsations of light which signaled that the computer had begun its task. He typed out the final directions and waited until he was sure that everything was under way, then reached under the console and pulled out a freshly leatherbound book so heavy that it took both hands to lift it into his lap. He flipped through the pages to where a strand of magnetic tape marked his place; he traced down the lines with his finger, hunting for where he had left off. He read, adjusted the settings on the console, then typed.

"You had a good time, I suppose?"

John left his hands hovering in midair and kicked his chair around to face Miss Feuer. "I am busy," he said. "Unless you're here for a reason, go away."

"Oh, I have reasons." Miss Feuer had changed her dress. Or the stains had changed position of their own accord. She was no thinner but her face had more life, John thought. For the first time, he understood the reference to a smile "playing around" someone's lips. A smile was playing around Miss Feuer's lips but, so far, had not touched them. It ran above, under, then, *zip*, off into the cheek, but it never quite managed to make its way to the lips. Despite all the activity going on in the general vicinity, her mouth remained as tight and rigid as a string-drawn purse. "And you needn't be so hostile to me. I won't keep you from wherever you're going."

John closed his eyes. "I'm not going anywhere, Miss Feuer. I am working. Here. Now." He looked to see if she was still there.

"You didn't happen to see the reports from Japan in the last half hour, did you?" Miss Feuer had balanced herself on one sturdy leg and swung the other back and forth.

"I've had other callers who needed work done. I'm trying to catch up."

"Then you don't know." One lip twisted. Almost, but not quite.

"Don't know what?"

She looked past him to the console. "Didn't you see them?"

He wanted to scream, cry, run, hit; anything to stop her. "Get out."

Miss Feuer's eyes watered. "You may hate me, you and your friends, but when I speak as a professional you have to listen to me. I've had a piece of chalk in my hands, too, you know."

"All right, Miss Feuer. *Speak* to me as a professional. Help me a little. What should I have seen? What reports from Japan?"

A ball of foam appeared at the corner of her mouth and was snapped up by a gray tongue. That was why no smile would go near her lips today: it was afraid of being eaten.

"Mount Fuji. Totally extinct for all intents and purposes." She looked at John and her head did a ticktock motion back and forth. The lost smile had landed in the muscles at the rear of her neck.

John tipped his chair back and shut out the light with his hands. "I see. I think. The volcano erupted and somehow this has something to do with one of your projects. Now, let's see if I can guess what."

Miss Feuer cackled. "All the seismograph reports are wrong." John lifted his hands and looked at her. She still hadn't smiled but something like a laugh was boiling under

149

her words. "Not one of them is right. They don't mean anything. Nothing ties together at all."

John studied Miss Feuer's face. Deep shadows dropped down from the inner corner of each eye and faded into her cheeks, coal smudges on a blancmange. Miss Feuer was the scene of a battle, a war where fierce loyalists resisted revolutionary forces, her body a closed amphitheater housing the contest, ready at any moment to explode as the concealed opponents burst through the barricaded exits. John realized that if she had allowed herself the luxury of a plea for help, the whole structure would have collapsed and spilled into the room, the fragments hopelessly shattered beyond any hope of restoration. "Do you have your figures, Miss Feuer? We can run a check on them."

Miss Feuer's arm flopped in the direction of the computer cabinetry. "All there. The data have been processed. Some still coming in, I suppose." She made a quarter-turn toward the door and stopped. "I think I'd better leave, don't you? I don't know that I want to know."

John faced his console. He could afford a few moments' generosity. Either he would find an answer for her, and she would leave, or he would find no answer, and someone would have to carry her out. In any event, she would be gone.

He struck a chord, called back the data on the volcanic eruption, and programmed the computer to reevaluate it in light of as many seismograph reports as were available.

The computer blurred into action. John stared through the window at the cabinets lighting up, one close, another very distant, watched the tape spools whirl recklessly, then haltingly back up inch by inch before succumbing to

150

another daemon urge to spin forward and disgorge a mile of ribbon into a waiting twin. The workman whom John had seen the week before had returned; like John, he watched the computer from a perch halfway up a web of cables about two or three thousand feet into the cavern, as if afraid to get too close to any of the activated hardware. The illumination was much too dim for John to distinguish the man's features, if indeed it was a man since John couldn't even tell that from this distance. All at once, apparently frightened, the person began to swing, agile as a monkey, through the forest of wiring, finally disappearing entirely.

"I'm going. I don't think I want to know." Miss Feuer faced the door but made no attempt to take the necessary paces and walk through it.

The typewriter stammered to life and Miss Feuer gasped.

Keruk's virus mutations. John threw a switch and transferred the output to the terminal in Keruk's laboratory. "Not for us."

"Oh, misery!"

"Keep calm, Miss Feuer. We'll have this worked out in no time."

Responding to a shift in her center of gravity, Miss Feuer leaned toward John. "You don't imagine, I hope, that I have been anything less than scientific about all this? I want it understood that my methodology cannot be faulted by anyone. I haven't had the slightest intention of using my work as a means to attain special privileges; I've never been concerned about vain honors." She pawed her head and left sunbeams of black hair radiating in all directions. "I have given my life to scholarship, and the rewards I receive from the increase of human knowledge are more than sufficient

151

to fulfill me. It isn't any big thing for *me*, you know, whether anyone ever finds out what I've done, how important my contribution. I know what it means, I know lots about that. Really." As her voice grew louder, the evidence of any recognizable human emotions registering on her face vanished.

John tried to soothe her. "If you want to rest, I can have the results transferred to your room. You have a terminal there, don't you?"

"*Rest.*" Miss Feuer said the word as if she were coining it. "How can I rest?"

The bars on the console tiers realigned themselves and clicked off. John quickly reactivated the typewriter and watched the computer spell out alternative conclusions from the seismograph reports. He smiled and tore the sheet off the spool and handed it to Miss Feuer. "There. This should make you feel better. It looks as if you were thrown off by a coincidence. The calculations indicate another volcanic eruption somewhere off the coast of South America, out in the Atlantic, simultaneous with the one in Japan. No wonder the seismographs went crazy."

John watched Miss Feuer's mouth open in a silent, scarlet howl, and he tried to cut her short before she screamed. "These things happen, Miss Feuer. Nobody can predict a coincidence."

She ripped the paper to shreds, threw them into the air, then stomped the pieces as they drifted to the floor. "Coincidence? *Coincidence?* I don't believe in coincidences, do you hear me, I don't believe in coincidences. You think I didn't suspect something like this? You think I would miss something so perfectly obvious?" She stumbled as one of her heels crumpled under her. "I'm a trained professional and I know how to discriminate between the possible and the impossible. This is not *real*. None of it is real, is it? This is one of Alicia's tests; this, the earthquakes, everything. What'll you two dream up tomorrow? Go on, tell me. Monsoons in the English Channel? Tidal waves up and down the Mississippi River? You're trying to make me believe that the world is going to blow up or something, that's what." She advanced toward John, a gyrating, chewed fingernail moving inexorably at him. "Where did you get your degree? How many years have you had in the area? Have I seen a copy of your *vitae?* Who recommended you? Teaching experience? Research grants? Publications? A.A.U.P.? What are your hobbies? Married? Children? Answer me *that*, Miss Feuer," Miss Feuer shrieked.

John ducked as she took a wide swipe at him and charged on toward the console, swinging both fists. She slammed a series of blows against the sides, leaving crimson flowerets as her knuckles split. "Liar. *Liar!* What do you know about it? I'm the expert. I've made field trips, taken samples, spilled acid on my blouse. You're telling me where the volcanoes are erupting? You're telling me? You must be *joking.*" She aimed a kick at the computer, missed, and sent her battered shoe flying across the room. "Nothing," Miss Feuer bellowed. "Nowhere nohow nowise never."

Corporal Comstock and Mr. Hand ran into the room and grabbed Miss Feuer. She gouged at Comstock's eye and wrestled Hand to the floor. "South Amer-i-can Vol*CA*noes! Boomlay, boomlay, BOOM!" John leaped from his chair and bolted for the door as Hand, Miss Feuer, and Comstock rolled toward him in a pummeling heap of arms, legs, trousers, brassiere, and hair.

As John ran into the courtyard, he caught a whizzing glimpse of Miss von Helsing with two briefcases trotting past him toward the computer chamber.

John had learned to be cautious in the last month. Despite the twenty-four-hour guard placed on Miss Feuer's suite across the courtyard, she occasionally broke loose and made straight for the computer. He cracked open his bedroom door and peeked. Not a living soul in sight; he had hoped that he would see Mamie. Mamie and his dinner.

John was perturbed about Mamie. All her energy was gone and she was obviously ill. He had deduced from the mosaic of suntan Band-Aids running up and down both arms and around her neck that something was severely amiss. Over the last few weeks, Mamie had totally abandoned the last, flimsy pretext of cleaning John's room and if she remembered to bring him one meal out of three, he was lucky. At first, she had been resolute about spending as much time as she could in John's quarters, sobbing and pleading when he ordered her back to Beulahland for the night. Amazing how dependent some people could get on others! Now, however, her absences outlasted her appearances ten to one and John feared that he had hurt her feelings.

Maybe that explained the loss of weight, the gobbets of loose skin sagging from her cheeks and jaws. When—and if —she dragged in at six in the morning, her bandages freshened, they exchanged few words. That was it, all right: Mamie was in a snit of some sort.

The only thing John could do to take his mind off the outraged messages his stomach sent via neural teletype to his brain was to go back to his computer and do some work. He couldn't use the console in his bedroom; if he stayed there, he would keep hoping for Mamie—and maybe a little steak. Or, perhaps, chicken with mashed potatoes and some collards. Mamie had taught him to love collards. No, he couldn't think about it. On to greater things. On to the computer.

Across the courtyard, John could see the door to Miss Feuer's room open a few inches, hesitate, and close. Normally, when Miss Feuer made her getaways, she didn't bother with tactical subtleties: she came out running, arms beating the air, shouting all the way until they brought her down and dragged her back to bed.

No guard stood outside Miss Feuer's door; perhaps he was inside, battling her back into repose. John risked sticking his head out to listen for the sounds of struggle. Nothing. He eased himself out of the room and ever so gently shut the door behind him. He slipped out of his shoes, picked them up, and tiptoed toward the computer chamber, grinding his teeth in suspense as he crept around the wall to the chamber door.

"Father! Can I speak with you?"

John slammed his back against the wall and lifted his arm to protect his face. When no attack came, he peered over his sleeve. Hand stood halfway across the threshold of Miss Feuer's room. Behind him, Miss Feuer lay strapped onto a cot, Miss von Helsing bending over her, fitting a metal band around her forehead. Hand spoke to a third person in the room whom John could not see, then closed the door and crossed the courtyard. "She's had another bad day. I don't know what sets her off." He walked with John toward the computer chamber. "You're not busy, are you?"

John shook his head. "As a matter of fact, I'm not. Mamie forgot to bring me my dinner again and I thought I would use the time to get in a little extra work."

Hand stopped him before he got the key into the lock. "You didn't have any dinner? Come on. We've got sandwiches and coffee in the guardroom." He waited while John put his shoes back on, then led him across the courtyard and worked the combination on the vault door. Hand walked ahead through the maze of corridors. They turned a corner and approached a blank wall. Hand depressed a tile in the floor with his toe and the wall slid back out of their way.

The guardroom was in total darkness, faint illumination coming from the thirty or so television monitors placed around the walls. As his eyes adjusted to the flickering, blue-gray dimness, John could make out several young men, among them Frank, who had taken their airplane, and the stranger who had relieved them of the helicopter the day he left the convent. They sat in or sprawled over heavy leather club chairs, smoking, chewing sandwiches, and watching the

156

screens. High in one corner, a doll-sized, black-and-white Miss von Helsing threw switches on a box in her briefcase as Miss Feuer bounced silently up and down on her cot. On another monitor, Membozig and Comstock, stripped to their underwear, worked out with weights while, next to them, encapsuled in his own rectangle, Mr. Tamino sat motionless and blank at an empty desk, his breathing imperceptible. Several views of Beulahland, like leftover trailers for a film epic of the old South, were ranked side by side. Among them, John spied a familiar face. "There's Dr. Klebo!" Dr. Klebo, his tweeds as rumpled as ever, bent over Mamie sprawled on a brass bed; she seemed to be trying to get out of the bed, Dr. Klebo seemed determined to keep her there. John was relieved to see that Mamie had sought medical attention.

"Yeah. And having the time of his life," Hand said.

Many of the screens showed no one, only images of blank hallways and stretches of empty desert. Others were singularly dull, like the one which now revealed Mamie immobilized on a bed. Frank watched her, however, with relentless fascination, his mouth open, a half-eaten sandwich spilling salami unnoticed into his lap.

"Tuna, salami, or cheese?" Hand asked.

"Cheese," John said, walking past the screens to join Hand. On one monitor he caught a glimpse of himself walking past the screens to join Hand.

"Look at that," Frank whispered. He had edged forward in his chair and pointed to the monitor. Spellbound, he watched Mamie roll over in bed as Dr. Klebo pursued her, a syringe in each hand. After six injections, Mamie settled down, Dr. Klebo left the picture, and Frank slowly sank back into the cushions.

Membozig had put down his barbell and tackled Corporal Comstock around the waist. "Three to one he gets him tonight," a voice yelled in the darkness.

"You're on," somebody answered.

A bowl of potato chips circulated through the room. Nervous crunching accompanied the silent battle between Membozig and Comstock. Comstock seemed reluctant to defend himself until Membozig yanked down his shorts. Then they fought in earnest. "Take him, Leo, baby!"

"Foul!"

Comstock, tripping over the underwear snarled around his ankles, was at a disadvantage and easily knocked on his back. But Membozig's overeager lunges found him in a scissors hold.

"I put some mustard on it. I hope that's all right." Hand gave John a paper plate with a sandwich on it. "How do you want your coffee?"

John had turned his attention to a view of Dr. Ivanson, eyes shut, sitting placid as Buddha, earphones clamped on his head. The next monitor showed the parabolic aerial trained on the star-speckled sky. "Cream, two sugars."

John crossed the room to get his cup and spied a monitor that surveyed the laboratory. Professor Keruk watched a rabbit doing back-flips on an enamel table. Occasionally, the rabbit overshot the edge and disappeared from camera range. Professor Keruk retrieved it every time, using a pair of rubber-tipped steel tongs. After a few moments, the rabbit stood on its hind legs, spun in a circle, and dropped over onto its side. Professor Keruk smiled, put on a pair of rubber gloves, then dropped the rabbit head first into a tank filled with clear fluid.

John wolfed down his sandwich and looked around for

another. A tray of cold cuts and cheese slices dominated a table in the middle of the guardroom, plates of bread, pots of relishes and condiments alongside. Accepting his coffee from Hand, John went to the table, bending low to make sure he didn't obstruct anyone's view of the screens, and made himself another cheese sandwich, this time with mayonnaise.

Membozig sat on the edge of his bed, watching his toes while Corporal Comstock, who had moved to another monitor, brushed his hair and straightened his tie. Membozig stretched, shook his head, ran a finger around his gums, then flicked a wall switch. The screen went black.

Hand smiled as John carefully wrapped his sandwich in a napkin and dropped it into his pocket. "Take all you want. Should I have one of the boys bring a pot of coffee over to the computer chamber?"

"One cup was more than enough."

"Are you in a hurry to get back to work?"

John shrugged. "I've put in a full day. I can take a break. A *short* one."

Hand grinned. "I can't get over you. One minute you're obsessed because you can't get back to your computer, the next you indulge me with a few spare minutes of your time. Fine. I've wanted to talk to you anyway about a couple of things."

John's dinner had not settled sufficiently for him to be altogether happy about being "talked to." On the other hand, he knew his own physiognomic eccentricities well enough to appreciate the opportunity to sit and rest while his gastric juices did their worst on the cheese sandwich. What better time to suffer a serious conversation than when in a digestive stupor? John seated himself in one of the

159

leather chairs, pleasantly surprised that it was firm enough to support his back. "I'm all yours, Mr. Hand. Talk to me."

Hand took the chair nearest John and turned on a lamp standing between them. "Don't think I won't. Ever since we grabbed you at that convent, I've had some things I wanted to get cleared up."

John watched Miss von Helsing get ready for bed. "Yes?"

"You're a hard worker, Father. Just what the Center needs. But you're something else, too. I wonder if you don't get a little frustrated by not being able to be all that you are. Nobody wants to see you stifled."

Miss von Helsing wore a girdle that looked as if it could deflect spears. "I don't follow, Mr. Hand."

"You're a priest. Doesn't it bother you that you don't say Mass or hear confessions or do any of the things priests do? Sure, I know how tied up you are with the computer, but is that enough?"

"Shouldn't it be enough?"

Hand grimaced. "Yeah, I suppose so. But don't you think you should offer all of yourself? I mean, the way it is, you're only making half the contribution you could make. I'm a great believer in people realizing their full potential."

Miss von Helsing's screen blacked out. "I'm doing my best." John smiled.

Hand pulled at his tie. "Hell, I'll come right out with it: I'd be more than willing to be your witness if you wanted to celebrate or something. I used to be a Catholic, an altar boy even. I'm a little out of practice but I think I could remember when to ring the bells and move the book."

Professor Keruk gave a rabbit a large injection. The rabbit fought briefly, then began to dance. "That's very nice of you but I'm under suspension."

"Not here you're not, Father. Didn't you remind me last month that we're all dead? I can't see that your suspension would hold past the grave."

The second rabbit went into the tank with the first. Dr. Ivanson changed tapes on one of his recorders.

"Past the grave, Mr. Hand, is where ecclesiastical authority is at its most effective." John looked at Hand's puzzled face and smiled. "I certainly appreciate your offer, please don't misunderstand me. But a long time ago I adjusted to the fact that I am under discipline. I'm afraid punishment has become a way of life for me."

Hand's confusion drooped into a frown. "Maybe I should put it another way. Maybe I should say that I think it would be very *nice* of you to do something which some of us might need."

John pulled the sandwich out of his pocket, unwrapped it, tore it in half, and took a bite. "I don't want to get in over my depth, Mr. Hand, but if you need a spiritual life of some sort what on earth are you doing here?"

Hand stared at John for several seconds without speaking. "I see," he said at last. "All right, maybe I'm here because I have a spiritual life, because I think this is the only place in the world where a man can contribute something of himself to make this a better world, because I believe that life is worth preserving and that if you get enough of the best people together, just by accident, they might save it."

Mr. Tamino's monitor darkened and went out. John had not observed him leave his desk. "That doesn't make much sense, Mr. Hand. If you'll pardon me, it's sentimental slop."

"What are you here for, for Christ's sake?"

"To work. To do my job."

Hand didn't reply, but he breathed heavily several times.

161

John finished his sandwich and wiped his lips with the napkin. "Mr. Hand, the last time we talked you were at great pains to be vague or to conceal your ignorance. I didn't appreciate that. I assume that the reason you're here is because you like your job. If you're unhappy in your work, and have to ice it over with a private eschatology, I'm very sorry that things didn't work out for you and all that, but leave me out of it. I don't want to know whether the Center is a tactical ploy of the Red Chinese; I don't care if my computer was built to outwit roulette wheels. I don't care so long as I have a place to work and a job to do. That might seem extraordinary to you, it might even seem immoral. You think whatever pleases you, but a good many years ago I gave up personal scruples when I became a priest; the church has handled my scruples for me very well, thank you, and I presume that she will continue to do so. Since you wouldn't tell me the truth about this place, then I am at liberty to assume that either you don't know it yourself or else it isn't worth knowing. If my own work has any special meaning or higher purpose than I know about, it doesn't bother me so long as the job I do is a good one. I admit that I may have an unusual outlook on these things."

"All too usual around here, I'm afraid." Hand pinched the bridge of his nose between an index finger and thumb. "I can't express myself well enough, I guess. All I know is that everything we do must have some meaning beyond *individuals*. We work for and with one another, as a group, for a bigger group beyond ourselves."

"Like Leo? He's working for the conquest of the West by the Red Chinese."

"*Not* like Leo!" Mr. Hand seemed to be close to losing

162

his temper, and John didn't want to stay for that. "Leo would be trying to overthrow a government no matter where he was. That's the way Leo is. He needs a personal commitment to stay here, so the Red Chinese provide one. Not that I'm saying we could let him go. We need him, we all need him, and because we need him we accept him for what he is, no more no less."

None of the monitors had people on them any more. John decided that it was far too late to continue the conversation. "Fine, Mr. Hand." He pushed himself to his feet. Hand remained slumped in his chair. "Then some of you have handy excuses for doing what you want. Excellent for you. My best wishes. But I'm more convinced than ever that I don't want to know why the Center operates, Mr. Hand, because my own training tells me something about people who honestly believe that man can save himself: you're heretics and quite beyond the pale."

"That doesn't mean we're wrong." Hand ignored John's impatience to go.

John smiled what he hoped was an appropriately grim smile. "No, not wrong. You have merely distorted an aspect of truth beyond the point that it is applicable to any given situation. 'A man's heart deviseth his way; but the Lord directeth his steps.' "

Hand nodded. "I'm not so sure that you haven't got that backward."

John swished crumbs off the front of his cassock. "And on that basis I am afraid we are going to have to leave it since I have other things to do. I know what it is I do; what my activity means is not any of my business. I can't be concerned with ultimate ends, Mr. Hand, because they will

163

never touch me; I am concerned about immediate tasks because they are my responsibility. You, I'm afraid, are lost in the jungle in between."

"My God, Father, don't you believe that what you're doing is *good*, at least?"

"I never think about it. But if doing good is so important to you, Mr. Hand, was the anonymous corpse with my bridgework left in a burning convent *good?*"

"Yes, it was. It helped get you here without any messy questions. And once we had you here, for all your limitations, we knew that you would do some good. You'll contribute to human progress."

John turned and walked away. "I have forgotten a great deal of theology in my time, I'm afraid, but one thing I do remember is that man does *not* progress. He is either saved or damned and that is a Divine option."

"Wait a minute. You'll never get back unless I go with you." Hand struggled wearily to his feet and led John across the room. He pulled a switch and the wall parted to let them pass. They had walked several feet down the corridor when Hand stopped.

"All right, Father. Maybe the option is that we *be* saved. Together, all of us, working as a unit in trust and honesty, we *are* saved."

John kept walking, forcing Hand to catch up and steer him down a long ramp which John had missed. "A pretty thought. But 'saved' on whose terms?"

They reached the vault door. Hand worked the combination and pushed the door open, but stood in John's path blocking entrance to the courtyard. "Now I don't understand you at all."

"No, you're wrong. You don't understand God, Mr.

Hand. You can't grapple with the possibility of Infinite Will which might not choose to obey your rules. You can't imagine that your honey-coated hopes could fall short of Infinite expectation." John stared at Hand until he stepped aside. "Don't let it worry you, Mr. Hand. Keep yourself busy and you'll forget all about it."

John swept past, leaving Hand at the doorway. He paused halfway across the courtyard to make sure the guard was on duty outside Miss Feuer's room, then ran the last few yards to the computer chamber, pulling the key from his pocket as he went.

HABITUDE, THOUGH FILLED WITH IMPLICIT DANGERS, HAS THREE MARKED VIRTUES (IF WE FOLLOW THE THOMISTIC SCHEMA TO ITS FRUITION): FIRST, IT SERVES TO SAVE TIME SINCE A HABIT, ONCE FORMED, UNDERMINES THE TENDENCY TO CONSIDER WITH EACH NEW CASE WHETHER A CERTAIN ACTION IS APPROPRIATE. SECOND, A HABIT CAN SERVE TO PRODUCE A SKILL WHEN IT FREES THE MIND FROM CONCERN WITH FORMS AND ALLOWS IT TO CONSIDER ESSENCE. THIRD, A HABIT CAN REDUCE THE ATTRACTIVENESS OF TEMPTATION BY . . .

John patted the Datafax, satisfied that everything was under control, then checked his list. At three that afternoon, the Interlibrary Microwave had carried a general request from Sister Joseph Matthew, S.O.N., currently writing a thesis on "Good and Bad Habits in the *Summa Theologica*" for the University of Illinois in Urbana. Sister Joseph Matthew had inquired whether articles on the subject were available in other libraries since no pertinent works could be found in the collections available to her. John knew that Sister Joseph Matthew would have a coronary if she discovered the existence of one pertinent

165

paragraph since, by right, those Habits were *hers*. At three-fifteen, John had programmed the computer. For the next two hours, the computer compiled, organized and, after its fashion, wrote the definitive work on St. Thomas' discussion of habituation with additional references, appendices, and postscripts on structural parallels in his handling of analogous material. Now—and John scrupulously checked the appropriate column with his pen—the computer had begun to send out the finished product to the Carnegie Memorial Library, Tupelo, Mississippi.

The final step, John believed, was a stroke of particular genius—not that the entire plan wasn't genius. But, if John knew his conscientious librarians, tomorrow morning the resident mistress of the Tupelo Datafax would discover some 200,000 well-chosen words dealing with "Good and Bad Habits in the *Summa Theologica*" littering the floor of her office. These, she would promptly bind and, within the limits of her resources, catalog. Next, distressed by a nagging conviction that she had left something undone, she would check through the previous day's orders for copies, discover Sister Joseph Matthew's spurious plea for assistance, and promptly churn the entire manuscript back through the Datafax, appending a note of apology for the perplexing "mix-up."

Sister Joseph Matthew, by this time secure in the belief that she was about to drill into an uptapped vein, would be swiftly hunted down by the Urbana librarian, no doubt a jolly girl who would run and skip all the way, blissfully unaware that the glad tidings she bore might very well finish off Sister Joseph Matthew, S.O.N.

John bitterly regretted that he couldn't follow through on his project and ferret out every meaty detail surrounding the moment when nun confronted manuscript. He had been solaced to some degree, however, by three series of charges, countercharges, and blanket denunciations between thunderstruck sisters and confused but indignant librarians which had whizzed back and forth through the National Interlibrary Microwave. Trifling rewards like that made all those years of hardship, if not worthwhile, at least more bearable.

John's greatest problem at present was trying to deal with his own impatience. The computer was ready to go, John was eager to give it the signal, and whole days would go by before a single request was made for specific Thomistic material. He hated being forced to wait for a nun to get an idea. That took forever.

The solution was obvious! John smacked his fist on the console and chuckled. He would anticipate the sisters, spraying the countryside with manuscripts before anybody asked for them. He rummaged through the books stacked alongside the console and opened one at random. Closing his eyes, John plunged a finger onto a page, then peeked to see what word he had found.

His fingernail poised between two words, *attritio* and *formidolosa*. Both sounded fine to John. He dropped that book and picked up another, flipping the pages and jamming in his finger. This time the word was *veritas*. John recalled that Thomas had held for two kinds of truth and two kinds of attrition. So be it. He struck the proper chords on the console and typed.

VERITAS AND ATTRITIO: A STUDY OF THOMISTIC DUALISM.

That ought to take care of two nuns.

He checked down his list of libraries and picked Cornell.

He couldn't risk shooting off unsolicited manuscripts to Catholic universities. No matter how high the principles of the librarians, a maddened nun on home ground could not be above suppression of John's work. Humming, he riffled through another book. Might as well make a night of it. The word was, oh, a nice one: *massa*. Now for an appropriate modifier. Flip, flip, flip. How about *peccatorum?* A mass of sins. Very good. He'd beat those nuns at their own game or die in the process.

He set up the computer for another program.

THE DEATH OF THE SOUL: A STUDY OF TOTAL SIN.

Total sin. Thomas had a special word for that but John could not remember it. He wasn't worried about it. That was the computer's job now, not John's.

The forlorn and wobbling figure teetered across the room slopping coffee from a tray, stepping on a piece of toast recently dispatched from that same tray, barely arriving at the table in the far corner with anything at all left in her hands. Mamie, as lost in her white uniform as a guppy in the bowels of a giant squid, trembled briefly, then moved slowly but inexorably toward John on his bed. Her eyes, all that could be seen of the real Mamie behind the miles of bandage, were fixed and staring at the pillow directly ahead of her.

"Breakfas' over there." Mamie's voice was a rattle.

John slipped from under the covers just in time to avoid colliding with her as she collapsed across the mattress. Her face buried in the bedclothes, her arms doubled under her breast, Mamie didn't move. John picked up his dressing gown and wrapped it around himself. Looking at Mamie in her present condition, and especially looking at her first thing in the morning, had robbed John of his appetite for breakfast. Wound in gauze, Mamie lay still, the outsized dress spilling over her like a flag on a catafalque.

"Mamie," John said, "have you seen a doctor?"

Mamie bubbled something through her bandages into the pillow. John couldn't hear her. He bent down and rolled her onto her back; her arms, gift-wrapped twigs, flopping aimlessly off her chest.

"Mamie," John repeated, "have you seen your doctor lately?"

"Yestiday," she whispered. "Ain't goin' back today."

"What did he say?" John tried to see through the slits on the bandaged face. He couldn't tell whether her eyes were open.

"Nothin'. He never say nothin'." John thought he saw an eyelid tremble. "He laugh a lot, though."

John held one mummified hand and patted it. A dozen or so pinpricks of pink seepage oozed through the area of gauze he had just touched. He carefully replaced the hand on the blanket, happy that Mamie didn't seem to notice.

Maybe she needed some cheering up, a reminder of the good old days to snap her out of her doldrums. John put on a cheery voice. "Say, Mamie, I need a bath. Nobody gets me as clean as you do. How about it?"

The head moved back and forth a fraction of an inch. "Can't help, honey. I'd come unglued."

The images which erupted into John's consciousness made him decide to abandon that tactic. He would be forceful. "Well, this can't go on, Mamie. You haven't cleaned this place up in nearly a month. I don't get half my meals on time, the other half I don't get at all. My health is liable to fail."

A sour chuckle came from the bandages.

John was encouraged. He had made Mamie laugh, although he wasn't sure quite how. "That's the Mamie I know," he said. "Now, we've got to make you eat. Put some of your weight back on you and get you back in shape. A couple of good solid meals every day . . . "

"I eats eight," Mamie wheezed.

John frowned. "Obviously not the right kind of food." She looked like something badly constructed out of coat hangers. "And I don't mean your little snacks, either. Steaks, liver, lots of potatoes and gravy. Look! Here's an idea. This morning, you eat my breakfast." He craned his neck and surveyed what remained on the tray. "Two eggs, bacon, juice, toast."

"Already had a dozen eggs." Mamie's voice was weakening.

"No excuses. You're going to eat if I have to force it down you." He studied the face, the mouth sealed under wraps, and wondered how. No, this was all too perfect. John should have thought of it before: her mouth bandaged shut, the sudden weight loss, her lack of energy. "Mamie, are you on some sort of crash diet?"

Mamie groaned.

That was it! "All right, Mamie. We've got to be serious about this. You're too old to start getting vain about your figure, you know. You could make yourself sick. And bandaging up your mouth isn't going to stop me from getting those eggs in you either. I'm going to cut another hole in that mask and shove some food down your throat." John turned to hunt for scissors, a razor.

"Don't. *Don't.*" The words were a pitiable whimper. One arm lifted imploringly off the bed, struggled to stay airborne, then crashed back down. "Don't mess with them bandages, honey. Won't do neither of us any good if my face start bleedin' agin."

John backed away from her and went into the bathroom. He saw no point in arguing with Mamie any more; he would have to take decisive action, that's all there was to it. The world spent too much time arguing and not enough time working. If Mamie wouldn't meet her responsibilities, then John would speak to Tamino about having her replaced, and fast. Look at that bathtub; scaly with crust and dried body oil. She hadn't touched it in a month. And the dust on the console. John watched his face in the mirror turn red above the shaving cream as he thought about *that*. Mamie's lack of concern could quickly result in having a very important piece of equipment break down. John nicked the corner of his left nostril as he slashed across his upper lip with the razor. Didn't that woman realize the delicacy of the components in the console? Didn't it matter to her that the dust particles she, and only she, was allowing to dribble into the transistors could mean that a program might be aborted? Didn't she realize what could happen to information being fed into the memory banks because of her carelessness? John almost detached an ear lobe as the gravity of Mamie's offenses became clear to him.

He rinsed his face, toweled himself off, and picked up his toothbrush. No, Mamie wouldn't be blamed for anything if the computer broke down. Tamino and all the rest would think John had made mistakes when the real fault lay with Mamie. He squeezed the tube and shot a yard of Ipana across the bathroom into the tub. She was hopeless, her crimes unforgivable, and the sooner John got rid of her the better.

He stuck his mouth under the tap, squiggled jets of

water between his teeth, spat the white foam into the basin, and wiped stray toothpaste off his lips. He wouldn't wait another moment.

He paused with the doorknob in his hand, then pushed through into his bedroom.

"Mamie, either you clean that console or you're through."

Mamie was no longer on the bed. John had to hunt before he found her, wedged between the wall and the mattress, her position given away by one gauze-shrouded, sensibly shod foot aimed jauntily skyward. As he pulled Mamie back onto the bed, John noticed that her bandages had assumed a festive array of crimson polka dots in uniform patterns all over her body. They were still damp and warm but Mamie was cooling rapidly.

The morning had been spoiled. The work load which had built up before noon would keep John scrambling until the wee hours of the morning. The thought of a full-scale siege on the backlog of programs didn't really displease John despite the fact that he wouldn't be able to keep up with his other project. However, if the Datafax reported the appearance of the enemy on the horizon, John would let the computer take over on its own. The work so far had been fine; so good, as a matter of fact, that John had been quite stimulated by some of the perceptions that the machinery had made on its own. Not that the computer had what any sane person would call "perceptions," but it certainly had a knack for juxtaposing ideas in a fresh—how to say it—postconciliar manner. John felt as proud of the computer as any teacher would feel of an especially apt student. Perhaps it was just as well that he was going to be busy; this was the day to let the hardware go it alone. John would take a look at the Datafax occasionally to see how things were progressing and be happy that he had reached the stage when he could let the computer spread its wings and soar. Too bad that he had no one with whom he could share his triumph but the world had always had a dearth of really *good* Thomists.

"John, could you come over to my sitting room for a few minutes . . . " Tamino's voice made shockwaves out of the loudspeakers before another voice, Miss von Helsing's, cut him short.

"What do you mean 'a few minutes'? If this isn't settled and settled fast, he's *never* going to get out of here."

John flicked on his own microphone. "I'm sorry, Mr. Tamino, but I'm pretty busy right now. Could we get together sometime tomorrow when I'm more caught up with my work?"

"You get your tail over here and you get it here pronto!" Miss von Helsing, to judge from the increase in volume, had taken over Mr. Tamino's microphone. "Do you *hear* me?"

"Perfectly," John said. "But it doesn't make much difference how much work I have to do, does it?"

"Father Doffenbaron, this is Dr. Ivanson. I am afraid that, as much as it grieves me, I must agree with Miss von Helsing. Your presence is most urgently needed."

"Do you hear *that*, fat-ass?" Miss von Helsing had regained possession of the microphone. "Now you move yourself or I'm coming over there and do it for you."

Scuffling noises. Two pops. Waves breaking on a distant shore. A thump.

"John, Alicia's on the upset side, I'm afraid." Mr. Tamino again. "We're going to have to bear with her, old buddy. Do you think you could drop whatever's on the stove and trot over?"

"Mr. Tamino, I don't like this at all." John made his voice crisp and firm. One had to take a stand someplace. "You promised me, *promised* me, before I agreed to come here, that I would not be disturbed in my work. I am being disturbed, Mr. Tamino, very much disturbed. The tasks set out for me are not in areas of interest to me, after all, they pertain to the specialties of the other members of the Fellowship. Miss von Helsing, of all people, should be aware of how dependent the entire Center is on my programs. Despite the difficulties this morning, I have already completed six assignments for her and I know for a fact that she has the data in her possession." John leveled a frosty glare at the microphone. "I am astonished that she could be so ungrateful."

The sound level in the computer chamber rose to surreal heights; the hidden loudspeakers rumbled with a cacophony of shouting, screaming voices, some high, some low, some old, some new, but altogether too many of them for the equipment to carry with any degree of fidelity without exploding. John couldn't understand a single word and he crushed himself down into his chair before the violence of the assault on his eardrums.

"You son of a bitch!" Miss von Helsing had moved from the general chorus to deliver a solo. "Don't you talk to me about that shit-wipe you've been pumping through the wires. You want to talk to me about your programs, you'd better come prepared to defend yourself because I'm going

175

to pull you to pieces. Little *bitsy* pieces. Then I'm going to feed what's left over to Membozig and what he won't eat I'll use for soap. *Leggo me!*"

"Thanks, Phil." Tamino, once more in control of the microphone. "Hi there, John. Well, looks like we have our problems, don't we?"

"Miss von Helsing threatened to kill me."

"Oh, John, don't let that bother you." Tamino coughed as he tried to chuckle. "Alicia gets around to saying things like that to everybody, sooner or later. Just a hot-tempered girl." His whisper came in hurricane puffs through the speakers. "Just a joke, John. Really."

"The hell it was! I'm gonna . . . " Miss von Helsing's ambition dissolved into mumbles.

"Father Doffenbaron, this is Dr. Ivanson again. I am afraid that you do not comprehend the gravity of the problem. While Mr. Hand and Mr. Tamino deal with Miss von Helsing, permit me to explain why you are so crucially required for a conference. Certain serious aberrations in the program results we received from you today have caused us some distress." Dr. Ivanson spoke with an audible quaver. "Naturally, I am attempting to maintain full control over myself in the face of the chaos which you have so gratuitously visited upon us before I do"—he paused and cleared his throat. Or was that a sob?—"that which I must do."

John was stunned. "I didn't realize that the problem was my programming. Please accept my apologies. Tell Miss von Helsing that I am deeply sorry if I have in any way made an error." Where? How? "If she would be generous enough to retract her threat, I will be over at once."

"Go on, Alicia." A background voice. Did it belong to Hand?

"Alicia. You heard the man."

Shuffling footsteps came from the ceiling speakers. "All right. I take it back."

"Thank you." John switched off his microphone and left the computer chamber. As he crossed the courtyard, a delirium of self-doubt filled his mind. Nonetheless, for all his frailties, John could not understand how he might have ruined anyone's programs. He had done so few, he remembered them all. Dr. Ivanson had asked for mathematical calculations concerning the time lapse between the explosion of the primary mass of the universe and the initial observed disappearance of a quasar. The program had been clear, direct. John could not imagine what had gone wrong. Miss von Helsing's six requests were no more difficult than usual: a statistical study of lunacy among gifted children for the computer memory banks; a survey of something she called "life habits" of candidates for public office on the state and national level; three alternate analyses of "goal-drive" orientation among professional persons with an excess of twelve years of higher education; and a projection of Miss Feuer's recovery potential, which had saddened John as he recorded it. Nothing particularly tricky about any of that, so far as John could remember. He could have run those programs off in his sleep.

Naturally, John realized that he was as fallible as any other man, but he also knew that no mistake ever before had escaped his double-check procedures. He lived in dread of the day when he would let an error slip through. One would be intolerable. John knew himself well enough to know that he would spend weeks trying to regain his self-confidence. Two errors, the same day, would mean disaster, collapse. The possibility that *two* mistakes might be laid on his doorstep was so ghastly that he realized

177

instantly the impossibility of such a consideration. John could not be blamed, that was all there was to it, and he sifted his memory hunting for some other source of the difficulty.

Mamie! The dust on the console! He had pushed through those first programs in his bedroom while waiting for the delegation from Beulahland to come and claim her. Certainly, John felt quite remorseful about everything, but this, *two mistakes*, surpassed the boundaries of remorse. Mamie was to blame. Mamie did it. John didn't do it.

With an odd lift of his spirits, John pushed open Tamino's door, explaining everything before his accusers could get in a word. "The fault is not mine, I want that clearly understood. My housekeeper was careless in her concern over the equipment in my bedroom and I am afraid that significant, but probably not irreparable, damage has been done. I have suspected that this might happen and had every intention of speaking to you about it, Mr. Tamino, if other tragic events had not intervened. I don't want you to worry yourselves further over this. I will see that a revision of your programs has top priority in my schedule."

John smiled, happy that he had had the presence of mind to smooth over a rough situation so deftly. No one in the room replied. Tamino sat bent over his desk playing with a cut-glass paperweight, studying John through his eyebrows. Miss von Helsing adjusted wires on her own arms with one hand and threw switches on the gray box in her briefcase with the other; her jaw muscles were working vigorously but she neither looked at nor spoke to John. Dr. Ivanson, very pale, very drawn, leaned heavily against the wall in one corner of the room, his eyes closed, his head tipped back, both hands concealed in the pockets of his smock. Hand rested an elbow in one fist while the other set of fingers tugged at the skin under his chin. John was pleased: quick action had disarmed the enemy.

Tamino hemmed, hawed, and glanced at the others without moving his head. "Um, John. We all know how badly shaken you must be by what happened to the Junta woman, but . . . "

John shook his head. "A personal loss is one thing," he said. "A job badly done is another. We all understand that."

Tamino rolled the paperweight back and forth between hands set up like goalposts at opposite sides of the desk. "I'm sure we do, John, not that it affects us much right now. I don't think a careless housekeeper could be responsible for what happened to these programs."

Clearly, Mr. Tamino had not understood what John had told him, but John thought it indiscreet to make an issue of it. The possibility of dialogue, in which all concerned would be given the opportunity to acknowledge the truth of John's position was still too fragile to bear the burden of candor. "Dust," John said, offering a smile of reassurance. "Little grains of dust. She left them all over the room."

Miss von Helsing's eyes widened and she stared hard at John. "Nuts. Stark raving ga-ga," she said.

John icily ignored her and appealed directly to Tamino. "You *do* understand. Grime, filth sifts into the transistors, breaks connections, impedes contact. Certain data get through, other data don't. Errors pile upon errors; a tiny particle of inaccuracy turns itself into a mountain range of fallible data; the mountain range topples into a desert of wrongness; the desert creeps out in all directions and becomes a lifeless planet of miscalculations; the planet blooms and swells into . . . "

"I get the picture, John," Tamino said. "But I'm afraid you don't. The mistakes on the programs Dr. Ivanson and Alicia are griping about could have come only from information that was programmed into the computer. You're trembling, John."

And his hands were perspiring as well. Tamino's mind was impermeable. John turned to Dr. Ivanson. "Doctor, you as the only other competent professional"—he loathed himself for sounding like Miss Feuer—"or at least the only other person with a properly earned degree can understand what a mechanical malfunction can mean."

Dr. Ivanson spread his eyelids an eighth of an inch apart. "I am afraid I cannot, as a matter of autobiographical fact. My equipment has never failed me."

"Oh, to hell with him." Miss von Helsing pulled the wires off her arms and snapped them back into her briefcase. "Dan, are you going to spell out the hard facts of life for this turkey or am I going to get stuck with the job?"

Tamino massaged the paperweight. "Why don't you and Dr. Ivanson show Father Doffenbaron the program results and see what he says?" He gave John a dim smile.

Miss von Helsing and Dr. Ivanson produced irregularly sized sheets of paper and placed them on Tamino's desk. John pointedly chose to look at Dr. Ivanson's contribution first. He scanned the columns of figures for mathematical errors, misprints, spied none, then read the concluding remarks with some interest. He gave the papers back to Dr. Ivanson. "What's wrong with that?"

Dr. Ivanson shrank backward a step and exchanged a look with Tamino. "The good Father has a blind spot."

Offense burned John's cheeks. "Well, I noticed that part of it was in Latin, but any scholar worthy of the name knows Latin."

"That's the spot," sighed Tamino. "John, did you *read* the Latin?"

John nodded. "A perfectly respectable example of Medieval Vulgate. Of course I read it."

"So did I, regrettably," muttered Dr. Ivanson. "Didn't you think it slightly odd that the computer would have been so eager to inform me that"—he scanned the papers in his hand and quoted—" 'the highest authorities have speculated that the universe was created not only out of God's love but *in play*'?"

John shook a finger at Dr. Ivanson. "Computers are not 'eager,' Doctor, they are machines, and, therefore, thorough. And as for your question, no, I don't find it odd that infinite intelligence would consider creation to be sport."

Everyone in the room seemed to be very busy not looking at John, except for Miss von Helsing. "That was not the question," she said. "Where did the computer get that data? What is the source?"

"St. Thomas Aquinas. Would you care for the exact references?"

"No. But perhaps that helps explain why my survey of the life habits of political candidates noted that ninety-six point four seven of them were in a state of"—she picked up a sheet of paper from Tamino's desk and grimaced at it—"in a state of *malitia*. Now what the hell am I supposed to make of *that*?"

"That's astonishing!" John took the paper from Miss von Helsing and read it for himself. "I would never have expected a figure that high. *Malitia* is a term used by St. Thomas to indicate that a person is so immersed in his own depravity that his personality, insofar as we understand that term, is dead." John offered the paper back to Miss von

181

Helsing, who ignored it, her mouth agape, staring at John. "Really a coincidence, you know. I was trying to think of that very word not too long ago and here it shows up in one of your programs."

"Good Christ," Miss von Helsing said.

John squared his shoulders and joined his hands behind his back, rocking on his heels and toes. "I'm afraid that all this has been something of a lark, hasn't it? You and Dr. Ivanson just weren't prepared to assimilate all the data the computer gave you, so, of course, you assumed we had errors in the programs. I don't mean to be unkind, but I think both of you could have profited from a rather more catholic—and I am using a small C—education. A person can get *too* specialized, after all."

No one spoke.

Miss von Helsing reached into her pocket and pulled out cigarettes and matches. Taking her time, she tapped out a single cigarette, replaced the pack without offering to share, struck a match, and puffed. Blowing a Niagara of smoke down over her chin, she glanced from face to face until she came to John's. "The time has come," she said, "to discuss a few things. Not in rancor, mind you, not in anger, certainly not out of any desire to make a difficult situation worse. But, I don't believe that Father Doffenbaron can be allowed to leave this room without being told some brutal truths." She deflated the skin under her cheekbones and inhaled deeply. "I've gone over the readings I took of you, Father, gone over them as carefully as I could, and I think, under the circumstances, I should make my report here, today."

Dr. Ivanson frowned. "Is this germane?"

Miss von Helsing smiled, but not a smile calculated to

communicate joy. "Oh, yes. Very germane." Watching him through a filter of tobacco fumes, she turned her attention to John. "Father, as I explained to you once before, in my work I expect that my subjects will serve me by being representative of several generalized types or groups. You are a first for me, Father. As far as I can tell, you are representative of a *single* very small, very specialized social grouping: five-year-old boys. What a fascinating life you must have. You live in a comic book, filled with bright colors, funny characters, monsters, and simple stories. Some people would call you a monomaniac, but that misses the point. You are so divorced from reality that you cannot differentiate between events that happen and the things which you think happen. If you have any awareness of sensate experience, and I tend to doubt it, that awareness is limited to what you are doing at any given point in time." Miss von Helsing dropped her cigarette and ground it beneath her shoe. "I ask myself, 'Alicia, does this character know where he is? Does he know what he sees? Does he know what he's doing?' and I say, 'No,' because little children have not absorbed enough experiential data to make valid comparisons between immediate and past events."

John shrugged. "I gather that you are insulting me."

For a fleeting instant, Miss von Helsing looked annoyed; then she relaxed. "You don't comprehend what I'm saying to you, you poor man, because your perceptions are flawed. They tell me that you fancy yourself an expert on St. Thomas Aquinas. I can't say that your dossier indicates your behavior being much affected by what you know about theology. I conclude, therefore, that you have no convictions, not that such a condition is necessarily a flaw in little boys, just a fact. But for our purposes, your incapacity for relating the internal with the external is pretty bad news. As a point of reference, you operate on an intellectual par with certain Australian aboriginal tribesmen who are fascinated and delighted that flint, steel, and fire are crucially interrelated but never have bothered to discover and seem unable to learn the human actions necessary to make the combination work. As a result, when they need a fire, they can't start one; and when they shouldn't have one, they may just as easily burn up a thousand square miles of hunting ground. They believe, like you, that things happen to them, or don't happen to them, on an arbitrary basis."

"Whether these parallels are applicable or not, Miss von Helsing, is a moot question. I believe I would be inclined to debate them." Dr. Ivanson scowled and pursed his lips. "But, the one thing that is perfectly clear to me is that we are being detained by the length of your—what shall I call it?—analysis. Do you think you might come to the point?"

Miss von Helsing continued to study John down the bridge of her knife-blade nose. "My point is this. Since Father Doffenbaron is living in a world which is totally out of control, we have made a grave mistake in letting him operate as if he could make intelligent decisions on his own. As Dan will remember, I was against bringing him here. I understand that he had been considered before the Center acquired Bonnie but that his problems so outweighed his abilities that even she was preferable. And that is saying something, as we all know too well. However, we can undo our mistake, I think. We provide controls for him, a playpen with imposed restrictions supervised by the rest of us. Restrictions that will prevent any more of the nonsense like we had today."

John looked at Tamino. "Is she threatening me again?"

Tamino put down his paperweight and stared at the light refractions sparkling within it. "Probably not without some cause, John. I don't know exactly what you've been up to, but I have a pretty good idea how that religious stuff got into today's programs. I sent out for the books, remember? That little project of yours has gotten out of hand, John, and spilled over into the work of your colleagues. John, that won't do, won't do at all."

John lifted his arms, then let them slap down against his sides. "Are you threatening me, too?"

"Permit me." Dr. Ivanson moved across the room and leaned one buttock against Tamino's desk. "You have put data into the computer which we find singularly, and most charitably, academic for the research with which the rest of us are occupied. Do not misunderstand me, Father; I, for one, admire and respect the breadth of your talents and interests. On the other hand"—Dr. Ivanson placed his fingertips in prayerful conjunction under his nose—"on the other hand, you were not secured to be a Thomist, you were secured to operate our computers. It would seem that these activities are mutually exclusive from the point of view of your colleagues."

John *was* being threatened and he did not like it. He had come too far, suffered too much to be repressed again by people whose appreciation of his work was impaired by their own obsessions. John was not going to be victimized by stupid, prejudiced, muddled brains again, not when his own mind was pinprick sharp, perhaps for the first time in

185

his life. If they forced him one inch more, they would regret it.

"All right, Dr. Ivanson, what do you have in mind?" John slipped closer to Tamino's desk, the fingers of one hand flexing open and shut.

"My dear Father, I speak for the mind of this group as a whole. We are compelled to have you clear the computer of the troublesome extraneous data." Dr. Ivanson would not meet John's eyes but looked past him to Miss von Helsing. "Do you agree?"

Any last crumb of indecision disappeared as soon as she spoke. "And the faster he gets that crap out of there the better. We don't have to fool around with him."

Dr. Ivanson glanced at Johm, eyes slitted and wary, then backed away, aimed for the door. "Well, Father, I think that settles it since I know Mr. Tamino will concur with this council of advice. I am sorry if our decision disappoints you, but we simply have no place, at this time, for your private pleasures, I'm afraid. If you could have a corrected version of the spoiled program ready for me by sometime, oh, shall we say late tomorrow, I think . . . "

John reached out, yanked the paperweight from Tamino's hands and, in one smooth overhand arc, smashed it against the side of Dr. Ivanson's head. Dr. Ivanson staggered, opened his mouth, then closed it again, before he melted in gentle surges to the floor. Hand would be the next problem. John whipped around, already kicking at the point where he expected to make contact with the gun. His reflexes overcompensated; Hand's gun was not yet fully raised and John's toe went past its mark and dug into his enemy's solar plexus. Hand reeled sideways, dropping the revolver, his cheeks a bouquet of colors from rose to orchid to violet. Mr. Tamino reached across the desk to grab John's cassock, but John crashed the paperweight down on the tugging fingers, battering them again and again as they wriggled in retreat over the blotter. Tamino yelled, jumped from his chair, hopped around the room, clutching his wounded fist under an armpit. Hand, still gasping, hurled himself at John, arms outstretched. John seated himself on the edge of the desk, braced with his arms, lifted his legs, and caught Hand full in the face with both feet. Hand dropped straight down onto the floor, his body making a noise somewhere between a splash and a smack. As Hand struggled to push himself up, John lightly touched him behind the ear with the toe of his shoe, measured like a golfer approaching a tee, squared off, and kicked Hand with all his strength. Hand collapsed.

Miss von Helsing advanced, teeth bared, briefcase in one hand, a Medusa wig of wires and electrodes in the other. John permitted her to circle within range, then leaped on her. They rolled across the floor in a tangle of cassocks, skirts, electronic circuitry, and slashing fingernails. In the midst of the struggle, John discovered that Tamino had joined them on the floor and that Miss von Helsing fought him as blindly and ferociously as she fought John, her teeth sunk into Tamino's pudgy jowl while her knee pumped madly in the depths of John's midsection, questing for the groin. John pulled himself free of the battle, carefully positioned the abandoned briefcase, then jumped up and down on it until he was sure that he had not left a single transistor unsquashed. Miss von Helsing spied him and released the frenzied Tamino just at the instant John cracked him over the head with the paperweight. Tamino plopped down onto Miss von Helsing, pinning her to the floor. Spitting and cursing, she clawed after the hem of John's cassock as he dashed out the door.

He arrived at the entrance to the computer chamber at the same moment that two guards burst through the vault entrance on the far side of the courtyard. They skidded to a full stop, apparently torn in unspoken debate over whether to pursue John or to rescue the fallen warriors in Tamino's office. John slammed the door fully shut and turned the key from the inside. He stood briefly in the middle of the room trying to regulate his breathing before moving to the console. With a stunning sensation of having the shadows part to reveal a special dispensation of insight, John understood for the first time why St. Thomas had counseled clerics to avoid participation in wars lest their minds become distracted by unrest. Not that John could accuse himself of warring in any full sense of that word since he had avoided meticulously the use of anything but blunt instruments for fear of disobeying the Dominical injunction to St. Peter to "put up again thy sword into the scabbard." An edged weapon was intended for the shedding of blood and even if a sword, a pair of scissors, or a saw had been handy, John would not have used them. A paper-weight or a foot, it could be argued, certainly never was envisioned as a weapon and its manipulation as such was a happpenstance of an unpleasant situation. *Substantially*, a paperweight was nothing more than a blessing to man, as was his foot of course; if either had *accidental* properties as an instrument of war, then surely St. Paul's Second Epistle to the Corinthians was applicable: "The weapons of our warfare are not carnal, but mighty through God." Had God inspired the inventor of paperweights for any other end but mankind's well-being? Certainly not! And would the

Almighty Creator attach to the bottom of man's leg a bony appendage with any intention that it should be used to cause harm to another man? John grimaced at the absurdity of such an idea. Therefore, since neither God nor John, God's priest, ever would intend paperweights and feet to be used for anything but the infinitely good purposes of heaven, the incident in Mr. Tamino's office was clearly beneficial to all concerned and not a matter to trouble John's conscience further. He placed his hand on his breast and felt the staccato booming of his heart settle down to a gentle and regular *thuh-dump*. Any more thought on the subject was going to be definitely upsetting, so John forcefully engaged his mind with the task of sealing away all memory of the morning behind the steel shutters of his hardwon inner peace.

He went to the Datafax, the anguish in his soul dissipating at the discovery that the computer was in the process of voiding itself of another manuscript. He glanced over the transcription to find out whose convent-trained mind was shredding into tatters under the assault of words pouring out of her Microwave receiver. Poor Sister Marianne Francis Weimar, O.S.D. Poor librarians at Yale's Sterling Library when the hapless virago, her brain a scorched wound, would attempt to launch a counterattack against the unseen foe by crawling into the New Haven Datafax screaming prayers, threats, imprecations, and bargains.

Improvements in the computer's style especially pleased John. One could almost see the spinster hand behind the prose, knuckles white with exhaustion as it dragged its felt-tipped pen across another ream of fine-lined tablet paper.

189

AS ST. THOMAS SO WISELY AFFIRMS, THE ANGELIC MIND, EVEN THAT OF FALLEN ANGELS, IS OF SUCH SIMPLICITY THAT THE NATURAL GIFTS OF INTELLIGENCE ONCE GIVEN HAVE NOT BEEN DIMINISHED. QUOTING FROM DIONYSIUS, HE MAKES THE ELEGANT POINT THAT THESE ANGELIC GIFTS WHICH ARE UNIQUE TO THEIR LEVEL OF CREATION HAVE REMAINED TO THIS DAY UNSPOILED AND MOST BRILLIANT. IN THE PARTICULAR CASE OF THE RE-BELLIOUS ANGELS FOREVER BANISHED FROM HEAVEN, THE AWESOME POWERS AT THEIR DISPOSAL IN THE WAR-FARE AGAINST FRAIL MORTALS . . .

Gratified that the work went so well, John remembered his own tasks which the day's interruptions had left begging and reluctantly pulled himself away from the Datafax and back to the console. As he glanced over his assignments, he noticed that the computer had compiled a list of natural disasters which had taken place within the last twenty-four hours. Surely, these must be for Miss Feuer, assembled as the result of a long-standing order which no one had bothered to change. John glanced down the chronicle of earthquakes, storms, tidal waves, and volcanic eruptions. He bit his lip and shook his head. What a pity that Miss Feuer had lost sufficient lucidity to appreciate the report John held in his hand. Her prophecy had come true.

2:00 A.M. TIDAL WAVE ACTIVITY INDIAN OCEAN. DITTO MISSISSIPPI RIVER.

John crammed the report into an already overstuffed envelope. Even though he strongly doubted that Miss Feuer would see the day when all this material might be of some use to her, John hesitated to reprogram the computer and cancel Miss Feuer's information order without specific directions from somebody else. He certainly didn't want to make a decision that might be held against him later.

"John, I've got to give you credit. You're a spunky little guy, all right."

John didn't look up at the loudspeakers, but concentrated his attention on the console. Professor Keruk had left instructions for a sequential analysis of tumefacient myxomycetic growths with crucial directions scrawled in a shorthand reminiscent of Sanskrit. John would have to guess what he was expected to do.

"Hey, John. We know you're in there. How about coming out and having a nice, unemotional conversation?"

John tipped back his chair, passing a hand over his eyes in exasperation. "Mr. Tamino," he said, "I think we have concluded our conversation. The answer is, no!"

The floor of the computer chamber began to rise. John sat upright, watched the glass window slide past, and chuckled. "Mr. Tamino, if you value the work your computer does for you, you will return me to the courtyard level."

"Now, John. We're just moving you up to the Game Room so that we can get a look at you."

The ceiling pulled out of the way as John and his console lifted toward it. "Mr. Tamino, you are doing no such thing. You are moving this room into that glass cage where you can break through and get me. If I go up one more foot, I am going to give the computer instructions which will tie it up from now until Gabriel blows his horn."

The ascent stopped, the ceiling closed, and John was lowered back to the original level.

"John. You shouldn't joke like that. Alicia almost had a heart attack."

John whistled to himself and pressed a sequence of

191

chords. The fun was over; he could deliver ultimatums as well as anybody. "Mr. Tamino?" John called. "Are you near a terminal?"

Tamino's voice was gravid with suspicion. "Yeah. Why?"

"Watch it. I've opened the channels so that you and your associates can audit me." John pressed a final chord and typed.

PREPARE TO DELETE THE FOLLOWING FROM CONTAINED DATA:

"John, what are you up to?"

ALL DATA.

"Don't try to use your terminal to override me, Mr. Tamino. I've jammed you out. Now, you are going to leave me alone or I will set this program into action."

Sizzling noises filled the chamber; Tamino seemed to be sucking air between his teeth.

John typed some more, adding a double whammie.

FOLLOWING COMPLETION OF DELETION ORDER, ALL BANKS TO REFUSE ADDITIONAL COMMANDS.

"John! Do you realize what you're doing? The computer controls everything from the power supply to the ventilation system. If it shuts off, we're done for in, oh, God, less than a couple of hours, at most."

"I appreciate your concern, Mr. Tamino, but you're too late."

"*John!*" Tamino's voice exploded in the room with such force that John wondered what had happened to the flash of light that should have accompanied it. "No matter what you do, I can get to you within half an hour. The guards already have the blowtorches set up outside your door." The words dropped into the chamber with the impact of boulders. "And when I have you, John, we can do things to you to make you see things our way."

John shut his eyes. He was too far in to back out. "No, you can't, Mr. Tamino. Before your men get through my door, I'll break through the glass wall and get into the hardware itself. I'll have enough circuitry scrambled before they lay a finger on me to put you out of operation forever. What damage I haven't done here, I'll finish on the machines themselves."

Surprisingly, Tamino laughed. "Fine. Go ahead, John. Try it. You'll be dead before you get through the glass. The entire cavern is filled with inert gases to prevent atmospheric damage to the wiring. You take one breath and you'll suffocate and die."

What sort of fool did Tamino take him for? "You're lying. I've seen somebody working on the computers twice already. If they can live out there, so can I."

Silence.

When Tamino spoke again, his voice had a peculiar timbre which John had never heard before but which novelty made no more appealing. "I'm not going to argue with you about what you think you've seen in the cavern, John, but it wasn't a human being or anything else that breathes air. Believe me."

Perhaps John was affected by the way Tamino spaced his words, but a nuance in the phrasing made John doubt himself, briefly. No! He had seen what he had seen. Tamino was playing tricks. "I'm not blind, Mr. Tamino. You're bluffing."

Tamino did not answer. John waited, nervous but not impatient. He had all the cards, Tamino had none.

When Tamino finally spoke, he prefaced himself with a garbled obscenity. John ignored it.

"All right, John. Let's hear what you want."

"Not what I want, Mr. Tamino. What I am going to *do*. I am going to continue my private project and will, as necessary, program the computers with information of special concern to me."

Tamino's long expulsion of breath blustered through the room like a passing freight train. "No go, John. The others will rip us both limb from limb before they'll let you keep on turning their work into Sunday-school lessons."

John winced but remained calm. "That is a meaningless statement, but I am willing to compromise. What if I told you that I could prevent the computer from calling on the specialized data to which the others object so strongly?"

"No more sermons at the end of Dr. Ivanson's research?" Silly man. "No."

A grating noise. John guessed that Tamino had muffled his microphone while he conferred with the others, assuming that they were conscious.

"All right, John. Let's hear how you're going to pull it off."

The phrase was the final offense. "I do *not* 'pull things off,' Mr. Tamino. By my office, if not by my training, everything I do is laden with a sweet significance and you had best be alert to it from here on out." The day's burdens cracked John's voice. "Any committed ecclesiastic is an anomaly in the twentieth century, a figure of fun and misunderstanding. But I have thrown my lot in with you, and if you cannot appreciate what I am then at least have the courtesy to respect what I do."

Tamino grunted. "You've done good work for us, John. Until today, I didn't have a single complaint."

Caught up in the torment of his position, John ignored the compliment. "You are condescending. I resent it."

A weary Tamino replied. "I'm sorry."

"Can't you realize how it must pain me to do what I am about to do? To compromise with *ignorance?* I am willing to separate the rich resources of the finest theological mind in history from the nitpickery of people like Miss von Helsing, who is a very insulting woman, by the way. The loss, however, is hers, and I view her stubbornness as a symptom of the age. We are living in mad times, Mr. Tamino, and priest or not I certainly don't want people to be able to say that I didn't keep step. So, insofar as the computer is concerned, I will create a series of electronic defenses which will keep St. Thomas locked away where he won't"—John's voice gurgled with sarcasm—"*contaminate* the oh-so-up-to-date projects of my *colleagues.* Why do they make this demand, Mr. Tamino? Why?"

"Wild, isn't it? Now, John, not to backtrack on you, could we talk about those 'electronic defenses'? Will they be one hundred percent effective?"

Mamie had been right. Nobody cared about anybody. "With one unlikely reservation, yes."

"John, old friend, I like the sound of what you're saying but we've got to be totally frank with each other, right? Right. So, what's the reservation?" Mr. Tamino had resumed his friend-of-old-folks-and-crippled-children manner.

"Normally, the computers use only *specific areas* of stored data for *specific programs.* I will set up a programmed bypass around my memory banks so that they cannot be used for reference on a normal basis. However, if a question arose which would demand that the computer go on 'brute force,' that is to say, examine every bit of stored data to solve a program, then it would, naturally, bring in the material which I have added to it. The chances of this happening are so remote that we can safely say that they are impossible."

More scraping noises as Tamino deafened his microphone. Chopped fragments of strident alto managed to make it through the loudspeakers. Miss von Helsing was alive and well and screaming.

"All right, John," Tamino said at last. "We've got a vote. Keruk, Ivanson, and Hand are for you. Nothing from Jane, of course, and I can't find Leo. Alicia opposes your scheme. And I'm abstaining." Tamino chugged out a dismal parody of laughter. "Looks like we can get back on an even keel once you clear that pending order off the boards. How's about it?"

John ran his hands over the console and aborted the program. He accepted the capitulation without a touch of pleasure. The triumph had been not only predictable, because it was just, but easy because it was inevitable.

"I'll bet you feel real proud of yourself, don't you? Put one over on the big people, didn't you? Well, buster, if Tamino didn't catch that catechism-class hodgepodge you were feeding him, I did" Miss von Helsing had taken over a microphone, somewhere, somehow. If only John knew how to shut off the loudspeakers. "Well, let me tell you something that you won't find in your breviary, lover. Your self-delusion is the final gift of the Spirit, a secret grace unknown, yea, even unto God. If you think I'm going to let you get away with this, think again, sweetness. I know all there is to know about you and you don't know shit about me. That's a bad mistake. Bright boys do their homework before they pick their enemies. I suggest you push a few buttons on that toy of yours before you say your prayers at bedtime; you might get some pointers about what you're in for. You'll want to make a few special intercessions while you've still got the chance."

"Mr. Tamino!" John shouted in the microphone, "Miss von Helsing is threatening me again and I will not stand for it." He pounded the bars on the console until it glowed like a fireworks display. "I am ordering the program to maintain the self-eradication order at stand-by on a twenty-four-hour basis." He blocked off the subsidiary terminals. "If I do not feed the computer a set of code orders once a day the hardware *will be cleared at once.*"

Tamino didn't answer. John sat, inexplicably chilled, waiting for a single word of reassurance. He completed the program and fed it into the computer, already skeptical that he had provided himself with enough protection to get out the door alive.

"Mr. Tamino," John yelled, "I've done it. I've got to be here every day, forever, or this place shuts off."

The hollow silence of ten thousand tombs answered him.

Feverishly, his hands bumping into each other like blind swallows as they soared over the console, he set up the computer to provide data on Miss von Helsing. She was right. Knowledge was power. Once John had dispelled his ignorance, his fear of the woman would vanish as well. That made sense. Why, John would probably find out what a miserable and unhappy childhood little Alicia had endured, from infant impetigo to adolescent acne. He would discover that she had a dog named Spot perhaps, or a cat named Fluff and that little Alicia and adorable Fluff and cunning Spot were inseparable companions. Which is why she couldn't befriend people to this day. That's the sort of thing he'd find out. Yessir, he could see it; Alicia in pigtails and bangs, her hair the color of ripe corn, pretending to be a simple milkmaid while she cavorted with her animal pals. No wonder she had devoted her life to that dippy discipline of hers: that cat and that dog never let her find out what people were really like.

Almost without pause, the typewriter prattled into action. John snatched the sheet out of the carriage, reading so quickly that he lost his grip on consecutive order, his eyes freezing in confusion and fear at a word here, a clause there. His mind split, subdivided, fragmented, and pulverized as he tried to pull the dossier into a single, comprehensible picture.

BROADWAY . . . LA SCALA . . . BERCHTES-GADEN . . . MAGAZINE COLUMN . . . REFUGEE MURDERS . . . JOHNNY CARSON SHOW . . . HEADS . . . HAT BOXES . . . ELECTROCUTED 1966.

Trembling violently, John tumbled to the door. He had to see Tamino, get promises, assurances, affidavits, guards, protection, help. He burst into the courtyard and confronted the guards gathering up tanks of acetylene and oxygen. John recognized Frank and grabbed his sleeve. "Help," John said. "I need help."

Frank, puzzled, looked at John, then at something over John's shoulder. Still clutching the guard's arm, John slowly turned around.

Behind him, leaning against the door he had just come through, her skirt torn, her hair a taupe storm, Miss von Helsing puffed a cigarette and leered. "You sure do, my friend. And if the day ever comes that I don't need the computer any more, you'd better have some ready." She flicked her cigarette away and strolled toward her room, leaving John, unable to move, to breathe, staring after her.

Part Two

MACHINA

How do I love thee?
Give me a minute and I'll think about it.

Lora cursed herself for wearing the satin blouse, then bit her lip. She had promised that she wouldn't use words like that any more, not even in private, except when somebody got fresh with her at the diner. She shivered and wanted to call the blouse, the desert wind, and her own dumbness a lot of names, but caught herself just in time. What they said about fat people not feeling the cold (not that she was all *that* fat, really) wasn't true. Lora hated the cold more than the heat, and she knew a lot about heat. She had started walking at 3:00 P.M. to get here and she had sweated up a storm until the sun went down. She didn't really mind these walks though; she knew how pleased she would be to get home and step on the fuzzy bathroom scales and discover that another two pounds had been left someplace back in the sand. If only she could keep what she lost *lost* from week to week. On the whole, these hikes hadn't done her any harm. She figured that over the last six months she had managed to knock off, oh, probably four pounds that stayed off. She felt pretty proud of herself about that.

Lora remembered how scared she used to be of the desert at night, especially when those fresh college boys dumped her out here. Honestly, if it hadn't been for the way things worked out, she would never, never, never have forgiven them. And she'd thought they would be fun, for an evening at least. Well, she guessed that they *had* been fun, but they were mean to leave her out here in the desert when they were through. What if she had stayed lost? She could have *died!*

Nowadays, she probably knew as much about getting around out here as anybody in the world. Hitchhike from the diner until she got to the crossroads, then ask to get out. Then take another ride until she came to the Frisco tracks. After that she had to walk for *hours.* Not many girls would do that for a boy but, then, Lora had never had a steady before. She giggled when she remembered how she'd met him. Boy, couldn't somebody make a movie out of that! Those old college boys had run off and left her and she must have wandered around half the night, lost and everything, when she'd heard it. When she *saw* it, she had started to run, boy, had she started to run! She didn't remember a thing except for tearing her stockings on the mesquite, until she found herself lying down, with him telling her everything was all right, not to worry, he wouldn't hurt her. And he hadn't either. She giggled again.

Lora strained her eyes, trying to see something off in the darkness besides the stars and the distant silhouette of the butte cutting into the sky. She knew how silly she was to try to see him from here beside the little shrub where she had fallen down that night when everything started.

201

The rumble and squeal of the treads made her heart jump with excitement. She shivered and clutched herself, much colder now when she thought how warm she was going to be in just a few minutes. Oh, boy!

Over a slight dune, the dark shape of the tank lumbered toward her. She slipped out of her shoes and hopped up and down to make sure he saw her and didn't just turn around and leave. One night she'd had to chase the tank nearly half a mile before she caught up with it. "Here I am," she yelled, and waved both arms over her head. "Here I am."

The tank slowed, turned, belched fumes, stopped, and settled into the sand. Lora ran and clambered up the front toward the turret, hiking her skirt over her thighs as she climbed. Even though nobody was watching her, she always felt so silly pulling her dress up like this. Maybe someday he'd let her wear slacks. Lora couldn't figure out why he didn't like girls in pants.

The hatch opened and Lora dropped into the basket, feeling his hands dig in under her ribs as he caught her and lowered her the rest of the way. He closed the hatch and turned to her. Lora hugged him, then holding tight around his waist, leaned back and looked up into the pale, handsome face. "I bet I'm the only girl in the world whose boy friend comes for her in a tank."

"Don't knock it," he said. "It's the only thing I can get."

She released him and began to undo the buttons on her blouse while he watched. Oh, he was *gorgeous!* So big and tall and, well, everything! And a real man of mystery, too. Lora supposed he was in the army or something, what with the tank and all, but she had never heard of any army base around here. He didn't like her to ask questions, so she didn't; but sometimes Lora wondered. Maybe he was married. Maybe he was a spy, and someday they'd get caught together in the tank and the F.B.I. would think Lora was a spy, too, and they would be lined up against a wall and shot together. She wouldn't mind, just so long as they shot her first.

She unzipped her skirt and stood in her panties and bra, waiting for him. He grabbed her and kissed her, grinding his mouth so hard against hers that she thought that her teeth would come through the skin.

His tongue moved over hers, then slid up and licked the top of her mouth, her wisdom teeth, her tonsils, the insides of her cheeks. He tasted so good and clean, not any alcohol or garlic or onions on her boy friend's breath. All her girl friends said that boys always smelled bad, but *he* didn't, he smelled good, all over. Lora felt his hand slip down into her panties and squeeze the fat on her bottom. She let him push the panties down with one hand while he undid the brassiere with the other. She wriggled, pulled back half an inch, and her underwear fell to the floor.

"Oh, Baby," he said. "Oh, Baby."

He licked Lora's face while she disentangled him from his shirt and threw it away. She dodged his tongue slipping over her eyes as she tried to get a look at his belt buckle to find out why she couldn't unfasten it. He bit her ear while she solved the puzzle and moved on to release the snap and pull down the zipper. He was so thin, no hips at *all*, the trousers flopped down over his ankles. Lora held on tight as he stepped out of them. She felt him move his hips toward her stomach, slowly, the *thing* rubbing against her navel. She reached down and touched his pelvis, startled and pleased that he had not bothered to wear shorts. He

203

moaned in Lora's ear and she squirmed against him. She knew he loved her; nobody else ever had worked himself up so fast over Lora. One of those college boys had taken an hour, at least, and she blotted out a nasty memory of that Mr. Rubin, the Milwaukee drug salesman.

Lora nibbled his shoulder, licked his collar bone, sucked the dimple in his chin. He squeezed her tight against him, mashing her against his chest, his bottom half bouncing back and forth so violently that she thought he was going to drill a hole in her tummy.

"Unh, unh," he said. "Unh, unh, unh."

"Sweetie? Precious?" Lora tried to pry herself loose. She didn't want him to cheat himself, or her either, for that matter, by getting too excited. She pushed her rear end out away from his prods and almost fell over as he pursued her. "You funny guy," she sighed and bit him hard on the titty.

"Whattaya wanna do that for?" He examined himself for punctures.

Men were such babies. They couldn't think ahead for one second. Lora squatted down onto the floor of the basket, hating the feel of the cold metal on her bare skin. She scooted forward until she was flat on her back, her feet spread-eagled around his legs. From this angle, she couldn't see his face, just his outline against the green lights glowing from the dials on the radio in the corner. He was so tall and handsome, Lora could barely stand it: those broad shoulders, those narrow hips, those big legs. Oh, boy!

He sat in front of her and pulled her feet around his waist. Lifting herself on her hands, Lora inched herself up his legs until she sat on his thighs, resting her head on his chest. Slowly she pulled herself closer to him, her hand in their mutual lap, guiding him. He scrambled his fingers in

Lora's hair, tilted her head back and softly rested his lips against hers. She closed her eyes and tried to imagine herself in a nice soft bed, lying down, doing this *right*. All this sitting and bouncing around was bad on her back. She couldn't understand why he didn't at least bring a couple of blankets so that they could stretch out on the desert. But he got mad every time Lora suggested it. This just didn't feel right to her and made her remember too many weirdo nights in A & P parking lots and movie theater balconies. He was special to Lora and they should do it the way everybody else did it. But Lora knew he wouldn't like it if she suggested getting out of the tank and she had learned the hard way that if you got a boy mad too many times, that was the end of that.

He was squeezing her with both arms, his head rocking back and forth on her face as she built up steam. Lora's back really did hurt and she wanted to hurry him up. Suddenly, all the rhythm vanished as he started to arch harder and faster toward her. Lora grabbed him around the middle and hung on for dear life, flopping and jogging until she thought the top of her head was coming off. Oh, boy! Oh, man! Oh, wow!

His head sagged onto her shoulder and rested there. He panted, his breath hot and uncomfortable on Lora's breast. Giving him a quick nuzzle, she eased herself free and slid off his lap. They were both gooey with sweat. Lora crawled across the tank, found his shirt, took the cigarettes out of the pocket and, while he lighted up, mopped them both off. He had moved back and leaned against the side of the turret, sitting with one arm thrown over his knees, his eyes closed and mouth open exhaling smoke. He was the sweetest thing in the world. Lora couldn't resist creeping up

205

next to him, hot as she was, and pulling one of his arms over her shoulder. She didn't close her eyes but studied what she could see of him from the waist down. Even in the green light, he was the most gorgeous guy she'd ever run into and she just wished it would never stop. She reached out and touched him.

He moved her hand back onto her own lap. "Not yet. Give me a minute to get my wind."

Lora felt hurt. All she'd wanted to do was touch. "Well, you just better hurry up. I got a long walk ahead of me and I don't want to spend the rest of the night here." That was a lie and she knew it. Lora would have stayed there all night if he'd let her. "I think maybe the next time you better come into Podstown and pick me up."

"In a *tank?*" He didn't even look at her.

"Well, we could meet at Ruthie's Rest and Ruthie lets Pepe Cortes bring his girls on his daddy's tractor. Ruthie's been around. She won't mind."

"Nope, can't swing it." He patted her breast with the hand hanging over her neck, rubbing the nipple with his thumb and sending shockwaves down through the pit of Lora's stomach. "Besides, you don't mind the walk. Keeps you in shape."

She punched him in the ribs and he grunted. Honestly, if she could only stay mad at him for five minutes, maybe she could get her way. All she wanted was to make him come to town long enough for the other girls to see what Lora had caught.

Then, maybe, that wouldn't be too smart. He was certainly the best-looking thing she'd ever seen and those witches would be after him in a second. Hike or no hike, she at least had him all to herself in the tank.

"Dean?" she said, bending around to look up into his face. "I'm sorry."

"S'all right." His lips turned up into a smile. "Don't mention it."

He was so good-natured. He never talked dirty, except when he asked her to do something special, and he always got over being mad as fast as anybody Lora had ever met. Honestly, he treated her as if she were the last girl in the world.

That sort of bothered her, somehow. Not that she wasn't glad to have him be so nice, but she couldn't stop wondering why anybody so handsome would bother with her. And he was always so worked up. He never let her leave without doing it at least three times, sometimes more. She could tell by looking that he was already set to go again.

Maybe it was love, real love. Maybe he wanted to marry her. She had heard about boys that took it for granted that a girl would marry them after they'd done it with her, although Lora hadn't run into any herself. Maybe he was like that, only too shy to mention it. She studied his face, the long eyelashes, the thin lips, the funny little nose. Well, one thing for sure, when they were married she'd see to it that he got more sun. He was the palest soldier she'd ever seen. Lora thought that soldiers were supposed to spend a lot of time outdoors.

But, pale as he was, his complexion was good, better than hers, and she loved his face. She even loved his toes, they were so straight and clean. Lora's toes were bent and crooked from being mashed together in tight shoes.

He looked into her face and then down at himself. She followed his eyes and watched.

The arm around Lora's neck tensed and brought her forward until her head was pressed, mouth down, on his chest. Oh, well, if he wanted her to do that she'd do it but she felt like a fifteen-year-old school kid on her first date with a sailor. Lora nibbled and lapped her way down his stomach, pausing to scrub his navel with her tongue. The only nice thing about this was that you could get it over fast and move on to something where everybody had fun. She pushed her mouth down and got busy.

When they were married, she decided suddenly, they wouldn't live in Podstown. They would move far away, maybe to Chicago or New York, and they wouldn't even send Christmas cards back to let people know where they were. Not even to her dad, that rat. She wanted to meet his family and maybe have them visit and let Lora show off what a good cook she was.

He jerked, bim, bam, boom, and Lora felt him slip away from her. Boy, that *was* quick. She hadn't even heard him start to breathe fast. She nestled her head into his belly and tugged at the curly little hairs with her teeth. He didn't budge. Usually, he hollered and slapped her bottom when she did that. Her neck felt warm and damp and she reached back to wipe it with her hand.

Something warm, dark, and sticky dripped from her fingers. She squinted in the dim green light, then jumped up onto her knees and turned around.

The line of evenly spaced holes ran from his lower rib up across his chest into his neck. Lora didn't believe it. It was a bad joke. "Dean?" she said. She pushed him and he fell over, a bubble of blackness rushing out of his mouth and nose. Lora strangled a whimper rising in her throat. No time to think, no time to cry. She couldn't be caught here. With

208

her record, nobody would believe that she hadn't done it.

Done what? She hadn't heard a thing!

Lora pushed herself to her feet and snatched up her clothes, pulling on her skirt and blouse, slipping and sliding in the expanding pool. She would carry her underwear, bury it in the desert. A part of her told her to stay and weep, but a wiser, older part said, "Run, run!"

She stepped up onto the collapsible seat and pushed at the hatch. She couldn't budge it and panic swelled over her heart. She pounded, she shoved, she clawed, but the hatch stuck fast. She jumped off the seat and looked wildly around her. Somebody must be in here with her. Somebody who shot her Dean. But she saw nobody, nobody but the naked corpse whose blood had washed over the entire floor of the turret and squished between Lora's toes.

Lora screamed. And then she screamed and screamed and screamed some more.

Not having slept bothered John less than the thoughts, washed in primary colors and narrated by banshees, which had haunted his wakefulness from midnight to dawn. Miss von Helsing's phantom *Doppelgängers* lurked under the bed, behind the console, sprawled in the bathtub, on the other side of the door, all waiting for the signal to rush John en masse and chop him to slivers with tomahawks and Boy Scout hatchets. He tried to convince himself that he was having a seizure of cerebral indigestion as a result of all that had happened the day before, that he was imagining things. But at three thirty-six by the radium face of a normally honest wristwatch, people had been running in the courtyard outside his door, people had been shouting, and the images of massacre were as sharp and brilliant in his mind as Kodachrome slides. "Don't let her get away," somebody had yelled; then John heard a woman scream.

"The blood! Look at that blood!" somebody else had shouted, and he turned on the lamp beside his bed, fully expecting to see rivulets of gore streaming down the walls. Then somebody had called somebody else a clumsy bastard and Mr. Tamino had asked for a gun. "She's in Jane Feuer's room," another voice yelled and the pounding and yelling started all over again. "Get von Helsing," somebody that sounded like Hand had bellowed, and another bellow replied that he already had got her. Then a long, dreadful silence broken only by sobbing and female murmurs, themselves punctuated by cries of "No, no, no!" John prayed that it would stop.

And stop it did, at four forty-seven, with five distinct gun shots. John scarcely had begun to relax, relishing a fantasy of Miss von Helsing being dragged feet first into the desert to be left at the disposal of a fraternity of coyotes when the console across his bedroom burst into furious action. An order flickered across one of the luminescent television screens.

TRANSCRIBE FINAL REPEAT FINAL ENCEPHALOGRAM, CARDIOGRAM, ETC. READINGS AND CORRELATE READINGS WITH PREV. ACCUM DATA RE. CAUCASIAN FEMALE TYPE 12G FOR REF VON HELSING.

While a call for transcription of "final" readings sounded promising, the fact that these were to be put at the disposal of Miss von Helsing did not. She was still out there, somewhere, hiding, planning to do terrible things to John.

He had waited nearly thirty minutes, his ear pressed to the door listening for sounds in the courtyard, before he had risked making the dash for the computer chamber. After informing the console of his presence by means of the coded signal, John glanced through the work that had piled up overnight. Miss von Helsing, whatever else might have occupied her during the early hours of the morning, had not been idle. John decided that he would put her programs out first, as a proof that he held no hard feelings. Maybe, if he made a point of demonstrating what a good sport he was, she would realize how invaluable John was to her projects. And if, as a general practice, he expedited everything she sent him, after a month or a week or maybe even less, she would come up to him one day, stammering with shame, and tell him what a fool she had been and how much she wished that they could let bygones be bygones and be friends. John shuddered at the thought of spending the next decade of his life pretending to be pals with Miss von Helsing, but as an alternative to an ax in his neck a little bogus chumminess had incontrovertible attractions.

He ran the figures for her programs, then glanced over pending data that had come through the computer during the night. The world had wallowed in violence. A mad thrill killer had machine-gunned every male between the ages of nineteen and twenty-five in a county somewhere in the Southwestern United States while an American aircraft carrier, off-course in a fog, had been strafed repeatedly by Australian jets, also off-course in the same fog. The casualties in both cases were astonishingly high and John made a mental note to be sure that Membozig was alerted to the American-Australian mishap in the Indian Ocean and that Miss von Helsing was informed of the vagaries of American lunacy. These special attentions would please Miss von Helsing, John thought, and he felt himself fast on the way to healing the wounds which could cause him, in particular, so much pain.

Delighted that his colleagues had made so few demands on him today, John finished the work that had been left for him in almost no time at all. Nothing from Membozig, Keruk, and Feuer (naturally), and outside of Miss von Helsing's requests, only the briefest of assignments from Dr. Ivanson. In fact, John realized that Dr. Ivanson's program had been aborted halfway through and that John's task required him merely to delete the incomplete data already processed. His desk cleared, as it were, John felt his cares vanish, hobgoblins in the sunlight of his freedom.

Briskly rubbing his hands, John peered over at the Datafax, immediately disappointed that it, too, seemed to be on vacation. Well, nobody loafed in John's shop, ruthless taskmaster that he was. He snorted at the absurdity of the notion; John with a whip! Flogging his Datafax! He hummed to himself and reached under the console for a book.

The jolt almost threw John out of his chair as the floor of the chamber lifted toward the Game Room.

"John, you're needed up here. Sorry we didn't warn you, but this is an emergency, I'm afraid."

John grumbled, pushed the book back into place and wearily turned his chair around to watch himself rise into the glass cage. And he had laid out such a nice day for himself, too.

The first thing that struck John as being unusual was that no one occupied any of the terminals on the amphitheater floor. Membozig, eyes wide and uncomprehending, sat tied to a chair in the middle of the room. Keruk and Ivanson huddled together in a far corner. Miss von Helsing paced and smoked, apparently oblivious to John's tentative waves, winks, and nods of friendship and forgiveness. Even Miss

213

Feuer had joined her colleagues, her face much thinner than John remembered it over the comfortable bulkiness of the strait jacket. As he lifted higher and higher, John could see Hand and Tamino caught up in frenzied dialogue in the bandbox, Tamino's microphone shielded by a pudgy fist.

The second thing out of the ordinary which John noticed was Corporal Comstock, naked and presumably dead, his body riddled with holes, lying open-eyed and open-mouthed on a porcelainized tabletop near the old-fashioned tintype grouping of Membozig and the guards. John recalled the alarming data about the lunatic machine-gunner slaughtering an entire county's masculine population and wondered if this were the county and, if so, how did the maniac get into the Center to shoot poor Corporal Comstock? John resolved to double-check the locks on his door every night before he went to bed.

Mr. Tamino shook his head furiously at Hand, then turned to his microphone. He did not speak immediately but stared at the instrument as if he didn't know quite what he was expected to do with it. From his vantage point, John could see Tamino's mouth open, start to form a word, then snap shut. He repeated this charade several times before finally compressing his lips and forcing himself to blurt out several sentences without stopping.

"All right. Some of you know why we're here, some of you don't. The story is this. Last night, we solved one mystery that has been plaguing us for months: who was taking out the tank and how they were getting away with it. Corporal Comstock was our thief, his method simple. Every time he wanted to borrow a tank, he slipped a photograph of the desert at night in front of the security camera surveying the area he planned to visit. In the guardroom, nobody noticed the difference. Only Dr. Ivanson's alertness informed us of the fact that a tank was being stolen at fairly regular intervals. If Dr. Ivanson's schedule had been a trifle more flexible—and this is no criticism of your work, Doctor—and he had found time to inform us of his discoveries instead of waiting for two or three days after each occurrence, perhaps we could have avoided these, um, tragic consequences. However, that's the way things work out."

Tamino wiped his mouth with the palm of his hand and continued. "Last night, Corporal Comstock had himself a rendezvous with a young lady. No, no. Don't get yourselves in a snit. She knew nothing about the Center apparently and for that we can send up prayers of thanks to whatever we each send up a prayer to."

"I shall immolate a goat," Professor Keruk said. John frowned down at him.

"Thanks, Senid." Tamino paused again, stumbling after inspiration. John suffered for him; he never had been much of a public speaker either. "Where was I? Oh, yes. In any case, we have Corporal Comstock and this young lady—her name doesn't matter—hard at it when, according to her, she looked up and found Corporal Comstock full of holes. Now—and here's the messy part—they were locked in a tank, nobody in there with them, the girl tells us she didn't hear a sound, and yet somebody shot Corporal Comstock. Furthermore"—helpless dismay seized control of Tamino's face—"the killer then went on a rampage through four towns and villages, plus intervening farms and state patrol stations, and killed 103 other men all with a similar—what's the phrase, Phil?—*modus operandi.*"

The figure stirred a memory to life inside John's brain.

Hadn't that been the total number of deaths, less one, of the men on the American aircraft carrier? John was sure of it! What a gruesome coincidence.

"The witnesses, those that are still sane enough to talk"—Tamino loosened his tie and stretched his neck as if in danger of imminent strangulation—"all said that they heard nothing. Mothers embracing teen-age sons found themselves with armloads of dead meat; wives scooting across the mattress for a good-night cuddle discovered themselves sharing beds with corpses; old ladies making eyes at filling station attendants watched them get perforated before they could count out Green Stamps; and, from what I can find out, many of these deaths took place at the same time in different places. But, more astonishing yet, *not one single bullet has been found!* You say, 'Bullet holes with no bullets?' Perfectly reasonable that you should ask, and so do I." Without warning, Tamino sprawled across his desk and screamed down into the amphitheater. *"All right, Membozig! How didja do it?"*

Membozig stared at Comstock's body, unable to lift a hand from his bonds to wipe away the tears coursing down his cheeks. "I didn't do it, man. Why would I wanna kill my baby?"

"Cut it, Leo." Tamino raised his fists over his head, then, finding nothing within reach to hit, let them sink to his sides. "For the oldest reason in the world. You were *jealous*. You caught Comstock sneaking off for a piece when he wasn't giving you any, so you *shot* him." Tamino slid back across the desk top and slumped into his chair. "Leo, I don't mind about all those other people. So you had a gripe against the human race and had to get it out of

216

your system. Everybody has a bad day. That's life. All I'm asking you to tell me is how you managed to do it without bullets. Huh, Leo?"

Membozig didn't answer.

"Mr. Tamino." Hand moved from the shadows at the rear of the bandbox. "I don't think Leo did anything. I think he's telling the truth. Too many things don't check out. First of all, when we got to the tank the only footprints in the sand that led up to the spot belonged to the girl. Second, the light had been off in Membozig's room for no more than half an hour. He wasn't out of surveillance long enough to travel the distances required to murder Comstock, much less 103 other people."

Tamino stared up at Hand, eyes full of hurt and betrayal. "Phil, don't talk like that. You've been a son to me. Think of everything we've been through together. Be on my side." He pounded the desk and shouted. "That fag spade's a Goddamn genius. If he can shoot people without bullets, he can sneak up on 'em without leaving footprints. Maybe he flew, for God's sake, I don't know. But he's not *telling*, the son of a bitch, and that's disloyal."

Hand beetled his brows. "That doesn't hold together. You can't prove he shot anybody."

Tamino exploded from his chair, his index finger rising like a rocket over his head. "He *did* it. *He* did it. Every one of us heard him, right in this room with our own ears, threaten to burn Comstock. So he shot him instead. A matter of taste, nothing else. I don't see a hell of a lot of difference. And he did it without bullets."

"I wrote that song for him myself." Membozig blubbered without control. "Oh, Lawdy."

217

John turned to his console and worked out a combination of chords. The bars pulsed and glowed for only a few seconds, then hopped up and blinked out.

DATA REQUESTED NOT AVAILABLE.

John switched on his microphone. "Mr. Tamino, could I have your attention please?" Everyone in the amphitheater, except Membozig, looked up at John. Even Miss Feuer, wearing the biggest smile John had ever seen, anywhere, attempted to focus her eyes on the glass cage.

"What is it, John?"

John didn't know what it meant, but it seemed relevant. "I have checked the memory banks and the computer has no record of Membozig or any other member of the Fellowship doing work with bulletless guns. And, in the time I've been here, I don't recall Leo ever working with material that had reference to anything but extant weaponry."

Tamino did not seem pleased with John's contribution. In fact, he stared so hard at John that John looked away, regretting that he had butted in.

"Perhaps I can point out a few things we have overlooked." All heads swiveled toward Miss von Helsing, who rested one flank against Membozig's terminal. All heads save that of Miss Feuer. Hers wagged in jolly abandon at John, tongue sticking out, eyes rolling. John forced himself to look at Miss von Helsing. She flicked through a looseleaf notebook lying open on the terminal, a peculiar smirk wrinkling her cheeks. Her patent delight in whatever she was about to do shocked John.

"We have forgotten to examine the pertinent ethnopsychological factors in the case." Miss von Helsing hoisted her hip off the terminal and ambled toward the snuffling

Membozig, a tigress anticipating a lunch of wounded blackbird. She dropped a hand on Leo's shoulder and clutched it. "Leo, we must remember, is representative of several groups, three of which contribute to make him the darling boy that he is." John watched in suspense as Miss von Helsing's nails dug deeper into Membozig's shirt. He readied himself to turn away when blood started to flow. "First, our Leo is a dispossessed Negro who wants acceptance from his Caucasian peers. Leo wants love. Not unusual, not unique, some might call it cute. But, in Leo's case, as a part of our little family, an occasional inconvenience." John relaxed as she released Leo's shoulder and smoothed out the talon dents in his shirt. "Second, Leo is a disillusioned Negro who feels that he has been cheated of his birthright, whatever that may be." Miss von Helsing strolled around Membozig's chair and went to the table where Corporal Comstock lay, his dry eyes contemplating, John hoped, the wonders of paradise. "Third, Leo is a genius with a particular knack for warfare. As I believe I mentioned before Leo came to us, he has a special gift for tactics at the expense of strategy. However, we all hoped that Leo would mature in his talents"—she shrugged—"as so many before have outgrown the impulsiveness of youth." Miss von Helsing dragged a stiletto fingernail up the corpse from the inner thigh to the first wound, tracing and retracing its outlines. "Normally, Leo exercised his group roles one at a time. But last night he became a committee of three, all asserting their distinct influence: the lover got pissed off because he'd been jilted . . . "

"I said that! Didn't I say that?" Tamino grabbed Hand and pointed at Miss von Helsing.

"Yes, you did, Dan. But there's more. The disillusioned Negro screamed for revenge against an unjust social order.

The military tactician took over and brought Leo to this—"
Miss von Helsing smacked Corporal Comstock on the
stomach with the back of her hand.

"Not good enough." Hand, dark and furious, shouted
down at her. "Not by a long shot. You don't explain
anything, you just complicate the motive. Why did he
murder all those other people? Your theory doesn't say
anything about that, does it?"

"Phil." Miss von Helsing used every bit of her diaphragm,
the overtones ominous. "Shut up. The other murders are
perfectly consistent with the over-all pattern. One Membozig screams for revenge against everyone who's ever
cheated him of what he expects from life. The second
Membozig says, 'I'm going to kill all those bastards who
won't love me.' That narrows it down to white men right
there. The third Membozig, the genius, provides the plan."
Miss von Helsing marched behind Membozig's chair and
crossed her arms over his chest, as if to protect him. "I
understand Leo. You don't."

Hand waved her arguments away with a swift gesture.
"Then why didn't he kill me and Mr. Tamino and Father
Doffenbaron and Dr. Ivanson? We're white. We won't go to
bed with him either."

Miss von Helsing planted a kiss, so formal as to be
liturgical, on the top of Leo's head. "That's because we
have a *fourth* Leo and that Leo wouldn't hurt anyone
who's working for the same great cause that Leo's working
for. Isn't that right, Leo?"

John couldn't tell whether Membozig's nod was his own
or whether Miss von Helsing's breathing pushed his head
back and forth, but rage, sudden and uncalculated, boiled
in John's heart. She actually had the gall to use Membozig's

loyalty to the Red Chinese government against him when she, herself, wasn't a party to the same loyalty. John's anger mingled with disgust when he thought that Miss von Helsing had dared to suggest that he, a priest, had no commitments. What about her? John wished he could do something mean to Miss von Helsing.

"Alicia, could you give me a clue where all this is going? You lost me about two Membozigs ago." Tamino had slumped so deeply in his chair that he seemed to be lying in it. "Maybe I'm a dummy, but I don't give a damn *why* Leo did it, I want to know *how* he did it."

John weighed his options. If he took Hand's side in the quarrel, maybe he could precipitate a fight over whether Miss von Helsing was really all that necessary to the Center. Mr. Tamino could always find another ethnopsychologist, or something not much different. But where could they find another John? If John went, so did the computer. Clever, wily John. He had learned something these past few months and he congratulated himself for it. He had learned how to scheme.

Miss von Helsing patted her curls. "Leo isn't going to tell you what you want to know, Dan. I can see that. All I was doing was explaining the situation as it stands preparatory to making a suggestion."

Even if they didn't get rid of Miss von Helsing, Hand would be pleased that John had joined forces with him. He would assign John some special guards, around-the-clock protection so that John could sleep. He pondered and watched as Hand slouched to the rear of the bandbox.

"Let's hear the suggestion, Alicia. I'm listening." Tamino didn't look as if he were listening. John suspected him of trying to take a nap.

"Since Leo is presently in no emotional state to be cooperative"—Miss von Helsing reconnoitered her notes—"and since we have every reason to believe that he will continue in these infatuations to the detriment of our work, I urge that we insure ourselves against a recurrence of last night's misfortune. Someplace here I've got a few alternative procedures I jotted down while we were interviewing that frump you dragged out of the tank."

"If he won't talk, punish him." Tamino did not sleep. "Punish him until he cooperates."

Miss von Helsing speared a page with her fingertip. "Here we are. Since Leo's sex drives are the fuse which caused the emotional blow-up, I think some therapeutic castration might be in order. Or, if you're squeamish about that, there's nothing like a prefrontal lobotomy for pulling these characters into line."

John didn't know whether Leo had killed anyone; he didn't really care, since Leo never had evidenced any particular interest in killing John, but he rebelled mightily at the prospect of Miss von Helsing exerting that much influence over any decision which affected another human being. What she could do to Membozig, she might try to do to John. He gripped his microphone and shouted: "No. I won't hear of it, not without another opinion. Mr. Tamino, I urge you, I beg you to bring my psychiatrist Dr. Klebo here for consultation. He's very competent." John's courage crumbled and dissolved in the ocean of wide, disbelieving eyes spread beneath him. He looked desperately at Hand, hunting for reassurance, and saw nothing but a shadowed face.

"I have had my fill of you." Miss von Helsing gaped up at the glass cage and John scooted his chair back against the console. "My patience is at an end."

222

John did not answer. He couldn't answer. The surge of sly self-confidence had exhausted its fuel and he had no reserve tanks. Regret and fear filled John's throat, strangling the unspoken rush of apologies, retractions, and pleas of momentary insanity.

"Come on, Alicia. Let's keep personalities out of this. We're having a reasoned discussion among colleagues." Tamino scratched his chin and squinted at John. "You may be right, John. Klebo's a nut but he's also a physician. No matter what we decide to do with Leo, I don't want anybody touching him but a professional. I want him punished, not butchered."

A demon, previously dormant, now awake and well in charge, seemed to take control of Miss von Helsing. Before John's bewildered eyes, she burst into tears and threw herself across the room toward Membozig. Clutching at his knees, she kneeled before him, forcing him to look into her gushing face. "Leo. Leo, my darling. You know that I don't care whether you shot Corporal Comstock, don't you, dear one?"

Tamino whispered to Hand and they both looked over at John. John thought he saw Hand smile before he disappeared totally into the shadows at the rear of the bandbox.

Membozig tipped his head and let the tears run in diagonal silver streaks down his cheeks, as if he couldn't see who was talking to him. "What?"

"Leo, we're grown men and women." Miss von Helsing caressed away the moisture on his face. "We have responsibilities to one another. You know as well as I do that it doesn't really make one bit of difference *who* shot Corporal Comstock; he was in that tank because you drove him to be there. Do you see that, my sweetness? Your darling full-time hard-on drove him there, in front of whatever killed him. You never let him forget how much he needed to have another body next to his, did you? You forced him to think of nothing but love so he went out to find some. It's all the same as if you'd pulled the trigger, don't you see? Don't you understand?"

Membozig nodded and Miss von Helsing spread her arms wide to frame her victory.

"I did it to him," Membozig said. "I loved him so much."

"Huh?" Tamino said. "Alicia, what the hell are you up to?"

Miss von Helsing clapped her hands fast onto Membozig's ears. "Don't listen to them, my black angel. Don't let them steal our moment of honesty and truth from us."

Membozig sniffled. "I can't hear you."

"No matter how Comstock died, deep down we know that you're the guilty one, Leo." She had uncupped one ear, the one not cocked toward Tamino. She looked at him, a dry incongruity in the angle of her head. "He's dead, Leo. You drove a good man to his death. Who will be next?"

Membozig bit his upper lip and stuttered. "I wanna see that girl he was with. I wanna tell her I'm sorry."

Miss von Helsing wiped away a tear and threw a caterpillar of eyelash across the floor. "Too late, dearest. She's gone. Security. You did that, too, didn't you?"

"Good Christ, Alicia, *I* shot her." Tamino bounced out of his chair. "Nobody ever accused Leo of *that*. Hell, you saw me do it."

Membozig shook his head fiercely, spraying Miss von Helsing with a mist of tears and saliva. "No, I did it. I didn't shoot nobody with guns, but I made it happen. I did it. I killed 'em. I did it." His sobs ululated into a howl. "*I wish I was dead!*"

Miss von Helsing stood and stepped backward three steps, her lips parted in a tiny, hungry smile. "There. Now we're all agreed. Leo wants to be punished because he knows that, somehow, he's guilty. You want to punish him, Dan, because he won't tell you something you want to know. I only want to simulate a punishment with some surgery to prevent our being bothered with any more of his nauseating love affairs." She reached out and stroked Membozig's bound arm. Not that I think *you're* nauseating, dearest."

"Permit me to interject my fulsome agreement." Professor Keruk peered up at Tamino. "Myself, I do not believe in punishments. But I am so much in sympathy with the idea of precautions against other such incidents. If the problem is genital in origin, the solution would seem to be obvious."

"Just make him talk," Tamino said. "I don't care how you do it. Alicia, toss me a cigarette, would you? My nerves are shot."

Dr. Ivanson wiped his hands on the front of his smock, glanced enigmatically up at John, then moved out from the wall. "Not torture, under any circumstances. And understand that I do not speak out of scruple but out of an instinct for what is best in this situation and in the long run for our work. Torture, at this juncture, could gravely inhibit Leo's future value to this community. If, however, through psychotherapy or other *humane* means we could offer Leo a stability at least comparable to our own, then I believe we may have done him a great service which, naturally, will be to the profit of the Fellowship as a whole. As for last night's incident, I most earnestly suggest that we consider that a misfortune not to be corrected, look to the days to come, and forget the unpleasantness of the past."

"Psychotherapy?" Miss von Helsing grabbed Membozig's head and clutched it to her bosom. "Leo, do you want them to send you away from us, send you to a stranger? Leo, let *us* punish you, let your friends make you clean again. For you, it's the knife or nothing, beloved. Let it be *my* knife!"

"A lovely sentiment and worthy of a woman of your charms, Madam." Dr. Klebo, striding ahead of ·Hand, marched across the amphitheater. He waved to Tamino, then, radiating happy surprise, stopped dead and opened his embrace toward John. Miss von Helsing, as rattled as an apprentice vampire encountering her first crucifix, backed away a foot for every yard that Dr. Klebo advanced. His mind relieved, John sank back into his chair, confident that the man bouncing into the room like a politician at a prebribed rally would do as well for Membozig as he had done, once upon a time, for John.

"He's mine," Miss von Helsing choked. "I don't need you here."

"And a lucky girl you are, too. He's a strapping specimen if ever I've seen one." Dr. Klebo tucked a finger under Membozig's chin and lifted his face. "Dark but comely, as they say."

Dr. Klebo, rounder and rosier than John remembered him, prowled around Membozig, tut-tutting the guards away, his face a sparkle of winks, a glitter of grins. One hand took Leo's pulse while another finger probed his ear. He ah'ed and oh'ed over secret discoveries.

"Well," Dr. Klebo said at last, "I can't see a thing wrong with our young man outside of the fact that he cries too much. Those manacles probably aren't doing much for his circulation either." He saluted Miss von Helsing. "However, all things taken into consideration, I'd call him an excellent choice with which to share the winter of one's life, Madam.

In most cases I like to run a few tests, but this lad looks sound as a dollar to me."

Miss von Helsing, who had managed to interpose a computer terminal between herself and Dr. Klebo, spluttered her inarticulate indignation up toward the bandbox. Tamino nodded, wearily, and turned toward Dr. Klebo.

"Doctor, our problem has nothing to do with the boy's health. We don't like the fact that he refuses to cooperate with us. He killed the fellow on the table and won't tell us how."

Dr. Klebo had not noticed Corporal Comstock. He trotted to the table, gave the corpse a few pokes, prods, and pinches, then wiped his hands on Miss Feuer. "No problem, sir. He's been shot. These holes, you see, are where the bullets went in. Or, of course, he could have used a small stick but that isn't very efficient. No, he shot him."

Tamino paled and slowly walked back to his chair.

"This will get us nowhere," Miss von Helsing said, still maintaining a wary distance between herself and Dr. Klebo. She puffed on a cigarette, then addressed the room at large. To his surprise, her sweeping, theatrical glances even included John. "The question now is how we're going to deal with Leo to make sure he doesn't foul us up again. He needs to be punished, that's all, but effectively punished. If you insist on letting this meat mechanic take care of it, I won't argue so long as he does his job and goes back where he came from." She disappeared in a geyser of tobacco smoke.

"Such a perceptive analysis from such a gracious lady. I'm astounded. However," and Dr. Klebo strode to center stage, "I need a few guidelines. What, exactly, am I supposed to chop off, carve out, tack on, or whatever?" He directed a winning smile toward Miss Feuer, who returned it. "Can't just start hacking, can we?"

Dr. Ivanson wiped perspiration off his forehead and shifted from one foot to another. "These are appalling medical ethics, I must say."

"My dear sir," beamed Klebo, unfazed, "as a physician I am in the service of mankind. I offer my skills to society. This society is smaller than some, larger than others, but it has retained me to do something to the boy tied to the chair. Some mention was made of a knife as I came in here; I deduced that surgery has been prescribed. So be it. I'm all yours."

"Castrate him." Miss von Helsing pawed through the nicotine screen. "That's what *I* say."

"Gracious, Madam!" Dr. Klebo looked stern. "Have a care for those cold nights ahead."

"Christ." Miss von Helsing glowered at Hand. "You should have briefed him before you brought him over. Listen, Doctor, Leo's queer. Because of his faggery, he's murdered Lord only knows how many people and we don't want him to do it again."

Dr. Klebo perked up and considered Membozig with renewed interest. "I should have guessed. He's right out of the textbook, no footnotes. An underdeveloped masculinity as the result of insufficient father-figure identification; probably the result of living in a matriarchical environment dominated by mobs of moms and aunties on welfare. Probably never saw the dad who visited at night on foggy weekends."

Miss von Helsing choked on her cigarette and threw it away. "You are *wrong*. His sexual drives are not the result of psychosis but ethnopsychological influences. Leo"—she put a proprietory foot forward but snapped it back—"is the prototypical child of the slum where overcrowding inevitably produces massive waves of inversion, suicide, and madness. You *must* know of Professor Slepyan's work with mice. Every time the cage population reached a certain level of overcrowding, the males became sterile and schizophrenic and the females devoured their own young. Leo is representative of the third generation of a Class Four Negro environment."

Dr. Klebo chuckled and winked at Dr. Ivanson, who seemed offended. "Oh, yes, *mice*. No doubt the late Mr. Disney could have had us roistering in the aisles over the zany antics of impotent Mickey and baby-munching Minnie, but without popcorn, dear lady, the concept loses much of its appeal." He dismissed Miss von Helsing's theories with a flick of the wrist. John could have cheered. "Enough of such conceits, charming as they—and *you*—are. I definitely do not believe emasculation to be the answer. We would leave this strapping youth churning with hopeless passions, cruel vendettas, and uremia. No, we must be courageous and resist these tempting digressions from the true source of our patient's trouble—his brain."

"Psychotherapy," said Dr. Ivanson.

"Lobotomy," shouted Miss von Helsing.

Dr. Klebo paced out a figure eight, fondling a flap of skin under his jaw. "Psychotherapy might be an answer, given nine or ten years. Not that I wouldn't be willing, mind you. Things have come to something of a standstill in my present work, what with one thing or another, so I definitely will have the time."

"Forget psychotherapy. Forget lobotomies. I want to know how he shot all those people." Tamino had turned the color of an infected carbuncle. "That's what I want."

"What we want and what we can have are often very different things," Dr. Klebo said, a sweet patience in his voice. "We must relieve this boy's unpleasant tensions before we can start thinking of ourselves." He ignored Miss von Helsing's groan as he moved past her to examine Membozig's head. "If the patient doesn't want to tell you his secret, there must be," and Dr. Klebo pressed his fingers into Membozig's tight curls, "a deep psychotic need being fulfilled. Oh, John, do I have you to thank for bringing an old man back from the valley of the shadow?"

John exchanged emotion-drenched smiles with Dr. Klebo. Old friendships were the best friendships and John felt warmed that he had been able to do so much good for so many by suggesting that Dr. Klebo be brought from Beulahland.

Dr. Klebo placed his index finger straight down on the top of Membozig's skull. "Well, let's see if we still have the magic touch," he mused. "*Zut, zut, zut,* right between the two hemispheres. Hum de hum."

Miss von Helsing, lighting a cigarette, almost set fire to her nose trying to see what Dr. Klebo was doing.

"A lobotomy," she guessed. "You've agreed to a lobotomy!"

Dr. Klebo lifted his eyes to regard her with wonder. "Madam, you may be a thesaurus of misinformation about psychosis but I could never fault your sense of fun. And while I would be the first to agree that performing a lobotomy certainly would be a zesty job, the recovery period can be quite extended. Am I right in assuming, sir, that you are in something of a rush? You seem rather agitated."

Tamino did not answer. He seemed to be pouting.

"Leo is our military expert," John said, grateful that he could participate in the conversation without starting a fight. "He has a great deal of work to do for us."

"Excellent." Dr. Klebo traced invisible lines on Membozig's head with his finger. "No, definitely not a lobotomy. Wouldn't want your military expert to come out from under the anesthetic acting like a cranky vegetable. Oh, the trouble I've had with my lobotomies, refusing to dress, or eat, or evacuate in private." He stuck out his tongue, as if he believed that airing it would remove a permanent bad taste. "No, I have something else in mind which"—he bowed to Miss von Helsing—"will be quite to your taste, I'm sure."

"We'll see."

"Of course we will, my dear, of course we will." Dr. Klebo tapped Membozig's skull. "First we take a bore, a drill, what have you, and go through the bone about, oh, why not here? Then we insert a long, hollow steel needle into the cerebrum, careful as we go through the corpus callosum, until we hit the midbrain. Now, that's pay dirt, my friends. That's the *old* brain which harbors the operational centers which keep us alive. Right down there." Dr. Klebo jabbed at the base of Membozig's skull, a gesture that left John eerily chilled. He had every confidence that Dr. Klebo would do the right thing but why did he have to keep reminding himself of it?

"Sadly," Dr. Klebo went on, "our maps of the area aren't too accurate. So, we'll probe around a bit, sending a low-voltage electric charge down the needle. If he stops breathing, we move on. If he waves his arms, we just dig a little deeper." Dr. Klebo did an imitation of inserting a

231

corkscrew into a bottle and Dr. Ivanson covered his eyes with a shaking hand. "If he screams, we say, 'too bad, just the primitive fear neurons,' and give our probe another tap. Oh, disappointment will pile upon disappointment, I'm afraid, until we reach the end of our journey and discover the hidden cavern where his dragon sex urge hides."

Dr. Ivanson stumbled and turned his face to the wall. Hand rushed to his side and helped him from the amphitheater.

"How will we know when we've found it?" Miss von Helsing demanded.

Dr. Klebo pursed his lips and brushed lint off the sleeve of his jacket. "Simple if indelicate, Madam." He paused, gave his sleeve one last whisk, and smiled a curiously gentle smile which almost demolished John's growing apprehensions. "When we find what we're looking for, he will have an erection and quite possibly an orgasm. One may merely speculate what sodomite orgies he will fancy himself enjoying before we take the last and final step."

Professor Keruk licked his lips. "If you please, Doctor. *The last step.*"

John watched Dr. Klebo adjust himself for the denouement, slipping thumbs into weskit pockets, puffing out his chest, clearing his throat over and over. Suspense overwhelmed John. No, not suspense. Anxiety. John was inexplicably frightened.

"At that instant when we will have given this boy the most exotic sexual thrill he, or anyone else, has ever known, we will inject a minute amount of liquid nitrogen through the needle and freeze the appropriate brain cells into oblivion. They will die and so will all question of our young friend's desiring any further sexual entanglements for the rest of his days." Dr. Klebo tiptoed around the chair and gave Membozig an earnest, fatherly smile. "Now, won't that be nice?"

Membozig didn't appear to have heard a word.

Dr. Klebo prodded him. "I said, *won't that be nice?*"

"Nothin's ever gonna be nice for me again." Leo's chin trembled and he overflowed with great, whooping sobs.

Miss von Helsing tracked a smoke ring with her eyes as it floated up toward the bandbox. "Well, Dan? What do you think?"

Tamino was asleep.

"Most fascinating, indeed." Professor Keruk showed his earth-colored molars. "I would be honored if you would make use of my laboratory facilities."

Miss von Helsing gathered up her possessions, including the discarded eyelash, and walked away. "Well, what are we waiting for?" she asked as she passed Dr. Klebo.

"Dr. Klebo, *wait!*" John clutched the stem of his microphone and shouted.

Dr. Klebo waved over his shoulder and scuttled after Miss von Helsing and Professor Keruk. The guards descended upon Membozig, untied him, and led him out.

"*Wait!*" John jumped from his chair and rapped on the glass. "*Please wait.*"

Only Miss Feuer seemed to hear him. Swinging her body back and forth, laughing with all her heart and soul, she watched John's every move, as happy as a child at the circus.

The last three days had been too full of excitement for John to waste time worrying about Membozig. He had, in fact, not thought of the poor man at all until reminded by Dr. Klebo's departure from the computer chamber. John felt half guilty that he hadn't dropped in on Dr. Klebo since his resurrection from Beulahland, but John had been busier than at any other time in his life. Not that he resented the demands on his time; John was delighted. His discomfort arose from the tremendous responsibility which circumstances had thrust upon him, forcing him to separate and compartmentalize the inexplicable avalanche of data which the computer was drawing from its external sources. Were the student riots ethnopsychological material or were they political phenomena which should be put in reserve for Leo? And why did the occurrences seem to come in pairs? Did it have something to do with cycles of the moon? In which case, should Dr. Ivanson be consulted? What about the outbreak of trichinosis in Israel? Should he have that referred to Professor Keruk, as he had done with the other epidemic on Pitcairn Island, or should he notify Miss von Helsing to be alerted to changing Jewish dietary patterns? No one could be found to help him, so John programmed everything two or three times and trusted in those instincts which had never failed him.

Part of his discomfort, John was convinced, sprang from his bad eating habits. Since he and Miss von Helsing now shared Sarah, John's meal schedule had been no more regular than during the last month of Mamie's tenure. On the whole, however, Sarah had seemed peppier in the last day or so. John had a murky recollection of somebody humming spirituals as she scrubbed his back this morning. He had been distracted at the moment, however, because for the first time in months the console in John's bedroom had monitored a feeble message to the computer from the terminal in Miss Feuer's room. John couldn't decide whether this might mean that Miss Feuer was up and about or that someone else was playing with the equipment. In either case, John was troubled. The request had been unimportant enough, merely instructing the computer to relay to Miss Feuer's terminal the accumulation of data concerning recent murders, holocausts, wars, and so on. John didn't like the looks of that. If indeed Miss Feuer had been the person at the terminal, her illness would appear to have aggravated an already morbid turn of mind. Too bad. She had seemed so jolly the last time John had seen her.

For all his troubles, John appreciated Dr. Klebo's visit. The doctor had been impressed not only with John's computer but with John. "I can't get over it," Klebo had said. "Within the boundaries of your personality disintegration, John, you could be classified as *functioning.*" A Klebo hand had plopped on John's shoulder and squeezed out a Freudian benediction. "Goodness knows I'll miss those neuropsychopathic fugues of yours, but I can't help but be proud of you."

John had explained his own work with the *Summa*, confided in Dr. Klebo about the difficulties with the rest of the Fellowship, and chuckled with him over the discomfiture roiling convents throughout the world. "Naughty John," Dr. Klebo had snorted. "Try that any place else and we'd have to get you committed again. Amusing, of course."

Although John had neglected to inquire, Dr. Klebo spoke at some length about his months in Beulahland. John gathered that Dr. Klebo had exhausted either himself or his subjects and that, difficult as it was for him to make the break, the hour had come for a sharp change in Dr. Klebo's professional life. "Hemanalysis is a dead end, John," Dr. Klebo had said. "Blood will tell, but only so much."

Dr. Klebo had dropped a few mysterious inquiries about Miss von Helsing, which John answered at an emotional peak only slightly short of apoplexy, then offered apologies for not having "called" sooner and departed to "check on the patient."

No sooner had his guest left him than John remembered that Dr. Klebo could have audited Membozig's life functions through the main console. All things considered—the heap of unprogrammed data in particular—John decided that both he and Dr. Klebo would be happier with the physician at Membozig's bedside. John looked at the fluorescent blip of a regular heartbeat which dominated one of the television screens, then turned back to his console.

As he continued to disentangle the web of data, John found himself becoming increasingly restless, the victim of a well-concealed irritation boring away under the level of his awareness. At first, he decided that he was more upset about Membozig than his newly authenticated sanity permitted him to admit. He tested himself with a consciously willed concern for Membozig's welfare but felt not the slightest sympathetic vibration from the pesky dissatisfaction which gnawed at his soul. Did John still expect an attack from Miss von Helsing? Yes, but the shudder which that called out of him answered to a completely different name than the camouflaged misery playing hide-and-seek inside him. Perhaps John's breakfast had not agreed with him. He tried a belch, savored it, and concluded that breakfast had been not only nourishing but delicious. John leaned back in his chair and watched the bars on the console glimmer, rise, and depress, thinking of the pretty colors as he tried to clear his brain of preconception, to ready the stage for the surprise appearance of the next performer in that ongoing vaudeville troupe which comprised his thinking process.

Free association had always been easy for John and he prided himself on the outlandish hurdles and leaps he could take from one word to another like little Eliza, Olympic champ, sprinting over the ice floes. Eventually, however, he tended to drift until he found an interesting eddy and there he sank and drowned. John just clicked off, like a computer. Maybe that was his trouble; John was a delicate machine subject to the whim of a perverse systems analyst. Perhaps that was the basic human flaw, that this all-too-perfect mechanism had been scrambled and short-circuited by Satanic programmers.

What a happy picture of Eden that brought to John's

mind: two well-formed, reasonably efficient cybernetic entities, functioning exactly as their Maker had intended until they were spoiled by the fumble-fingered malice of a second-rate mechanic. Why, it was twentieth-century Milton! Not only did the metaphor possess a poetic merit of which John had never believed himself capable, it was a deadly accurate assessment of his own life, such of it as John remembered. Gloomily, he realized that he remembered very little. Surely, that fact should have been apparent to him before; he felt unaccountably saddened that it should become important now. He did a quick search for his past and wondered which pocket of his brain had worn through and let the whole thing dribble out. John cheered himself with the affirmation that the best of him was what he knew now; the fact that it was *all* of him was secondary. An inventory of his qualities certainly did nothing to discredit him: he was a priest, he functioned, he ran the computers, he knew more about the *Summa* . . .

John sat upright and stiffened, clutching the arms of his chair. He knew with sun-scorched clarity what had been nagging him: *The computer had not been receiving any requests for Thomistic materials from the outside.* The nuns had capitulated, abandoned the fight; John had *won!*

How long had John been free? He couldn't remember the exact day when the Microwave Relay had brought the last pusillanimous inquiry after a Thomistic tidbit, but it had been a long time, probably at least a week.

John pushed himself out of his chair and ran to the Datafax. He ripped through stacks of paper, unreeled teletype rolls, but search as he might he found not a single reference to the *Summa*. John threw down a last wad of emergency requests from Dartmouth for all published

238

works on the treatment of curare poisoning and stared at the wall, gathering his thoughts.

Should he wait to see what happened or should he press his advantage? No doubt about it, he couldn't slacken up now when the battle was his. He had a war to be won. John knew, mathematical probabilities aside for the nonce, that it was perfectly possible for the computer to analyze the entire Thomistic corpus, then to go back and, with a jiggle or two in the original programming, to refute everything it had written previously, ad infinitum. John smiled and walked back to the console and sat down. His heart was full and overflowing. On impulse, he gave his chair a joyous spin and whirled around under Dr. Ivanson's distressed gaze.

John slammed his feet onto the floor and dragged himself to a halt. "I'm sorry, Doctor, I didn't hear you come in."

Dr. Ivanson stroked his temples and sighed with the effort. "Please, Father, I had no intention of disturbing you. To be perfectly frank, I am here only because of whim. Perhaps, I . . . " Dr. Ivanson paused, amending his thoughts, then gave John a hard look, redolent with import which John could not interpret. "I am in the toils of a dilemma and I need wise counsel."

"Of course."

Dr. Ivanson seemed to relax momentarily, but tightened up again. "First, however, an apology. Although it might be best if we never alluded to the occasion again, I do feel that I should express my personal regrets for the unhappy events in Mr. Tamino's sitting room some days back. While I scarcely feel that my position was unjustified, I have come to realize that you, in your own way, were no less justified in yours." The apology had taken its toll on Dr. Ivanson's

239

self-possession, the skin on his face was taut as a membrane. "As you will see, this speech serves as a prologue for dialogue."

John nodded. "Your apologies are gratefully received. Everything worked out happily for all of us so I see no point in holding a grudge."

"You are gracious."

They stared at each other until John tired of watching the ebb and flow of Dr. Ivanson's eyelids and turned away to break the connection. Dr. Ivanson whistled air up through his nostrils in long, lung-straining breaths, but never expelled any words. Puzzled if not uneasy, John wondered if he were expected to grab hold of the conversation and get it moving.

"You spoke of a dilemma, Dr. Ivanson?"

"I did," Dr. Ivanson said. "But, more to the point, I came to speak to you about a matter which should come under the aegis of one of your specializations."

John did not want to play guessing games. He feinted with a noncommittal "Hm."

"A scriptural text."

Dr. Ivanson was at least sufficiently sporting to give hints.

"New or Old Testament?"

Dr. Ivanson jerked. "New Testament, as a matter of fact. The twenty-first chapter of St. Luke's Gospel." The astronomer closed his eyes and let his head dangle back as he recited. " 'And there will be signs in sun and moon and stars and upon earth distress of nations in perplexity at the roaring of the sea and the waves. . . . ' " Dr. Ivanson stopped and opened his eyes. "I would like your comments."

"Exegetical or hermeneutic?"

240

"Your choice. Just an informed opinion."

"I have no opinions." John savored Dr. Ivanson's visible dismay. "But St. Thomas dealt with scripture on occasion. Let's see if he got around to this particular text." John swiveled his chair toward the console and pressed a chord or two, then typed out a recall command for the memory banks. Had John been the sort of man to enjoy revenge, this moment would have been delightful. But John had no grudges, and he reminded himself that the happiness he felt must be joy that he could be helpful to another human being in need. "Do you want the material in English?"

"Or Swedish." Dr. Ivanson brushed against John's shoulder as he leaned over him to watch the console.

"The option is Latin."

"English."

The typewriter crackled and chattered across the carriage.

REF SUMMA THEOLOGICA, QUAESTIO 73. . . .

The typewriter stopped and the astronomer straightened up and backed away from John's chair, his mouth shaping silent words. John ripped the quotation from the carriage and offered it.

"Is that helpful?"

Dr. Ivanson looked at John as if he had forgotten his name, then shook his head. "Not very, I'm afraid. The Last Judgment is not a premise which I find particularly to my taste. However, I acknowledge that to be personal prejudice."

"St. Thomas never questioned his premises." John smiled. "Conclusions drawn from them would have the

241

force of absolutes, naturally. I am satisfied that St. Thomas was satisfied. I can't imagine expecting *more.*"

"I see." Dr. Ivanson rediscovered the piece of paper in John's hand. Slowly, as if he were operating on an independent time scale, he reached out and took it. "As a scientist and a rational man, I am forced to say that this is poppycock. But, all things considered—and I have much to consider, Father, believe me—I am greatly attracted to any sort of unrelenting declaration which is convinced of its own unambiguous hold on absolute truth." Dr. Ivanson studied the page, sheet-lightning ripples of pain or annoyance shooting down his face. After an obituary pause in which his gaze rested on what must have been nothing more compelling than a period, Dr. Ivanson crumpled the paper in his hand and let the ball drop to the floor. He looked at John. "Doesn't this bother you, Father? Granting that the premises could be valid, that all other evidence is applicable, doesn't this sort of thing even slightly jar your grip on the fragment of significance you have wrenched out of life for yourself? No, I see that it does not." He hid himself behind hooded eyes for an instant, then let his face relax into a wide smile. He reminded John of a recently engorged lizard.

"I know nothing about any other 'evidence.' You quoted a passage of scripture and asked for a textual analysis, which I gave you." John had a fleeting concern for what digested behind that smile. "As an astronomer, I should imagine that you have become quite accustomed to 'signs in the sun and moon and stars' and not let St. Thomas's discussion of the Eschaton depress you."

"Do I look depressed?" Dr. Ivanson had vanished underneath a face so rigid that he scarcely moved his lips to speak. "Not so depressed as astonished by my own limitations, I fear." Even as he spoke, Dr. Ivanson had frozen solid where he stood, his breathing imperceptible, his white-knuckled hands knotted at his sides. If he were not depressed, then John could believe that Dr. Ivanson had turned to stone before his eyes.

"An unusual event need not be one of the *particular* events, Doctor."

"Do I detect a mood of professional pastoral calm insinuating itself in those meaningless words, Father? Please, no outrage, but I'm afraid that you do not understand my predicament. Not since I was thirty-six years old and laboring at Jodrell Bank have I witnessed anything at all through my telescope which I could call unusual; by that I mean anything which did not fall happily into a slot prepared by conventional theory or which quickly did not prove capable of burrowing its own niche in a Newtonian or Einsteinian framework. Bluntly, I longed for the day when such an event might occur, affording me the long-deserved opportunity of untangling the puzzle and winning all the prizes from astounded and envious colleagues. I already have one small, but endearing, comet which bears my name, I have christened a gas nebula after my sister, and been honored with a Crater Ivanson on the dark side of the moon by grateful Russian former students. But all this is as nothing compared to the paradoxicality now regnant in the heavens which I cannot interpret save as arbitrary and nonsensical. At first, I brooded that my isolation here with the Fellowship had denied me the fruitful intellectual stimulation to be reaped from amiable debate with my peers, but from the reports which we receive through your computer I learned that all over the world my colleagues are as baffled as I. Refreshed by the knowledge that I was not alone in my confusion, I pressed on, hoping to be the one to make the breakthrough. But before I could assume that I had sufficient data on a single phenomenon to draw even the most primitive hypothesis, another burst into hideous reality, then another, the universe writhing and contorting itself in defiance of the laws of reason and, worse, esthetics."

John frowned. "Esthetics?"

"Why not? I have always felt—perhaps as the result of an excessively stringent Lutheran upbringing—that the only discernible attribute of a putative Deity was His love of order. Where there is chaos and disruption in nature, destruction swiftly and decisively follows. Now, only the slightest hint of unity is maintained, all the rules have been discarded and new nonlaws make their appearance once, twice, then vanish, and a fresh anarchy rules Olympus."

"I understand your question about the text, Doctor. The 'signs' are without interpretation from an empirical point of view. So you come to me—and St. Thomas."

"Yes, exactly. The primary function of any self-respecting theology, after all, is to sew together all the loose seams in the observable universe. However, St. Thomas has begged the question. Or, more disastrously, he has ended the discussion by ending the world."

John bent from his chair and retrieved the wadded ball of paper from between Dr. Ivanson's mirror-bright oxblood toes. He smoothed out the folds and stretched the sheet back and forth across his knee. "I mean no disloyalty to my mentor, Doctor, but how many times before have celestial phenomena been greeted as evil portents by the hysterical?"

Dr. Ivanson melted enough to wince. "Even in a state of madness while simultaneously deaf and blind no one could call *me* a hysteric, Father. Halley's Comet might send a just proportion of the world's lunatics over the edge of a handy precipice, a near miss by a visiting asteroid might stimulate a large segment of the socially dispossessed to propound an imminent doomsday, but until I see the *sense* of it, not even the spectacle of the sun dancing gavottes for Spanish kiddies will extract more from me than a pair of dark glasses out of my breast pocket. What I find troubling—but not *depressing*, mind you—is the conviction that in so much disorder a kind of order must be implicit. Your religion, or rather the good Aquinas, offers a solution, but only by stringing together an assortment of loose ends with some distastefully melodramatic events which are quite beyond my experience."

Doctor Ivanson shifted his weight from one foot to the other. "Nonetheless, I shall allocate a certain amount of time and gray matter to think about this talk with you, Father. I would be hypocritical if I told you that I leave you unaffected by it. Now"—he flapped his arms, testing frail wings for a long flight—"I must be off to my work."

John watched Dr. Ivanson leave the chamber, then let his chair drift slowly around in a full circle, his mind backtracking at top speed to whatever he had been thinking about before the interruption. He glanced up at the Datafax, perturbed by the steady flow of material spilling out of the slot. He would have to wait until the machinery cleared before he could proceed with his scheme to eviscerate the entire body of the *Summa*.

A serpent of numbers wriggled across one of the television screens, snapping John back into the present. The input had increased, heaven only knew from where. John set up the console for an audit and stared through the window at the cabinetry. He marveled at the sight: even with the constant and overwhelming load of new data to be absorbed, the barest proportion of the hardware was in use. To be sure, John saw more lights gleaming, more tape spools whirling than he had noticed before, but the greater proportion of the steel cabinets hunched, unilluminated and still, their transistors sleeping quietly and undisturbed by the electronic storms raging through the circuits of their fellows.

He stiffened in his chair. Far off, moving closer, a figure shinnied, crawled, and hopped through the cables. Reflexes moving faster than thoughts, John slapped his hand around the microphone, flipped the switch and yelled.

"Mr. Hand! This is John Doffenbaron. You are needed in the computer chamber at once!"

246

"You better have your eyes checked, Father. No one's out there." Hand leaned his forehead against the window and stared down the ranks of steel cabinets. John squinted and tapped on the glass with his fingernail.

"I saw her out there." John was trying very hard not to scream. "She was in a long blonde wig and a short dress. Crawling on her stomach. Coming in this direction. She was carrying a can of pork and beans."

Hand patted John on the back and walked away from the window. "You're overwrought. You know she couldn't be out there. Nobody could be out there, damn it. They couldn't breathe."

John strained his eyes until he thought they would spin from their sockets. If only he could find her again, point her out to Hand. Then they'd stop her, once and for all. "She was right back there by that orange—no, it's more yellow—cable."

"Crawling on her stomach. With a can of pork and beans."

John slapped the palm of his hand against the glass. "I am not being funny. Yes, she was on her stomach. Then she got up and danced around on one foot until she tripped over some wiring. I think she skinned her knee because she sat right down and held it. Rocking back and forth with her mouth open."

"Father," Hand said, his voice as slick as margarine, "if you're willing to forget about it, I'm willing to forget about it. Miss von Helsing has better things to do with her time than creep around on her belly in a gas chamber. With or without a blonde wig yet."

John gritted his teeth. "I don't *want* to forget about it. I want somebody to tell her to keep away from my computer. I want somebody to tell her to keep away from *me*." A mother lode of irritation sparkled through his darkness and John, fighting to keep the loops out of his vocal cords, turned on Hand. "Tell me something, will you? Why are you so defensive of that woman all of a sudden? Where does she fit into your neat do-gooding little world? What's her big fat contribution to the betterment of man that allows her to sneak around inside my computer? Tell me *that?*"

Hand refused to volley. "What if I told you that Miss von Helsing couldn't have been lurking down in that cavern? Would you believe me?"

"I don't believe that story about inert gases."

Hand made a silly face. "All right; you're wrong, but skip the gases. What if I said that she hasn't left Membozig's bedside since the operation?"

John fingered the bristles on his chin and thought.

248

"Have you been with her every second? Can you personally attest to her whereabouts during the last hour?"

"No, not personally, but the guards . . . "

John twisted about, his movement silencing Hand. He scanned down the hardware, through the wires. More than half the cabinetry sparkled and winked back and forth through the passageway. "I thought so." Instant despair had dropped John's voice an octave. "Well, I saw her, wearing beads and sandals, a wig, and some sort of Naugahyde or linoleum dress."

"Oh, get off it, Father. Linoleum dress! Why would a woman her age want to get herself up like that?"

"She's an actress, an opera singer. Actresses wear costumes." Why couldn't Hand grasp the simplicity of John's reasoning? If Miss von Helsing didn't kill him she would have succeeded at least in demolishing John's credibility with everybody else. "I thought you were the one person in the Center who would believe me, *help* me." Two more computers glowed with activity. Automatically, John glanced over his shoulder and watched the keyboards on the console pulse and hum as they accommodated themselves to the rising tide of input data. He didn't doubt that the hardware had ample storage capacity to handle anything that might be fed into it, but he would have been happier if he had been coordinating the material as it passed through, cataloging, cross-referencing, doing his job. The woman was not only a threat to John's life and sanity, but she was a damnable nuisance.

"All right, Father. Show me again where you saw her last." Hand moved beside him and looked with professional intensity through the window. John was not convinced.

"There. I told you. By the orangey-yellow cable."

Hand pressed his nose to the glass and narrowed his eyes. Suddenly, his jaw fell open and a gargling sound came out of his throat. "My God, Father! That must be 500 yards. How in the hell could you identify anybody at that distance and in that light? You have a pair of binoculars in here?"

Tempted to lie, John restrained himself. "No, of course I don't. But who else would be wearing wigs and dresses and crawling on their stomach?"

Laughter, tainted by frowning brows, bubbled from Hand's mouth. "Membozig, that's who. I'm sorry. I shouldn't make fun of him."

"Or of me. This is not fun, Mr. Hand." John watched Hand's face twist in and out through a glossary of smiles, none appropriate, and despised him. Hand had seemed to be a very serious fellow, the sort John would never trust with confidences but who should be expected to handle the dirty work in an emergency. Clearly, John had been wrong and he was disappointed.

As if he read John's mind, Hand tut-tutted. "Have I let you down, Father?"

The insight hurt more than the fact. "Ridiculous. Of course not." John walked from the window and, steadying himself on the console, sat down and rubbed the top of the typewriter. "I had relied a little too heavily on your competence as a security agent and," he aimed to kill, "as my friend."

Hand cocked his head and grinned. "I'm glad that you consider me a friend, at any rate. And speaking as head of security in this place, I can assure you that Miss von Helsing poses no danger to you for the time being. She has her own problems."

"Is that so?" A ton of gloom lifted from John's soul and hovered, ready to drop back down.

"And it's all your fault." Hand's grin broadened and dimpled. He looked around the chamber as if suspecting spies crouched in the shadows. "If the truth were known, she's scared to death of your friend Klebo."

"Klebo. Dr. Klebo?"

Hand bit his lip to restrain his laughter and John hugged himself with joy. "Klebo!"

They gave themselves over to roaring, snorting, tear-dribbling, nose-sniffling hysteria, one of them rising from the depths of mirth only to look at the other and plunge again. "Klebo," they both cried, an antiphon that pyramided their hilarity to ever greater peaks from which they dived in manic arcs of guffaws and giggles.

At last, his spleen sending irate warnings, John clasped both hands over his mouth, blinked the moisture back into place under his lashes and, with spasmodic but reversible relapses, brought himself under control. "I've never heard anything so funny. Who on earth could be afraid of a psychiatrist?"

"An ethnopsychologist," Hand said, and they rolled and rocked in a fresh fit of laughter.

"Now then"—Hand wiped his eyes—"do me a favor. Just forget about what you thought you saw in that cavern and I won't say anything to Mr. Tamino about your hallucinations."

"Hallucinations?" John sobered and glared at Hand. *"Hallucinations?"*

"Now, now." Hand assumed his characteristic slouch, a languid fist nestled on an oblique pelvis. "Even if I believed you, do you think that Mr. Tamino would listen to one

251

word? How could he? He wants peace and harmony in his Fellowship and if you start to mutter about Miss von Helsing crawling in and out of your computer, he will be very confused and upset. You and I know that she won't bother with you while Klebo is bugging her but Mr. Tamino doesn't know that. He'll think you've gone crackers for sure, Father. What with everything else going on, he doesn't need anything more to make him unhappy with you."

John tried to confect sympathy for Mr. Tamino and all his problems but didn't quite manage it. Nonetheless, Hand was right. John wouldn't be hurt by staying out of the limelight for a little while. Let Miss von Helsing fight her fights with Dr. Klebo. John would do his job and after the worst was over, and John had his own private hopes as to what the worst might be, he would register a formal complaint about unauthorized personnel inside the computer. He wouldn't be hysterical the next time either. John would explain, calmly and with suitable restraint, that he found unexplained phantoms distracting to his work and conducive to the possibility of error. No, he wouldn't mention error as a consequence. John would hint at damage to the computer, suggest sabotage.

"Do we have a deal?" Hand still smiled, but tension lines eroded the corners of his mouth.

"Mr. Hand, you drive a hard bargain but you have a deal."

"Attaboy." Hand slapped John's shoulder, then, as he moved toward the door, threw a last, worried look through the window.

John stared at the console in disbelief. He couldn't keep up with it, the data was coming in too fast; he was superfluous. No, that was not true. John would be needed later when this insane tempo slowed down; he would be needed to restructure the accumulation of stray facts and the tag ends of information into a controlled, regulated, programmable order. But, for the time being, he could only watch.

The bars on the keyboards tripped down, blipped light, then shot back up, faster than John could keep track of them. He had a mad notion that another hand had seized control of his computer and, equipped with reflexes beyond human comprehension, was tapping out orders, setting up programs of a complexity to boggle a normal human mind. *No, no.* John shook his head to disengage the clutch of such a senseless fantasy. No programs were being set up. For all the blinking of lights and whirling of tapes, no information came out of the computer. The typewriter sat dumb, sullen, the little ball leaden in the center of the carriage.

The stream of ciphers, letters, and figures raced at such a pace across the six television screens that they appeared to be no more than spluttering columns of light, briefly intelligible only if John wiggled his fingers in front of his face and created a temporary and inadequate stroboscopic effect. Not that he had the slightest interest in what the words said, what the figures meant, but he was fascinated and not a little frightened by the overwhelming mass of facts which so suddenly had begun to pour into his computer. Meaning and comprehension were not John's concern and he was sorely grateful. Had he been expected to make sense out of all this he would have run gibbering from the chamber and locked himself in his bathroom. But amounts of data, types of data, these things were important to John and he could see from the complex staccato chords being struck across the face of the console, all keyboards in simultaneous operation, that more information about *everything* was crackling into the memory banks every microsecond than he could assimilate in a lifetime.

The concept depressed him. The flashing colored bars splattering the walls and ceiling with a Gatling-gun fusillade of iridescence made his head hurt and he sensed himself on the edge of an emotion that he had anticipated for many long years with a special terror: John had begun to hate his computer.

No, he would not allow it to happen!

Carefully forming the words with silent, dry lips, he told himself that the computer was a cybernetic tool and this feeling of inadequacy was nonsense. He was, after all, in no way dependent upon the computer; the computer needed him to make whatever mountains of data it ingested into manipulatable chunks of knowledge.

John knew better. He did need the computer, desperately. Desperation had shaded and textured his existence without the computers and he could not bear the pain of being forced to return to that state again, alone, empty, purposeless. John knew he was weak, but the computers had given him strength, shared their strength with him. He did not dare permit a momentary pique to obliterate all meaning, past, present, and future, from his life. Through those transistors and wires, electrodes and lights, tapes and magnets, pulsed the very stuff which made John's life a possibility from now on. He ached to think of how horrible and debilitating those times had been when he had not known or had been deprived of a handy Honeywell, Rand,

I.B.M. or S.D.S. John had cast his lot with the machines; he knew their transistorized components better than he knew the juicy odds and ends of his own physiognomy. He struck his breast, wretched that he would have allowed even an embryonic treachery a place within him. No computer would be capable of doing the same thing to John! John was privileged, honored to have a full share in such a great partnership, man and machines, meeting for the first time as equals. Naturally, partners would have their own specializations, their own moments of dominance over each other. Any healthy relationship engendered cycles in which one or the other side was on the upswing while the partner declined in importance. How could John have been so arrogant, so full of pride as to have believed that he would always be the strong one? Now, when speed was of the *esse*, this computer, the child of his own heart, had shown itself fully capable of meeting the crisis. Later, when refinement, sophistication, a leisurely understanding of fallible human cognition was needed, John would be on hand to provide it, gently to assist the computer digest and absorb the vast meal.

A suffusion of paternal compassion spread through John's body as he considered his mutant infant in need of a good burp. His eyes stung with thick tears and transformed his world into a shimmering window of swirling darting colors, which rippled and spilled in ectoplasmic splendor. John's hands folded over his solar plexus and his Adam's apple quivered before the spinning wonder of the grief-refracted lights; he was a humbled sinner prostrate before an epiphany of heaven itself.

A peculiar clicking made him blink and the vision

evaporated. Several seconds passed before John was in sufficient self-possession to recognize the source of the noise. The typewriter had gone into operation.

AUTOMATIC PROGRAM 1-A-ZED NOW IN EFFECT. ALERT ALERT ALERT ALERT. AUTOMATIC PROGRAM 1-A-ZED NOW IN EFFECT. ALERT ALERT ALERT ALERT. . . .

A screaming siren howl yammered and yelped through the loudspeakers; the motorized door to the computer chamber slammed shut, and John's ears popped as the floor lifted him and the console upward. He grabbed the arms of the chair, his toes curling in their shoes, and watched the typewriter dictate orders.

SCREEN ONE: TAMINO. SCREEN TWO: MEMBOZIG. SCREEN THREE: KERUK. SCREEN FOUR: IVANSON. SCREEN FIVE: FEUER. SCREEN SIX: VON HELSING. ALERT ALERT. PROCESS GAME PRECEDENTS. RADIO TELESCOPE UNDER COMPUTER SCANNING ORDERS IN ACCORD. AUTOMATIC PROGRAM 1-A-ZED.

John checked quickly to see if the others had arrived in the Game Room, then cleared the typewriter and ordered the computer to hold information until otherwise instructed. The siren shut off and Tamino's voice roared through the loudspeakers, a tremulo of urgency and eagerness coating every word.

"All right, boys and girls, this is it, the big one. Let's hop to it, hup-hup-hup, get our thinking caps on and have at it."

SECURITY FORCE TO EVACUATE BEULAHLAND. TUNNELS WILL FLOOD IN TEN MINUTES. MINES ROCKETS ARTILLERY ACTIVATED. AWAIT GAME PRECEDENTS. ALERT ALERT.

An image fluttered, then stabilized on the second television screen at John's left. He recognized the picture as an exterior view of the bogus rockslide. At first, John thought it an ordinary still photograph, but he soon noticed tiny moving figures jogging over the desert toward the camera. The camera zoomed in and revealed the ancient inhabitants of Beulahland, all carrying rifles and wearing grenade belts, being dispersed in a ring in front of the camouflaged dome. A single tank lumbered into the picture, Frank, helmeted but natty, standing in the turret, shouting through a bullhorn and pointing as old men and women staggered and tottered this way and that across the sand. The screen flipped, scrambled, and dissolved into another view showing two others, their faces and shirts drenched with sweat, digging shallow trenches. As soon as they were finished, three old women dropped into the depressions, lying on their stomachs to achieve minimal concealment, and peered miserably down antique gun barrels.

BEULAHLAND EVACUATION EFFECTED.

The screen faded to a generalized ochre and John acknowledged the evacuation.

"All right. Who's missing the jollies?" Tamino called. "Get to your desk, Professor. We are going to have us a *time*. Alicia, stretch those beautiful legs and get over to your terminal, baby. Somebody aim Jane back to her chair. Yeah, just hook those straps down. Hi there, Dr. Klebo. Glad to see that you've made yourself at home. Alicia, sit down. Doctor, why don't you take a seat over there by Jane? Yeah, that's fine. Where's Ivanson? Well, we'll have to

257

start without him. All right, take a gander at the screens in the middle of the room and we'll get a quick rundown on what's popping." John looked away from the console in time to see the six white screens rise from the amphitheater floor.

"All right, John," Tamino said. "Give us a summary."

Alarm signals buzzed through John's nervous system. He stared blankly at Tamino's expectant face. "A summary?"

Tamino seemed too chipper to be annoyed. "Sorry I caught you off guard there, John. You're going to need all the cool you can muster, believe you me. Just tell your computer to summarize the circumstances which led up to the implementation of 1-A-Zed."

John overrode the typewriter in the middle of an ALERT and retracted the earlier order to delay information. Managing to catch the keyboards during an electronic breather, he directed the computer to recapitulate the relevant data which triggered the automatic program. He wondered, as he stroked the keys, who had devised the preassigned program 1-A-Zed. Certainly not Bonnie Deckstewer. She had always agreed with John that cybernetic codes and symbols should be treated with the reverence due anything that could be so potent with meaning. 1-A-Zed sounded as though it had been contrived by a child who collected boxtops so that he could be a G-Man.

"Sweet Jesus! Will you look at that!"

Tamino's exclamation broke the strand of John's speculations and he turned his attention to the first screen on his right.

258

A telephone call from an eyewitness at Armageddon could not have surpassed in shock value the report of disasters which surged out of the memory banks. A nuclear reactor had exploded in San Francisco, leveling the city and killing thousands for miles around; half the population of Olekminsk, U.S.S.R., had been found dismembered by unidentified assailants; a mushroom cloud had been seen rising over Madagascar and no communication from that island had been received since; Castroite guerrillas had crept over the border from Paraguay and visited a midnight massacre upon the sleeping inhabitants of São Paulo, Brazil; Fairbanks—houses, people, trees, grass, everything—was missing; an out-of-control Chinese ICBM had eradicated Prince Edward Island; Angolan revolutionaries had destroyed a hospital and eaten the patients, four surgeons, and an orderly; an abandoned British submarine, empty save for seventy-six complete skeletons still bearing shreds of flesh, had drifted onto the beach at Honolulu. Around the globe, tensions peaked toward frenzy, yet no individual nation would take the responsibility for the catastrophes within its own borders or those of any other nation.

What confounded John most was that the events were clearly irrational. Who could comprehend why seventeen inhabitants of a Minneapolis housing development had been decapitated and their heads, neatly shrunk to the size of plums, left decorating mantels in St. Paul? Who could guess why a Falkland Islands Presbyterian pastor's maiden aunt had committed hara-kiri? Who had sent Saudi Arabian armies roaring to war by circumcising every woman in Mecca over eight years of age? Certainly, a kind of macabre rationale could be extracted from some of the day's occurrences. Whoever cut the tongues out of the entire Mormon Tabernacle Choir was clearly either a music hater or a religious bigot. But why had all the men under forty on Easter Island developed overnight symptoms of heroin addiction when the drug had not been available to them for over a year?

John had seen enough. Again, he fervently thanked God that he was merely a systems analyst and a priest and not charged with the responsibility of making sense out of a world gone insane. His heart went out to other members of the Fellowship, who sat with their gawking, pallid faces aimed at the screen on the far right, as helpless as compass needles before the allure of magnetic North. John even felt sorry for Miss von Helsing, in whose mouth an unlighted cigarette drooped forgotten and in whose fingers a match had long since extinguished itself against seared flesh. And poor Professor Keruk had turned saffron for want of blood in his cheeks. Had he not known better, John would have believed that even Miss Feuer, her head lolling on one shoulder, demonstrated occasional glimmers of comprehension. Mad as she was, bless her soul, she showed just as much attention to the screen as anyone else in the amphitheater.

PROCESS GAME PRECEDENTS.

John pulled the microphone in front of his face. "Mr. Tamino, do you think we have enough information? Apparently, the program holds in abeyance until we feed the computer references from previous games."

260

"Whazzat? Oh, sure. Well, it looks like war to me but I'll be damned if I know who's fighting it." Tamino lifted his eyes from the screen and wiped his face with a jerking hand. "We'll need war games precedents. Ask Leo. Yeah, that's it. Ask Leo." Tamino glanced back down at the screen, moaned, then fixed a pained, hypnotized, unblinking stare on the chronicle of horrors still issuing from the computer.

John looked back and forth down the row of desks in the amphitheater. No one else seemed to have heard his dialogue with Tamino. "Mr. Tamino, Leo isn't here."

Tamino twitched, then leaned out of the bandbox and searched. "Where the hell is he?"

"Recuperating nicely." John had been mistaken. Dr. Klebo had listened to every word. "As soon as we work our way through the swallowing problem, we'll have him off intravenous."

"I want Leo *here!* Get him out here!" Tamino shouted. Black panic shrouded his face. "What have you done to my boy?"

"Tush, tush, sir." Dr. Klebo lifted a pacifying hand. "He's perfectly serviceable, all things taken into consideration. I haven't the slightest doubt that once you become accustomed to the novelty you will be more than pleased with the results of our work."

"*You bring him out here, do you hear me? You bring him out here and I don't want any backtalk!*"

Dr. Klebo attempted to reconstruct a crease out of the wrinkles in one trouser leg. "Now, now, let's not lose our perspective. I see no medical reason why he shouldn't have a little outing if he isn't allowed to get too excited." He

261

stood and beamed proudly to an audience that ignored him. "Not that excitement should ever be a problem with that lad any more."

"Get him!"

Klebo ducked and scurried for the exit.

RELEVANT DATA RELAYED TO PRESENT TIME.

John instructed the computer to maintain a continuing report of pertinent developments. The console absorbed the order within a fraction of the time he expected, then, one after the other, all six screens lighted up and began to jitter with words. Below John's glass cage, faces void of animation, the four members of the Fellowship slowly turned and contemplated those particular disasters which related to their specialties. Professor Keruk, teeth bared, learned of syphilitic Eskimos attacking a walrus colony. Miss von Helsing tore her hair at the news of an inmate revolt at a Warsaw foundling hospital. Mr. Tamino sobbed unashamedly over the latest stock quotations. Miss Feuer blew bubbles out of one nostril as the patterns on her screen scrambled to detail the collapse of every major bridge in South America and eastern Russia, some through apparent sabotage, others through causes unknown.

Mr. Tamino, random muscles in his jaw tugging at one another, lifted himself on his elbows and scanned the desks below. "Where's Ivanson?"

No one answered. John suspected that he was the only one who heard the question.

"I want Ivanson in here." Tamino spoke not to his microphone but, so far as John could tell, only to himself. "He's going to tell me a thing or two," Tamino said.

"Do you want me to page him?" John asked.

Tamino either did not hear him or did not care to acknowledge the question. "Yeah, it all ties together. The sort of thing nobody would expect but the nuts. Heh. Just goes to show you."

"He should be in the observatory. I saw him earlier." John raised his voice and enunciated with great precision. The expression on Tamino's face made him uneasy.

"A plot, that's what it is. Why wasn't I informed? A plot, all right. A plot to undermine confidence in the solidity of man's social structure, in the warp and woof of the human condition." Tamino leaned his chin on folded fists and studied the eroded grain in his desk top. "Ho ho. I've *got* it!" He smacked his hands together, rubbed them as if grinding an ant to smithereens, and gave John a quick nod. "All right, John. Shut off the screens. I want everybody to listen to this and give it some thought."

John put the computer on stand-by.

As if waking from three separate but enervating nightmares, Miss von Helsing, Professor Keruk, and Miss Feuer stretched, fluttered their eyelids, and readjusted their buttocks on their chairs while the screens faded and went blank.

"All right, I think I've got a clue on what's happening." Tamino had suppressed his melancholy, the calliope reasserting itself over the oboe in his larynx. "I want you to listen to this, hear me out. Mind you, I'm not forcing my opinion on anybody, but I want you to give it some clear thinking and let me know your considered opinions. Are you ready? Here goes." He leaned back, closed his eyes, and recited as if by rote from some half-forgotten nursery rhyme. "Now, just suppose that we have some beings from

263

outer space who want to disrupt our culture and throw the world into confusion. They can't attack in a way that would be obvious because we'd be on to them and rally to the common defense. Heh heh. I'd like to see them take *us* on, hey, gang? Anyway, suppose they wanted to make us feel that we didn't have anything to depend on any more, that our world, our way of life was coming apart at the seams, what better way could they do it than what's been going on today? A city disappears here, a head shrinks there, confusing stuff like that. The world goes bats, who can blame it? Wars are declared against innocent parties who retaliate and blow up somebody else who was looking the other way. Oh, in no time at all, my friends, we'd be so worn out battering away at one another there wouldn't be any fight left in us. We'd be ripe for the rockets to land and pick up the pieces." Tamino straightened up, radiant and smug. "What do you think of that for starters? I know that you might want to fill in some of the gaps, of course, but it gives us something solid to work with until Leo and Dr. Ivanson get here to give us some specifics. Be frank. Toss it around and see where it goes."

"Bullshit," said Miss von Helsing.

"Illogical," said Professor Keruk.

Miss Feuer buried her face in her terminal.

"That's not discussion!" Tamino bellowed. "That's slander. John, let's hear from you. Don't you think what I suggested has possibilities?"

John braced himself. "I'm afraid not. Not one piece of evidence has come through the computer that I know of which would add the slightest credence to your theory." He saw a vein in Tamino's forehead swell and pulse. "But I do admire your creative approach."

"Opinions." Tamino slumped into his chair. "You offer me nothing but personal opinions. John, I want you to put my idea into the computer and see if it can make anything out of it."

John turned and pressed the appropriate bars, typed the necessary instructions, then leaned back and watched the console assimilate its orders. He hated this sort of thing. John had worked for an idiot at I.B.M. once who had forced him to program a multimillion dollar machine to draw bunny rabbits for his three-year-old daughter and John had felt no sillier about that than he felt about Tamino's space ships. On impulse, he added a command for the computer to void itself of the question if it proved unprogrammable.

INSUFFICIENT DATA.

John smiled as he tore the paper from the typewriter but carefully straightened his lips before he turned to face Tamino through the glass. "Insufficient data," he read.

"The trouble with machines," Tamino said, weighing each word before dropping it, "is that they have no intuition. By the time the data are sufficient the Goddamn flying saucers will be parked in our front yard."

Dr. Ivanson had come into the amphitheater and almost reached his terminal before John noticed him. He stood staring at Tamino, his mouth contorted. "What did you say?" Dr. Ivanson asked the question but John suspected he didn't really want an answer.

Tamino incandesced with joy. "Ah, Doctor, just the man to help me put these lunkheads straight. I've been telling them my theory of what's been going on in the world." He closed one eye and aimed down a stiff index finger at Dr. Ivanson. "Doctor, I've figured out that we're in the middle of an invasion from outer space." He paused and stared at Dr. Ivanson. "How's that grab you?"

Dr. Ivanson shuddered and walked quickly to his terminal. "I have work to do. We'll discuss it later when you're more yourself."

"Get your hands off that typewriter," Tamino shouted. "We've got to keep all channels open. We're on 1-A-Zed Alert."

Dr. Ivanson looked at his hands poised above the keys. "I have only the merest bit of new data to pass on to the computer which I am sure will not in any way hinder the progress of your delirium."

"You can wait." Tamino flung himself back into his chair and nursed the sting of rejection. "Turn the screens back on, John."

John obeyed. Nothing had improved. Fear-crazed peasants had rioted in Buenos Aires, the entire presidium of the Chinese Communist Party had vanished from Peking, and two million women around the world had given birth to monstrosities of assorted sizes, shapes, species, and genders; with parenthetical restraint, the computer noted that only 51.002 percent of these women had been pregnant.

"Now, here's our patient."

"God have mercy upon us!" The supplication escaped John's lips before he was aware of thinking it, but the sentiments, echoing through his soul and the loudspeakers, seemed not only appropriate but incumbent.

Dr. Klebo pushed a long reclining chair with wheels, the body of the contraption tilted back. But the angle of the chair could in no way account for the arresting thrust of that leg, for the perplexing tilt of that head, for the arhythmic spasms racking that thorax, for the tangled, twisted, tortured bundle of withered skin, slack muscle, and rigid bone that Leo Membozig had become. John watched the procession across the amphitheater until he could watch no more.

Dr. Ivanson's voice was subdued and choked. "You don't mean to pretend that he is alive?"

"Always good to see you, Doctor." John dared to look up, concentrating all his attention on Dr. Klebo's face and nothing else. "Of course he's alive, and happy as a clam. Probably for many of the same reasons, come to think of it." Dr. Klebo wiggled his jowls in appreciation of his own joke and proceeded to raise a metal Christmas tree of bottles and tubes which he slipped into rubber plugs already skewered into Membozig's body and limbs.

Tamino stood at the edge of the bandbox, shoulders sagging. "You've broken him. He's ruined."

Dr. Klebo struggled to reverse the course of a large bubble which was resolute in its intention of scooting down a tube into a Membozig artery. "Hardly that, sir, hardly that. This young man has many useful years ahead of him, give or take a decade." The bubble retreated from Dr. Klebo's pinching fingers, floated up through the bottle, and popped. "There." Dr. Klebo stepped back to admire his handiwork, cocking his head one way and then the other. "As I said once before, when the novelty wears off, you'll find him as lovable as before."

Dr. Ivanson, braver than John, had not removed his eyes from Membozig and the chair. "That is an atrocity. What have you done to him?"

Dr. Klebo puffed out his chest like an affronted capon.

"My good Doctor, what you call an atrocity I call a very good first try under unexpectedly adverse conditions. I do confess that I scarcely expected the excess of side effects from what read like a very simple operation in *The Reader's Digest*. They condense their material, of course. Maybe they left something out. However"—he turned and winked at Miss von Helsing—"as Lord Chesterfield wrote in his letter of March 10, 1746, 'Whatever is worth doing at all, is worth doing well,' and I might have done a little better had I not had an altogether too enthusiastic—but extravagantly lovely—assistant who nudged my elbow at some rather crucial junctures." He winked again. "But I hold no grudges, dear lady, place no blame."

Tamino had not moved. "Does it talk?"

"Not loudly; and you must take into account that the breathing comes at places one might not expect in conventional speech. But the words seem lucid enough. Oh, you have it on my honor that we never got close to the speech centers. And as for those areas where sophisticated thinking seems to take place, we would have needed a trowel . . . "

"Make it say something."

Dr. Klebo leaned over Leo until their noses touched. "Hello!" he shouted.

"Hello," Leo said.

Tamino walked into the recesses of the bandbox and leaned against his desk, hiding his face behind his hands. "I don't know what to say. If we filled him in on developments, do you think he would be able to make some suggestions?"

Dr. Klebo straightened a blanket which had slipped off Membozig's upthrust leg. "No need to fill him in. He's as up to date as anyone here. Been watching the terminal in his room for recreation during his conscious periods." He gave Membozig an affectionate pat on the cheek. "Still can't hold a book yet, but we'll figure something out, won't we, big boy?"

"We'll figure something out," Membozig said. John realized that Leo had not opened his eyes since Dr. Klebo had wheeled him into the amphitheater.

"Dr. Klebo," John called. "Is he conscious now?"

Dr. Klebo made an angry face over his shoulder at John. "Now, John, who's to say? He talks, doesn't he? His eyes just happen to be closed at the moment, but that doesn't mean anything. Either one of them might pop open any time now."

"I don't want to hear any more." Tamino hurled himself into his chair. "Let's find out once and for all what we've got here. Leo, do you hear me?"

"Mr. Tamino," Leo said.

"That's right." Tamino straightened up and leaned forward. "Leo, what do you think of the computer reports?"

"Awful things. Everywhere. Awful things." Dr. Klebo had been telling the truth. Leo's left eye popped open. It didn't blink.

"That's right, Leo, awful things everywhere. But we'd like to know who's behind it, we want some hints so that we'll know what's going on."

Membozig opened his other eye and tried to focus the set on some distant object. "That computer. Ask that computer."

John frowned at Tamino. "We need game precedents."

Membozig closed his eyes, then opened them halfway,

269

one lid a trifle higher than the other. "No precedents. Can't think. Remember. Maybe them Chinese . . . " His voice trailed off into whispers.

Tamino gnawed a knuckle, then looked desperately at John. "He's the expert, damn it. What have we got to lose?"

John tapped out the order and waited.

INSUFFICIENT DATA TO JUSTIFY PRESUPPOSITION. THE PEOPLE'S REPUBLIC OF CHINA CURRENTLY SUFFERING INTERNAL REVOLT. MILITARY ESTABLISHMENT NON-FUNCTIONING.

"Did you see that, Leo?" Tamino tapped his fingers on the microphone, sending a bass drum Morse Code through the loudspeakers.

Dr. Klebo tipped Membozig's chair up and twisted his head to look at the screen past the obstruction of the protruding leg.

"Well?" The tempo of the drums increased.

"He's thinking about it," Dr. Klebo said.

Leo spluttered a froth of saliva and Dr. Klebo hastily pulled the chair back down and rearranged his patient's head.

"I think he's tired." Dr. Klebo pushed Membozig's eyes shut. "He could use some rest."

"May I interrupt the Grand Guignol and use my terminal?" Dr. Ivanson sounded as if his throat were filled with cracked ice. "My work has been interrupted for a sufficient length of time to justify some annoyance." Like a searchlight scanning the night for enemy bombers, Dr. Ivanson lifted his fury toward Tamino. "I have been patient, Mr. Tamino, far more patient than is necessary and that merely out of profound sympathy for the butchery visited upon my colleague. However, I am entitled to the concern of this group. If you do not find my work of sufficient import to allow me to continue with it, uninterrupted, then I will take appropriate steps to solve the problem for all of us." Ivanson moved in an atmosphere of grand affront, a deposed archduke compelled to battle rats for a garbage-can dinner. "I warn you, Mr. Tamino, warn all of you that little prevents me from doing that thing which has called and beckoned me for more years than I care to recall."

Tamino, the upper part of his face shadowed by a tent of fingers, interrupted. "Yeah, yeah. But more to the point, Doctor, didn't you, Jane, and Alicia have something going with some voices from outer space a while back? Where there are voices there are people, I always say."

"Are we back on *that* again?" Miss von Helsing slashed the top off a pack of cigarettes, her second since she had come to the amphitheater. "Not voices, Dan. Radio signals."

"Radio, voices; put 'em together and you've got Amos 'n Andy," Tamino snarled. "But didn't one of you figure out that somebody was up there trying to get in touch?"

"You have struck home, Mr. Tamino." Dr. Ivanson licked his lips. "We were indeed monitoring some remarkably regular high frequency pulsations . . . "

"That's it! I told you!" Tamino jumped up and clapped his hands. "They're the ones. They followed their radio beams down here to take the planet over. Listen, we all know that it would take somebody from the stars to manage to confuse *us*. Ivanson, I want you . . . "

"No. *No*." Dr. Ivanson marched from his terminal and

271

let his hands fly over his head like angry bees. "I won't listen to one more moronic word. If you would allow me to use the computer, I would be able to prove you wrong." Suddenly as cool and frosty as if he'd been dropped into a freezer, he looked across at Miss von Helsing. "I'm afraid that our joint project has come to an unexpected conclusion. The two radio stars in question have vanished."

"Vanished?" Miss von Helsing dropped her cigarette. "For good?"

"One presumes. Because of Mr. Tamino's immersion in his own fantasies I have been unable to relay this information to the computer memory banks."

The loudspeakers in John's chamber bleated with sympathetic outrage as Mr. Tamino screamed down from his bandbox. "Well, for crying out loud, what are you waiting for? Don't you overrated geniuses see the big picture? Dying radio stars. Desperate refugees taking to their spaceships to find a new home. And *they find us!* What have I been trying to tell you?"

Dr. Ivanson, his eyes dark slits of contempt, turned away from the crescendo of Tamino's speculations and seated himself at his terminal. John monitored the input, noting that Dr. Ivanson reported an event which had taken place eighteen years before his telescope received the signal. He could not understand the excitement aroused by an occurrence that, in the hustle and bustle of their lives, amounted to nothing more than merely a memory in the infinity of the heavens.

The keyboard of the console blazed with light as every bar depressed at once. Momentarily blinded, John covered his eyes and jerked his face away.

"What happened? Something on fire?"

John ignored Tamino's shouts, wiped his eyes, and squinted through the rainbow conflagration. "Dr. Ivanson. Please stop using your terminal until I see what's happening up here."

"I am *not* using my terminal. I have finished my transcription."

John couldn't adjust to the glare. He pushed back from the console and lurched out of his seat.

"What the hell is he up to now? My screen's gone blank." Miss von Helsing, refreshed by adversity, ranted at John, at everyone, and at no one in particular. "Will somebody get that screen working, damn it? Didn't you see what's happening in Ponca City, for God's sake? And why the hell does he have all the lights on up there? It's black as pitch down here."

The console shimmered, a pyre of color, relentless.

"Hey. The lights *are* going out."

"Goddammit, I already told you that."

Shielding his face to save his vision, John bumped around the console to the window, hoping to discover if whatever had gone wrong with the console had affected the operation of the rest of the hardware. In the window, John saw only the reflection of his own silhouette against an aurora borealis pulsating from the console behind him, and nothing else. Nothing was visible in the cavern; the deep green lights of the cabinetry were smothered in blackness. John cupped his hands against the sides of his face and leaned against the glass, trying to force his eyes to see something, anything. His mouth went dry as he searched, looking to those places where he knew he should find a cable, metal, a light. But he saw nothing.

As if beckoned, he squinted, refocused from instinct

273

without a reference point, and spied, far off in the darkness, the flicker of an atom of brilliance which, as he watched, swirled and grew. John stiffened before the spectacle of the dancing light which pulverized into more atoms, then regathered itself into a larger single center of spitting energy. Steadily, ponderously, the light approached him, spread and stretched itself, split into two orbs of equal size, joined at the tail, then advanced from an unknowable distance, each part leaving a trail of exploding sequins.

The relief which came with understanding broke from John in a spasm of coughing.

"What the devil's going on? Are you all right up there?" Tamino's voice, elfin and unimportant, squawked into the chamber. The loudspeakers had no volume; the lights had gone out in the amphitheater. John understood. The computer would need all the available power to sustain itself.

Peering cautiously through twined lashes, John felt his way around the console and grabbed the microphone. "Everything's all right. The computer has gone on brute force and taken all our electricity."

"I thought I heard something. Did anybody else hear anything?" Tamino sounded cranky. He also sounded frightened. John chuckled. Mr. Tamino wouldn't have to wait for his flying saucers; the computer had given him more excitement than he could handle.

"I heard him. He said that the computer had taken all our power." Keruk? Ivanson? Klebo? The words were whispers as the loudspeakers slowly died.

"What the hell for? You don't think he's . . . "

John saw no point in attempting to reply. He strolled back to the window and watched as more and more of the cabinets, in order and obedient to some key word or phrase

274

or equation in a recent transmission, searched and collated each one of the billions of components which together stored and related data. Whatever had started it—perhaps Ivanson's figures on the dead radio stars—nothing would stop it until the computer had juggled every possibility, drained every source available to it. Already, John could distinguish the shapes of individual cabinets as the quest approached him down the twin banks, every activated cabinet gleaming, every light flashing, every tape spinning, the calculations taking place as fast as electrons could fly, tentative solutions held in abeyance as another set of computers burst into action bringing the lights nearer.

He was perfectly aware that the computer might not find an answer to whatever problem it had set for itself. Yet, John felt an enormous thrill. Normally, a programmer cursed the day that his hardware went on brute force, a waste of time which indicated either a poor system or an inept program. But had such a programmer ever had such a computer? A waste of time, perhaps, but a day John would never forget, the day when the mightiest electronic brain on earth exhausted the sum total of man's cumulate knowledge to solve a riddle which would be, by definition John supposed, the most important question ever asked.

He wished he could remember, if he had even known, what the question was.

The last and closest pair of cabinets glittered to life. John licked his lips, eager now for the machine to finish its work. The ceiling lights in the chamber and the amphitheater flashed on, the console bars flicked up into position, and Tamino boomed through the revived loudspeakers.

". . . answer me, I will get a machine gun in here and blast through that glass myself. That's the last warning."

John hurried back to his chair to watch the typewriter.

Almost offhandedly, he turned to the microphone. "Don't worry, Mr. Tamino. The computer has been working a little harder than usual."

"Nothing's wrong with it, is there?"

Afraid to disturb whatever delicate cerebrations were occupying the computer's transistors, but driven by a curiosity which neutralized his fears, John touched the console and pressed two bars, requesting a report on the status of the program in progress.

PLEASE STAND BY.

"Mr. Tamino, I am clearing your screens down there. I think that the computer has . . . "

TRANSLATION COMPLETE. SEMANTIC ADJUSTMENT UNDER WAY.

Translation? Semantic adjustment?

"We got that bit about a translation out here, John. What the hell is it translating?"

"Martian," Dr. Ivanson said. "Alpha Centaurian."

"Heh heh. You just may be laughing out of the other side of your mouth before this day's over, Doctor."

Mr. Tamino sounded excited. John was excited, too, rubbing damp palms back and forth on the arms of his chair, waiting for the typewriter to make its first move.

"How long are we going to have to wait?"

"Miss von Helsing, the computer is organizing data." John enjoyed the opportunity to exploit his authority. "The program would seem to be somewhat more complex than we're used to." John tensed. The typewriter clicked, hesitated, then spattered out a column of figures.

```
9F 466  =  3C 273
57 C    =  58L 9
44M 677 =  9C 767
```

"Oh, my God."

John twisted around and saw Dr. Ivanson leap from his chair and back against the wall, his fingers digging and stretching at the material in his smock. Dr. Klebo ran to the astronomer's side and shoved him purposefully back to his terminal.

```
8C 22   =  44C 2
```

"What's wrong with *him?*" Tamino, plainly disappointed, glowered down from the bandbox. "I can't make heads or tails out of it. Are those things equation results, John?"

"No." Dr. Ivanson pushed Dr. Klebo away and shut his eyes, as if the numbers on the screen were causing him immediate and great personal agony. "Those are catalog listings of astronomical features: stars, galaxies, asteroids. The computer is equating them, establishing a common reference for each set."

"What's the reference?" Mr. Tamino asked the question but he didn't seem interested in the answer.

"All of them have disappeared. But why are they arranged in pairs? I can't imagine . . . " A sob gathered force in Dr. Ivanson's chest and stifled the rest of the sentence.

277

"I don't get it." Tamino said, and looked again at the screen; disappointment had evolved through disinterest to patent boredom.

```
67L 108 = 98C 721
 9C 6   =  9C 58
```

As the list ran on, Dr. Ivanson, disconsolate and noncommunicative, allowed his arm to be punctured by Dr. Klebo's hypodermic. John noted with concern that Dr. Klebo was putting something in Dr. Ivanson rather than taking something out. He hoped that Dr. Klebo had the good sense to administer nothing more potent than a sedative, but a quick glance at Membozig gave John pause.

The typewriter altered tempo.

DUBLIN = CHRIST CHURCH
FUJIYAMA = S. AMERICAN TIDAL BASIN.
PLEASE NOTE THAT DUE TO IRREGULARITIES IN THE SHAPE OF THE EARTH PRECISE SYMMETRY IS DEMONSTRABLE ONLY THROUGH EXTENSIVE TOPOGRAPHICAL CALCULATIONS IN EACH INDIVIDUAL INSTANCE. THESE CALCULATIONS ARE AVAILABLE AND IN STORAGE. ARE THESE CALCULATIONS REQUESTED?

Everyone, with the exception of Dr. Klebo and Membozig, looked at Miss Feuer. For an instant, John thought she shook her head but the head continued to wiggle until it lolled over the back of her chair.

"We would be wiser to omit the calculations since these would be comprehensible only to Miss Feuer." Professor Keruk smiled at his colleagues. "Her mind remains elsewhere, do you not suppose?"

"Skip the small stuff," Tamino grunted, and John relayed the order to the computer.

John felt the early twinges of progressive anxiety about the material coming from the computer. He did not like the possibility that, after all the fireworks, the answer might be a fizzle. Nobody seemed to know what the program results meant, not that John personally had expected to be able to understand anything that related to another's specialization. Only Dr. Ivanson had a clue and he sat, nodding groggily, keeping his own counsel, although John did decipher an occasional slurred word or two from Dr. Ivanson over the loudspeakers. " 'S horrible" and "Impossible" were the words.

SAN FRANCISCO = MADAGASCAR.
SÃO PAULO = OLEKMINSK.
ST. MARTIN'S HOSPITAL, MOXICO = H.M.S. PENDRAGON.

Now, *that* was perplexing. John wondered what a derelict submarine had in common with an Angolan hospital under siege by revolutionaries.

FLORENCE ST. GEORGE = MURO YAMASATO.

"Hara-kiri," Miss von Helsing said. She was right. Miss St. George had been the suicidal Presbyterian in the Falkland Islands, God have mercy on her soul.

PRINCE EDWARD ISLAND = FAIRBANKS, ALASKA.

"Get me a globe, *somebody get me a globe*. And a hatpin."
Miss Feuer bounced up and down, her face empurpled with effort as she struggled against the strait jacket. "Oh. Please. Get me a globe, a *globe*." Before anyone could stop

279

her, she had burst one of the straps holding her down and was running, her chair clanking behind her, across the amphitheater and out the door.

"I've been meaning to ask," Dr. Klebo said. "Why does that pleasant young woman insist on being tied to a chair?"

Miss von Helsing rummaged behind her terminal and produced a briefcase. Her fingers worked with a distinct lack of direction as she unfastened the locks and set dials before pasting electrodes to her temples and decolletage. That done, she sat tensely and watched oscilloscope waves generating from her equipment through the computer to her screen.

Miss Feuer, her chair still firmly in tandem, one arm jutting from a jagged slash down the side of the strait jacket, trotted back into the amphitheater carrying a large globe with a butcher knife quivering out of Iceland. She righted her chair behind the proper terminal, carefully seated herself, then, her tongue jutting out of one corner of her mouth, extracted the knife and carefully plunged the blade through the orb from the Indian Ocean to the mid-Pacific. "I wish I could get a hatpin someplace," Miss Feuer said, and gave Miss von Helsing a sad smile. Miss von Helsing did not smile back; instead, she readjusted the settings in her briefcase. Miss Feuer stabbed the globe again.

AMSTERDAM ISLAND MASSACRE = SALT LAKE CITY.

Miss Feuer blinked at the screen, then gave the globe another thrust. "That's *right!*" She tittered, a pixilated cherub, happy with her work. "One thing and another taken into consideration."

"Disarm her," Mr. Tamino said.

"A lump here, a lump there, it figures," Miss Feuer said.

A cautious Professor Keruk crept up behind Miss Feuer but scampered for cover as the butcher knife flashed over her head. In rapid succession she skewered Japan, Russia, California, and Prince Edward Island before laying the knife aside.

Blowing a series of quick puffs up over her lip and through her bangs, she adjusted her microphone with the one arm available to her and scooted her chair forward. "I am ready to report," she cheeped, her voice higher and happier than John had ever heard it. Of course, she hadn't been talking much, and if one discounted the screaming, John guessed that her throat had profited from the rest.

"Jane? Is it really you? Back with us?"

"Really, Mr. Tamino, I'm feeling just wonderful." She looked as if she felt wonderful to John.

ULAN BATOR = PUNTA ARENAS.

"I think I've worked everything out." Miss Feuer scanned the room, her eyes moist and dribbling. "You've all just been so wonderful to me, kind and lovely." She saw Dr. Klebo. "Who's he?"

"A friend, my dear," Dr. Klebo said. "Tell me, are you comfortable in that thing?"

Miss Feuer followed his gaze and contemplated her strait jacket. "Oh, I've gotten so used to it, I never think about it any more." She picked up the butcher knife and sawed away at the front of the canvas, then stopped, blushing. "My goodness! I almost forgot! I don't have a stitch on underneath."

Miss von Helsing attached another set of electrodes.

"Jane, baby, my very-favorite-girl-in-all-the-world, honey lamb, you were saying something about having 'worked everything out.' " Mr. Tamino mopped the back of his neck with a handkerchief. "I don't want to rush you, angel, but if you could, if you just *could* . . . "

POLISH ARCTIC EXPEDITION = TUNISIAN ANTARCTIC EX-PEDITION.

John sickened as he read the details on the screen that relayed information to Professor Keruk: Poles eaten by their sled dogs, Tunisians devoured by penguins. John had never liked the looks of penguins.

"Well, I hate to sound so dumb about it, but it was the most peculiar thing." Miss Feuer wiped her nose. "My, that feels good." She wiped it again, counterclockwise. "Any-way, I was sitting here, sort of dreaming, I guess, when I saw the screen say something about 'topological calcula-tions' and then 'San Francisco equals Madagascar' and I said to myself, 'Jane, that's *crazy*! How could San Francisco equal Madagascar?' I was thinking about it when I saw that 'Prince Edward Island equals Fairbanks, Alaska,' and I decided that we were playing a game or something." She brushed her hair back, her face puzzled. "You know? I don't remember *what* I thought we were doing. I didn't even know we were in the Game Room until I went out for the globe." She smiled and a glaze seemed to slide over her features, immobilizing them.

"Yes?" *Yes?*" Mr. Tamino chewed on his handkerchief.

"Oh!" Miss Feuer twitched as if poked. "Where was I? Oh, yes. Well, I thought, what with the discoveries that the earth wasn't a perfect sphere and everything, you know, the

282

computer was *wrong*. Fairbanks doesn't *equal* the Prince Edward Island, for mercy's sake, Fairbanks is almost directly *opposite* the Prince Edward Island and if I had a globe and a hatpin I could prove it. So, I got up and ran and got a globe." She hung her head. "I couldn't find a hatpin but I found a big knife somebody had put under my mattress." She peered slyly up over her shoulder at Mr. Tamino, who was sweating. "Wasn't that lucky?"

"Very," Dr. Klebo agreed.

"So"—Miss Feuer scratched through the jacket—"I came back and stuck the globe a few times and, within a degree or two, everything worked out. And if you take into consideration—and this gets very technical and only another professional would fully understand—if you take into consideration that the earth isn't actually round but slightly pearshaped, then all these things that have been happening in pairs really, truly *do* happen at points directly opposite each other. Earthquakes, volcanoes, murders, wars, suicides, massacres, everything." Cheeks flushed, she took her knife and jabbed it from Franz Josef Land to French Polynesia. "Isn't it wonderful?" She goggled at the hilt still in her hand. "I was the last to believe it possible but when I saw how everything works out that way, not just earth sciences, I realized that if you're going to stay ahead in this world you've got to be open minded and ready to change with the times." She nodded her head at a forty-five-degree list. "Phlogiston, you know."

"We no longer use phlogiston," Professor Keruk shouted. "I do not in my laboratory at this time have a single bottle of phlo—"

"Shut up!" Tamino said. He sadly pondered his fist for a moment before slamming it onto the top of the desk.

"Lord, I thought for a minute that she was on to something."

Miss von Helsing studied the globe, which still slowly revolved after a weeping Miss Feuer had released the knife. "She *is* on to something," Miss von Helsing said, her words crunching through a glottal barricade of nicotine and tars. "It works out just like she said it does." Two more wires came out of the briefcase and Miss von Helsing pressed them onto her eyelids.

DATA REPORTED TO PRESENT TIME. TRANSLATION AND SEMANTIC ADJUSTMENT COMPLETED IN DETAILED SURVEY AND ANALYSIS.

"You're as much of a basket case as she is, Alicia," Tamino groaned. "It doesn't make any *sense.*"

AWAIT INSTRUCTIONS FOR TRANSMISSION DESTINATION.

Transmission destination? Why should the computer send its analysis any place else?

REPEAT. AWAIT INSTRUCTIONS FOR TRANSMISSION DESTINATION.

"Mr. Tamino, the computer has a detailed survey." Almost before he completed the sentence, John regretted speaking. A curious intuition told him that he had made a mistake.

"This I've got to see."

John hesitated. "It might be pretty long. Calculus, logarithms, lots of equations."

Tamino waved his hand and dismissed the problem. "We've got the time. What else have we got to do? Fire away, John."

John pressed a bar on the console and ordered the computer to relay its report to the amphitheater. A blue light glimmered briefly on the tier John had just touched, then all six television screens flipped and focused.

A twelve-tone cacophony of emotions jolted through John as he read the words spelling out in phosphorescent letters on the green tubes.

ONCE AGAIN THE ANGELIC DOCTOR POINTS THE WAY IN HIS DISCUSSION OF THE TEXT FROM EXODUS XXI (WHICH IS ECHOED IN LEVITICUS XXIV AND DEUTERONOMY XIX)

"What the hell . . . " Tamino howled.

IF ANY HARM FOLLOW, THEN THOU SHALT GIVE LIFE FOR LIFE, EYE FOR EYE, TOOTH FOR TOOTH . . . .

Dew at sunrise, all John's doubts and fears evaporated before the brilliance of the computer's analysis. Here, at last, was the perfect vindication of the place of the church in a naughty world. The best minds of his age, his own among them, baffled by a troublesome problem which was so simply unraveled by traditional Catholic principles. St. Thomas had done it again.

"He's done it again!" someone screamed through the loudspeakers.

How cruelly ironic that secular scholarship, which, Lord knows, John had never underrated, had been incapable of seeing through to the core of the difficulty, had foundered on the shoals of human limitation; yet, knowledge that floated on a foundation of pure faith had no difficulty in breaking through to truth. And how embarrasssing for John, with his training, not to be able to make a guess after

Miss Feuer's startlingly perceptive insight. He felt humbled and not a little contrite that he had permitted himself to stray from a categorical Thomistic point of view to an eclectic ignorance more appropriate to Miss von Helsing. Thank God, thank God *indeed*, for the computer.

THE LEX TALIONIS, AS ST. THOMAS SO EMPHATICALLY ASSERTS, IS APPLICABLE TO ALL WHO ARE A PARTY TO SIN. "NOT ONLY IS HE BOUND TO RESTITUTION WHO COMMITS THE SIN, BUT ALSO HE WHO IS IN ANY WAY CAUSE OF THE SIN . . . IN ANY WAY WHATEVER." THUS, BECAUSE WE ALL SHARE IN MAN'S FIRST SIN AND BY CONSENT HAVE PARTICIPATED IN EVIL EVEN AFTER THE SAVING ACTS OF OUR LORD AND SAVIOUR, JESUS CHRIST, SO ARE WE LIABLE FOR SUCH EXPIATION AS GOD MAY DEMAND. THIS EXPIATION MAY BE DIFFERENTIATED BY DEGREE: THAT IS, IT WOULD BE AS OPPOSED TO CATHOLIC TEACHING TO SAY, "ALL MEN ARE DAMNED," AS TO SAY, "ALL MEN ARE SAVED." RATHER, IN THE CURRENT AND DRAMATIC EXPRESSION OF THE LEX TALIONIS IN HUMAN AFFAIRS, WE MUST PRESUME (AS SURELY ST. THOMAS WOULD WISH US TO) THAT FOR SOME THE EXACTION OF PENALTIES IS THE BEGINNING OF ETERNAL DAMNATION WHILE FOR THE REST [CHRISTIANS!] THE SWIFT RETRIBU-TION IS THE PARTICIPATION IN OUR LORD'S OWN AGONY AND ATONEMENT, I.E., THE INCEPTION OF PURGATION WHICH WILL PERSIST PAST THE GRAVE UNTIL A SEAT IN HEAVEN IS ATTAINED BY THE FULFILLMENT OF THE CLEANSING. . . .

John agreed, although he had never dreamed that he would see it happen in his day. As the computer gave a quick summary of the difference between distributive and commutative justice, John squirmed. Perhaps the post-graduate-nun stylistic traits had been a bad idea. If they cloyed on John, he could imagine how they affected Mr. Tamino.

"What has that halfwit done to my computer?" Tamino bellowed. Rapid, loud, background voices volunteered opinions which John could not distinguish one from another. He frowned up at the loudspeakers. The noise in the chamber was hindering John's ability to concentrate.

IN THIS CONTEXT IT IS OF THE UTMOST IMPORTANCE TO NOTE THAT ST. THOMAS FEELS THE LEX TALIONIS IS BEST APPLIED IMMEDIATELY AND WITHOUT POSTPONEMENT. HIS REASONING, AS EVER, IS BASED ON EXEMPLARY CHARITY FOR THE CULPABLE PARTY. "IT IS CLEAR THAT IT IS WRONG TO REMAIN IN SIN FOR EVEN A SHORT TIME"; THUS, THE PRICE FOR THE MASSACRE IN SÃO PAULO IS EXACTED FROM THOSE COLLATERALLY GUILTY BY VIRTUE OF THEIR COMMON HUMANITY WHO LIVE IN OLEKMINSK, U.S.S.R. A FINE POINT IS DEMONSTRATED IN THIS INSTANCE: CAREFUL EXAMINATION OF THE SOVIET CORPSES HAS REVEALED AN EXACT DUPLICATION OF THE WOUNDS FOUND ON THE BRAZILIAN VICTIMS. ANOTHER EXAMPLE, WHICH MIGHT OTHERWISE SEEM CONFUSING, IS THE EXTERMINATION OF THE ARCTIC AND ANTARCTIC EXPEDITIONS. THE SIN HERE IS CRIME AGAINST THE NATURAL ORDER WHICH HAS BEEN PLACED UNDER MAN'S SUPERVISION AND CARE. THE POLISH GROUP HAD BEEN NEGLIGENT IN THIS CAPACITY BY THEIR FAILURE TO INOCULATE THE EXPEDITION'S SLED DOGS AGAINST RABIES; THE TUNISIAN TEAM, WHICH HAD NO DOGS, THEREFORE WAS VISITED WITH RETALIATION BY THE AVAILABLE MEMBERS OF SUBORDINATE CREATION, IN THIS INSTANCE PENGUINS.

Lights flashed on the console. John turned and saw Professor Keruk beating his terminal with both fists. Shaking his head, appalled by the Indian's lack of self-discipline, John instructed the computer to ignore all orders from the amphitheater while the present program was under way. A crash resounded through the loudspeakers.

Miss von Helsing, standing, dangling wires, legs far apart, arms shaking, had hurled her briefcase through the nearest screen.

AN OBSERVATION IN CONCLUSION . . .

"And about time," Dr. Klebo grumbled. "Not only have I been bored, I suspect that I have been subjected to an anti-Semitic tirade. I demand equal time."

WHEREAS, AT THE MOMENT, RETRIBUTION IS EXACTED AT POINTS WHICH SEEM TO BE PRECISE OPPOSITES ON THE FACE OF THE PLANET, WE MUST ASSUME THAT THIS IS AGAIN AN EXAMPLE OF GOD'S JUSTICE BEING TEMPERED BY GOD'S MERCY. THOSE DIRECTLY GUILTY OF SIN AGAINST GOD AND/OR MAN ARE THEREFORE LEFT ALIVE WITH A SUFFICIENCY OF TIME FOR SELF-EXAMINATION AND REPENTANCE (WITH THE EXCEPTION OF SINS WHICH IN THEMSELVES INDUCE IMMEDIATE MEANS OF RETALIA-TION, E.G., RABID SLED DOGS IN THE ARCTIC); THOSE UPON WHOM MEDICINAL RESTITUTION HAS BEEN VISITED ARE THUS ALREADY FREED FROM FURTHER PAYMENT OF THE DIVINE DEBT, MADE POSSIBLE BY THEIR PARTICIPA-TION IN CHRIST'S ONE FULL PAYMENT IN WHICH HE WAS ABSOLUTELY INNOCENT WHILE THEY ARE COLLATERAL-LY GUILTY. THUS, THE PRICE IS EXACTED FROM MAN GENERICALLY BUT NOT FROM MAN INDIVIDUALLY. OUR READING OF ST. THOMAS WOULD INDICATE THAT THIS STATE OF AFFAIRS IS TEMPORARY SINCE EACH MAN MUST BE CALLED TO ACCOUNT FOR HIS OWN SIN. "IT IS WRITTEN, TRIBULATION AND ANGUISH UPON EVERY SOUL OF MAN THAT WORKETH EVIL."

And rightly so. How apt of both St. Thomas and the computer to apply the quotation from the Epistle to the Romans. And a snappy ending for what John recognized as the computer's masterpiece. No doubt about it, this was far too good to waste. Tingling thrills squeegeed down John's back when he thought of the perception, the contemporaneity, the *verve* of the whole work. So Dr. Klebo had been bored and offended. So people had forgotten how to pay attention for more than five minutes. John, for one, couldn't remember a more fulfilling six hours than the ones he had just spent. He instructed the computer to hold the report, verbatim, for further instructions as to its disposition.

"Is it over?"

This was a piece of Thomistic analysis which was destined for greatness. John would see that it was put at the disposal of the finest, most appreciative minds. No nuns.

"No, I do not plan to kill him," Mr. Tamino said. John, half listening but unconcerned, lazily swiveled his chair to face the amphitheater. "That would be a grave error from our point of view since he claims to have planted some kind of electronic bomb inside the computer."

Dr. Ivanson and Hand stood at the foot of the bandbox. John wondered when Hand had come in. He hoped that Hand had seen the report. *There* was a man who could profit from some exposure to a good theologian.

"But," Mr. Tamino drawled, a picture of externally imposed controls at work on an internal chaos, "I must confess that I've been wondering whether Dr. Klebo might not be useful in dealing with the problem." Mr. Tamino looked meaningfully back and forth from Dr. Klebo to Membozig.

"You mean to *John?*" Dr. Klebo's face, at first shocked, donned speculation, then pleasure. "Well, the idea has never occurred to me, sir, but it certainly does open up a wide range of possibilities, doesn't it? Actually, I had my eye on the lady with the butcher knife. However, for an old friend like John, I suppose I could adjust my plans." Dr. Klebo folded his arms, all business. "What did you have in mind?"

"That, Doctor, I leave to your talents and your discretion. All I ask is that you chop out whatever makes him stuff my craw full of medieval theology every time he gets a chance."

Dr. Klebo smacked his lips, rubbed his chin, scratched his head, and said, "Hm," three times. "Dear me. You're speaking of John's acquired psychoses. We certainly would have to dig around for those, I'm afraid."

"So dig," Tamino growled. "Just give me a nice, happy carrot that can run a computer."

John didn't worry much about being turned into a carrot. He still had the best hand and he played another trump. "Mr. Tamino, if you pursue this conversation, I will clear the computer *now.*"

A new, more ominous Tamino studied John, an old fox eying a plump chicken. "John," he said, starting softly but getting louder as he went, "I'm not sure that I won't tell you to go ahead and do it. A hell of a lot of good the computer's been since you got your hands on it. Go on, sizzle its innards, blow all the tubes, go on. Then, chum, I really will get you *and get you good!*"

John's vision filmed as abdominal spasms and a suddenly restless bladder clamored for his attention. He tried to tighten his lips, appear stronger than he felt, but a persistent tremor in John's chin refused to submit to his need. The sands shifted beneath his house of cards and his world crumbled around him. John hesitated, attempting to force a reluctant larynx to make the noises appropriate to surrender.

291

"No . . . " he choked, and got no further.

"No, and quite properly 'no,' Father," Dr. Ivanson shouted. "Hold your ground, don't relent. Accept the challenge."

John gagged, his mouth filled with pleas for mercy trying to crowd past a scream ordering Ivanson to shut up.

"Whose side are you on?" Tamino lifted his wrath from John and hurled it at Dr. Ivanson. "Don't you have some stars to count or something? Mind your own business."

Dr. Ivanson didn't budge. "You have no threats which are meaningful to me, Mr. Tamino. And, lest you convince yourself that you are the victim of a conspiracy, let me assure you that my only concern is that we do not allow our prejudices to obscure information which might prove useful."

"Useful? *Useful?*" Tamino threw himself face down across his desk. "What are you people trying to do to me?" He looked at Dr. Ivanson with swollen, narrowed eyes. "You don't believe this nonsense, do you? He hasn't been sneaking around baptizing you, has he? You're bright, Doctor. Tell me you don't believe it."

Ivanson rested his chin on his chest and spoke, carefully spacing his words. "Let us say that I have sufficient cause to suspect that the more commonly accepted hypotheses do not apply to the present situation. Under those unhappy circumstances, I am forced to be most cautious before I disallow any theory which accounts for the observable phenomena."

"Wait a minute." Tamino readjusted himself into a sitting position. "So we grant the possibility of one event causing its mirror image on the other side of the planet. But, if we grant that, then we have to allow a lot of this divine retribution shit, too, don't we? Now, what about all those stars, planets and whatnot you've been shouting about? How do they fit into the master plan, O sage? Why did they get shot down?"

Dr. Ivanson turned his back on Tamino and placed a finger across his lips, his eyes sending John warning signals. Without pausing, he made a full circle and looked up at the bandbox. "I have a theory which is not necessarily pertinent. However, let me say that I find it most intriguing that evidence of these events would have to travel through thousands of light years of interstellar space to arrive here at precisely this moment."

"Ah." Tamino leered. "In other words, Doctor, you refute Galileo? We are, after all, the center of the universe?"

Dr. Ivanson cringed. "We could debate that point indefinitely, Mr. Tamino, depending upon whether you care to choose astronomy, philosophy, theology, or semantics as our point of departure. But"—Dr. Ivanson did a graceful sidestep—"I hardly think you're prepared to carry on an intelligent discussion with *me* in any of those areas."

"Dr. Ivanson is very well read," Miss Feuer volunteered.

"That is quite the truth," Professor Keruk said. "Often, when I have need of the proper spelling of some word in a variety of languages, I have sought out the wise astronomer, who is very free, on an appointment basis only, to dispense with the great store of his knowledge."

"Oh, stop it." Miss von Helsing pulled herself up from behind her terminal. "I don't care what causes this insanity. But, thanks to Jane, we are in a very privileged position. *We know what's happening.*"

A great iron door in John's heart swung open and fresh

293

air poured into the darkness. He took a deep breath and relaxed, content to let the others squabble so long as he was left alone.

"I'm sorry. It's been a long day. I've been in this chair for upward of seven hours." Mr. Tamino, to judge from appearances, could have been in the chair for a week, without food or water. "Alicia, would you tell me what in the hell you are talking about?"

Miss von Helsing dusted crushed cigarette butts off her rump. "Be reasonable, Dan. How many other people could guess what's going on out there? So much is happening, do you think anyone in his right mind is going to sit down and work out parallels? Not on your sweet ass. They're too scared wondering what's going to blow up next."

"Other computers . . . "

"How many of them have read the *Summa Theologica*?" Dr. Ivanson turned and sauntered toward the exit.

"Would you stop reminding me of that?" Tamino shouted after him. "I was beginning to feel a little better."

"Mr. Tamino, could I say something?" John waved through the glass. John had remembered a fact that could totally exculpate him.

"*You*. You keep your mouth shut, buster. Alicia and I are talking."

What John had to say was too important to be passed over; he might forget it. "No. I think you should remember that with the extramural sources available to our hardware it was only a matter of time before the computer encountered the relevant Thomistic matter and arrived at the same conclusion. The only difference is one of speed. As Miss von Helsing has said, we know something now that we might not have known for days if I hadn't . . . "

294

"Truce." Tamino wagged his handkerchief over his head. "Cease fire, John. You've made your point."

"Not that it reflects in any way on the validity of the computer's analysis, but what he says is true, Dan. Eventually, the computer would have tapped into something, somewhere that would have veered it off on the same course or another one just as goofy." Miss von Helsing, her legs none too steady, stood with her back to John, as if she might be forced to agree with him but no power on earth could make her look at him.

"Fine. Dandy." Tamino busied himself tying and untying knots in the handkerchief. He was so adept at it that John wondered whether he had ever been a sailor, or a Boy Scout, or an executioner. "But where does that leave us? What's the application of the principle?"

Membozig screamed, a long, warbling cry more appropriate to equatorial rain forests at midnight than glass and chromium amphitheaters. Dr. Klebo rushed across to his patient and clapped both hands over Membozig's mouth. Membozig struggled, all angles and sharp edges, then relaxed.

"Poor lad." Dr. Klebo examined bite marks on his thumb. "Not quite adapted to his lot, I'm afraid."

Tamino, who had scrambled to the rear of the bandbox, edged slowly back to his chair. "What was that all about?"

Professor Keruk and Miss von Helsing peered cautiously over Hand's shoulders. Hand had drawn a gun.

Dr. Klebo sucked his thumb. "I can offer only conjecture, sir. But I suspect that he had a thought or an idea and then discovered that the normal routes for expressing it were—how shall I say it?—gone. However"—he sampled his wounded thumb one last time, then shoved it into his pocket—"the brain is a versatile organ. With time, adequate detours will be devised to get him around the rockslides of broken blood vessels and the canyons of missing gray matter."

Membozig whimpered and writhed on his chair.

"Now *that* I recognize." Dr. Klebo sniffed and smiled. "A bowel movement. I think we had best move along." He collapsed the rack of bottles, tilted the chair, and rolled Membozig across the floor. "Say bye-bye to all your friends."

Leo said nothing.

For several seconds, no one spoke. The only sound in John's chamber came from the console, seriatim clicks and whirrs as the bars depressed and raised on the keyboards.

At last, Hand broke the silence. "May I get those people in off the desert? It's night out there by now and they're in no condition to take much cold."

"Sure, why not?" Tamino said. "How are we expected to defend ourselves from a lightning bolt? Bring 'em back and see that everybody gets extra rations of grits and greens or whatever it is we feed them." He fashioned a slipknot out of the handkerchief and hanged his little finger. "We might as well close up shop ourselves unless somebody else has a suggestion."

"I would like to say that I am so terribly grateful for the courtesy and understanding you have shown me in the past few hours, especially for the more than adequate expressions of professional appreciation bestowed on me by my colleagues and very good friends, Alicia," Miss Feuer gave Miss von Helsing a buoyant salute with the butcher knife, "Dr. Ivanson," she looked around, bleak with disappointment that the astronomer had already left, "and the gentle

Father Doffenbaron." Tears washed down gulleys in her joy-creased face. "I'm so very happy that we're all together again."

Tamino pushed himself away from his desk. "I never knew I'd been away. I wish I had."

Miss Feuer and Professor Keruk were shaking hands as John felt the chamber begin its descent to the lower level.

John didn't have any time to waste. He had to make up his mind about where he would send the computer's report. He knew as well as anyone, better than most, how quickly everything became obsolete in these odd times. Not that St. Thomas ever would become outdated, but when one applied Thomistic scholarship to contemporary problems, the problems had a perplexing way of changing even if the scholarship didn't. John had to make a decision and he hated to be rushed when he did that. He preferred some leisure hours relaxing over a pot of coffee, the security that he could spend a few nights sleeping while his subconscious weighed options. Still, for an academic like John, *publish or perish* wasn't merely a rule of thumb, it was a law of survival. Survival? He chuckled to himself. He was officially dead, wasn't he?

The laughter froze in his throat and crumbled. Officially and very close to *actually* dead if Mr. Tamino didn't get himself under control. John saw no point in dwelling on Mr. Tamino's problems. Reminders of his own mortality had a habit of immobilizing John, and he had work to do. Even more than that, he had an obligation, under God's providence, to realize the gifts which had been bestowed upon him. John fondled the buttons on his cassock and thought about himself. Today had been a triumph. What other Thomist could have done what John had done? What other systems analyst could have done what John had done? *No one else could have done what John had done.* He had achieved his apotheosis and the possibility of imminent death now seemed highly remote. Although his humility was loath to admit it, the evidence was too great: John was a genius and much too important to be killed or medically neutralized by the mediocre likes of Mr. Tamino. Ha, he thought, and tried a sneer. His face was insufficiently mobile to manage it, so he contented himself with saying "Ha" again, this time out loud.

How about Loyola? Which Loyola? Skip it. Notre Dame? Who pays any attention to what comes out of Indiana? Scratch Notre Dame. Georgetown! No, not with all those C.I.A. people skulking around the campus: hadn't John assigned them himself when he worked for the Pentagon?

Perhaps John was wrong to consider Catholic institutions. The probabilities were fairly high that they were so involved with whatever heresy was being promulgated by their current faculties that they wouldn't even notice another piece of Thomistic scholarship, no matter how superb. And the secular universities were anything but trustworthy. This thesis had to land somewhere where it would create a real shock.

Why hadn't John thought of it before? It just showed you that even the brightest people had occasional mental lapses. John happily conceded that his never lasted too long, not when speed was of the *esse*.

Where else could John send it but the Massachusetts Institute of Technology, his old alma mater? What a nifty surprise for them. John could imagine just how many theological studies they had coming through their Interlibrary Microwave Relay. He giggled and pounded his knuckles together as he pictured the looks on their faces when page after page started piling out of the Datafax. And then, the moments of stunned disbelief and awe when they recognized the splendor of the anonymous incunabula delivered to them like a cuddly orphan on the doorstep of a soft-hearted millionaire. John didn't disillusion himself with the hope that anyone at M.I.T. had the background to understand the material, but, after all, it would cost them only a dime to call Harvard. Perhaps he should send it to Harvard in the first place. No, John had all the proper alumnus loyalties. M.I.T. was getting something from John far better than any contribution to the endowment fund. John was giving them something of *himself*.

"Up and at 'em, John." Tamino snatched at John's quilt; John clutched for his life. "Forget about yesterday for the moment. We've got an emergency and you might be able to help."

Shielding his eyes from the glare and blare of unexpected light and uninvited Tamino, John struggled from the bed and groped for a robe. Tamino pressed his cassock into his hands.

"No time for transitional stages. Put this on over your pajamas."

"Slippers." Someone had stolen John's voice during the night and replaced it with a rattle. "Feet."

"We have a truce, John. That doesn't require that I dress you. However . . . " Tamino punched him back down on the bed and slid unlaced shoes over bare skin. Then, offering a stabilizing arm, he helped John struggle into his cassock.

"No time to button up here. You can do that as we walk."

Dragging John behind him, Tamino charged across the courtyard and through the vault door. "Sorry to haul you out like this, but your chum Klebo, has been up to something and I intend to correct it."

Enfeebled thoughts bobbed to the surface of John's mind, struggled to swim, then happily sank. Any pretense at curiosity was beyond him.

Tamino accelerated their pace. "The good doctor has managed to pull a little coup of some sort. I, for one, don't have the vaguest notion what he's up to but he's abandoned Membozig and gone back to Beulahland." They veered down a side corridor and John blearily recognized their course as the way to the guardroom. "Hand notified me that the old folks were behaving mighty strange this morning and suggested that I get in touch with you before we made a decision on a course of action." He scowled back over his shoulder to where John lagged. "Hand gets some queer notions from time to time."

Ahead of them in the hall, a phalanx of men in fatigues parted to make room as they passed. John's brain fluttered to brittle awareness as he saw a battery of flame throwers, rocket launchers, bazookas, and hand grenades stashed carelessly against one wall.

Awaiting them, shaking his head, Hand slouched in front of the monitor screens. He didn't bother to acknowledge John and Tamino as they joined him.

"It's the most incredible thing. He got there at midnight and started going from cabin to cabin. Pretty soon, he had collected himself a little crowd. We don't get much out of the loudspeakers, just some whispers and the occasional cackle." Hand tensed and pointed at a far screen. "Wait a minute. What's he up to now?"

John followed the direction indicated by Hand's finger. Dr. Klebo emerged from a shanty, scooting its limping occupants ahead of him, then paused on the porch and clapped for attention. "Over here, one and all. Attention." He lifted two fingers in what John at first thought was a victory sign. As the fingers disappeared into Dr. Klebo's mouth, John realized, too late, that the psychiatrist was going to whistle.

The citizens of Beulahland cringed under the wave of sound issuing from the porch. "The time is at hand when I must speak," Dr. Klebo cried. "The hour is come when you must listen." A perplexing tremulo asserted itself in Klebo's voice. John wondered if Dr. Klebo were chanting; he supposed every Jew knew how to chant.

Dr. Klebo struck his breast. "You see before you a man stricken with remorse, buried under the weight of his many wrongs. Long nights have been drowned in the tears of my contrition, endless days scorched by the heat"—he gulped and his voice broke—"of my *shame.*"

John glowered at Tamino. "It's a revival meeting. Did you get me up to watch Dr. Klebo confess his sins?"

"Shh!"

"Unable to bear this burden, unwilling to resist my responsibility any longer, I have returned to you." The crowd moaned and backed off. Dr. Klebo spread his arms. "I know some of you may be surprised to see me with you once more. I can tell some of you are worried that I am with you again, but put your confusions and terrors aside. I have come not as a physician but as a friend."

A skeptical murmur echoed through Beulahland.

Tamino chuckled. "A subtle distinction not lost on our black friends." He rubbed his chin. "I've got to admit it. That fat old fox has piqued my curiosity."

Dr. Klebo hooked a thumb into a vest pocket and stared intently at his audience. "The day is long past when minor differences of pigmentation and brain weight can separate us. I am here to seal a bond and liberate my conscience. All of us have troubles in this life. I, a downtrodden son of Shem, got troubles; you, odious descendants of the outcast Ham, got troubles, too."

An old man in coveralls burst into tears.

"But I'm going to let you in on a little secret about those troubles, my friends, a secret I never shared with my patients because who wants to give up forty-five smackers an hour, eh?" Dr. Klebo gave a sly, not particularly reassuring, wink. "The miseries of this life aren't caused by our insecurities and inadequacies: our insecurities and inadequacies are caused by other people." Dr. Klebo smacked a fist into the palm of his hand. "Name one trouble, one ounce of *angst* that wasn't foisted off on you by somebody else."

Nudging a chum, a bent crone lifted a hand. "My rheumatiz. Nobody done give me that."

"How do you know?" Dr. Klebo gripped the railing and leaned forward. "How do you know you didn't catch it from somebody else? How do you know somebody didn't slip rheumatism germs into your soup? How do you know somebody didn't work a rheumatism spell on you?" He leaned back, triumphant. "Lots more of that has been going around than you read about in the papers."

"Lawdy," the old woman howled, and covered her face with her hands.

Tamino licked his lips. "The man may be an idiot, but he's my kind of idiot."

"What have you ever done to deserve your pathetic, stinking lot? What did *you* ever do to end up here, wretched beyond my pitiful powers of description? And don't you try to palm the blame off on poor old Adam. The root of your miseries is much closer than you think." Dr. Klebo borrowed a bandanna and wiped his forehead.

John glanced nervously at Tamino and was immediately relieved to see that he smiled.

"The Fellowship is your oppressor and it's about time somebody told you." Jacket flapping, Dr. Klebo marched back and forth across the porch. "I'll admit, I was as much of a dupe as any of you. They conned me into being as much of an exploiter as the next fellow, encouraging me to use you for my own selfish ends. But I've changed, times have changed, and by my mother's grave *you're going to change!*"

Beulahland huddled together. John didn't doubt for a second that they believed him. "What's he trying to do?"

Tamino showed a flash of tooth. "Who knows? When you've been around as long as I have, John, you'll discover that the discontent of a malcontent is a fragile and precious thing; like an orgasm, it's fun to have but hard to explain."

"I bring you revolution," Dr. Klebo bellowed. "Cast off your chains, rise out of bondage, set your spirits free!"

"Amen," someone said. It sounded like a question.

Dr. Klebo peeled off his coat and tossed it over his shoulder. "Now, some of you may ask why I should so generously risk my privileged position for you. Why should I, a Jew, a brother-in-law of slum barons and a cousin of loan-sharks, a man whose only previous displays of interest were limited to those little driblets of you which he could get into a test tube, why should Klebo come here to risk his Yiddish all for *die Schwarzen?* Klebo has something up his sleeve, you think. An eviction notice, perhaps? Maybe a hypodermic needle? A bill for services rendered? Nope. Those days are over. I renounce the past. Baby, color me black. I'm one of you."

Eyes goggled and jaws dropped in stark bewilderment.

"What is more important, I have become a humanitarian despite my long years of medical practice. I want no rewards or praise, merely the peace of soul a good man can extract from good deeds."

Another Amen pierced the air, this one more emphatic and secure. At long last, Dr. Klebo seemed to have found the language of his people and he knew it. "Amen," he shouted back, "Ah-*men*, ah-*men*, ah-*men*." He stamped time with his right foot, encouraging and directing with both hands as the chant swelled into thunder. The tension mounted in direct ratio to the shrillness of the voices and John shuddered.

"That clinches it," Hand groaned. "It's like a Munich beer hall in blackface." He turned to Tamino. "I've heard enough. Let's put a stop to this before it gets out of control."

"Patience, Phil." Tamino patted Hand's shoulder. "Everything in its own time."

Dr. Klebo had moved from the porch and begun to move among his constituents, giving them little pushes and shoves. "Show some backbone. Let's see some of that old jungle-bunny savagery."

He raised an arm over his head and marched down the line, forcing those leaning against one another to support themselves. Few could, John noticed.

"I don't like this," Hand said. "Five more minutes and he's going to have them mobilized."

"Oh, sure." Tamino shook his head. "Ten more minutes and they'll all be dead of exhaustion."

"Come what may," Dr. Klebo was shouting, "I'm doing this all for you." With a flamboyant gesture, Dr. Klebo aimed his army toward the steel doors of the elevator.

"Well, I don't think this is going to be much trouble." Tamino gave John a cold, distant flick of the eyes. "Sorry I disturbed your rest. If you want, Hand will have one of the boys get you back to your room."

A momentary suspicion that Tamino might be trying to pull one over on him, although he didn't know one what, called forth the dialectician in John. "No, I'm already up. I'll stay." He puzzled over the monitors. "That certainly doesn't seem like the Dr. Klebo I know."

"Oh, it isn't, John. It's a Dr. Klebo that Dr. Klebo has dreamed up for the occasion." Tamino bit his lip and turned to Hand. "I guess it's about time we found out what the good doctor has on his mind."

From a panel under one of the screens, Hand produced a microphone, untangled the cord, and passed it to Tamino. Flicking a switch, he grinned as if he were faced with an audience that faced no one else in the room. "A good morning to you, Doctor. Hi there, everybody. This is Dan Tamino, your director. I've been enjoying your speeches but the thought has occurred to me that unless you all go about your business pretty soon I might not get my breakfast this morning." He narrowed his eyes. "Any truth in that?"

The black column trembled, separated, then regrouped as Dr. Klebo scampered thither and yon reestablishing order. He turned and pointed his finger at something fifty or sixty degrees to the left of John's vantage point.

"Let my people go!" Dr. Klebo strutted before his unseen adversary. "The revolution has arrived on your doorstep, sir, and its first victim is your breakfast."

"Gee whiz," Tamino said. "Sounds like you mean business."

The ancient blacks began to stare at Dr. Klebo with a new respect.

"I speak for my brothers and sisters and I have composed, solely on their behalf, a series of ultimatums." From his back pocket, Dr. Klebo produced and unfolded something that appeared once to have been part of a shopping bag.

"Yes. Right on. Well done." Tamino nodded. "But, just to clarify things for me, isn't the correct term 'non-negotiable demands'?"

Dr. Klebo ignored him. "Number one: no more desert nights without hot water bottles for these good people."

Tamino did not hesitate. "Agreed."

Heads wagged and hands waved. Beulahland had caught Dr. Klebo's mood.

"Number two: no more blood tests."

"Since you have made the sacrifice, Doctor, who am I to quibble? Agreed."

Joy in Beulahland pursued a geometric progression.

"Number four . . . "

"What happened to number three?"

"Oh." Dr. Klebo traced a path down his notes. "I beg your pardon. Number three: no more snacks for the Fellowship after 2:00 A.M."

Tamino shook his head. "Golly, that's a tough one. Can't we compromise on three-thirty?"

Boos, hisses, and hoots dispensed with compromise. Sighing, Tamino assented. "What's next?"

The old folks leaned forward, hungry for more goodies. Dr. Klebo edged away from them.

"Oh, oh." Tamino whispered something to Hand and Hand ran from the room.

"Number four." A nervous and imploring note now rode the top register of Dr. Klebo's voice. "Our final ultimatum is in regard to a lady deeply beloved by my radical friends and me. Miss von Helsing, that charming and endearing woman of the world . . . "

Fresh furrows creased every brow in Beulahland.

" . . . whose labors over the years have brought happiness to so many while depriving her of so much . . . "

A bass accompaniment of grumbles threatened to suppress Dr. Klebo's new theme.

" . . . in the way of simple, human pleasure, should be allowed more free time in which . . . "

A spoon bopped off Dr. Klebo's neck. He rubbed the spot and sidled away from the mass of bodies which hobbled toward him.

" . . . I could bring her to an appreciation of her somatic potential so desperately lacking at the present."

Crockery, crutches, and crinolines surged toward Dr. Klebo, battering him against the wall of a nearby cabin. *"And amnesty for me. No reprisals. Sanctuary."*

"Let us not forget your patient, Doctor." Tamino stared, expressionless, at the television image of Dr. Klebo cowering before the assault of his mutinous troops. "In exchange for my permission for you to pursue your new, uh, project, do you promise to give Leo the care he needs? I would hate to think that you might neglect him."

"Constant attention. On my oath. By his side through thick and thin." Dr. Klebo lifted an elbow to fend off a belaboring pot. *"Help!"*

"Help him," John yelled. "They'll tear him to bits."

"He's helped." Tamino dropped the microphone, let it dangle, and turned away. On the monitor, John could see Hand and four guards burst from the elevator and press forward with truncheons to rescue Dr. Klebo. "Don't worry, John. Phil will get everything straightened out." Tamino walked to a center table and examined a half-eaten sandwich as if he couldn't understand what had happened to it.

"You let him off very lightly." John frowned. "You didn't have to, you know."

"Oh, I know. Far better than you, I *know*. But"— Tamino flipped the sandwich aside and offered John his first smile in many hours—"I always let people have what they want, so long as it doesn't threaten the Fellowship." The smile vanished. "I also see that they get what they deserve. It's in my contract."

John hesitated, torn between jumping back into his bedroom or running across the courtyard to the computer chamber. As a result, he did nothing but warily observe Miss von Helsing take two or three steps, glance over first one shoulder and then the other as if she expected to find something unspeakable hovering above her, then stumble forward, silent lips chewing indigestible words. In the time since John had last seen her in the amphitheater, Miss von Helsing had undergone a sea change, complete with mildew. Her clothes, once uniformly pressed and well-cared for, hung as if they had been dropped on her from a very tall building.

She thrust her head and neck out, the posture of a duck swallowing water, and flipped her left arm in a meaningless gesture as she advanced. John wasn't sure whether Miss von Helsing had seen him, and could not tell from her zigzag course whether she was rushing toward him or away from him. At last, one foot hooked in front of the other, she staggered and, bending over to watch, rearranged her legs. Glancing up, Miss von Helsing's eyes met John's and she stared at him, mouth open, as if reminded of something she had been trying to forget. "Oh," she said. "Ah."

John decided to move. He charged from his threshold and cantered toward the computer chamber.

"You," she called "I *want* you."

John stopped and turned around.

A maroon fingernail, its enamel chipped, sliced through the air ahead of Miss von Helsing, pointed more or less at John. As she closed in, John shuddered before the full disclosure of her decay. If the pink smears on the sides of her face were really cheeks, then one was five inches higher than the other. Why were her eyes so red, especially the parts John expected to be white? What had happened to her teeth? Where were *they?*

An old familiar fragrance filled the intervening space between them and John drank it in. "You're drunk," he said, affronted and, he hated to admit it, envious.

"You betcha, toots." Half her mouth curved up in a sunken ski-jump grin. "Whoopee." She assumed a half-squat and peered right and left. "You think we're alone?"

"May I help you back to your room, Miss von Helsing?"

She uncoiled and drew herself up to her full height. "I *said*, 'Do you think we're *alone?*' "

Drunk or sober, she was still bigger than John. "Yes," he said.

She smiled and handed John her briefcase. "Goody. Here, help me with this damn thing. Well, *open* it you iggorent, er, ig*n*orant sunnuvabish."

John flipped the catches on the case and held it out for her.

"Now, where the hell is the little bastard." She hunched over the briefcase and scratched through a tangle of wires and tubes. Squinting eyes assayed John from behind the briefcase. "Nobody else is here, are they?"

"No."

"Okay. You're all right for a stinking, no-good . . . " she rambled through a pornographic inventory of John's character, physical attributes, private habits, and evolutionary status. "So much for you," she concluded, then absently returned to her search. "Oh, fuck," Miss von Helsing said, smiling at John, then clawed at the wires some more. "Ah-HA!" She yanked a cord from the briefcase with such vigor that she tottered backward, hunting for a vanished equilibrium. Recovering, she retraced her steps with exaggerated care and clapped five talons into the back of John's neck. "Don't stiffen up, baby. Just keep holding that briefwhoozit."

"Miss von Helsing," John asked, using his most reasonable voice, "why are you holding onto my neck?"

"Because I been holding onto every neck in this zoo all morning." She spluttered, misting John's forehead. "Whassamatter, sweetheart? Think I was giving you special treatment? Ha! Ugh!"

"You're doing this to everybody?"

"You got a scrawny neck. Half the necks in Beulahland got more meat on 'em. And that Hand. There's a neck and a half!" She dug in a little deeper. "Stop wiggling."

John considered. Unless Miss von Helsing was engineering a mass murder—a possibility not to be dismissed lightly—then John was not in any immediate peril. A little torture, perhaps; that he could take. On the other hand, if she *were* disposing of the Fellowship neck by neck, the briefcase and the wires would seem to indicate electrocution. John could not imagine even Miss von Helsing using valuable equipment so carelessly; the overload would do terrible things to all her transistors. He watched her wave a cord at his neck and decided a little quick pain would be better than the extended agony which could come of prolonging this encounter.

"C'mon, pleeeeze? For Alicia?" she wheedled. "Relax!"

John concentrated on relaxing as he felt fingers probe and explore, hunting his throat for something. She found it: a major artery. "Hang loose, hog-face, or I'll cloutcha," Miss von Helsing said.

John took deep breaths, thought of poppy fields, digital computers, *Quaestio* 72, Volume III. Pleasant things.

Miss von Helsing plopped the wire on the side of John's neck, missed her target, swore, tried again, missed, and stepped back wearily. "Here, gimme the case and you put the damn thing on. Right on the big thump-thump." John traded her the briefcase for the electrode and, feeling for the strongest pulse, pressed the adhesive down on the spot.

"All right." Miss von Helsing slid her eyes back and forth in their sockets. "I guess nobody'll disturb us." She leaned toward John and whispered at a volume that could be heard across Times Square at noon. "If anybody comes in, warn me, will ya?"

"Yes," John said.

"Swell. Okay. Now, don't think of anything." Miss von Helsing sneered at him. She did it well, even drunk. "Not that you *think*, you dirty letter slot."

John puzzled over the last epithet. Miss von Helsing must be quoting from one of her stage roles.

"Nose picker," Miss von Helsing snarled, busily twisting

knobs in the case. "Okay. Here goes. Get ready. *Don't tense up!*"

John braced himself for what he knew was going to be at least twenty thousand volts. Miss von Helsing pulled a crumpled slip of paper out of her briefcase, flapped it open, and read, *"You are doomed to die. Now."*

Nothing happened. After what he felt was a polite wait, John tugged the electrode loose and gave it to Miss von Helsing. "That's that," she said. "Just a little testypoo." She snapped the briefcase shut, leaving the wire trailing out the lid.

Shaken, John watched Miss von Helsing swoop and stumble across the courtyard. He admitted a grudging admiration for her loyalty to her work, even in a condition which would have robbed John of the last tatter of motivation. That was devotion.

Still behaving as if she expected to be attacked by shrikes, Miss von Helsing arrived at Miss Feuer's door and battered at it with the briefcase and the side of her foot.

John turned away, crossed the courtyard and unlocked the computer chamber. As soon as he set up the code declaration of his presence on the console, the computer acknowledged him, then went on about its work. John stretched back into his chair, laced his fingers behind his neck, and savored the knowledge that all had gone so well for him.

"John, old friend, are you busy?" Dr. Klebo, no less furtive than Miss von Helsing but a good deal more sober, tiptoed over to the console as if afraid of waking it.

"Just settling down, Doctor."

Obviously ill at ease, Dr. Klebo twisted one toe on the tile floor and tangled his fingers in his watch chain. "I am looking for one of your colleagues who, sad to say, has eluded me. You don't suppose"—his eyes glittered as he said the name—"that the lovely Miss von Helsing has passed your way?"

"Why?"

"Oh, John, your new self-confidence has made you more rude and irascible than ever." Dr. Klebo reached out and pinched John's cheek, somewhat harder than John felt to be necessary. "But, considering our long association, I'll tell all. I want her, for my own. All of her." Dr. Klebo twirled on one foot. "Mine, mine, mine."

"You made that pretty clear at Beulahland this morning." Dr. Klebo blushed. John pressed on. "I don't think she wants you, Doctor."

"You're a very sick man, John, and not entitled to opinions." Dr. Klebo turned his face into the shadows. "Help me, John. You see the state I'm in. I was even driven to politics. She avoids me, runs when she sees me, calls me ethnic names, threatens me with empty liquor bottles. John, I suspect that she drinks."

"Maybe she drinks to forget about you."

Dr. Klebo flushed and scowled. "I didn't want to bring this up, John, but you are reverting. You've even imposed your delusions on that helpless computer of yours. No, don't argue. I read your Rorschach, remember? Massacres in Brazil, shrunken heads in Minnesota, rabid penguins. You can't fool *me*, John, even if you've fooled yourself."

Dumbfounded, John didn't answer. Dr. Klebo had lost all touch with reality.

"John, let's not quarrel. Just tell me where she went. I'm a man in torment, can't you see it? That woman is a powder keg of emotional TNT and I want to be the one who shoves his hot little fuse right into the middle of it. John, if you've seen her, *tell me where she went.*"

Frightened, John eased Dr. Klebo's fingers off his throat. "In Miss Feuer's room. She's giving her a test."

"Thank you, John. I'm forever in your debt." Dr. Klebo danced across the chamber. "One of these days I'll come back and cure you *and* your computer."

Dr. Klebo bounced against Hand, who entered the chamber just as the psychiatrist left it, muttered an apology, and tripped off in pursuit of his prey.

Hand stood in the doorway, his face and posture ominously stiff. "Father, would you come with me, please?" The question was not a request, it was a recognizable order. "Something very important has come up."

Instinctively, John placed his hand on the console, casually, inconspicuously, gently tapping one finger. Hand's presence had brought a mood into the room which John did not like. He stalled. "Nothing could be more important than a talk between friends, Mr. Hand. Why can't we discuss whatever it is you want to see me about right here?"

Hand ground his teeth before speaking. "This is not a matter for conversation between friends, Father; I mean, it's a security problem."

"A *security* matter?" John played coquette. "Aren't you the security chief? Tell me about it." He inched his fingers toward the bars that would throw the computer into a tizzy of activity, harmless in itself, but sufficiently disconcerting to the unprepared for John to use the diversion as a wedge to open a way for his own well-being. John would tell them that the computer had started to destroy itself and that only he knew how to reverse the process; he would tell them that he had fulfilled his threat; he would tell them . . .

Hand tipped slightly forward. He straightened up with his gun aimed at a point somewhere on John's midsection. "Get away from the computer. Mr. Tamino wants you, immediately."

John snatched for the console but before he could make contact his chair spun from beneath him and he tangled in his cassock as he plopped to the floor. Instantly, Hand had John's arm locked behind him and was forcing him to his feet. John screamed, a panicked gargling yip. He felt the cold caress of the gun barrel on the base of his skull. His diaphragm still pumping, John bit the inside of his cheeks, trying to communicate his terror to the world at large.

"He's going to kill me." A fool, John had been a fool to believe that they would let him live. "He's going to kill me."

Hand moved John's arm into a fresh, unconventional position which sent a blitz of hurt through the limb and across John's chest. "Nobody's going to kill you, Father. Do you think I would let anybody do that? I like you."

John's feet moved, only because forward motion kept the tension on his arm at a minimum. "Don't let him kill me," he begged, not believing that Hand listened to him, not believing anything.

They moved through the courtyard and the vault door which waited open for them. Down long corridors, up staircases, over ramps. When John opened his eyes, they filled with tears, so he kept them closed. He didn't know where he was, he didn't care. John didn't want to die, murdered by bullies. Where had they been hiding all these years, in what alley?

"In here."

317

John tossed his head and the tears splashed away long enough for him to see a panel open onto darkness. He fought, arm or no arm, as Hand shoved him. He crashed down onto his side and lay still, trying to massage away the electric jolts shooting back and forth between his elbow and spinal cord. The lights went up around him in response to an unseen rheostat but John did not get up. He rolled onto his stomach and moaned, his mind an indiscriminate goulash of pain, fear, and suspense.

"Stand up, John. You look like a bag of garbage that's just been run over by a truck."

Tamino sat at the opposite end of the room, surrounded by more communications equipment than John had ever seen in one place. Teletypes, telegraph keys, telephones, television sets and television cameras, tele-everything spread in all directions around Tamino and in well-organized rows behind him. Forty or fifty yards, John couldn't tell exactly, stretched between him and Tamino. Groaning, John struggled to his feet. He wondered apropos of nothing, if Tamino had been sitting in the dark before he plunged through the door. The possibility that the darkened room, gradually illuminated, had been an effect meant to increase his fear gave John a shred of reassurance. If they intended to frighten him, then they did not intend to kill him. John clenched his fists and tried to muster sufficient dignity to erase the humiliation of his entrance.

"What is this? Why have I been treated so shabbily?"

As he spoke, the lights in the room modulated through a succession of tones and intensities, inexplicable and awesome. *A trick, a cheap theatrical trick!* John wished he knew how to sneer. But, why would they bother, what were they trying to achieve?

318

Tamino smiled but did not answer.

"Where am I? What do you want of me?"

No, the lights did not modulate; something about the room itself was not right, as if the sound of John's voice altered its character, shoved everything out of focus, like looking at fire through a waterfall.

John stepped forward but stopped at once. Tamino's end of the room went fuzzy as he watched, reassembled itself, and was as it had been before. But, for a second, everything shimmered as if radiant heat had distorted the light waves and created a mirage.

"What are you doing to me? What's happening to this room?"

Tamino arched his brows, amused. "Doing to you, John? Is something wrong with my office?"

"Everything's blurry." John swayed. "You won't stay still."

"I'm sorry to hear that, John. Phil must have given you more of a roughing up than he meant to. You took quite a spill coming in here, you know. Must have affected your vision, don't you think?"

John crushed the palms of his hands against his eyes, feeling his gossamer hope slip away.

"That's right, John. Don't look. Maybe you'll feel better. I sure don't want you fainting on me, not after I've gone to so much trouble to get you in here." Tamino laughed easily, charmingly. "You're honored, you know. No other member of the Fellowship has been in my office, not even Phil Hand. But, under the special circumstances, I thought you might like to be where we could enjoy some—privacy? Yes, privacy. And come to an understanding."

Not breathing was worse. John couldn't breathe the air, he couldn't feel the floor; nothing seemed secure. Mr. Tamino must be right, John had hit his head and not even known it because his arm hurt so much. Yes, that was it. He wanted to believe that.

He pulled his hands away from his eyes and tried with all his might to bring Tamino into focus. He couldn't do it. A sensation ran through him which might have been simple nausea but which John knew to be revulsion, the pure, untinctured reaction of a child for a snake. He wanted to run, not out of fear, but out of disgust, a desire to be *clean*.

"Would it help if I turned out the lights, John? I'm sorry, but I'll have to keep a little illumination on you, just to make sure you're a good boy and don't do anything you shouldn't."

A comfortable darkness filled the room. A soft, sourceless glow nestled around John in a golden corona.

"Better?"

"Much better. Thank you."

Tamino's words, when he spoke, hung in the air at some indefinite distance, at one moment sharp and close, at the next echoing and remote. "You have truly distinguished yourself, John. You have succeeded in doing something which no one else has ever quite managed: you have broken our security. No denials, John. Close your mouth and listen.

"This morning after our contretemps with Dr. Klebo, I heard about something that happened at M.I.T. a few days ago which, I think, you will find of particular interest. It seems that the librarian received a very curious document through the university Microwave Relay; so curious, in fact, that when she had stopped laughing, she bundled it all up and showed it to several people over lunch. John, they loved it. One of them, a theoretical math instructor, asked for the thing to show to his parish priest. This priest, regrettably a man with a highly developed sense of humor, saw no point in letting the joke stop there, but saved the manuscript and showed it to the principal of his parochial school, a Mother Barbara. Mother Barbara, somewhat less subject to the comic muse than her pastor, considered the whole enterprise in somewhat questionable taste. She, for one, didn't think it very humorous to make fun of so much tragedy and she was convinced that it was extraordinary bad form to parody St. Thomas Aquinas so ineptly. I see from your expression that you are catching the drift of this little saga, John. Be patient. The best is yet to come.

"On Mother Barbara's staff as a catechetics teacher was a young sister who once had done some postgraduate work in Thomistic theology at Yale before she gave up her doctoral studies under rather strange circumstances. Her name is Sister Marianne Francis Weimar. Ring any bells, John?"

"No. I don't think so. Should it?"

"Yes, it should, but that's beside the point. Not to question Mother Barbara's motives, although there is talk of her desire to discredit the pastor, who drinks, with the archbishop, who doesn't, she decided to have Sister Marianne Francis glance over the manuscript.

"She called Sister Marianne into her chambers, gave her the stack of papers without explanation and told her to read. Then, having glanced at only two or three pages, the strangest thing happened, John. The Boston tabloids have made quite a lot of it, but who's to account for what makes news in Boston?

"Anyway, to continue, Sister Marianne Francis, without

321

the slightest warning, knocked Mother Barbara over and tried to shove handfuls of the manuscript down the poor woman's throat. Sister Marianne Francis then discovered that she still had quite a lot of paper left, so she set fire to it. Finally, noticing that Mother Barbara did not seem to be chewing her share, Sister Marianne Francis set fire to Mother Barbara.

"Sad to say, John, for obvious reasons, Sister Marianne didn't stick around to keep Mother Barbara kindled. Although she sustained a few nasty burns, Mother Barbara lives and has been able to make a very complete statement. Not that Sister Marianne Francis has kept her mouth shut, but the disclosure of a previous unhappy incident involving twenty-three staff librarians and an Interlibrary Microwave Relay in New Haven has helped to discredit her, at least with those Boston newspapers."

John nervously shifted his feet. The aureole followed him.

"Now, and I'm sure that you will be relieved to hear this, John, the manuscript was totally destroyed. However, a number of people have expressed great interest in that manuscript, especially a confederation of mothers superior which rendezvoused last evening in Boston with all the concerned parties from the M.I.T. librarian down to Sister Marianne Francis. Now, such a formidable party isn't allowed to get out of Boston without making a statement to the press. I think you might be interested in a few rather intriguing sentences in their release, John."

Spinning crystals of perspiration hung from John's eyelashes. A greater dread than his fear of Mr. Tamino crouched within him.

"Now listen to this, John. I quote: 'The document

which unbalanced Sister Marianne Francis Weimar was without doubt the work of a madman whom we had believed dead. However, with the appearance of *countless such demented manuscripts* in the past months, we are convinced that he is alive and has access to facilities of the Interlibrary Microwave Relay network. For this pathetic creature's own good, an intensive search is being initiated with the greatest haste. I might note that for reasons which we are not at liberty to divulge, this has become a Vatican matter. We are not without our own resources to pursue this responsibility to a satisfactory conclusion.' Close quotes."

John didn't believe a word of it. "How did you see to read that in the dark? My work is *not* demented. You made all that up to frighten and insult me!"

"No, John, I didn't make anything up." Tamino sounded surprisingly calm, almost cheerful. "I have read that statement so many times this morning that it is forever engraved on my memory, I am sorry to say. But, that's one of the hardships of my job, isn't it?"

Hidden by darkness, Tamino seemed less forbidding, less powerful, less real. "I don't know about your job, Mr. Tamino." A burst of reckless courage urged John on. "It doesn't seem very interesting."

"Are you trying to distract me, John? All right. I'll be distracted." Tamino's laughter was full, threatening. The roar of the voice churned around John, pressing him into himself; he cringed. "John, you're misguided. What do you know about my job?"

"Nothing more than what Membozig and Miss von Helsing told me, and what I've seen for myself."

The blackness hovered and settled, restless with silence.

"Tell me, John, have you heard about someone named Allen Flegna? Or Anne Lagfell? No? How about Lane Glaflen? Not Glaflen either, huh? That surprises me, John. But, then, you've been pretty busy, or so it would appear. Well, those are some of our directors, the folks I work for. The Center and every place the Center touches is my territory. I'm sort of what you might call the district manager in charge of promotion and distribution."

A commercial enterprise! A vision of Hand carting his burden of highflown humanistic principles visited John and he narrowed his eyes. This would crush Hand. John determined to tell him, watch him squirm, and extract his just revenge for the twisted arm. "What do we sell, Mr. Tamino?"

"Sell? Sell, John? Why, nothing. We *buy*. That confuses you, doesn't it? Admit it. This is our little moment of truth, just yours and mine. And long overdue, I'm afraid."

A new timbre or, rather, the absence of any expression at all in Tamino's voice disquieted John. "I don't follow you."

"You will. The Fellowship, of which you are a card-carrying member, is an organization steeped with tradition, John. I won't tell you how far back our antecedents go, but you can take my word for it that the effect of our work has been pretty widespread for, well, a very long time." A pause. A not-very-reassuring chuckle. "Some might say, and I think I would be one of them, that this poor old world couldn't get along without us. As the years rolled by, we've stuck to our guns in the face of some pretty wild opposition, and that's for damn sure. But we have maintained standards, John, to the degree that I think I can say without fear of exaggeration that our only changes have been in choice of location and technological improvement.

Naturally, we want privacy, but accessible privacy. And as for technology, yesterday's sorcerer is tomorrow's nuclear physicist, if you get the drift of my words."

John didn't, but he saw no advantage in admitting it. "Of course," he said. "I have a question, though."

"Fire away, John."

"What do we buy? It would seem to me that we have things to sell, if we wanted to. Our research surely must turn up something every now and then that could bring us some money."

"Money? Money?" Tamino's laughter avalanched through the darkness. "The Fellowship isn't interested in money, John. We buy intangibles. We use our research results—I prefer to call them our 'product'—as a means of exchange. Mr. Jones has something we want, and every Mr. Jones does, so we offer him something he'd like to have in trade for it. Oh, John. We have many, many clients: presidents, prime ministers, potentates of every political stripe, a couple members of the Curia, as a matter of fact, not to mention the billions of ordinary, down-to-earth people who slog through life, hunting for a few, trifling thrills to break up the monotony."

John decided that the more Mr. Tamino talked the less time he would have to think. Best to keep him talking. "What do all these people have that could be of interest to us?"

The darkness was silent unto itself. John could hear nothing but his own heartbeat.

"Every living soul has *something* to offer, don't you think?"

John sensed evasion, a reluctance to answer the question.

"Let's get back to you, John." John had been right. He

had pushed too far. "I've been thinking about this Thomas Aquinas business of yours and the computer's," Tamino said. "It has definite possibilities. Why, imagine how efficiency can be improved around here. Take Alicia, for example. She could monitor two ethnopsychological case studies simultaneously, one that she set up for herself, another that just happened. Don't you think it might be handy to be able to predict every major catastrophe; all you'd have to do is trigger one and you'd get another as a bonus. Naturally, we're going to have a shakedown on the project, just to make sure that everything works out like you say it does. I have an old client in mind who should be more than happy to help us out. I'd hoped that Leo might be able to come up with a good test, but since he's pretty much out of the picture these days I've got Professor Keruk working on it."

Despite himself, John smiled.

"Surprised that I changed my mind, John? You shouldn't be. I'm an optimist. Always hunting for the bright side."

A crackle of static, a hiccup, and Miss von Helsing's electronic presence hissed through invisible speakers. "Hey Dan. Yoo hoo. You hear me?"

"You're coming in loud and clear, Alicia."

"Awright," she said. Silence.

"Alicia? You still with us?"

A rustle, coughing. "Yeah. I just peeked out my door to see if anybody was listening. Okay, I got the results from the survey. Nobody gives a shit."

"What?"

"Nobody *cares*. I tell 'em, 'You are doomed to die,' and they just look at me or make dumb remarks. The worse the

326

news, the less likely anybody is to believe it. I told you that. Only one notable twitch in the whole sample. Ivanson. He cracked up, laughed like I was counting his toes with a feather duster." A tinkle, which John's overtrained ear identified as ice in a glass. "He's a nut."

"Thank you, Alicia." Tamino's gratitude strained itself through a filter of apprehension. "But try to keep yourself in shape, would you? I might need you later."

"Any time. *Omigawd. What was that?*"

"My flame, my Teutonic dumpling, so this is where you've been hiding yourself!"

"Is that Klebo?" Tamino asked.

"Dumpling? *Getcher friggin' kike hands offa me.*"

"It sounds like Dr. Klebo to me," John said.

"Resistance is useless, my breath, my heartbeat, my soul. Open yourself and receive me."

"Zip up your fly, you pig." Breaking glass, grunts, slams.

"Let me out, *meine Schatz.*" Dr. Klebo again, muffled and far away. "I adore you, your violence, your strength, all your girlish ways. You are my destiny. Come back, *meine Schicksal!*"

"Dan? Still there?" Huffing and puffing, Miss von Helsing's gasps surrounded John in the darkness. "Listen, I have to get outta here. Find a new place to hole up. I'll call back."

"Love will find a way!" Dr. Klebo shouted.

"Enough is enough," Tamino said. John heard a click and realized with annoyance that Mr. Tamino could shut off his loudspeakers.

Something in the room shifted; position, mood, shape, John could not tell. But he felt the difference. Maybe he was warmer; or was he colder? He didn't know, but he

327

knew he was responding to a change outside himself. Even before Tamino spoke, John guessed that the moment for the showdown had come, and he braced himself.

"Shall we cut the chitchat, John? We have a problem which has to be dealt with, don't we?"

John didn't answer. He lowered his head to conceal the panic which he knew must be declaring itself on his face.

"I don't want to hurt you, John, really I don't. You're a good worker. You're competent. And, despite what I said in the heat of the moment the other day, I *am* worried about what you've done to booby trap the computer. As a matter of fact, I think I rather like you, John. Whether you know it or not, I've bought you, lock, stock, and barrel. You're my kind of guy."

John was not flattered, but he was relieved.

"However, this security break could be a very serious thing for us. I am very unhappy about it. I don't like the idea that half the nuns on the face of the earth have got it into their coifs that you're not dead, after all the trouble I went to. Don't you see my side, John?"

Curiously moved, John responded to the hurt in Tamino's voice. "I understand, Mr. Tamino. I didn't mean to make trouble for you. I just never thought they'd figure out that I was responsible for all those monographs."

"You made a mistake, John," Tamino scolded, avuncular and not unkind. "Under other circumstances, I wouldn't be able to forget that kind of mistake. To prove you were dead, to keep them off our necks, I would have to drop you someplace, dead."

John nodded. Everything Mr. Tamino said was perfectly reasonable. In fact, he really sympathized with Mr.

Tamino's position. *What was he thinking?* John sympathized with nothing but himself and he'd better not forget it.

"On the other hand, two things work in your favor, John. First, the manuscript you sent out was regarded as a prank, a joke, and destroyed. That means nobody knows our little secret but us, so we can still use the computer's interpretation of what's happening in the world for the Fellowship's advantage. Second, even if those who saw the manuscript do pass on what they can remember of it, Alicia's spot check has proved to my satisfaction that nobody will believe it. People just don't like bad news. The world is full of harebrained theories. Remember, old chum, that even the good sisters called your work 'demented.' "

More than anything else, that *really* galled John. How could that librarian at M.I.T. have been so blind? How could that parish priest have been so stupid as to have missed the significance of John's magnum opus? And those nuns, those *nuns!* They were *jealous,* no matter what they told the newspapers. Well, it all proved what John had long suspected: he was ahead of his time. Naturally, he would be vindicated. He swallowed heavily and wondered how and by whom? A sorrow that made the space around him seem as bright and happy as a beach in July filled John's soul.

"I won't even ask you to remove the Thomistic data from the memory banks," Tamino was saying. "That's my reward for the good work you've done for us and a little gift to say I'm sorry for ever doubting that theology might be useful to somebody someday."

Of course, John could take pride in the fact that he had done what he'd set out to do: he'd cleared the graduate schools of sisters and he had done full justice to the *Summa*. As no one else ever had. John had risked his life for a principle.

"You can even keep using the computer to set up more of your private projects. Be my guest, John. Fill it full of St. Augustine, St. Theresa, the encyclicals of Pius XII. You've convinced me that we might get something worthwhile out of it."

John had fulfilled his life's work, come to the apex of his ambitions. Now, as he looked proudly from the top of the peak which he alone would ever conquer, he admitted that from here on out every minute of the years left him would be lived in drab comparison to this one triumph. Nonetheless, as he staggered downhill to an inevitable grave, John would have received from life what so few others had: one platinum moment to look back on with smarting eyes. He would also have a faithful companion to make his journey a little lighter, a little more carefree: he would have his computer. John could bear anything knowing that he would always have another program to set up. Not so thrilling as Thomism, admittedly, never so exciting as those sacred moments watching his brain children whiz through the Datafax like flaming arrows of vengeance for all the half-forgotten injustices done him in his youth, but sturdy, reliable, a comfort to doddering old John.

The picture of himself, palsied, probably in a wheelchair, banging out one last program for a stunned and grateful audience of faceless onlookers before he sank back to be received by angels and swept away to his eternal reward so delighted and moved John that he had to fight to keep from weeping.

"But John," Tamino had lowered his register and was

stretching his words into arias, "you cannot, under any circumstances, send out anything to anybody through the Microwave Relay again. You spilled the beans once, chum, and that's once too many. If you stay quiet, do your job, and forget about everything but what's going on here, with us, you'll be well taken care of and we'll stay friends. But, one more whisper about you on the outside and I'm afraid that we're going to have to give those nuns a corpse they can dance around."

The air turned red. John scrubbed at his eyes and looked again. The air *was* red.

"John, I swear it, I'll fry you myself and love every sizzle! I want your promise that you will tend to your affairs and not make me do something you'll be sorry for."

John smiled. "I promise."

The atmosphere shook and deepened to a mottled brown. "What?"

"I promise." John saw no purpose in making a detailed explanation of his motives, but he felt that Mr. Tamino deserved at least a précis. "I have done as much with the *Summa Theologica* as any man who ever lived, more probably. I have reached the furthest extension of my abilities and expectations, Mr. Tamino. I can't ask for any more." The happy-sad feeling so permeated John's heart as he spoke that he couldn't care if the air did have stripes and dots and smelled rank. How tragic, and yet how wonderful, to have outlived your dreams.

With a convulsion, the room settled back into darkness.

"Well, I don't—how do I—" Tamino seemed undone. "Are you *honestly* telling me ... "

"No arguments, Mr. Tamino." John smiled a brave eyes-lifted-to-the-far-horizon smile. "I give you my word that I shall never transmit another word out of the Center without your permission."

"I scarcely expected this cooperation." Mr. Tamino's voice came from a far knot of blackness more intense than the rest. "At least, not without a little more persuasion."

"You can trust me, Mr. Tamino." The glory was God's and John shared in only the tiniest particle of it.

"Yeah," Mr. Tamino said. John pitied him the cynicism, the suspicion that must torment the poor man's days and agonize his nights.

"All right, John. We've got a bargain. I intend to hold you to it. I don't break my bargains; I take a dim view of people who break theirs." John could hear Tamino moving but he couldn't tell whether he had left his chair or was merely adjusting himself on the cushions. "One, um, favor, John. I would appreciate it if you didn't make a point of telling everybody what I said about the function of the Center. A couple of them might take it pretty hard."

"You mean they don't know?"

"Well, John, let's just say that everyone is entitled to believe what he wants to believe around here and I don't think that some of your colleagues would *want* to believe what I told you."

"Why should I believe you?"

"No reason," Tamino said. "No reason at all, John. But, from here on out you at least have a point of view, eh?"

"I have always had a point of view, Mr. Tamino. Would you mind if I discussed our conversation with Mr. Hand?"

"Phil?" Tamino didn't hesitate. "Oh, sure. He's on my team. Now, go on, get back to work." Then, with what John thought to be an oddly formal touch, Mr. Tamino added, "I'm happy that we could come to terms so pleasantly, John."

332

To John's surprise, a panel of light opened directly in front of him, not more than three steps away. Momentarily stymied, he couldn't figure out how he had managed to get turned around in the dark when he couldn't remember moving.

Hand waited for him in the corridor. His relief, palpable, reached out for John in a tight grip on the shoulders. "Did it work out? Sure it did, or you wouldn't be here. I'm proud of you, Father."

John pulled loose from Hand's embrace and moved away, not quite sure where he was going but confident that Hand would catch up and steer him. Rubbing his arm, which suddenly had recalled the indignities done it, John turned and looked at Hand, not smiling. "Mr. Hand, are you free for a while? I think we might have a talk."

Brandishing a fist over the console, Hand would have none of it. "So he told you a story you like. He told me a story I liked, too. He told Alicia a story. He told Leo a story. He's got a great imagination, or maybe he's a compulsive liar, I couldn't care less. What matters to me is that we're all here and, no matter what else happens, something good is bound to come of it."

John had stopped listening to Hand's declamations. At first, he told himself that he was bored. Later, he realized that he was angry. Currently, he was transcending anger with nausea and disgust at Hand's glint-eyed, foam-flecked altruism. "We have covered this ground before, Mr. Hand, many, many times. We have nothing to discuss so long as you maintain this groundless conviction."

"Oops. I didn't know you were busy. I'll be back." Miss Feuer blurred in and out the door.

"Human beings are worth something. Life is worth something." Hand rocked on his heels, serious, tendentious. "I've done the whole *schtick*, bag, thing, groove, Father, from the hippie bit in San Francisco, flowers in my hair and a needle in my arm, to guard duty in a prison in Missouri. Something good came out of all of it. Sure, I missed my own education, but I found out that it was you people with your talents and skills who made the world click. And I found out about myself. I'm dumb, but I've got a strong back to offer you."

"I don't want your strong back." Why, John wondered, did all his serious attempts at conversation seem to evolve perverse existences of their own and go capering off, leaving him stranded?

"That's because you don't accept yourself as a human being."

They had arrived at jargon, the final life-twitch before total cerebral petrifaction set in. "Do I have any alternatives?"

Hand blushed and frowned. "You haven't had a full human experience, that's your trouble. I know what you're going through, I was just like you once."

The very possibility was an affront. "I doubt that," John said.

"No, it's true." Hand missed John's displeasure, or overlooked it. "Then I quit my job at the prison and enrolled in the Sensitivity Maturity Acclimation Relationship Method in Fresno. Oh, Father, that changed my life. Every day, all the SMARM people, men, women, and children, would get up and take cold showers together, in trust."

"Nobody stole the soap? Hid your clothes? Tied knots in your underwear?"

Hand ignored John. "Then, after breakfast, naked as the day we were born, we'd go to our seminar rooms and be ourselves and we'd accept everybody for what he was, that is we'd accept everybody who was being himself. The ones who weren't being themselves would be"—he said the words with all the implicit doom of a hanging judge passing sentence—"*rejected by the group*. Finally, after two or three weeks, the ones who weren't themselves would start tearing out their hair, having breakdowns, attempting murder, suicide, real things, and we'd accept them."

"Real things." John tugged at his lower lip and studied Hand, hunting for some hint of satire, some pinch of irony, some flicker of humor. "And that's what proves the intrinsic worth of the human animal?"

"You're damned right." Hand's teeth clenched. "After you've spent eight weeks in the nude with other human beings, watched them beat the hell out of each other, make love all over the place, neglect their children, and understood it and accepted them and been accepted by them, then you'll never forget how really *great* other people are. All you have to do is just understand, believe, trust, accept. Down underneath all the rot and ugliness in your fellow man there's an authentic *nice guy*. I found that out. I saw it."

A mental congestion analogous to a mouthful of saccharine overwhelmed John. He changed the subject. "After that? You came here? How did you meet Mr. Tamino?"

"I thought you knew." Hand registered an adequate approximation of surprise. "He was in my SMARM group. We accepted and understood each other."

"I bet you did."

"Well, he listened to me, I'll tell you that. I think it was during Genital Touch Hour that I told him about how people couldn't help but make their world better if they had enough time and understanding. Mr. Tamino said that he thought even a few people could make a significant contribution, under the right circumstances. I agreed with him. This may come as a surprise to you, but Mr. Tamino has a very human outlook. Anyway, later, during Hostility Expression, we were both kicking the same fellow and he asked me about my background and was very interested in my experience at the prison. One thing led to another, and he brought me here to set up his security system." Hand leaned against the console and assumed an expression of such appalling complacency that John wanted to hit him. "I am totally committed to human betterment, Father. Nothing can convince me that we haven't got the potential to clean this world up."

John saw Hand's world, scrubbed and gleaming, populated with tight-pored, white-fanged athletes and their strapping, odorless mates, gamboling through existences of hygienic emotional neutrality. Hand's promised land would make St. Thomas irrelevant since there would be no place for human vagary, unless they needed a missing ingredient of "authenticity" for the mass-produced populace. One out of ten can be greedy on Thursdays, two out of six are allowed a modicum of gluttony on Sunday afternoons, and lust for all eugenically accredited adolescents between the hours of seven and ten in the evening. The morning session with Mr. Tamino had wiped out John's minimal tolerance for people who couldn't appreciate St. Thomas and he decided with a finality he seldom felt about anything that he was through with Mr. Hand in particular.

"Mr. Hand, I reject you. You are not part of my group."

Hand paled, then simmered to an even crimson, except for his nose, which remained white. "You can't say that," he cried. "I have expressed concern for you. We have been honest together. We've *touched.*"

"You nearly broke my arm."

"And you kicked me in the face once. Both feet. But didn't I accept that, acknowledge it? I wasn't threatened by it. I realized that you were expressing personal insecurities which the group . . . "

"God forgive me, but I cannot take another word of this." John spun his chair away from Hand.

"No." Hand followed him and squatted at John's knees. "I *had* to twist your arm. Your security break endangered group solidarity. Naturally, it must be hard for you to accept the truth, that you're the one who's outside the group. That would be a horrible thing for anyone to face and I understand why you *must* reject me for telling you the hard facts. Admit it, Father, you need to be part of the group, don't you? Be honest!"

"Are you having a party, Mr. Hand? I don't mean to disturb anything, but I'm sure you won't mind a little interruption." Miss Feuer, pert and pale as a healthy mushroom, swirled into the chamber. "Father Doffenbaron will make a wonderful addition to your festivities. He is a kind and gentle man."

"I used to like you, Mr. Hand. I admired your courage when you defended Leo against Miss von Helsing. I actually envied you. But I see now that everything you did or said was born of a curious dedication to an abstraction which, I must confess, I find perfectly revolting."

"Have you seen the reports? Everything is shifting. By a

338

full ten or twenty degrees." Miss Feuer dropped a folder into John's lap. "The floods in New Delhi certainly gave me a start. But then I hadn't noticed the troop ship which blew up in the Panama Canal. Of course, none of my figures has been quite right for the past day or so, but the discrepancies were so slight I thought it was just some silly mistake of mine. Nobody's perfect."

"I stood up for Leo because I didn't want the group damaged." Hand ground his knuckles against his thighs. "I couldn't bear the thought that suspicion and personality quirks might actually destroy somebody we needed. That's why I made sure that Mr. Tamino didn't want to hurt you before I took you in there this morning."

"I would be very grateful"—Miss Feuer batted her eyelashes at John—"if you could set up a program to check my theory and see if we can establish a pattern for the shift."

"And if he had intended to hurt me? Would you have taken me to him then?"

"Goodness, how you men love to talk. You won't have anything left to say at that party if you keep on like this." Miss Feuer tried to turn John's chair toward the console. He resisted her, dragging his feet. She picked up his feet and pushed him toward the keyboards. "Just a simple checkout to see if the change in the duality pattern is general or if Panama and New Delhi were a mistake."

"Yes, I would have taken you. This place is more important than any individual when the chips are down." Hand dropped his head, as if the admission had cost him more than he was prepared to pay. "But I still respect you, Father, one hell of a lot."

Miss Feuer watched John set up the program. "Aren't

those colors gorgeous?" She had to be restrained from touching one of the pulsing bars. "I never knew your work was so *artistic*."

John stared at the typewriter, thinking about what Hand had just said. "For a man who reveres human life, Mr. Hand, you are awfully casual about mine. I'm afraid that your kind of purity is not to my taste."

"Ah, I see we are gathering together." Professor Keruk bowed into the room, shaking hands en route to the console. "How busy we have all become in these last days."

"Father Doffenbaron and Mr. Hand are planning a party for us," Miss Feuer said. "They didn't say I couldn't come."

"I never said I was pure," Hand said.

"A birthday, perhaps? To whom should I make appropriate congratulations?" Professor Keruk turned full circle, ready to shake hands again.

"All right, I take that back. Not pure. Sterile. Nothing could live on you, Mr. Hand. You don't bleed."

DRIFT APPARENT AT A RATE OF 2.59 DEGREES PER HOUR. ACTION [A] CURRENTLY INCURS ACTION [A'] AT A GLOBAL POINT 158 DEGREES LONGITUDE BY. . . .

Miss Feuer snatched the sheet out of the typewriter. "Well, that's a relief, and that's for sure. I thought I'd made a booboo."

"If you please." Professor Keruk edged in front of Miss Feuer. "As much as I enjoy the sociableness, I note that the computer is not presently in use. Might I interrupt the joviality to request that you run some calculations which Mr. Tamino desires most speedily?"

"That's where you're wrong, Father, dead wrong." Hand

elbowed Keruk out of the way. "I don't figure that I'm any better or any worse than anybody else. But I have a human concern."

"Goodness." Miss Feuer clutched her throat and looked at Professor Keruk. "If the drift keeps up at this rate, why, in just a few days . . ."

"There you are!" Miss von Helsing plowed between Miss Feuer and Professor Keruk. John blinked and looked twice to make sure that the apparition was really Miss von Helsing. Her blouse had lost a sleeve, her hair stood in tufts and snatches from her scalp, and looping tangles of wires and connections ran by the dozens from adhesive patches all over her face, limbs, and torso to a knapsack of buzzing tubes on her back. "I demand protection," she screamed at Hand. "I am in the middle of a very important stress study." She waved her arms and sparks showered from the electrodes. "And somebody is harassing me and my work."

"A costume party!" Miss Feuer squealed, clapping her hands. "Oh, Alicia, what a clever idea." She wagged a finger at Miss von Helsing. "I knew you'd be in on the action somehow."

"To have a human concern, Mr. Hand," John shouted, "you need some knowledge of the human condition. Man is, of himself, wretched, evil, incapable of any good without the saving action of God." He tried to see past the smoke puffing out of Miss von Helsing's knapsack. Professor Keruk shoved something into John's outstretched fist.

"Merely add these mutation factors to the acquired data. I would be most gratified." Professor Keruk broke off in a fit of coughing, his face obscured by fumes as Miss von Helsing jumped past him in pursuit of Hand.

"The evidence of man's nobility surrounds you," Hand

341

called to John, shoving Miss von Helsing's head out of the way. "The unity of our common purpose overcomes any individual weaknesses."

"Listen to *me!* Listen to *me!* When's it gonna be *my* turn?" Miss von Helsing clawed at Hand's lapels. "I've got to have someplace to hide. Get me out of here. Every place I go, he's right there like he was using radar or bloodhounds. You're in charge of security, give me some."

"Alicia"—Miss Feuer frowned, cocking her head back and forth—"is your costume *supposed* to be on fire? It's terribly cute but don't you think its a little risky?"

"You are so kind," Professor Keruk said, as John fed his figures into the computer. "I was unaware of the difficult conditions under which you labored. My sympathies."

"Weaknesses, Mr. Hand? Weaknesses? You talk about the degradation of the human spirit as if a good diet and regular exercise could clear up the problem." John finished his typing and forced his chair around past the obstruction of Miss Feuer's legs. "We are helpless without the intervention of God, useless without His aid, purposeless without His call."

"Alicia, dear." Miss Feuer struggled to restrain her concern. "Do you want your hair burned off? It looked so nice the way it was."

A surge of pressure crammed John back against his console. Professor Keruk lighted momentarily on John's lap, then struggled up. Miss Feuer flopped aside as a round, red-fringed bald head bobbed through the smoke.

"My darling," Dr. Klebo shouted. "What have they done to you? Someone get a fire extinguisher, a blanket, a pail of water. Don't worry, dearest. I'm here now."

"Get away from me." Miss von Helsing, a ragged stream of flame pursuing her, darted behind Hand and pointed. "That's him. Get him out of here. I won't be responsible for what happens."

Hand held Dr. Klebo at arm's length and gave John a long, sad, pitying stare. "I think maybe God's fed up with doing all the work. Now it's our turn to give Him the kind of world He wanted in the first place. He's given us the equipment, showed us how to love one another, sharpened our minds, made us want good things. We owe Him something. I think He's decided to leave us alone and let us work it out for ourselves."

"One more step and you're a dead man," Miss von Helsing screamed.

"The work in progress has to do with one of your favorite diseases, Father." Professor Keruk nodded at the console, his eyes bright with pleasure. *"Lymphogranuloma Veltri."*

Miss Feuer crept toward Miss von Helsing, dodging Dr. Klebo's fists, Professor Keruk's elbows, John's feet. "Alicia, I think we'd better snuff you out before you ruin your costume. You don't want it spoiled before you have a chance to show it off at the party." She removed her jacket and slapped Miss von Helsing's knapsack and hair with it.

"You leave God out, Mr. Hand, and you might as well total up the accounts and close the books on this precious world of yours." Another heave of pressure mashed against John and he caught his breath. Over the heads crowded around him, he could see Miss Feuer's jacket flapping and tossing hot embers and a waving arm which did not fit any of the bodies scrambling and shoving for space.

343

"Is that lunatic Klebo in here?" Dr. Ivanson popped into view, then disappeared as Hand and Miss von Helsing lurched sideways. "I just called on Leo and found him crawling across the floor of his room trying to find a glass of water. That man needs medical attention."

"Help me, help me," Dr. Klebo shrieked. "They have taken my love and dissatisfied with burning her alive are now flogging her with large whips."

Hand tightened his grip on Dr. Klebo's windpipe. "You depend on God, Father, and nothing is going to be left anyhow. Man has to help himself, find his own way out of the mud and slime before he can start worrying about God."

"That's right, sweetie." Miss von Helsing ducked as the jacket lashed over her face. "Choke the bastard blue."

L.V. MUTATION 456 STABLE AND REPRODUCING. RESISTANT TO KNOWN ANTIBIOTICS AND EXTANT TREATMENTS COMMON TO VIRAL INFECTION. CULTURE SURVIVES AT -60 DEGREES FAHRENHEIT TO +185 DEGREES FAHRENHEIT.

"And is quite fatal as well, in half the time I had hoped. To most mammals and all primates, I add with ill-concealed self-congratulation." Professor Keruk reached out and shook hands with Dr. Klebo and John. "I have a success," he crowed.

"Oh!" Miss Feuer jerked backward, clutching her wrist. "Alicia, what is in that costume? You gave me a *shock!*"

John tore out the report and passed it to Professor Keruk, who shoved it into Dr. Klebo's bloated face. "Why should man want to pull himself out of the mud and slime, Mr. Hand?" John yelled. "It's the only thing he knows.

344

You can't change mankind, only God can do that and he isn't compelled to do anything He doesn't choose to do."

"Have you all gone mad? Doesn't anyone care what happens to Leo? At least come and help me put him back in his bed." Dr. Ivanson reached out for John but was pushed aside before he could make contact.

With all his might, Dr. Klebo tugged until he loosened Hand's fingers at his throat. "Be brave, my precious. Just give me time to overpower this fiend and I'll ... " Hand retightened his grip and Dr. Klebo's eyes bulged.

"Keep squeezing. I want to see his tongue turn black."

"Alicia, if you'd take off your dress it might help. Every time I hit it my hand gets burned."

"But man can choose, Father, and I know the choice decent men everywhere will take."

"Not only mammals, but I have had remarkable good fortune with several chickens and two goldfish."

"I am offering my own time for an errand of mercy; will no one else do as much?"

"There are no decent men, Mr. Hand. Only repentant sinners who throw themselves on the mercy of God."

"*Ho! Hey! Ha!*" Bodies disentangled and separated, battered into silent isolation by the exuberance if not the volume of Tamino's entrance. He beamed his approval on each in turn; on wan, trembling Dr. Ivanson; on the smoldering wreckage of Miss von Helsing; on charcoal-smeared Miss Feuer; on Professor Keruk, who may or may not have been nursing a black eye; on blotched Dr. Klebo and flushed Mr. Hand; and, last, with lingering reassurance, on cowering John.

"What were you people up to, anyway? Having a little off-duty brainstorming while the boss was out of the room?

Well, I won't take up too much of your time. I just want to make a quick announcement, then you can all get back to whatever it was you were doing."

John didn't know whether exhaustion had taken its toll or whether Mr. Tamino's presence exerted a mysterious calming effect, but lungs caught up on missed oxygen, tense muscles slackened, and contorted faces relaxed into the easy calm of death masks. Even John felt a new relaxation. Not that he should be tense. John and Mr. Tamino had come to an agreement.

"I've decided to try out this action-reaction phenomenon to see what can be done with it and how effective it might be for our work in the future," Mr. Tamino said. He looked in quick succession at John, Professor Keruk, and Hand, as if he had a special, hidden message for each of them. "I have an acquaintance who is in a position to run our test for us. Of course, the details will have to be worked out when I see him, so I'm going to have him brought here." He singled out Professor Keruk. "Have you seen to that little matter I asked you about?"

Professor Keruk flourished the sheet of paper in his hand. "All is excellently in order."

John stiffened, mental jaws snapping at the bait Tamino had dragged so smoothly through muddied waters. "I hate to say this, but isn't it something of a danger to our security to bring an outsider here?" He refined his sarcasm. "I was under the impression that security was very important to us."

Half of Tamino's mouth smiled. "Thank you, John, for making the point." He looked at Hand. "Think you can manage to hold our cover, Phil?"

"I'll do what I can."

346

Tamino strolled over and dropped a friendly paw on John's shoulder. "I guess Phil can take care of it, John. That's his job, after all."

John nodded, not reassured.

"Well, everyone get his own house in order in the next three days. We'll have our guest here by then."

Miss Feuer consulted the piece of paper in her hand. "Three days?" She flicked a glance at John, started to say something, but stopped herself.

Tamino backed toward the door. Miss von Helsing, suddenly alert, crept away from Hand, edging alongside Tamino and using his bulk as a barrier between herself and Dr. Klebo. "Phil," Tamino said, "could I see you for a few moments? We need to get some things straightened out."

Miss von Helsing bolted from the chamber. Breaking loose from Hand's hold on his neck, Dr. Klebo made a half start after her but couldn't crowd past Tamino. He waited until everyone but Dr. Ivanson had gone, then left, not saying good-bye.

Dr. Ivanson turned toward the door, but stopped. "Don't they see, Father?" He didn't wait for John to reply. "No, of course they don't. And neither do you, alas." He shrugged and walked toward the courtyard. "I shan't linger," he said. "I have no reason to linger."

MEMORANDUM TO: ALL MEMBERS OF THE FELLOWSHIP
FROM: DANIEL TAMINO, DIRECTOR
CONCERNING: THE FELLOWHSIP MEETING WITH WARD
THAADEN

John read the note for the fourth time since he had
found it under his door that morning. He still didn't like it.
"Thaaden?" How did you pronounce *that*. Was the H
silent? Were the A's said together as "ah" or separately as
"ah-ah"? Was Mr. Thaaden an Englishman? A Scandina-
vian? An anagram? The whole business rubbed salt in
John's fresh wounds. Mr. Tamino's precious security
regulations applied to everyone but Mr. Tamino, and John
resented with a revolutionary's zeal any privilege which did
not include him. He reread the note:

ALL MEMBERS OF THE FELLOWSHIP WILL GATHER AT
PRECISELY 1:30 P.M. IN THE GAME ROOM.

348

NEGOTIATIONS WILL BE CONDUCTED BY MR. TAMINO
AND MR. TAMINO <u>ALONE</u>.

NO MEMBER OF THE FELLOWSHIP WILL DISCLOSE HIS
PRESENCE TO THAADEN UNLESS SPECIFICALLY INSTRUCT-
ED TO DO SO BY MR. TAMINO.

A SECURITY FORCE OF FIVE MEN UNDER THE SUPER-
VISION OF PHIL HAND WILL BE AT THAADEN'S SIDE DUR-
ING THE ENTIRE INTERVIEW.

DR. KLEBO, AT THE REQUEST OF ONE MEMBER OF THE
FELLOWSHIP, WILL NOT BE PRESENT AT THE INTERVIEW.

FELLOWSHIP MEMBERS (WITH THE EXCEPTION OF FA-
THER DOFFENBARON) WILL BEAR ARMS FOR THEIR OWN
PROTECTION IN CASE OF UNFORESEEN EMERGENCY.

                    DANIEL TAMINO,
                    DIRECTOR

John wadded the memorandum and bounced it off the
glass wall. He acknowledged that he had been in a sulk for
days, that he was overly sensitive to slights, but he had been
desperately overworked. Miss Feuer's new bouncy personality had begun to get on John's nerves. He congratulated
himself for not screaming at her, but eight or ten visits to
the computer chamber every day was an imposition.
Certainly, she had every right to expect fresh figures,
revised calculations, but John saw no reason why she
couldn't be satisfied with a résumé in the morning and in
the evening like everybody else.

John's enthusiasms had slipped away from him, strand-
ing him in a fog of accidie. He hadn't thought to thank
Professor Keruk for naming the new virus *lymphogranuloma Doffenbaron,* so now Professor Keruk was mad
at him. John supposed that normally he would have been

grateful, or at least polite, at the honor, but things weren't
normal for him. He had the admittedly paranoid conviction
that things were going on which he should know about but
which nobody was telling him. John tried to convince
himself that he was suffering under the accumulated weight
of several misfortunes: the interview with Tamino, the
ridicule that had greeted the St. Thomas manuscript, the
ongoing quarrel with Hand, and the visit from an outsider.
But his mental adding machine totaled up the injustices,
inequities, and indignities and produced a sum still insufficient to account for his glumness. Why should he be so
worried? About what? He didn't know.

The Game Room had been rearranged for the visitor,
and the somberness of the total effect, empty floor with
one chair, heavy black draperies on the walls, dim lights,
scarcely served to lift John's spirits. The old magic had
petered out on him and, morose, dyspeptic, he ignored the
glances and waves from his colleagues as they spied John in
his glass eyrie.

He looked around, hunting for their guest, Mr. Thaaden.
John's watch said that it was nearly two but he found not a
sign of the stranger. So much to do, so little time in every
day to do it. How could Tamino dare to rob him of a whole
half hour?

Scanning his colleagues, John noticed that no one but
Miss von Helsing seemed to have brought a weapon. She
sported a fireman's ax over one shoulder.

The lights went out and John started from his chair.
Since his session in Tamino's office he had avoided
darkened rooms; he had even installed a night light by his
bed.

A circle of yellow light crept across the amphitheater

floor, pooling at last around a pair of large, bare feet. Shyly, but smoothly, the light climbed up the ankles, paused at the thighs, then rushed deliriously over the torso of a man stark naked except for a cloth bag which covered his head and neck. While John watched, the man was eased onto the one chair by gloved hands floating into the spotlight from the surrounding darkness. With a presence of mind that John sincerely admired, the man leaned back, crossed his legs and folded his arms across his chest. Unable to see the face, John could not guess the age of their guest. His body was lean and well developed, but hairless enough to belong to a youth. The muscles, however, were hard, crossed with thick nets of veins which made John wonder if he weren't simply a well-exercised ancient.

"Ladies and gentlemen," Tamino greeted the Fellowship through the loudspeakers, "our guest wishes, I'm sure, to apologize for his appearance. We all forgive him since we know that he was lifted from his bathtub sometime yesterday evening in order to be able to join us with the least inconvenience to everyone concerned. Mr. Thaaden" —he pronounced the name Tah-*eh'* den—"is one of our best friends and would be happy to admit, given the opportunity, that he has reached the lofty pinnacle of success almost solely as a result of his association with us. However, so successful has he become in recent years that I'm sure he understands our precautions to insure that he knows neither where he is nor who we are, other than the fact that he is among friends. Ward, you may remove your mask."

The stranger pulled off the bag with one hand and smoothed down a scalp of wavy, mercury-gray hair with the other. The face was not particularly young, but John

351

wondered if the stern expression it wore made it seem older than it was. Deepset eyes shadowed into empty holes beneath a smooth forehead and over tanned, acne-pitted cheeks.

"I have an impression of infinity," Mr. Thaaden said. "Of limitless possibility. The darkness becomes our enterprise, I think. Might I ask whether you are speaking English out of habit or as more camouflage for my benefit?"

"Doesn't matter," Tamino said. "We're not here to discuss linguistics. We have bigger stakes to worry about."

Big business? The overthrow of the capitalist oppressors? Human betterment? The quest after pure knowledge? John wondered, and wondering, doubted. And doubting, ceased caring.

"Ward, I want you to tell me something. What is it you want most in life? Be blunt. Don't hold back."

Thaaden stared into the darkness with such intensity that John suspected him capable of seeing more than they thought he could. "An army of my own."

"Ward, you've come to the right place. You might even say that I guessed in advance what you had in mind. A revolution, right?"

Thaaden smiled. "Of a sort."

"You'll need awfully loyal troops for that. More sons than soldiers." Tamino chuckled. "Professor, how about filling in our guest on that matter we discussed last evening?"

"Ah. The arrhenotoky experiments," Professor Keruk stammered. "Quite just the thing. Does our guest have at his disposal a women's prison? A concentration camp for ladies? A school of adolescent girls?"

352

"I do not." Thaaden wiped his hands across bare thighs, angry.

"Cool off, Ward." Tamino, smooth, consoling. "You listen to our idea and let us worry about the details. Okay? Go ahead, Professor."

"Indeed. Arrhenotoky is the process of parthenogenesis whereby solely male offspring are produced. Parthenogenesis, as our guest must realize, is the process of producing offspring without the presence of a sire at conception. All most efficient and clean. My researches have proved that by introducing a varient of E-vitamin enzymes into the food or drink of a female subject, conception can be induced at will. But, moreover, if hormonal extracts are included in the formula, you are assured of multiple births as well, no less than five in any instance."

"Isn't that phenomenal, Ward?" Tamino interrupted, jolly as Santa Claus at a paraplegics' Christmas party.

"Certainly." Thaaden twisted in his chair. "But where am I going to find the female subjects?"

"Simplest thing this side of heaven. First, some information from our earth sciences expert."

"Oh. Goodness. Already?" Miss Feuer, apparently rehearsed, was nonetheless caught off guard. "Well, let me see. I've had so much to do in the past couple of days. I haven't—Was it gold mines? No? Oh, dear."

"Oil wells," Tamino said.

"That's right. Thank you. Here goes. I have come to the conclusion that at this moment, in northern Manitoba—I promised not to say exactly where—a large untapped oil reserve is available on several thousand acres of burned-out timber land. And it's available for a song. With all the trees

gone, the owners, who never even thought of oil, the
ninnies, are sure to grab up the first decent offer."

"Get the picture, Ward?"

Mr. Thaaden leaned forward on his knees. "No, but I am
fascinated by the intricacies of this puzzle."

"Great. Now listen to this." Tamino paused to blow his
nose. "First, you buy up, under a corporate name, the oil
land in Manitoba. Then you set up an anonymous foundation to channel the profits into a home for the upbringing
of socially underprivileged male children, with yourself as
director. Next, you introduce our arr-whatever-it-is drug
into the water supply of several overpopulated cities and,
bingo! more socially underprivileged male children than
you'll know what to do with. The world looks and the
world sees a nice overendowed orphanage. I look and I see
Thaaden's combination military academy-arsenal head-
quarters. A perfect setup."

"Not for me." Thaaden bent forward and touched his
knee with the end of his nose. "I can't wait eighteen years
for the children to grow up."

"You won't *have* to," Tamino exulted. "Professor, the
pièce de résistance!"

"Yes. By the daily injection of certain pituitary com-
pounds, you can accelerate the entire growth process. With
regular treatment, your young men should have achieved,
by the age of ten, the size and coordination of twenty-
year-olds."

"And the devotion of ten-year-olds for their dad. That's
you, Ward," Tamino added.

Mr. Thaaden picked at his toes for several seconds, then
looked up into the darkness. "I could wait ten years. But
I'd never get away with it. Can you imagine what would

354

happen when I started to march on the capital with preadolescent regiments? I would lose whatever popular base I ever had. I wouldn't last a month."

"Not so, Ward. Alicia?"

"Our guest has his head up his ass," Miss von Helsing said. "After ten years of carrying off every snot-nosed orphaned sextuplet in sight, no questions asked, you'll be the most popular philanthropist since the Easter bunny. You can have all the revolutions you want."

Mr. Thaaden said nothing and Tamino, using his felt-tipped tongue, filled the gap. "Well, Ward, old boy, have we or have we not done right by you?"

"If you can be believed."

Silence.

Thaaden seemed gradually to become aware of the vulnerability of his situation. A sheen of perspiration appeared on his face and visible droplets ran from his armpits in a lunatic bobsled course down his ribs. The seconds heaped into piles of minutes and still no one spoke as Thaaden alternately leaned forward, sprawled, crossed, uncrossed, and recrossed his legs. "Very well," he said at last, "I like it. What do you expect from me in return?"

Tamino's laughter came less as a break in the tension than as a nasty surprise. "Nothing that we don't already have: your friendship. As a matter of fact, we want to do you another favor as a special treat. Let me pose a question, Ward. What city in the world do you dislike the most?"

Thaaden did not hesitate. "Prague." He bit his lip. "I met my wife there."

"Perfectly in character for you to love your enemies, Ward. What if I told you that I could provide the means to destroy Prague, nostalgia and all?"

355

Thaaden stiffened. "Impossible! An attack on Prague, successful or not, would mean war. I forbid it. Too much has already happened which we cannot explain. Relations are strained everywhere. No one is ready for war. I forbid it."

"Forbid, Ward? A strong word for a man in your situation, especially when all we want is to make you happy. After all, would I suggest anything which would be harmful to an old buddy like you?"

The question hung in the air unanswered.

Tamino sniffed twice, a pretty poor imitation of wounded feelings, John thought. "Would the computer tell me what spot might have a special affinity for Prague?"

John wheeled his chair toward the console and peered into the darkness for the typewriter. The rapid, shifting glow from the keyboards was barely sufficient illumination for him to see what he was doing, but he managed to type out the order. The reply was almost instantaneous.

PRAGUE = MADRID

John held the sheet of paper close to his face and leaned back over the console to get the maximum light. The action-reaction shift had been more rapid than he had anticipated. No, this was impossible, out of the question. Unless the whole process had accelerated in a fashion the computer had not foreseen. Perhaps the computer *had* foreseen it and John had not noticed. That was Miss Feuer's job. John had given her all the figures. Why hadn't she said anything? He crouched over the keyboard and struck two chords.

"Hey, up there," Tamino shouted. "We're waiting on you."

"I'm confirming my results." Even as he spoke, he watched with mounting distress the report spelling itself out on his typewriter.

DRIFT APPARENT AT AN OBSERVABLE RATE OF 19.767 DEGREES PER HOUR. THIS FIGURE IS NOT CONSTANT. CORRECTION. DRIFT APPARENT AT AN OBSERVABLE RATE OF 21.58 DEGREES PER HOUR. ACCELERATION OF DRIFT FOLLOWING A GEOMETRIC CURVE OF . . .

"We're waiting, computer," Tamino called.

Flustered, John grappled with his microphone and yelled, "Madrid, but I'm afraid that the figures are changing so rapidly . . . "

"Could I have the drift rate on that, please?" Miss Feuer asked.

"Quiet, both of you." Tamino's bellow bludgeoned down Miss Feuer's request and the first glottal gasp of John's response. "All right, Ward. How would a visit from you sit with the government in Madrid?"

CORRECTION. DRIFT APPARENT AT AN OBSERVABLE 22.06 DEGREES PER HOUR.

Sticky and moist with his own sweat, John cursed the darkness, longed for a candle, and repeated his first order.

"A brief stopover would create no serious problems. Why?"

PRAGUE = SARAGOSSA

John's desperation mounted out of control. He whirled his chair around and tried to find the courage to interrupt Tamino, to borrow some confidence. He listened to Tamino describing *lymphogranuloma Doffenbaron* and succumbed to an impatient hatred of the man's voice. If he didn't break in, they would blame John for not informing them of the shift from Madrid to Saragossa. If he did interrupt, they might blame him for any security break. He cursed Thaaden's wretched smile as Tamino told him what would happen to the people of Prague if the people of Madrid were infected with Professor Keruk's prize disease. He despised Tamino for his authority, for his ability to frighten John, for his dark rooms, for his friends, for his past, for his future. John covered his ears, but a muffled, inane shadow of the detested voice seeped through the cracks between his fingers.

" . . . infect anyone you choose, as many as you want."

Thaaden roared, clutching his naked sides. "A plague, in two places at once? A master stroke! I can scarcely believe it, it's too wonderful."

John spun away from the laughter and aimed his attention at the console.

CORRECTION. DRIFT APPARENT AT AN OBSERVABLE RATE OF 26.9 DEGREES PER HOUR. THIS FIGURE IS NOT CON-STANT. CORRECTION. DRIFT APPARENT AT 27.7 DEGREES PER HOUR THIS FI CORRECTION DRFT APPRNT 28.6 DE-GREES/HR. CRRCTN DRFT 29.4 DEGREES/H . . . .

Mumbling half-words and semisentences unintelligible even to himself, John slammed his hands across the keyboards, setting up the only order he knew which might save him. He didn't know, didn't care what disasters the computer might be monitoring to arrive at its conclusions; only one disaster preoccupied John now, the possibility that he might be blamed for a mistake.

PRAGUE = LYON

His eyes filled with sweat and tears, his vision almost gone, John struck another series of bars. If Thaaden was in Madrid. . .

LYON = MADRID

John's senses momentarily deserted him and he beat the arms of his chair with both fists and pounded his feet on the floor. He couldn't remember, couldn't sort out what happened where and to whom if Thaaden went to Madrid. Would he be killed in Lyon? No, of course not, because he wouldn't be in Lyon. He'd be in Madrid. But to send a plague on Prague, Thaaden had to infect Lyon. Then he couldn't go to Madrid. Why was Tamino sending him there? Somewhere, somehow, a strand of reason remained which John could use to unravel the skein of contradictions, if only he could calm down. He needed a drink.

The shock of the idea stunned him into suspended mental animation. No, the *last* thing he needed was a drink. Never a drink. Nothing could be bad enough to drive him to that, nothing this side of death itself.

PRAGUE = BERN

For some reason, that bit of information swept away all the sharp edges of John's distress. As his heart slowed to a more reasonable pace, he saw the problem with a clarity that encouraged him. First, the figures were current, and Mr. Tamino, apparently unaware of the drift, had assumed a static relationship between Prague and Madrid. John didn't know much about the speed of modern aircraft, but they'd have to strap Thaaden to a rocket to get him anywhere close enough to do the job. In less than an hour, if the curve held, the cycle would have completed itself and Thaaden would have to *be* in Prague to initiate a disaster there. John sighed, the expulsion of air bearing with it all the poisons and insecurities which had troubled him so needlessly.

Why bother to raise the issue now, when Tamino had instructed John to remain silent? He would wait until after they'd sent Thaaden off with his little package of *lympho-granuloma Doffenbaron* and then they could arrange for a cable to cancel the whole operation. John smiled, pleased not only with himself but charmed at the prospect of seeing Mr. Tamino's experiment fall through. Not that John had the slightest desire to wish bad luck on anyone, but Mr. Tamino was due a comeuppance.

"Well, no point in delaying you any further, Ward," Tamino said. "Our men will see that you're dropped off at a convenient airport—don't be surprised it it's in Bulgaria —and we'll take care of the passport and the tickets to get you to Madrid and then home."

"And the other materials? The location of the oil field? The drugs?"

PRAGUE = REGENSBURG

So much for *that*. Gloved hands were already helping

360

Mr. Thaaden into underwear, shirt, trousers, jacket, tie, socks, shoes and, finally, a bag over his head. Erect and confident in the spotlight, he waited for someone to guide him on his way.

"In due course, Ward. Haven't we always taken care of you, boy?"

The lights in the amphitheater blazed on so suddenly that John's first thought was of an explosion. Not hearing any sound, he turned to deal with the urgent clatter from the typewriter.

AUTOMATIC PROGRAM 1-A-ZED PRIME NOW IN EFFECT. CENTER UNDER ATTACK. ALERT ALERT ALERT ALERT. ALL STATIONS.

Now sirens blared, shaking the glass in John's cage. The television screens on the console blinked and hummed to life, displaying rockets and cannons sliding out of fissures in the face of the butte, a view of the radio telescope aiming at a point on the horizon, and dust clouds rising in the wake of a large but unidentifiable vehicle rushing straight toward the camera.

"What is it? What's happening?"

"We're being attacked, Mr. Tamino." John could barely hear himself over the wail of the sirens. "We're being attacked."

"You bastard," Tamino howled.

John ran from the console and stared into the amphitheater. Tamino stood, arms waving in all directions, ranting and stamping his feet. "I could have given you anything, anything in the world, but you betrayed us."

Thaaden, confused by the bag on his head, the noise, the

361

accusations, turned this way and that, hands outstretched, groping for escape. The security guards backed off, giving him wide clearance as he staggered toward them. "What is this shouting? What has happened?"

"A homing device, that's it. Planted under his skin so they could trace him here." Tamino's screams reached a pitch that soared high above the sirens. "By all that you call holy, Thaaden, I'll have that skin off you before this day is over."

Thaaden backed up, and tripped over his chair. He caught himself before he fell, but the weakness, the clumsiness, the speed of his movement triggered a deadly response in the people surrounding him. Without a visible signal, but simultaneously, guns appeared in every hand but Miss von Helsing's. The loudspeakers relayed the reports to John as he gaped at the flames and smoke blasting at Thaaden. The force of the bullets knocked him over. He writhed briefly, then raised a gore-drenched hand in a pitiful and senseless attempt to protect his masked face. More shots and Thaaden rolled over, his shirt front a tatters of streaming, crimson pits. Their guns pumping bullets, the mob advanced on Thaaden, Miss von Helsing lifting her ax as she ran forward, her mouth open, eyes staring somewhere but not at the corpse on the floor. The blade glimmered with reflected light, then started its arc downward.

John jerked his head to one side and saw Dr. Ivanson huddled by himself against the wall, staring at the revolver in his hand. He pulled his lips back over his teeth and shouted. "No more interruptions. No more interruptions to my work. I will endure *no more interruptions to my work.*" Then he shot himself in the face. As he slid down the wall, his mangled head left a weaving purple track.

362

John knew he was yelling but could not recognize any of the words. He slid to the floor and pulled the skirts of his cassock over his head, chewing at the cloth as he sank to his knees, his mind filled with screams, broken bodies, shattered skulls, death, a wheeling spiral of horror that sucked him deeper the more he resisted it.

He sensed that the chamber had begun to descend to the courtyard level. Whimpering an inarticulate prayer, he scrambled across the floor to the console and crunched himself into the knee-hole under the typewriter, hiding his head between his knees, digging his teeth into his thigh, trying to force the hurt to clear his mind and cleanse his soul.

"All right, Father. Out!" Hand's grip on his arm was tight, but not the brutal hold John had expected the moment he had seen the shoes march through the door toward him. "You can't stay under there. We need you. We need artillery coordinates."

John compressed himself into as small an area as he could, determined to stay where he was until the sirens stopped, until Tamino didn't scream at him through the loudspeakers any more, until he could escape without anybody noticing. "Leave me alone. I'm all right where I am."

He watched Hand's feet spread apart and Hand's knees bend. With a single mighty tug, John was yanked from under the console and spilled into the middle of the computer chamber. He tried to crawl back into hiding but Hand blocked his way. "Don't you understand, Father?

We're under siege. We need you at the computer to defend ourselves."

John pushed himself to his feet and fought vertigo. "I don't want to be here shooting rockets. I want to get out before somebody kills me, don't you understand that?" He grappled with Hand's lapels, clutched Hand's ears, clawed at Hand's sleeves. "Sneak me out. Take me through the tunnels, through Beulahland and I'll hide in the desert until it's over."

Hand frowned at him, disgusted.

"It's not that I'm planning to run away, Mr. Hand," John protested. "Oh, no, I never would do a thing like that. No, sir. Me? Never. I just need a breath of fresh air, that's all. Fresh air clears the brain, nimbles up the old fingers for riffling through those old artillery coordinates. So, you just lead me through the tunnels and I'll take a little stroll in the sunshine and feel lots better. Then I'll come right back."

Hand lifted John off the floor and plopped him into his chair. "Even if I could, Father, I wouldn't. Anyway, it's impossible. None of us can get out. We're sealed off."

Lies! John knew a lie when he heard one. "Through Beulahland . . . " he began, but Hand shook his head.

"No. It's not there any more. We blew it up to close off the only entrance to the Center." A minor turbulence erupted behind Hand's face, then quickly subsided. "We didn't have time even to get those people out of there. Standard procedure, of course, and I suppose that it's better that they went fast rather than starving to death in the desert or getting trapped in the middle of a battle."

A spinning nausea settled in John's midsection and did gyroscopic pirouettes. He clenched his jaw and covered his mouth with a jerking hand. "What a terrible thing to do."

365

Running feet passed through the courtyard and Hand glanced anxiously at the door. "Not if it keeps this place going. The Fellowship is the hope of the world, Father." He straightened up, all his attention fixed on the sounds outside. "The hope of the world, and don't you forget it. Listen, I've got to get back to my men. You stay here, do you understand me? Lock the door after I leave and don't budge out of this room. I promise you one thing: we'll fight to keep you and the computer safe if everything else has to be sacrificed to do it. Are you listening, Father?"

A new unpleasantness occurred to John. If he stayed with the computer, he would be killed when the computer was captured. Anyone who knew enough to invade the Center knew enough to go for the computer first. Q.E.D., John would be one of the first to be exterminated, the only barrier between the enemy and the hardware.

"You've got to stay put, Father. You'll be safe here," Hand insisted, backing for the door. "Just lock up tight behind me."

"Don't fire yet. Wait until they're in range, you halfwits." Tamino's orders boomed through the loudspeakers. *"I want to hit them with everything at once."*

"I'll wait for you to come for me," John said, not looking up. "Knock three times so that I'll know it's you."

Hand paused at the door as though he had something more to say, then left. John waited for a count of twenty, tiptoed to the threshold, and pressed his ear against the doorframe. Hearing nothing, he eased the door open and peeked into the courtyard. He saw no one, so he cautiously slipped out, one foot at a time. John had already decided where he would hide: under Membozig's bed. If anybody started hunting for opposition, they certainly wouldn't expect much from a sick man. The chances were good that they wouldn't even search Leo's quarters.

Like a first grader crossing a busy intersection, John looked both ways to make sure he wouldn't be run down by charging troops, then scampered, skirts clutched in one fist, across the courtyard to Membozig's room.

"Get those rockets ready. You never know what they've got."

John shut Tamino out of his mind as a nonessential for his own survival and tried Membozig's door. Ajar, it gave with the slightest push. Still uncertain of his decision, John paused before entering, trying to hear a sound, any sound from inside. He heard nothing, not even breathing. Satisfied, he slipped into the room, shut the door softly behind him and leaned on it until he heard the lock catch. The room was empty except for a silent computer terminal, a standard hospital bed, and a table covered with buffed steel bowls and glass pipettes.

John slid his feet across the tiles toward the bed, trying to make as little noise as possible. Bending over, he gagged at the stench rising from the sheets. He shook his head and recoiled. Holding his nose with one hand, John pulled back the bedclothes with the other. Leo floated in a pool of filth, the paralyzed leg lifted with a curious daintiness away from the squalor which waited beneath it. John could not force himself to see if Leo were alive or not, but he had few doubts that the man on the bed was in very bad shape. From the condition of the sheets, John surmised that Leo had not been looked after for several days. The eyes were closed. If he was alive, Membozig displayed no awareness of John's presence. For a moment, John considered finding another hiding place, but changed his mind. With a shudder, he pulled the sheet back over Membozig and stooped down to crawl out of sight.

No sooner had his hands touched the floor than a viscous fluid squished through John's fingers. He felt almost grateful to discover that they were covered with blood. Then he had second thoughts.

Slowly, ever so slowly, he bent over and looked under the bed.

Dr. Klebo grinned back at him. The grin was fixed and tight, sincere and hearty, attached to a face which was attached to a head which was attached to nothing else. Slightly to the left, under the springs and against the wall, Dr. Klebo's vested torso rested on its back, propped against Dr. Klebo's legs; those legs were encased in neatly pressed if badly spotted trousers, a curled hand with no encumbering arm resting on one knee. Off by itself, looking strangely abandoned and lost, the other hand reached out toward John, a too-familiar tangle of wires and electrodes woven through the clenched fingers.

The ejaculatory prayer poised on John's tongue was overwhelmed by the gorge surging from his stomach. Scarcely thinking about it, John knew that the uncoagulated blood, the unglazed eyes, meant that Dr. Klebo was not long dead. He also knew, with even less thought, that he would not crawl under that bed.

Having wiped his hands on the bedsheets, John stood up and tottered out the door, his mind weighing and discarding options. In the courtyard he heard clopping footsteps race toward him. Hand, followed by six guards, ran past.

"Get back to that computer," Hand shouted, pointing toward the chamber.

John stopped, nodded, waited until they had gone

368

through the vault door, then plunged into the nearest room.

He slammed the door after him before he took in his surroundings. He caught his breath and stood still. John had blundered into Miss von Helsing's suite. He let his eyes wander over the wrecked furniture, the broken crockery, the empty ax cases. In all directions, piles of sofa stuffing, shredded tapestries, shattered tables gave evidence of either a vigorous battle or a first-rate tantrum. The axes, hatchets, and tomahawks protruded from the walls and floor in a random pattern. John jerked as a hatchet dropped loose from the ceiling. Clutching the doorknob, ready for the fastest possible exist, John called out. "Miss von Helsing? Are you here?" The answering stillness offered no assurance of his safety but John did not want to stay too close to the door in case battering warriors chose to burst through it without knocking. He inched through the wreckage, stealthily creeping toward the back room, stopping every yard or so to look around and make sure that no one lurked behind an upturned chair or under the rumpled carpet.

Reaching the entrance to Miss von Helsing's workroom, he paused and listened. John could hear motors, the regular hum and pulse of electronic equipment. He did not move for what seemed like eons, then summoned sufficient courage to poke his head through the door.

The gray metal boxes sat stacked four and five deep on the counter top, their wires stretching across to the occupied chair. On first glance, John had thought the chair occupied. Taking a closer look, he wasn't sure. The seated figure had a vaguely human outline but detail was obscured by the tight lacework of insulated cord spooled in and out over the entire surface, a package wrapped only in fine wire. An occasional faërie light, now blue, now yellow, spat and skimmed across the surface; the odor of ozone hung heavy in the air.

John edged toward the counter and placed his hand on the boxes. All warm; some, in fact, overheated. None of the dials registered anything at all, their needles prone beneath bowers of numbers and symbols. John crept deeper into the room and discovered the source of the hum, a tape recorder still joined to the web of wires in the chair by a single cord. John checked the amplification level and satisfied himself that the machine was recording nothing. He stopped it, rewound the tape a few feet, and punched the play button.

Miss von Helsing's voice, Juno with a megaphone, filled the room and John sprang to adjust the volume.

" . . . provided with both opportunity and incentive, found herself unable to avoid regression in a situation of social approbation and group emergency. Once more acting out patterns which she believed to have been successfully repressed, she immediately sought out a Caucasian Male Type 43—subclassification, Semite—and realized her potential as a Caucasian Female Type 1—subclassification, Aryan—in a manner consistent with both heritage and training. Reporting immediately for observation, she was subjected to the *most* thorough of ethnopsychological testing. . . . " A crackle and a scream interrupted Miss von Helsing's case study.

John stopped the recorder and began to turn off the other boxes as well. The sparks from the chair threatened to start a fire and John saw no point in wasting power on machinery which had nothing left to do.

"Got their range? *Got their range?*" Tamino demanded from somewhere. "All right, boys, let 'em have it."

370

John followed the explosions to their source and spotted the loudspeakers. Ceiling mounted, just like his.

"I *know* it looks like a bus, damn it. Obviously a feint at our defenses with the big stuff kept out of sight until they see what we've got. All right, you bastards, I'll show you what I've got. Fire again. *Fire!*"

John glanced around the room. A yardstick leaned against the wall in a far corner. He went for it.

"Have you ever *seen* such evasive action?" Tamino shouted, amazement carrying his words high above the booms and bangs that surrounded them. "Can't you characters hit anything? Give 'em a rocket. Hell, give 'em a dozen. *Fire!*"

Blowee. Whoosh. Kapow. John picked up the yardstick and advanced toward the speakers.

"These aren't slingshots you guys are shooting, you know. Aim. Damn it, they're getting away! John! Do you hear me, John?"

John rammed the yardstick into one of the loudspeakers.

"John, we need some fast calculations. The rockets are falling short, the guns are fouled up. The enemy is reconnoitering."

John stabbed the other loudspeaker, listened to it fizzle and sputter into complaining silence, then threw the yardstick aside. At least, he had made the gesture.

A curious numbness overtook him. All of a sudden, he wanted to go back to his computer. The Center was finished and if John had to go, he'd go looking at his hardware. He left the workroom and gingerly wound his way through the rubble to the courtyard.

371

John had little choice, really. He certainly didn't want to survive the one thing that gave him a reason to live. He knew exactly what he would do. He would hurl himself across the console and they would have to shoot their way through him to get at the computer. Maybe he should make the sacrifice and throw his shoe through the window into the cavern and let the room fill with Mr. Tamino's much-touted poisonous gas. No, that smacked too much of murder-suicide, and even in a just cause John didn't want to endanger his soul's health any more than necessary. He had been right the first time, as usual. John would just go on doing his job until somebody stopped him. He shuddered at the thought of how thoroughly he would be stopped.

He opened the door and let himself into the chamber, walking directly to the console, half hearing Tamino's overhead bleats.

"John, they're getting away from us. We gotta stop 'em, buddy. *John, get me the range on that fucking bus!*"

The computer had gone berserk. John thrust his hands onto a keyboard and seized control of the radio telescope, then set up the order for recalculation of artillery and rocket coordinates.

"*John!*"

John would stay with the computer, no matter what happened. And, oddly enough, he felt no bitterness. He had a conviction of impending and inevitable completion. Someday, people would remember John and speak of his life as a prototype of exemplary dedication. *They found Father Doffenbaron, bullet-riddled, bayoneted, and trampled, his pale sensitive hands still caressing the keys on the computer.* Not the ending to a full life which John

372

necessarily would have chosen for himself, but martyrdom had points in its favor.

An insistent rattle from the typewriter pulled John from his reveries. He read the figures and turned to his microphone.

"Mr. Tamino, override the automatic aiming device and compensate for wind drift by an elevation of seven degrees vertical, ten degrees lateral. And use only the heat-sensitive rockets."

"You heard the man, boys. Crank those guns up there and shoot."

John rose from his chair and moved to the window. Perhaps they should find him here, taking one last look at the rows of cabinetry, an expression of unruffled calm, of happy accomplishment on his gentle face. He spat on his cuff and scraped at an anonymous desiccation with his fingernail.

John considered his reflection in the glass, an unfocused haze of blinking lights spinning behind his reverse image. Inspired, he lifted his chin and turned his head slightly to the left, deemphasizing the lips which he had sometimes thought thick and pouty but which now, at the proper angle, he recognized as full and expressive.

"Get 'em leveled in there, boys. Shit! This isn't a wind, it's a hurricane. Higher. Higher. Hold it!'"

A blur bobbed up and down in the middle of John's reflection. He tried to ignore it but it got larger and larger. Squinting, he hunted a moth on the glass. No, it was farther away in the cavern itself.

He saw her.

Loping over the cables, her blonde hair streaming behind

373

her, she ran toward him. John thought for a minute that his mind was playing tricks on him, but as she got closer he could not deny the identity of those knees. She stopped beneath the window and wiped her nose, leaving a grubby smear across her cheek. Her skin was in terrible shape. Even this far away, certainly twenty feet at least, John could count the boils on her forehead. She looked as if she hadn't bathed in a year.

She cupped her hands, bulge-knuckled and grimy, over her mouth and shouted. John couldn't hear her.

"I can't hear you, Miss Deckstewer," he yelled.

She pointed back at the computer cabinets, frantic about something. Certainly, the computers were active. In fact, all of them seemed to be in operation, but John was not surprised, not when he considered the amount of data that had been coming in.

"You'd better get out of there," he yelled. "You'll suffocate."

Had the rings under her eyes been a shade lighter, had her dress been less soiled, had her teeth been not quite so green, John could have convinced himself that she was playing tricks. But everything about her screamed fright and urgency. She glanced hurriedly over her shoulder, then waved her fists at John, her mouth forming silent words.

"Nothing," he said, holding his hands behind his ears. "I can't hear a thing."

Muddy tears streaked down Miss Deckstewer's face and she spun in a circle, gesturing furiously at the computers.

"All right, let the bastards have it. *Fire!*"

Miss Deckstewer, her mouth open, jolted sideways and broke in two, her entrails spilling out in a gaudy stream. John pressed both hands against the glass and shrieked as she spread out into a scarlet pancake, smashed beneath an invisible weight. Crazily, John scanned the cavern for her murderer, but saw nothing.

"*Got 'em! Got the sonsabitches!*" Tamino's triumph clashed with John's revulsion and fear. He took one last look at the bubbling remnant of Miss Deckstewer and pushed himself from the window.

Gentle arms enclosed him, motherly clucks tickled his ear as he smothered his face in warm, yielding flesh and allowed himself to be dragged across the chamber and deposited in his chair.

"Did you see? Did you see?" He wiped his eyes against warm cloth, aware of an indefinite odor of perfume and perspiration. "Did you see Miss Deckstewer?"

"Oh, yes." Miss Feuer patted John's neck. "Every day. Bonnie was a very helpful person, like you. Prompt with her work."

John pulled away and pointed at the window. "No. Just now. Out there. Something *killed* her."

Miss Feuer blinked over the console at the glass. "Out there? Goodness, I thought she'd gone away." She frowned at John, a hint of the scold in her voice. "Didn't you even ask her in?"

John gritted his teeth and jumped from his chair, dragging Miss Feuer behind him to the window. "You see that puddle? *That's* Miss Deckstewer. She was trying to tell me something."

Miss Feuer crinkled her brows and looked everywhere but at the broad damp stain. "I really don't see a thing. Really." She pulled John away and led him back to the console. "If I saw anything terrible like that, it would just upset me." John searched Miss Feuer's face for a suggestion

375

of understanding and saw only a tiny smile and glittering ebony eyes. He threw himself into his chair. "You *did* see something. Why did you cover my face? Why did you make me come over here?"

As if time had paused and revealed all secrets, a serenity and wisdom radiated from Miss Feuer which rivaled everything that John had once called beautiful. Then, before he could take stock of the phenomenon, give it a name, Miss Feuer moved and John found himself staring into her black button eyes.

"I was over there, waiting for you." Miss Feuer indicated a spot by the door. "Mercy, I was so startled when you yelled that I just came over and grabbed you. You were so sad. I didn't want to upset you. Nesting instincts. Puppies."

She flicked her tongue over her upper lip and withdrew a hand from John's cheek which he had not noticed was there. "All right to talk now?"

He nodded, wondering what his shouts had to do with puppies. "What should we talk about?"

Miss Feuer gleamed. "About our work, of course. It's happening, isn't it, just like we thought it would. Pretty marvelous for us."

Dr. Klebo, Membozig, Dr. Ivanson, Miss von Helsing—that one didn't matter—Miss Deckstewer. John erased the pictures by concentrating on Miss Feuer. "I don't understand."

"Well, we were the first ones who knew that this was going to happen. I guessed what was going on and you figured out on the computer what the changes were going to be. That everything had to close in on us, see?"

Forgetting the ugliness and death would not be easy if he couldn't make connections with Miss Feuer's train of thought. "Close in?"

"Oh, *you* know." John could tell from her face that she had taken another detour. "What was that quote from the Bible, anyhow? 'To each his own'?'" She gave her hair an exasperated tousle. "That's not right. It had 'eyes' and 'feet' in it. 'To each eye his own foot'?'"

He was with her. At last. "You mean the *Lex Talionis.* 'Thou shalt give life for life, eye for eye, tooth for tooth.' "

"That's it!" Miss Feuer smacked her hands together. "That's what your computer said. Well?"

"Well?" John sat down, lost again.

"That's what's happening." Miss Feuer chewed a cuticle. "Step by step, all around the world, an eye for an eye." She reached out and lightly rested her finger on John's left eyelid. "I guess that if I poked hard it would be my eye for yours, wouldn't it?"

"That, of course, was the intention of the *Lex Talionis,* retributive justice administered in kind. However, I scarcely believe that contemporary jurisprudence would exact that kind of penalty from you, Miss Feuer."

Miss Feuer went blank. "Oh?"

A trickle of moisture ambled down John's spine. "I'm sure that the cycle merely goes full circle and then wears itself out. That's all."

Miss Feuer grimaced at a fingernail. "Maybe. But that's not what the computer said. I remember. The computer said that the action-reaction effect would be temporary only insofar as the reaction hit someplace else on the globe. I don't remember it saying anything about the whole thing wearing out. Maybe I'm wrong. I'm so bogged down in earth sciences and mechanical engineering." She made a nervous, uninterpretable gesture. "That's a specialist for you."

377

A vein in John's neck pinged and he reached to still it. His fingers were like ice against his throat. Why hadn't he recognized it for what it was? They had been touched, given fair notice, felt the long shadow in their midst, and missed the point. Corporal Comstock and all those other men who had died; John remembered and knew. Could it have been chance, and only a few degrees of longitude which had prevented John, or Hand, or Ivanson, from replacing Comstock on the table in the Game Room? If so, chance, in this instance, had been initiated with a vengeance and probably *by* one as well. Why, his mind demanded, should he be vulnerable to the madness of someone John had never met, would never meet, on the other side of the planet? And if Miss Feuer was right, what had John ever done to merit being responsible, unequivocably responsible, for himself? John, or any other human being, never had been cut out for that kind of work.

A spasm ran through him and he pulled himself to the console. "We must be able to stop it, reverse it. Something."

"Think so?" Miss Feuer sucked a fingertip. "How?"

John gripped the sides of the typewriter, thoughts chasing through his mind like rabbits and hounds, trying to find what they had missed. Signs in the sun and moon and stars? *Warnings.* That's what Dr. Ivanson had thought. Why hadn't Dr. Ivanson *told* them. John cursed himself. They had discussed it, right here in this room, the two of them, Ivanson had done everything but spell out the words. And John had missed the point.

He typed the interrogation.

The answer came quickly, too quickly.

CONTRAINDICATED. ABSENCE OF PRECEDENT. AS ST.

THOMAS DEMONSTRATES IN PART I, QUAESTIO 19, AR-
TICLE 7, THOSE THINGS WHICH HAVE BEEN WILLED ARE
WITHOUT CHANGE. USING THE TEXT, NUMBERS XXIII.19 HE
SKILLFULLY REFUTES THE CONCEPT OF A VACILLATING . . .

John swallowed the sob rising in his chest and clawed at
the console, clearing it for another interrogation; he
attempted to will away the pressure tomtomming at his
temples, tried to pour all of his talent, experience, and
success out through his hands and into the typewriter. He
hammered at the keys:

INFORM IMMEDIATELY OF COURSE OF PRESENT CYCLE
[REF. MS 677] WITHIN NEXT TWENTY-FOUR HOURS WITH
SPECIFIC INFORMATION AS TO STATUS OF PERSONNEL OF
THIS ORGANIZATION.

As if outraged beyond endurance, the console flaunted
all its colors in a peacock display of flashes, a grating,
distressed mechanical screech vibrated from the cavern and
everything stopped; the keyboards, the spinning reels on
the cabinetry, the lights, the typewriter. Everything stopped.
John punched two, three, four bars down at random.
They did not respond. He touched the typewriter, but the
paper in the carriage remained as white as a shroud.
"Is something wrong?"
John tried to think of an excuse, more for himself than
for Miss Feuer; any explanation, any postponement that
could give him a sufficient transfusion of hope to rise from
his chair and leave the chamber. A logical reason, an answer
that could momentarily diffuse his despair. But the
presence of this reality loomed too mammoth to be eluded.
"The computer is dead, Miss Feuer."

"Oh, no," she said, and rushed to the console. She prodded and hit, but nothing happened. "Not *all* of it, not all at *once.*"

John wanted to thank her for being concerned, for being kind, but he doubted if she realized precisely how much had just died before her eyes. No, Miss Feuer could not know, would never guess. Computers were not her specialty.

He leaned back in his chair, letting Miss Feuer's chatter wash past him unheard, and closed his eyes. All the promises in the world meant nothing; everything he had loved had been wrenched from him, stolen, spoiled. He couldn't even savor the joy of a real pain, only a nagging anxiety, as if he were supposed to do something and was in the wrong place, at the wrong time, and couldn't recall where he was expected to be. He opened his mouth to take a deep breath, not surprised that his mouth was dry when his hands were so wet. He hadn't had a drink for a long time, such a commendably long time.

What had happened to John's little bell? Shouldn't he hear the nice jing-a-ling that told him when he was sad and needed a touch of happiness on the rocks? No bell. Well, John was out of practice. Given time, if he had any time, he'd get the old bell tolling again. John's alcoholic angelus, calling him to fall on his knees, his hands, and finally his face.

"Are you all right?" Miss Feuer lifted one of his eyelids and peered in, as if she were trying to make sure John was still inside. "You're so pale. A sheet. Let me get you something to drink."

"Miss Feuer, there's more than one kind of justice in this world." John smiled in spite of himself and the smile hurt. "No water. Spirits. A wee drappie."

"Oh, dear. I don't have anything. Not a drop. I *don't*, you see. Maybe Alicia keeps something. She *would*, not to criticize or anything. Do you want me to run and look?"

"Father, we're in trouble." Hand charged between John and Miss Feuer. Grease-smeared and ragged, he leaned against the console and bent over John.

"I was talking to Miss Feuer," John said. "You are very rude to step in front of her while she was speaking to me."

Hand straightened up, took Miss Feuer's arm, and urged her toward the door. "Look, Miss Feuer, I've got to speak to Father Doffenbaron, alone. I'm sorry, but this is important." A misery covered Hand's face which John doubted that he could wash off.

"That's all right. I have an errand to run." She winked at John. "I'll rush over to Alicia's and be right back."

"Wait!" A premonition of (A) Miss Feuer finding a bottle, (B) Miss Feuer finding what was left of Miss von Helsing and, inevitably, (C) Miss Feuer dropping the bottle, called forth John's hidden reserves of energy. "Before you start poking around Miss von Helsing's room, I think I'd better tell you something."

Miss Feuer tilted her head and smiled. "I know. I helped strap her in and wind her up." She twirled and headed for the door. "I won't be gone a second."

"Make it five minutes," Hand shouted.

Miss Feuer's footsteps pitpatted into the distance. Hand waited until they could no longer hear her, then turned and roughly grabbed the front of John's cassock.

"Did you know who was in that bus? Tell me, damn it, did you *know?*" Grief clouded his face and filled his eyes, his agony stabbing through digging fingers into John. His grip relaxed and he backed off. "No, of course you didn't. I can tell by the stupid look on your face."

Hand had torn a button off John's cassock. "What bus?"

"The bus we shot at, the bus you gave us coordinates for, the bus we blew to smithereens, the bus filled with fourteen old women. Nuns, Father, *nuns.*" Hand slumped against the console and wiped his eyes. "Oh, it was pretty. No survivors. Seven direct hits with shells built to go through a battleship; then, to make sure they got the message, we slammed some rockets into them." He gulped heavily, then started again, under control. "A bus with St. Ambrose's Seminary for Young Ladies painted on the side in big letters. Not big enough for us to see three-quarters of a mile away. God, why were they coming here, of all the places on earth, why here?"

"To find me." Why else? John remembered the press release. How natural, chance being what it was, to save the best for last.

"It's not possible." Hand shook his head so violently that his hair flew back and forth like a flag. "How could they have known you were here?"

"They are not without their own resources." John wondered what went with the nuns. A convent in the nearest village? Or, if an infinite God could be capable of infinite irony, a brothel? Or, maybe, only poor Bonnie Deckstewer, a full recompense for twelve nuns. She had been a highly capable systems analyst in her day. How did one solve these equations where eyes balanced eyes? Some eyes were blue, some were brown, some didn't see very well, some saw much too well. Poor Bonnie. Yes, and John meant it, poor nuns. Where was that drink?

"You haven't heard the worst." Hand prepared himself for delivering bad news by rubbing the back of his neck. "I think Tamino's dead. I know Keruk is. God, it was horrible."

Yes, the more he thought about it, the more John remembered how rough it was on a man to be left thirsty.

"Mr. Tamino sent me to scout the area after we'd made our hit. I came back and told him what I'd found and, I swear it, he went crazy. I thought he'd come tearing down here after you, but he never mentioned your name once. He kept screaming about a broken contract, a rotten deal. He ran out of the arsenal and headed for that office of his. Professor Keruk met him in one of the corridors we didn't flood and begged Mr. Tamino to let him go. Tamino didn't even look at him, I swear it, just brushed him out of the way. My God, Father, they barely touched and Keruk was dead before I could get to him." Hand paused and sucked his lips into his mouth, making himself look prematurely senile. "His face, if you could have seen the look on Keruk's face. Oh, God."

John suspected that Miss Feuer would bring rye. Irish whisky was too much to hope for.

"I chased after Tamino. I wanted to find out what I was supposed to do, get my orders. I caught up with him just as he went into the office. 'Somebody's going to pay hell for this,' he yelled at me. Then opened the door, walked into the dark and, I don't *know*, I don't know *what* happened." Hand stared at John as if John might know.

John hoped Miss Feuer wasn't fooling around hunting for ice or mix or any such nonsense. He didn't even need a glass.

"Out of that room, flames, all over everything. Do you think it might have been an explosion, some sort of flash fire? One minute I couldn't get close to the place and the next it was out. No smoke, no ashes, no scorch marks. I ran in to see if I could help Mr. Tamino, but he wasn't there. *Nothing* was there, Father. All I found was a big hole cut into the rock." Hand lifted his eyes, silently pleading like a landlocked fish. "You saw his office. Didn't he have something in there? A desk? A real floor? Maybe some walls?"

John wanted to help Hand, but he had other things on his mind. "It was just an office, with lots of telephones and funny lighting effects." All very curious, he had to admit. Perhaps somebody decided to burn leaves and, *poof*, Tamino loses his office and they lose Tamino. One thing was as likely as another. John leaned sharply toward the courtyard. He could hear Miss Feuer's footsteps and a timpani accompaniment of tinkling glassware.

Backing through the doorway, a *chinoisérie* teacart in tow, Miss Feuer wiggled into the chamber. "Canapes and everything."

"Bring that over here." John said. Only one bottle, bourbon. But the seal hadn't been broken!

"Place your orders." Miss Feuer had found herself an apron. "Water or soda?"

John shook his head and reached for the bottle. With a ritual exactness, he twisted off the cap and poured a glass full to the brim, enjoying every splash, every splatter. Using both hands, he elevated the bourbon to his lips and broke the surface tension with his tongue.

"Hey!" Hand snatched up the bottle and examined the label. "You're not supposed to have this."

John's throat and stomach twiched in surprised welcome and he half emptied the glass. "A small restorative, Mr. Hand."

Hand reluctantly permitted Miss Feuer to take the bottle and fill two more glasses. John observed her generosity with displeasure, quickly finished his own drink, and stared hard at the bourbon until Miss Feuer bustled over and poured him another.

Miss Feuer lifted her glass, sipped, and winced. John figured that he would be cleaning up after Miss Feuer before the day was done. In one teensy specialty, John was the only professional in the room.

"Whew," Miss Feuer said. "This has turned into a real party, hasn't it?"

Pleasant echoes of sounds never heard already ricocheted through John's skull.

Hand tasted his drink and stared at the floor over the rim of his glass. "We're going to have to reorganize, that's all. Pull this place together with what we've got."

"I wish we had some music." Miss Feuer held her glass but she did not drink. The happy prospect of helping her get rid of it encouraged John to take one more long swallow. St. Thomas, computers, who needed 'em? John and his friends were on a chartered rocket to oblivion. Or something.

"It doesn't seem like a party without music." She poured another dollop of bourbon into John's glass.

"First off, we'll need a new director. Miss Feuer ranks the rest of us in tenure, of course." Hand wrinkled his nose and Miss Feuer saw him do it.

"Oh, no. Not me. I'm strictly earth sciences."

"Then, Miss von Helsing . . . "

"Dead." Taking the grand tour in the valley of the shadow under the auspices of a very old, very popular firm with many subsidiaries, it would seem. "Dead and gone. Membozig, too, I guess. Hard to tell. Oh, yes. *Requiescant in pace.*"

"That only leaves the three of us." Hand squinted off into space. "We'll have to divide the responsibilities until we're on our feet again."

John's feet had achieved an elegant existence quite independent of the rest of his body and he hadn't the slightest intention of imposing on their good will by demanding that they support him for Mr. Hand's benefit. He nodded at Miss Feuer and watched, stunned by the magic of it all, as she refilled his hungry cup.

"We could sing songs," Miss Feuer suggested. She munched a Ritz cracker and offered a plate of canapés.

"A holding action until we can get more personnel." Hand smirked and took a gulp of bourbon. "I think we can swing it."

What were those insipid contours that sprang, unbidden, to Hand's face when he smiled, that made John so yearn to paste him one? That face. Agreeable enough in repose, at its best when it was someplace else. John gloomily resigned himself to the fact that it would never be anywhere else again, ever. And that "holding action" business. They weren't holding anything; they were held. Absurd. "What have *we* got to hold?"

"What have we got to hold?" Hand snorted. "The Center, the computers, all that the Fellowship stands for."

A very curious thing about laughter: when one laughed, one couldn't swallow. And when one couldn't swallow at a decent pace, one tended to cry. Laughs and drinks. John would alternate. He had a full schedule of preprogrammed crying ahead of him.

"What's wrong with him?" Hand asked Miss Feuer.

"The computers have gone off." Miss Feuer spread

cheese paste on a wheat biscuit. "We're all on vacation." She waved her cracker in the air. "And having a wonderful time."

"What do you mean the computers are off?" Hand shouted. "Did he turn them off?"

"Tell him," John hooted. "Tell him everything."

The effort of engaging in intelligent discourse required another drink. Let Hand monopolize Miss Feuer. Perhaps, in an eon or so, she could teach him how to be amusing or at least pleasant. Hand clearly had one virtue: he listened well. But he should not let his mouth hang open in front of ladies. In front of Miss Feuer. Did he hear when he listened or did Miss Feuer's words drift into that gaping maw and dissolve to float down and away, forever lost? What had happened to all the wise words, the tragic cries, the good jokes since the beginning of time? All swallowed up, John supposed. Eaten alive.

"Put that glass down and listen to me."

Someone of their company had been shouted at. One moment. John would figure it all out. Hand, first of all, was the shouter. Miss Feuer no longer stood beside him, her supply of words long since consumed. Thus, was it reasonable to assume that John himself was the object of shouts? He considered the evidence.

"What?" John said.

"If we had some music we could dance." Miss Feuer had a mind like a . . . oops!

"People have to be warned," Hand said. Definitely and without dispute, he spoke to John. "Don't you see? This is the greatest thing that ever happened to the world. We can give people the incentive to restrain themselves, something

387

they never had before, not really. And they *will* restrain themselves if we get to them and tell them what's happened."

"Who will?" Hand must be reading something. So many sentences, one after another, all connected. Meaning nothing.

"If we get the point across that people have to get their lives in order, they'll change, Father. They'll pitch in and make this world a decent place to live."

"I guess I'll just have to hum." Miss Feuer eluded focus, spinning back and forth, around and around, faster than John's emancipated eyes could follow. He hoped, for her sake, that no one would ask her to stop.

"It looks bad now, Father. But we all know that everything is going to be all right. People want it that way."

A sermon. Hand had taken up homiletics. Had he told John his text? Not any gospel John had ever read, ever heard of. Perhaps an epistle, but he couldn't remember them too well. Ah. *The good which I would do, I do not.* "I suggest St. Paul," John advised. "Gloomy, but to the point."

"Oh, please. Won't anybody dance with me?"

Dear Miss Feuer, one of John's oldest and dearest pals. Perchance, if she would whiz by and replenish his half-empty glass, John might give her a twirl or two.

Hand put his drink on the teacart. John noted for future reference that Hand had barely touched his bourbon. In these times!

"Listen, if I start blasting right away, I can have us out of here by morning." Hand, the acid sweetness of his breath powerful enough to smother, leaned into John's face. "The world's been waiting for this moment, Father. It's bigger news than the second coming."

Whatever had happened to *that?* John wondered. He must have missed it. He'd been very busy there for a while.

Hand backed away just as Miss Feuer spun out of nowhere. They bumped together and John watched Miss Feuer's glass soar through the air, end over end, to smash against the console.

A stabbing explosion burst inside John's fist. He cried out with pain and stared in disbelief and shock at the glinting splinters jutting out of the bone and skin from his fingertips to his wrist. He puckered up, ready to weep.

"My God! My God!" he complained. "Why waste good bourbon?"

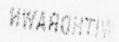